IRON & BONE

CAT PORTER

CONTENTS

PROLOGUE

Running.

We're always running from something. We convince ourselves we're free, but we aren't, not really.

Running from the bad things, running from the good things—they both have power over us. Both haunt, fluttering over us with vague glories, tinting us with deep failures.

Plenty of failures.

I doused my failures with gasoline. Held them at bay with knives, guns, my hands, my bike, my brothers.

My iron will.

But not my heart.

No, my heart was the flame that would light the match, ignite the blaze.

My heart made me hang on.

Because my mother's quiet faith and stubborn determination made me believe in a better day, someday.

Because, once upon a time, my cousin would hold my hand. Her trembling would ease, and so would mine.

Because my best friend had seen me through the worst, the darkest part of myself, the both of us dirty, bloody, bruised in the back of a truck heading out of Colorado and into the unknown. Because he'd killed for me, and I'd killed for him.

Because my friend Grace had come home and had risen from her ashes. She'd breathed new life into me, making me believe that there could be brighter days instead of the endless pages I had surreptitiously torn for myself from the notebook of my life.

I'd been running but essentially standing still for years. Left behind and edging forward on my own, I'd created my niche in my club, and I was content. I didn't need a hell of a lot, and I really didn't give it much thought. My way of life had become rote, straightforward, a day-by-day of not too much, not too little, and just enough.

Then, out of the blue, sixteen years later, on a weed-filled cracked sidewalk in a tiny Nebraska town on a cloudy afternoon, surrounded by suitcases, boxes, and crates crammed with her stuff—all of it obviously quickly collected—there she was.

The pixie, the angel, the herald.

Jill.

Grace introduced us. Tania, Grace's friend, held a baby—Jill's baby—settling her into a car seat in the back of Jill's shit-box car.

Her face was flushed, her strawberry-blonde hair knotted into two loose buns at the back of her head. Her shoulders were set in a rigid line. Dogged. Determined. Relieved.

She was running.

She'd been running a long time, too.

Her body stilled when she saw me.

It's you, isn't it?

Yes, it's me.

Ah, Jill, you've come back to haunt me. To pull things from me, damnable things. I don't want to look at them or touch them or feel them. Their spiky edges will tear my skin. I'd tightly bound them all in chains long ago and thrown away the keys.

I can keep you bound though, where you need to be, alongside the others and all my smoke. Otherwise, I will have to pay with what is left of me.

Pay with my scarred body.

Pay with my ripped, already severed soul.

ONE

JILL

"I'M A LITTLE OBSESSIVE. I admit it freely and openly."

"You can't live without these mochas, huh?" Matt asked.

"Guilty as charged." I led the way to the sugar and creamer counter, taking in the rich roasted coffee and cocoa fragrance rising from the white mug in my hands. "Only the Meager Grand Cafe's mochas. And my daughter is just as obsessed with their cupcakes."

He laughed. "Then, I'm glad I came here with you. If you like this place, it must be fantastic." He beamed his white smile at me, and my cheeks heated under his unabashed gaze.

Here was something new, something I wasn't used to—a nice guy liking me. A nice guy wanting to impress me. A nice guy doing nice things for me.

Time to get used to it.

Matt moved in closer to me at the counter and grabbed a few napkins from the dispenser, brushing up against me. That had to be on purpose.

With a sip of my latte, I squelched the tickle rising in my throat. Matt was cute and sweet, and every time he saw me at the rehab center where I took Rae—my ex-boyfriend's mother—he would be helpful and attentive, like he was being right now. Rae had just been diagnosed with multiple sclerosis and could no longer be on her own. My daughter—her granddaughter—and I had needed somewhere to stay, so we were currently living with her, and I'd help take care of her.

I tore open a Stevia packet, adding a bit to my decaf mocha.

Matt handed me a stirrer.

"Oh, thanks."

I took in a tiny breath. Who the hell handed you a stirrer when it was right in front of you? Only a thoughtful, kind gentleman— that's who.

This was why I had picked up and left Nebraska at a moment's notice, wasn't it? Because I was done with the wondering and the arguing and the wishing things were different, wishing that my ex, Catch, was different. I'd finally made a clean break with him, the one-percenter outlaw who'd cheated on me, was never really home anyhow, but we'd managed to have a baby together. Our relationship had once been passionate and fun, but both our insecurities and ambitions had chipped away at it until its luster had worn thin, and a mountain range of resentment had torn right through it.

Now, I was living the daydream I used to have while working at that launderette in Nebraska or pouring drinks for Catch's brothers at the clubhouse or planning a trip to the nearest Walmart, which wasn't very near at all, feeling as if it were a shopping trip to New York City. Back then I'd dreamed of being free from living my life according to the laws and demands of the monstrous global enterprise known as the Flames of Hell MC. I'd dreamed of not belonging to a tribe whose needs I had to usually put above my own. Most importantly, I'd dreamed of giving my daughter a real sense of family.

Here in Meager, I was truly happy for the first time in what felt like forever. I could sit in this great cafe and have coffee with a good guy who clearly liked me and literally not have a care in the world. I had even explained my surrogacy pregnancy for my friend Grace and her husband, Lock, to Matt last week. His eyes had widened as he'd emitted a long "*Wow*." The knowledge had only boosted his already eager attention.

Matt leaned in closer to me. "I meant what I said earlier, if you want to find out more about becoming a physical or occupational therapist for when you're ready, after the baby's born, I can introduce you to one of my old professors, take you on a tour of the school."

"You don't have to do that."

"Of course. You said you were interested."

I was interested in a lot of things, if only I could decide.

My thumbs rubbed the side of my hot mug. "I just finished this part-time class in social media marketing actually. I liked it." I fingered one of my dangling silver feather earrings. I enjoyed my little hobby of making charm bracelets, earrings, and necklaces, and in the very back of my mind I hoped to sell them online one day. That was my new secret idea.

"Mrs. Reigert just has a few more sessions at the center, right?" he asked, referring to Rae.

"Three more until her Medicare cycle is done."

"Am I going to see you after that?" His voice grew lower, dragging out the words, his shoulders rolling forward. "I mean, I'd really like to see you, Jill." His brown eyes held mine.

"Really?"

"Really."

I averted my gaze to the creamy swirls floating in my mocha latte.

"Jill, you want to see me again?" The soft lilt in his voice made me raise my head.

But instead of Matt's handsome face, my vision was filled with *his* face over Matt's shoulder.

Boner. One-Eyed Jacks Sergeant at Arms. One of Grace's closest and dearest friends. Among the club members, he was an easygoing eccentric of sorts, and when he grinned or laughed, which was often, that ease would show. However, with me, he maintained a shroud of seriousness. I just knew something else lurked underneath, and I'd remained fascinated since I'd first met him, which actually was many years ago and under emotional circumstances for the both of us. Death and regret.

Staring at me right now was that creature of the shadowy unknown. His gaunt face was set off by an incredible long mane of inky dark hair, a thin mustache and a trimmed beard. His eyebrows framed gorgeous green eyes that were a shade of beach glass. I had even looked up green gemstones on the Internet once to compare to that color. Jade. Peridot. Tourmaline.

Those remarkable take-my-breath-away eyes were piercing mine right now.

"What's up?" he asked in that familiar growly tone.

A stab of heat shot right through my middle and fired away down in my lady parts.

I choked back my hot coffee. "Hi."

He didn't move a muscle, not one, except for a slight twitch on his left cheek and his stiffening jawline. Those sharp green eyes of his claimed my breath and incited shivers as they traveled over me in one long sweep.

"Uh…you know this guy, Jill?" Matt turned in his seat, the unusually high pitch of his voice revealing an unexpected stress level.

Who wouldn't be stressed? I was stressed. I was stressed every time Boner came within a few feet of me. No, actually, every time he was in the same room with me, I got stressed. Very stressed.

I liked this stress though.

I'd become transfixed, addicted to it.

Last night, awake at three o'clock in the morning, I'd fantasized about him as my fingers took care of my stress level. Moaning into my pillow, I'd imagined Boner's lean and contoured body over mine, his ringed fingers clamping over my wrists, his long dark hair teasing my breasts, as his mouth traveled down my torso until it finally, finally reached my—

"Jill?" Matt sat up, brushing against me.

Boner's eyes narrowed, the ridge of his brows shadowing the green depths.

My back snapped up against the seat. "Boner, this is Matt. He's a physical therapist at the center where Rae gets treated."

"Hi." Matt rose to his feet, offering an outstretched hand.

Boner exhaled as he lifted his chin, studying Matt, as if scrutinizing a cockroach he was about to crush.

"This is Boner," I said.

Matt's gaze scurried over the many patches on Boner's worn leather vest.

Boner was a sight to see.

Over six feet tall, he wore faded jeans on his long legs ending in scuffed black boots, a ripped black club T-shirt, a tangle of leather bracelets around each wrist along with his bulky silver rings. A snake tattoo twisted up one of his sinewy arms. Two small silver hoops in one earlobe along with his exceptional hair and beard rounded off the image of the dark-road caballero, the insolent gypsy, the outsider rogue who wouldn't fit into any peg or give in to any rules, and that was just the way he liked it, damn it. And damn you if you didn't.

Ah, shit. Me, too. That's just the way I like it.

My sinful fantasy, my wicked addiction, my secret crush, my delusion.

I cleared my throat. "Working today?" *What a master of conversation I am.* I swallowed more of my mocha.

His brow furrowed as he shifted his weight. "Yeah, came to get coffee for me and the guys."

I swallowed him with my eyes as I licked the traces of coffee from my lips.

Holy hell, he's my mocha.

His large Adam's apple moved in his throat, his heavy eyes still on me, as if he wanted to say something but was busy talking himself out of it.

"Hey, there you are!" A tall brunette in a pretty light-blue off-the-shoulder asymmetrical top, big bangle bracelets, tight cropped skinny jeans, and high-wedge sandals clasped Boner's arm. She tossed me a quick look and then just as quickly ignored me.

I slightly slid down in my seat, and Matt's eyes widened for a second, as if the floor show had just gotten more interesting. *Was he envious? He should be.*

Mindy was a dancer at the local MC-owned strip club, the infamous Tingle. She was also Boner's latest woman and younger than me. Her toned, curvy shape pressing against Boner made me bite my lip as my hand went to my belly.

Boner glanced at her. "On a break."

"All set, Boner!" Erica, the owner of the Meager Grand held a full white paper bag out over the counter.

Boner nodded at her and went over and took the bag. "Gotta get back to work," he muttered at Mindy.

His eyes slid back to me, and Mindy and Matt faded into a fuzzy background. Boner lifted his chin and strode out of the cafe.

I watched through the big picture window as he headed to his Harley parked out front, Mindy on his heels. He packed up his bag of coffee, mounted his chopper, and seemed to shove at the vintage bike with a slight but cocky motion of his body.

I clenched my jaw.

Man and machine were one.

He flipped on his sunglasses, a pair that suited him so well, and I suppressed the groan rising in my throat. These shades weren't the athletic-style ones I'd noticed he used when he rode long distances. These glasses had a more delicate, sophisticated frame along with a purplish tint to the lenses, giving a refined, sexy note to his otherwise grungy vibe.

He stared straight at me through those glasses, right through the big picture window. I could feel the heat of his gaze as intensely as if he were next to me, touching me, his breath heating my skin. The clink of cups, the din of chatter, the ringing of the cash register—all of it faded under the power of that gaze.

He gripped his handlebars, and his engine erupted into a roar. Mindy gave him a quick kiss, and then she backed away, coffee cup in hand. Boner took off, pipes blasting, his hair flickering behind him like a dark flame in the wind.

"That guy's a real biker, huh?" Matt's voice snapped me back to my dull, cold reality. "There's a club in this town, isn't there?"

My eyes unglued from the fading vision ripping down Clay Street and returned to Matt.

Nice Matt. Cute Matt. Conscientious Matt. Friendly all the time Matt. Colorless Matt. Flat Matt.

I cleared my throat. "The One-Eyed Jacks."

"How do you know him?"

My stomach grew heavy, and my taste buds deadened. I pushed my coffee to the side. "He's a friend of a friend, that's all."

Yes, it was time to get used to that fact of my life. That was all Boner would ever be—a friend of a friend. That was all.

I needed to let go of my little secret obsession.

TWO

BONER

I had to get out of there.

Jill, on a date. Jill, smiling and laughing with a guy who had grinned at her like he'd do anything for her, like he'd wanted to gobble her up whole.

I knew the feeling.

I had stood there, and they'd both looked up at me—his face riddled with concern, hers with a kind of astonishment. Jill's initial expression was one of promise, shimmering with suggestion. I'd soaked it in, and then reality, my reality, had jerked me away.

I took the long way back to the clubhouse.

Every time I saw Jill, my insides would jolt and shove against each other, like some sort of seismic tectonic shift. That was me all right—pieces of cracked shell that rested on hot, molten rock. If I went back to work now, I'd be a moody mess and not get much done. I liked to keep my shit tight on the inside and easy on the outside.

I headed for the wide open spaces. The dried fields of brush and yellowed grasses sucked me in on both sides of the blacktop on the main road out of Meager. The sun poured its brassy heat over this stretch of farmland, over me, and I savored the warmth.

I hated small spaces, had for years. Living out here in South Dakota had changed that for me. I could open my lungs and breathe in this land's seeming infinity, the massive sky stretching over me, daring me to touch it, willing me to soar. The endless sameness of the prairie or the farms or the grasslands was my relief.

Just beyond, the Black Hills rose before me, the thick evergreen forest making the mountains look inky on the horizon. The air became cool and crisp as I gained elevation. The sharp freshness of the towering pine and spruce trees and the quiet whispers of those ancient hunks of stone soothed me as I wound through them on that black twisting ribbon of road. Riding here all these years had breathed fresh life into my lungs. The tremors that used to grip my gut just after I'd left Denver had faded as me and my bike had become one force in the wind on these roads.

Something about Jill threatened that.

I pushed my chopper into high gear over the smooth asphalt, the wind battering my skin, my focus trained on the hum and rattle of my engine. Jill's face wouldn't fade from my mind, though.

The first time I had ever laid eyes on her was a long time ago. A horrible time. Seventeen years ago, when my best friend had been shot and killed. The night of his funeral.

She was a teenager then, a strawberry-blonde *everygirl* wiping at tears on her face.

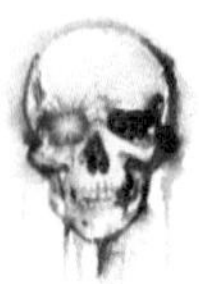

PAST

"Get the fuck out of here, you hear me?"

"Please, I need to see his wife. I need to tell her!"

I gritted my teeth as I dragged her away from the front gate of the clubhouse. "You will never see her or talk to her. You stay away from her, bitch!"

"You don't understand!"

We'd buried him only four hours ago, and brothers and old ladies from clubs all over were in the One-Eyed Jacks' clubhouse, dealing with their shock, sharing their Dig stories, drinking and eating, hugging, grieving.

Not another party crasher, not now.

I towered over her, my long hair swinging. "Oh, I understand real well. You're just some fucking groupie coming out of the woodwork like all the rest of 'em. There were plenty at the funeral, plenty more stragglers hovering the past few days, putting on their sympathy show."

"I'm not a groupie! I knew him. Please!"

"You all know Dig, don't you? Fuck off, little girl. Go find another club to blow."

"Why won't you listen to me?" Tears streamed down her crumpled face as she choked on her hiccupy breaths.

"Get out! Go!"

The viciousness of my yell pushed her, and she staggered backward under its force. I wiped off the wetness on my own face, my heart charged on adrenaline, on desolation.

My stomach clenched, my hands shook at my sides. I needed to eat, to sleep, yet both seemed unnecessary, unimportant. This burning, burning in my veins, in the pit of my soul—that was forever.

"Go!" I yelled.

She ran off down the gravel road.

Three months later, that girl was back.

There was a party. There had been plenty of parties to stem the tide of grief and despair. But it hadn't worked for me. I couldn't make sense of the way the currents had turned, sucking me under and then leaving me to float alone on the oily surface. Each party had blended into the next—a haze of faces, broken bottles, savage groping, bad jokes, forced laughs, burning lungs.

"Hey, hey, are you all right?" A small white hand firmly clasped my arm.

My head jerked at the touch, at the small hand's presumption over my ink. There was something irrational about those delicate fingers throttling the neck of my fanged snake.

"Hey, hey…" I mimicked her voice, laughing.

My eyes flicked over her. Medium height, pretty blondish-red hair in a mess of waves and curls tumbling over her shoulders, and a face like a doll's—pouty but serious. Her skin was pale with a spray of freckles over her nose and cheeks. Slate-blue eyes were trained on me, making my back straighten. That nervous jitter to her posture and her perfect pink lips made me lean in to her.

Motherfuck, it's her again.

"What the hell are you doing here?" I growled, my alcohol and weed–induced stupor abating for just a moment. "I told you to fuck off and stay off." I shook off her hand.

"Yeah, you did, but you wouldn't listen to what I had to say. And it's important."

"Important? What's so fucking important?"

"You were Dig's friend. He talked to you that day when I was with him."

I grabbed her arm and dragged her through the boisterous thick crowd toward where our cars and trucks were parked. I pushed her against the black Camaro. *His* Camaro.

"What don't you understand about, stay the fuck away? Look at you. This ain't a place for you. You're just a kid. What are you doin', huh? Go home. Get a life."

"I wouldn't have a life if it wasn't for Dig Quillen! He saved my life. And I know—I know—he called you on the phone to come help, to-to deal with the body," she whispered roughly.

My fingers grabbed her face, digging into her jaw. "Who the hell are you?"

"Dig killed that guy, Mole. Dig killed him for me."

Her words flared right through me, like an alternate oxygen, a compound that burned through my lungs, straight through to my brain cells, obliterating everything I'd thought I knew in its wake.

"Dig saved my life, and he got killed for it." Her eyes searched mine, the white beams of the overhead lights glaring down on us in the dark jungle of the club parking lot.

I peered into her face, my head hanging from my neck. "I saw that room, that bed. That was you?"

"Me." Her voice was firm, sure.

I was anything but. "You?"

"Yes."

"Tell me."

And there, against Dig's prized car, she told me every horrible detail of her abduction, every disgusting thing that fucker had done to her. How Dig had walked through that door, taken one long look at her, and changed everything.

"Yeah, he called me, and I went and cleaned it all up. No traces left, no body, not even those pizza boxes on the floor."

She winced, and her chest heaved. I grabbed her, her body wobbling in my grip. Her eyes shot open, and she pushed against me, a panicked moan escaping her lips.

"Who the fuck are you?" I whispered.

"Just a girl. Just a stupid girl."

"Why do you keep coming here, damn it?"

"I need to tell his wife. I need to tell her that I'm sorry. That-that it's all my fault." She leaned over, her body bowing as if she'd been pushed. She gulped in air, planting her hands on the hood of the Camaro. "That it's all because of me. I'm so sorry."

"She almost got killed, too, you know," I said. "Grace was pregnant, and the baby didn't make it."

"I know! I heard it on the news. She killed him, didn't she? The guy who—"

"She killed him."

"That's good. That's really good."

"You can't talk about this to anybody. You told your best friends? Your mommy and daddy?"

She violently shook her head. "No, no. Dig told me not to. Not ever. And I haven't. I won't."

The sound of her saying his name stung. "And how can I be sure of that?"

Her shoulders fell, her neck elongated. "I promised him. And I'm keeping that promise."

There was a force in her posture, a straight line that held firm.

She'd survived being kidnapped, tortured, sexually assaulted, and saved by an outlaw biker who had happened to be dealing drugs to her captor.

This girl couldn't be more than sixteen. Same age Grace was when Dig and I had first laid eyes on her a thousand years ago at a party of high schoolers, all innocence and sharp logic. Same age that Inés had—

My cousin Inés's adamant face seared my eyes. Defiance, despair, disregard. Even though I'd kept her safe. Even though she'd had me at her side, holding her up, assuring her with soft words, amusing her. My pleading, my strength hadn't been enough. She'd only slipped through my fingers. Nothing was ever enough for her.

I wasn't enough.

The girl's voice broke through my reverie. "I only came to see you. To explain. To find Mrs. Quillen, to tell her—"

"To tell her, what? Her whole life exploded in her face. What are you gonna tell her now that's gonna make that all better?" I shouted, my pulse jamming in my stiff neck. "Anyway, she's gone."

Her face paled. "Gone?"

"She left town. Up and took off. She ran away from all of us. Didn't even tell me." I shook, my whole body shook.

She lunged at me, her arms wrapping around my middle. I stiffened in her embrace, my breath snagging.

What the fuck was she doing?

"Forgive me. Forgive me," she said, her lips brushing against my shoulder, a hand tangling in my hair.

For one moment, I could believe this hug was real. It was her sorrow, but also my own. It was our confusion over this cataclysm in our lives. It was me and this girl out of nowhere, sharing this pain, this grief. It was me being lost and someone else getting it, holding it.

A shiver raced up my spine, and I swallowed hard. "What's your name?"

"Jill. Jill Loughlin."

"You can't be here, Jill Loughlin."

She let go of me and wiped at her face. "Okay."

"There's nothing for you here. Nothing."

She stared up at me, her gray-blue eyes glistening pools of wet, like stones in the sea. The tears, the choppy breaths had stopped. Her hand reached out and pressed against my chest.

"You loved him," she whispered. "He was a good man. A good person."

My heart raced under the pressure of her palm. She'd only spent a couple of hours with Dig, at best, yet she was so sure, so confident.

"I loved him like no other." My voice rasped in the cool darkness between us. "He was my best friend, my brother. I don't know how I'll live without him. I know I'll never forget him."

Her lips curved into the tiniest smile, her cheeks rising, her gray-blue eyes a force to be reckoned with. Her fingertips pressed into my chest. "You shouldn't ever forget him. I never will. Not ever."

I put a hand over hers and held it there, as if I could suck some of the Dig energy she'd absorbed out of her arm and make it flow into mine.

I squeezed her hand at my chest. "What did he say to you? He had to have said something—"

"He told me if the cops ever got involved, it would only make things worse for all of us."

"Yeah."

"And he made me promise to take care of myself, appreciate what I've got. And if I needed help, get it, and don't take it out on myself. 'Trust me on that one,' he said."

My stomach heaved, but I squashed down the physical drive to vomit. I only nodded, a strangled noise escaping my throat.

She moved her hand across my chest and removed it from me.

I shifted my weight. "You gotta go home. The Feds are hanging all over us. You got a car? How'd you get here?"

"I took the bus."

"Jesus." I wiped my arm across my face. "Where the hell do you live?"

"Ellston."

Almost three hours north of here. "I'm too fucked up to take you home myself, but I'll get someone who will."

"Are you sure?"

"Yeah, I'm sure. Gotta get you home."

"Thank you."

I only nodded, not sure what to do with her thank-you, her unflustered smile that lit up her whole face, her conviction, her trust.

I couldn't breathe.

"You remember, you don't say a word, to nobody. And I'll be watching out for things on this end. I'll keep an eye out. Know that I am. Don't you ever fuckin' dare talk to anybody—"

"I won't. I promise."

"Okay." I shuffled forward.

"Thank you."

I swiveled to face her. "Don't fucking thank me!" My voice came out harsh, mean. I hadn't wanted it to be though. I stood up as straight as I could. "Please, just don't thank me."

I had Dready take her home. I told him to get her talking, take down her address and phone number, find out anything else about her. He did.

And I kept tabs on her.

I'd kept eyes on her for the next year.

And Jill Loughlin hadn't disappointed.

"She saw me," Dready snorted over the phone. "She was hanging out with two girlfriends, waiting for the school bus, and I revved my engine. She spotted me right off, gave me a long look, and then got on her bus, not missing a beat."

"Good."

You couldn't miss Dready. Over six-three, all muscle, and reddish-brown hair in a mess of ratty dreadlocks.

"Get home," I said into my phone and shut it down.

I had kept my ears to the ground with the rival MC connected to the asshole who had kidnapped Jill and also his brother who had killed Dig. But things were quiet. Although both asshats were the nephews of that club's VP, there were no rumblings, no retaliatory maneuvers whatsoever.

But you could never be sure of this shit.

Every couple of weeks I sent Dready up to Ellston to check on Jill. Well, more like let her see him, let her know that the One-Eyed Jacks were a presence in her life. A teenage girl was an unknown entity.

It'd been about a year since she'd come to Meager and found me. She was in her senior year of high school now, went to church on Sunday with her parents, even went to youth group meetings and was a member of the track team. The all-American girl.

Jill didn't need me, and I had to stop being sucked in by the impulse to help, to save, to bolster.

I had to.

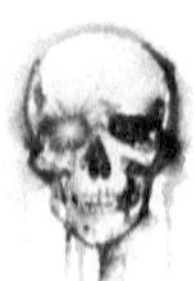

I pushed back the memories, got my head together, and finally made it back to the shop at the club. I left the bag of coffees on the strip of counter by the entrance.

"Where the hell have you been?" Dready opened the cover on the espresso I'd gotten him. "Fucking coffee's cold now. You suck, you know that? You get me addicted to this pricey shit, you insist on going to get it, and then you disappear and bring it cold."

"Had shit to do."

"Yeah, I'll bet."

I ripped my sunglasses off my face. "Fuck you. Go nuke it."

THREE

JILL

"YOUR TIRES ARE REALLY WORN OUT, JILL." Tricky glanced at me, his lips pressed together. "Good thing you brought it in today because, I'm telling you, looks like the left rear was ready to split. And your transmission…" He wiped at the thick mass of dark hair that had fallen over his eyes.

My ancient Honda looked old and tired next to the shiny hot rods being polished in the huge courtyard of the One-Eyed Jacks' repair and custom-detailing shop, Eagle Wings. Just beyond was the old go-kart track that was now used to test out bikes and cars. Lock was there with Travis, an Army buddy of his, not a member of the club, who was his hot rod specialist, their tall figures looming over the open hood of a freshly painted red muscle car gleaming in the sunlight.

Becca pulled on my hand, wanting to trot off into the bays where the men were working.

"I know, Tricky. I should've come in sooner. I just kept putting it off and I've been using Rae's car mostly and I forgot. Today, I could feel the difference once I got on the road, so I came right over. I didn't want to take any chances, especially with Becca in the car with me."

He wiped his hands on a rag hanging from his belt. "I'm gonna put in the order for the tires, and I'll give you a buzz tomorrow morning to let you know when I'll be ready to start, all right?"

"Thanks. I really appreciate it. Could you give me an idea of how much this is going to cost, so I can plan on—"

"No charge," said a deep voice behind me.

I swiveled around. Boner's green eyes swept over me, the muscle along his jaw pulsing.

"Oh, hey. You don't have to do that."

"We don't *have* to"—Tricky winked at me—"but that's the way it is. Gimme your keys."

I handed him my keys, and he opened the door, unhooked Becca's car seat, and planted it on the ground. He started my car and steered her to the side lot.

"You okay?" asked Boner.

No, not really—not with your tall, dark, bearded, long-haired magnificence studying me in that unrepentant way of yours.

Becca stilled beside me, her gaze glued on Boner. *Like mother, like daughter.*

"I'm great."

"That didn't convince me, Jill."

"Just haven't had my car looked at in a while, and it definitely needed a service check and new tires, as you heard."

Becca broke free of my loose grasp and lunged at Boner. "Ya! Hi. Hi." She embraced his legs.

"Hi, you." Boner's severe face broke into a grin, and he tousled her light-brown hair. "You keep growing, don't you?" He squatted down next to her. "Last time I saw you, you were this big!" He showed her an inch of space between his thumb and forefinger.

Becca's face lit up, and she grabbed at his thumb. "This big! This!" she stuttered.

Boner grinned and took her hand in his, and Becca swung their hands wide.

His green gaze fell on me. "You need a ride somewhere?"

Becca jumped up and down next to him, bringing his hand to her mouth.

There was no getting out of this now.

I adjusted the handle of my handbag on my shoulder. "A ride would be good."

"You heading home, or you got a doctor's appointment or something?"

"No doctor today. Thank God. I have to say, I see a lot of doctors these days between Rae's therapists, Becca's pediatrician, and my OB/GYN."

His face scrunched for a moment. Yep, there I was, babbling in his presence like some sort of infatuated teenager.

I was an infatuated teenager when it came to him.

Becca pinched his skin just over his wrist on the same spot where his tattoo of an angry snake slithered down his arm, baring its vicious eyes and long fangs.

My gaze followed the snake up his long arm to the black muscle shirt with the eagle logo of the club repair shop printed in red. His contoured shoulders and bare sinewy arms were taut as they held my daughter. His skin had a golden sheen to it from working outside and riding in the sun. His lean hips were cocked to the side, and his long legs were fitted in faded ripped blue jeans ending in black work boots. Although Boner was perhaps the least bulky of his brothers, he was muscular in a leaner, trimmer way than the obvious rounded bulk of Bear and Dready, two of the tallest and largest Club members, and Travis. Boner's muscles were perfectly proportioned to his frame. There was nothing overdone about him.

Well, except for that eerie stillness with which he looked at me, watched me, as if he were trying to burrow into my deeply held secrets. Yes, there was something out of balance about that.

But now, holding Becca's hand, he was relaxed, easygoing. *I guess he reserves the strange for me.* Who could blame him, after the intense start we'd had years ago?

I cleared my throat. "What I mean is, a day without a doctor visit for me is a really, really good day."

His lips twitched, and his cheekbones seemed to get more pronounced with that sudden swerve of his lips. "Right. I get that."

He lifted a hand, gesturing at my tummy. "You and the baby doing good?"

I took in a breath. "Yeah, I'm almost done with the second month, heading into the third."

His brows pulled together. "You puking every morning?"

I laughed.

Boner usually said what was on his mind and the way it was on his mind. It was refreshing.

"Actually, today, I didn't, which is pretty exciting. Although, I probably will later on today." I shrugged.

His gaze fell on me, and I straightened my posture under its weight.

"It's a real gift—what you're doing for Grace and Lock."

"I'm glad it all worked out. It's a gift for me, too."

We both averted our gazes.

"Well, my bike's out, obviously." He gestured toward his black chopper glinting in the afternoon sun.

My pulse spiked at the sight.

Thank God. Just the thought of getting on the back of his glorious self-styled chopper made my knees weak. It was a real signature piece with specially designed, by Lock, paint–detailing on his black gas tank of a red snake bursting forth from silver puffs of smoke.

I hadn't been on the back of a bike since I left Catch in Nebraska, and I missed it. I missed the exhilaration of the ride. I missed the thrill of hanging on to my man while I enjoyed that exhilaration of wind, speed, and metallic roar.

What I didn't miss, however, was clinging to a man I no longer trusted or had deep feelings for.

My gaze landed back on Boner. His eyes were on me, waiting for my response.

No, he wasn't Catch, nothing like him, and it sure wasn't the age difference either. Catch was the all-American boy next door gone bad—reckless, daredevil, seedy. Boner was the sage enigmatic phantom who visited you only in the shadows of the night.

His long-lashed extraordinary green eyes pierced me, and I felt that unique rush in my veins, leaving me breathless.

I cleared my throat. "Yep, the bike's definitely out. Unless you have one with a seat for Becca—"

He laughed. "My truck's over there." He turned back toward the open bays of the repair shop. "Yo, Trick! I'm heading out, giving Jill a ride."

Tricky raised a hand at us.

"Let's go." Boner handed me Becca and snatched up her car seat. He tracked toward his pickup, his long hair swinging over his shoulders in the hot breeze.

We set up Becca's car seat in the cab, belted her in, and climbed into his GMC.

He pulled out of the clubhouse property. "You need anything?"

I let out a laugh.

"What's so funny?"

"Everyone asks me that all the time."

He shot me a quirky no-shit grin. "That's good, right?" His attention went back to the road.

I took in a slight breath to deal with that smile and that tone of voice. That casual, comfortable of-course-you're-one-of-us-now attitude made a small part of me warm inside.

He was right. It was good. It made me feel like I belonged, was important to somebody—or several somebodies actually—after so many years of straggling, struggling, and drifting from one job to the next, one idea to the next, one set of pals to the next. *But this was only for a little while, wasn't it?* Until the baby was born. I'd always be connected to Rae and Tania because Becca was their blood, but how much of a real family member *I* was to them, I wasn't so sure. I was just the former girlfriend of Rae's son and Tania's brother.

My hand pulled at the seat belt over my tummy. "It's good for the baby, of course."

"Not just for the baby," he said, his eyes flashing at me.

"Well, yeah, okay, but I mean—"

"Not just for the baby," he said again, easing on the brakes at a red light on Clay Street in the middle of town.

My breath caught at his insistent, tenacious stare.

His head tilted. "Tell me you get that."

"Yeah, I get that."

"Good." His attention shot to the green traffic light. "So, you need to hit the supermarket?"

"Oh. It's okay."

"What does that mean?"

"It means, don't worry about it."

"I'm not worried, Jill. I want to help you. Do you need to hit the supermarket?"

"I'll grab Rae's car and go myself later. It's fine."

"Jill, where were you headed before you came by the club?"

My face heated. "To the supermarket," I mumbled.

"Right. Which one do you go to? Tibbet's or Safeway?"

"Boner, really, it's fine. You don't have to—"

"You got to do a full shop or grab a couple of things?"

"It's okay, really. Just take us home."

"Full shop," he said.

"I'll take care of it."

"Sweetheart, I bet you've been taking care of it on your own for a long time. Now, which supermarket is it gonna be?"

I sank back in my seat.

"Jill, baby, come on." His voice softened.

My stomach curled, and I glanced at him. "Safeway, please. They're having a sale on Becca's diapers this week."

"Safeway, it is." He licked his lower lip as he hit the left turn signal at the stop sign to take us to the main road to the store on the outskirts of town. "That wasn't too hard now, was it?"

"What?"

His eyes slid to mine, an eyebrow raised. "Telling me what you want."

I squirmed in my seat, my hand squeezing the seat belt across my chest. "Not too hard."

He let out a laugh. "Liar."

What was hard was being in a closed space with him. His scent was so interesting. It was spicy but earthy and mellow all at the same time. I cast a quick glance at him. The relaxed way he drove, one arm slung on the wheel, his long legs stretched before him, his other hand draped over the center console—it was downright sexy. All I wanted to do was stare at his profile and run my fingers through his long hair to finally know what it felt like. Just that—a touch—and I'd be happy. Maybe I should try bumping into him on purpose at some point. Then, my hands could get caught in his fantastic mane, and he'd grab me—

Shut up, Jill.

All this one-on-one attention from him was making my tummy do flip-flops in addition to the flip-flops it'd already been doing as I settled into the first trimester of pregnancy. Usually, Boner and I were in the company of others, never alone. Either at Rae's house, when he'd stop by with Grace, or at the club, if I'd stop by to meet up with Grace. I'd seen him in town many times, but I'd usually duck out, not wanting to bump into him.

I trained my gaze outside the window. *Get a grip. Get a grip.*

At the supermarket, he took Becca from my arms, fit her in the child's seat and took charge of the shopping cart. "You got a list, or we winging it?"

I waved the piece of scrap paper in my hand. "A list."

"Of course you do."

"Why, of course?" I asked as we strolled down the pasta aisle.

"I figured, with you having Becca, you living in a new town, being pregnant, taking care of Rae and her house, and it being just over two months in, and you're still walking and talking *with* a smile on your face, then you must be organized with a capital O."

He took the cans of tomato sauce I had piled in my arms and tossed them in the cart.

"You would be correct," I replied, adding boxes of ditalini, fusilli, elbow macaroni, and linguine to the cart.

"You liking Meager?"

"Actually, it's not much different from where I grew up, which is just north of here, so it feels comfortable to me."

"You ever go home?"

"No."

"Why not?"

"Are you always this inquisitive?"

"Usually helps being inquisitive when you're trying to get to know a person, don't you think?"

I stacked the tuna cans next to the tomato sauce in the cart. "I don't go home because there's nothing to go home to." I shot him the plastic smile that I'd perfected over the years, the one that kept the quivering emotions away. I turned my attention to the ketchup, my fingers brushing the bottles on the shelf.

Becca sang to herself. We turned the corner onto the cereal aisle. Suddenly, her back straightened and her eyes widened. She'd noticed the big colorful boxes with her cartoon heroes and heroines lining the shelves

"Uh oh," said Boner.

"Whatever you do, don't stop," I whispered. He kept the cart moving at a quick clip.

I twisted my shopping list in my fingers. "Are you from Meager originally?"

"Nope. Denver."

"Really? Nice. You ever go home?"

His eyes remained on Becca. "Nothing to go home to."

The flat tone of his voice had me do a double take. There was that severity again. He ignored me as he squeezed Becca's hand.

Boner and I had things in common.

Suddenly, dizziness and a queasy swell in my stomach gripped me. *That smell.* I grabbed the edge of the shopping cart, a cold sweat beading on my forehead. "Oh, no."

"What is it? Shit, you're pale."

"The rotisserie chicken from the deli department." I gulped in a breath, the nausea swirling up my throat. "Not good."

Boner immediately turned the shopping cart around and grabbed me by the arm. "This way, babe."

Half an hour later, I had filled the cart with everything on my list. "I'm done. Do you need anything?"

His eyes creased. "What do you mean?"

"Food, paper goods, household cleaning items, feminine products?"

His eyes lit up, and my insides warmed again.

"Yeah, there is one thing." He wheeled the cart to the household goods aisle and stopped in front of the slim selection of toys. "This." He grabbed a small baby doll packaged in a plastic box and handed it to Becca.

Her eyes widened. "Baby?"

"Yep. What do you think, Becs?" he asked her.

Becca hugged the box in a death grip.

"Say thank you, sweetie," I said.

Becca stared at Boner, her fingers whitening over the box. "Ank you."

"You're welcome." He tilted his head at me. "Done now."

He took us home and brought the bags into the kitchen.

Boner stared out the window. "This backyard needs a lot of work."

"Rae used to have this kid from down the block take care of it, but his family moved, and no one else is interested in helping out. Landscapers are a little expensive for her right now, with the doctor bills and all that."

"You ain't doing it either."

"No, no. I was going to put an ad in the local gazette and ask around. I just haven't gotten to it yet. Oops."

"I'll take care of it."

"You're going to do it?"

"No, I'll have one of the prospects take care of it."

"Are you sure? I mean—"

He faced me, his body brushing mine, as we stood at the kitchen window together. "What do you mean?"

His cinnamon breath from the gum he'd been chewing fanned my face, and prickles went up my neck at the dark shadow crossing the angles of his cheekbones and jaw.

"I mean, I'm sure your prospects must have more important club things to do than mow a local lady's lawn and weed her property."

"On top of the fact that Rae is good people and a solid part of our community, you're living here, too, and you're good people and a part of our community now."

"So, it's a good PR move for the club then?"

"PR?" His eyes narrowed, as if I'd said something unintelligible, and I instantly regretted it. "You mean, my boys get seen out here, raking and clipping while wearing their colors, doing a thorough job. Then, the neighbors see Rae's terrific new garden and ask her about it, and Rae sings our praises to the locals. Nothing better than that kind of word of mouth. That kind of PR?"

"Uh-huh."

"I wasn't thinking of the PR, Jill. If I know that Becca has a clean garden to play in, I'm going to feel good, knowing that she's happy and that her grandma's happy out there, in the clean garden, watching her granddaughter enjoy it all, and—"

My eyes bugged out of my head. "There's more?"

His hands went to his hips. "It takes one thing off your to-do list, which will lighten your load and make you happy, and then you'll be able to enjoy your daughter enjoying her grandmother's garden. That's why I'm taking care of it."

Something fluttered in my chest, and I tore my gaze away from his green eyes that were literally sparkling in the sunlight filling the kitchen.

"Well." I chewed on my lip. "That's a hell of a lot of happy."

FOUR

JILL

"LET'S HEAR IT for the dark-haired princesses. Right, Becca?" I clapped my hands, and Becca clapped with me. "Thank you for getting her the DVD, Rae. We love Snow White."

"My pleasure, honey. We're going to start her off with the classics. *Cinderella* will be next on our list."

I turned to Becca. "Oh, *Cinderella!* I love *Cinderella.*"

Becca's gaze jumped from me to her grandmother and back again. She clomped over to Rae, who sat in her electric lounge chair, and climbed onto her lap. My heart squeezed. I was so grateful that she had a grandmother whose lap she could climb onto, a grandmother who watched classic movies with her, told her stories, fed her, held her, laughed with her, shared her home with her and her mother.

Every day, I thanked God that I had landed in Meager, South Dakota. After Catch's sister, Tania, and her friend Grace had saved my daughter from a kidnapper in Nebraska, I had left with them and come to Meager where they lived. Tania had offered me room and board and pay to look after her mom and her house now that Rae was ill. It was a temporary solution that was working out great for all of us.

Catch and his family were estranged, so it was kind of ironic that I, his ex-girlfriend, was now a part of his family. I truly liked being a member of their circle. His mom, Rae, was an outspoken and smart woman, Tania was the same with a vein of humor and sass I really enjoyed, and his eldest sister, Penny, was a married mom to two boys, no-nonsense and practical to the core.

Tania and Grace had ended up saving my daughter from Creeper, a renegade One-Eyed Jack, and Grace and I had finally met by that stroke of fate. Her first husband, Dig, had saved my life by killing the man who had kidnapped me when I was fifteen.

A week later, Dig had been shot and killed by my captor's brother, in revenge for that act of salvation. Since Grace was unable to have her own kids, I had offered to carry her and her new husband's baby.

I was thrilled to be a part of their new start. It had been a new start for me, too, a huge positive. It was giving back with gratitude, coming full circle.

Now, here I was, a member of a family I'd never expected to have in my life, and it felt good.

Rae adjusted her electric reclining chair. "My mother used to sing that song to me."

"Which song?"

Rae began singing Snow White's song about her prince coming one day.

Becca raised her hands and laid them on her grandmother's face, enjoying Rae's clear, strong voice vibrating over her.

"My mother used to sing it to me, too," I said. "And I used to fully expect a man in colorful tights, a cape, and a crown on his gorgeous head to come knocking on my front door at any moment."

Rae's face warmed with a smile that told of a lifetime's worth of contented sighs and rich heartbeats. "Mine did."

"From everything you've told me about your husband, he certainly was a prince."

"A farmer prince!" Rae laughed.

I packed the DVD back into its case. "My mom used to tell me, 'He will come one day, and you best be ready for him.'"

"She was right. But that doesn't mean that you wait by the door with your coat in your hand, ready to take off the second Mr. Prince comes knocking. No, first, you need to be the person you want to be, and then you'll be ready for your proper prince. Otherwise, he won't be the right prince for you."

"Good point," I said.

Rae sipped on her tea. "It'd be unfair to yourself and to him—expecting him to make your dreams come true, to fill you up and make you happy. If you're not happy on your own, with yourself, you will never find it in someone else. It simply doesn't work that way."

Catch and I had done that, hadn't we? We'd had so many expectations for each other from the very beginning. As soon as all the little disappointments had piled up, the resentment had grown easily and created a thousand wedges between us.

"Look at Snow White," I said. "She had to deal with the huntsman, the dwarfs, and the evil queen before she was ready for that magic kiss, right?"

"Your mommy is *so* smart!" Rae said to Becca, who was gnawing on a graham cracker.

I glanced at my daughter. Becca wore the same adamant look of concentration on her face that her father did while he ate.

Rae stroked Becca's back. "You're young yet, Jill. You'll find someone else, and he'll find you. I only hope it's not too late for Tania. She's determined to follow through on her divorce. Who knows? Maybe she'll give Kyle another chance now that she's going back to Racine."

"Rae, she's going back to pack up her stuff and see her lawyer. She seems very sure. Upset, but sure about her decision, especially about moving back here to Meager. That's really exciting, don't you think?"

In two days Tania would be leaving South Dakota to return to Racine, where she lived with her soon-to-be ex-husband. Having Tania here the past two months had been great. She'd made sure that Becca and I felt comfortable, that her mom and I settled into a routine around the house and with Rae's various doctor and rehab appointments. I genuinely liked Tania; I would miss her. She was the older sister I'd never had, and she and Becca had fallen in love with each other.

"I just don't want her to have regrets," said Rae. "Ending your marriage is serious business. They've been married for just over ten years now. It's a shame. I mean, *now* they've figured out that they don't get along?"

"You get comfortable, even when you're unhappy, don't you think? Sometimes, it's really hard to take charge of your own unhappiness." I picked up Becca's jumbo Lego blocks from the floor and put them back in their plastic jar. "Better now than much later on, right? At least there aren't any children in the mix."

Rae's lined face etched into a tight frown that was more like a carefully constructed dam holding back an overflowing reservoir of frustration and disappointment. "They just kept putting it off. See how time flies away with you? I know, it's her life. But that's my headstrong daughter for you, barreling ahead, not much thought to the future."

I scooped up Becca in my arms. "I'm looking forward to having her back with us soon."

Rae sighed. "So am I. She'll be back before we know it."

My phone pinged a text notification. *I knew it.*

Can't make it today. Will call u

Typical.

This was the third time Catch was blowing off visiting his daughter. But now those visits included his mom, and Rae hadn't seen her son in years. She didn't talk about him much to me, which was just as well, but on occasion I'd hear her telling Becca stories about her dad as a boy. She was his mother, for Pete's sake.

"Rae? I don't think Catch will be able to come today."

Rae's neck stiffened. "Oh? That's too bad." She adjusted the small pillow she kept at her lower back.

I bit my lip. "He got sent out of town at the last minute. Can't say no to the boss."

"I suppose not." She busied herself with the television remote control. The news flashed by, a soap-opera, a talk show.

I put my phone down on the coffee table. "I'm going to change Snow White's diaper and put her down for a nap. Would you like me to make you another cup of tea first?"

"No honey, you go ahead and take care of our princess. I'll survive."

I headed into my bedroom with Becca. I needed to call Tania and let her know her brother wouldn't be coming. She'd be disappointed too, but was better at hiding it than her mom. And I'd have to find a way to explain it to our daughter, too. Catch really knew how to make the women in his life happy.

FIVE

BONER

"BONER, TAKE A PICTURE OF US, would you?" Grace handed me her cell phone and rushed back to stand with Tania at the front door of the office of Eagle Wings. Tania had come over to say goodbye before she took off for Wisconsin.

I dropped my phone on Grace's desk.

"Have you not heard of the selfie concept?" Tania asked her, brushing her black hair from her face.

"I want the real deal photo right now," Grace shot back. "I'm going to miss you."

"I'm only going back there to pack up my stuff and hire a lawyer. I'll be back before you know it—a month or two, tops."

Tania and Grace threw their arms around each other and laughed. You would've thought they were teenagers again.

I aimed Grace's phone and got the two of them in focus.

Whir-click. Whir-click. Whir-click.

"Wait!" Grace held up her hand. "Jill, get in here with us."

Jill glanced up at me and joined Grace and Tania, going between them. The three of them smiled huge, and I tapped on the screen.

Whir-click. Whir-click.

"Got it," I said, putting Grace's phone on her desk and grabbing mine.

The three of them yakked and hugged some more. Tania opened the front door of the office, and light streamed in, diffusing its gold through Jill's tumble of wavy strawberry-blonde hair.

I stood stock-still, taking her in: a curvy body in slim-fitting jeans, tired-looking black leather cowboy boots, a turquoise-blue T-shirt with a crisp white jean jacket over it. What little makeup she wore made those incredible eyes pop and didn't cover up those freckles.

Tania made some dirty wisecrack, and Jill threw her head back and laughed. That rich silky laugh of hers filled my ears, rippling through me. Her sweet face was relaxed, and her eyes, more blue than gray, gleamed in the light.

Whir-click.

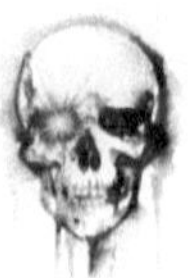

I grabbed a bottle of Miner beer from my fridge and drank, savoring the cold brew washing down my dry throat. I tossed my keys, my phone, and my gun on the kitchen counter, and then I drained the bottle. It had been a long day at work, and I was relieved it was finally over.

The *bip bop* from my phone went off. I opened my texts and saw Butler's code for me to call him back.

Butler had gone nomad last year after he'd been stripped of the presidency of our North Dakota chapter for colluding with a rival club and being totally off his ass on cocaine and whatever else he could find. Out on his own, he'd gotten clean with the help of twelve-step programs and the force of sheer will.

Over the past year, Butler had been doing freelance bounty-hunting for several clubs that were Jack-friendly all over the country. Our national president had given him permission to do so, loaning him out. But Jump, our chapter president and not a fan of Butler, had no idea. Grace had seen him with the Flames of Hell in Nebraska last year, and he'd asked her to keep it quiet, especially from Jump. She'd shared it with me though, and I'd been in closer touch with him ever since.

Butler's ultimate prey was Creeper, a former Jack who had worked with the same rival club as Butler last year but had gone over to their dark side after the dust had settled. He'd shot Butler and my prospect, Dawes, disappeared from the radar, and even kidnapped Jill's daughter a few months ago in retaliation for an alleged wrong done to him by Becca's dad, Catch, a Flames of Hell member.

I opened the bottom drawer and shoved aside the tray of screwdrivers, a small hammer, rope, and plastic ties, sliding out the burner from underneath.

I hit his number. "Hey."

"Creeper's with the Blades. They got him protected, on lockdown."

I drained my bottle. "Prisoner or guest?"

"Not sure yet. You know how these things go."

"Yeah." I rubbed a hand across my mouth. "Keep me in the loop."

"You be ready."

"I'm ready," I said. "By the way, Lock wants in."

"You sure about that?"

"He needs it. I'd like to give it to him."

"Let's give it to him then."

"Good. Later."

"Later, man."

I tossed the burner on the counter. It bounced off my phone, and the screen came to life. My camera was still on. The last photo I had taken appeared in the corner.

I tapped on it to enlarge it, bracing for what I knew full well would appear on the screen.

Jill.

That sensual smile was on her face, hinting at endless silky secrets, and her strawberry-blonde hair was covering one eye while the sunlight created a glow behind her. I enlarged the photo. Her lips were parted, her eyes innocent yet knowing.

Comfort on the edge. Yeah, that summed her up.

My pulse raced, my breath grew short. Fuck, what would she feel like under my hands? That pink mouth opening up to mine?

Unusual streaks of starlight shooting across my black sky—that was what it would be like.

My blood heated.

I closed my eyes as my fingers unbuttoned my jeans. My hand dived in and fisted my hardening cock. I opened my eyes, and they landed on her picture.

I stroked harder, my free hand planted on the counter as I leaned over. My gaze was pinned on her picture, my balls tightening.

My lips on her pale skin.

My tongue twisting with hers.

My hands on her naked flesh, kneading those incredible full tits.

Jill.

Her moans bursting between us, making me throb even harder.

I stroked faster, her smiling face encouraging me, her swollen lips teasing me.

My grip tightening on her soft full hair, the silky strands sliding through my fingers, over my chest, as she moved down my body.

"Jill—" I choked out.

Those grayish-blue eyes were on me, pleading for my touch, pleading for more. For me.

I came, my lungs contracting.

Fuck, she was going to be the end of me.

No, the end of me began a long, long time ago.

I cleaned up and grabbed myself another beer and drank, staring out the window over the sink. The late afternoon sun was burning over the grass, a final blazing hurrah before dusk. An ordinary afternoon, like every other. Ordinary like that horrible morning in Denver had been. It had started out bright and sun-filled like any other morning.

Only, it hadn't been.

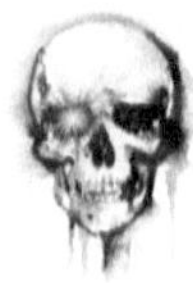

PAST

That morning I'd wanted to do something special for my mother. I'd woken up early for school, brushed my teeth, gotten dressed, packed my book bag, and even put matching socks on and tied my laces the right way for a change. I made her tea and toast with lots of butter the way we liked it, set our small table, and I waited for her to wake up. But all the time I sat in my chair, my eyes on her in the big bed, she didn't move. The blanket and the sheets didn't move. Her flannel nightgown didn't move.

I jumped up, knocking over the tea. "Mommy! *Mamá!*"

Two days later, at the funeral parlor, I bent over her casket and untangled the rosary from her rigid hands. I had to have it.

I managed to unlace it from her fingers while all the adults spoke loudly, away from the coffin. Only my cousin, Inés watched me, her eyes growing wider by the second.

My mother's fingers were as cold and hard as stone. I flinched, my heart slamming through me. I glanced up at her face even though I'd promised myself I wouldn't. It was pulled tight, her mouth drawn. This wasn't the soft prettiness of my mother.

This was what lifeless meant.

"Tu mamá está durmiendo ahora, está mirándote desde el Cielo."

All the adults spouted some variation of that line at me over and over again.

What baloney.

She wasn't sleeping or watching me from heaven. She was dead. And it didn't make me feel any better that she was somewhere else. I wanted her here with me—now. But she wasn't and never would be again.

This, *this*, was dead—her and me both.

I held back the tears stinging the backs of my eyes, but it was no use. Drops spilled down my face onto her stony fingers.

Two massive hands gripped my shoulders and hauled me back. The rosary snapped in my grip, the cross catching in Mommy's laced fingers.

"Oh, don't cry. Boys don't cry," said Uncle Johnny. "Enough. Leave her be. Come, take Inés's hand, and we'll go home now."

I was going to live with my mother's brother, Uncle Juan. Although, now that he was Americanized, he called himself Johnny.

I shoved the rosary in my pocket and took my cousin's hand while two fingers of her other hand were firmly planted in her mouth. She was nine, a year younger than me, but she still sucked on her fingers whenever she got anxious, which was a lot of the time.

I stole a last look back at my mother. She was just a thing now, a thing in a box. But something stabbed at me, spilling my insides on the floor of that dark ornate parlor room.

Good-bye, Mommy. I love you forever, my heart whispered to her.

My breath caught at the sight of the silver cross glinting at me from her rigidly folded hands. The shadows fell over her pale statue-like face, and the wooden top thudded into place.

Inés shuffled beside me. I took my hand from my pocket and peeked at my fist, the long chain of dark red beads hanging from it. The two free ends swung at my side. I'd broken her precious *rosario*. I'd ruined it. It was now just a chain of stones of dried blood, not beautiful any longer, its supernatural powers destroyed.

A moan escaped the back of my throat, and my lips quivered as a wave of emotion slammed into me. She was really gone, and I was alone. This broken chain was all I had left of her.

I sucked in a deep breath and stuffed the *rosario* back in my pocket. At least I'd gotten something of hers to keep. She could have the cross. She would need it to protect her in that box in the ground.

I'd get by.

SIX

BONER

"TANIA'S HERE!" Grace shut down her phone and slid it in her pocket.

"She's back?" I asked, taking the work orders I needed off her desk.

"She's back. Finally. It's been two months too long," Grace said.

Becca held her arms up at me. "Bo!"

I lifted her high up, her legs and arms swimming in the air, and then I squeezed her in my arms.

"You're going to spoil her, always picking her up every time she bats her eyelashes at you," Grace said.

"Ah, I'm a sucker for this girl. End of story."

Whenever Grace had Becca at the office, I'd sneak in to see her. She remembered me from our trip to the supermarket a while back and liked all the funny faces I made at her. Not to mention, when I held her on my lap, we'd play peekaboo, and she'd hide behind my hair.

One afternoon, maybe the second time I'd seen her at the office, Grace had asked me to watch her for a few minutes when an important call had come through.

I'd taken Becca in my lap. "*Becca, Boner,*" I said to her, popping the B's of our names really loudly.

She'd become fascinated with my lips, and I kept doing it.

"*B-ecca, B-oner!*"

Becca's face had lit up, and she shrieked, her hand going to my mouth, pulling on my lips. I did it again and again, both of us laughing in our corner of the office.

Then, it happened.

"*Bo! Bo!*"

"*Yeah, yeah, okay. Sure, Bo-Bo, it is.*" I tweaked her chin.

"There she is." Grace's voice snapped me back to reality, her eyes trained on a vehicle entering the open gate in the distance.

She turned to me. "You got Becca, or should I—"

"You go ahead. I've got her."

Grace dashed out the door toward the yard where Tania's Yukon was pulling in. A bike suddenly roared around Tania's vehicle and came to a stop by the line of our bikes.

It was Butler.

"Fuck me," I muttered to myself. "Oh, sorry, Becs. Damn."

With Becca in my arms, I made my way out the door to the thick of the yard where Butler swung off his bike.

"Dude! It's about time!" Dready hollered.

Butler ripped off his lid, and his face split into a grin a mile wide. Dawes, Bear, Kicker, and Tricky came out of the clubhouse and the shop, crowding around him, hugging him. Lock stood to the side, his arms folded.

Time might heal all wounds but way the fuck slowly for some of us.

I clamped a hand on Lock's shoulder. His teeth dragged across his bottom lip.

Last year, Butler and Grace had had a short-lived fling before she and Lock had finally gotten their act together. It had turned out to be more fucked-up club business than personal feelings—at least for Grace—but thank fuck all that mess had finally been put to rest and was behind us.

"Give her to me," Lock muttered.

I handed Becca over to him, and she immediately squashed her face in his broad chest. He put his hand on her back and made his way toward Grace and Tania.

I headed for Butler. "Well, well, well."

That huge white-toothed grin of his beamed at me, his light-blue eyes dancing. "Get over here, you crazy fuck," he growled.

We lunged at each other, hands slapping backs. He'd been an unruly prospect when he first started out, a temperamental and sometimes self-indulgent one who'd met with many holes and ditches on his road, but in the end, he was a good brother, a good man. I was glad to see him again, here where he belonged.

"Jump around?" he asked about our president.

"Yeah. Actually, he's—"

"It's about time. Where the fuck have you been?" shouted Nina, marching toward Butler.

Nina, our surprise guest, had arrived the other day with her bodyguard, Led, announcing herself to the club. Led was Flames of Hell. Turns out, so was Nina.

Butler froze. "What are you doing here?" His voice was suddenly several octaves lower.

A hush settled over the yard. Jump appeared, crossing his muscled arms with a sneer on his face, like he'd bitten into broken glass yet actually enjoyed the crunch. "What's the matter? Not happy to see your old lady?"

Butler's eyes drilled into Jump and then shifted to Nina.

Butler had an old lady, a woman with a family connection to the Flames of Hell, and he hadn't even bothered to tell me about it.

"When did you get here?" Butler asked her, his voice sharp. "We'd said next week."

"Led and I thought we'd come early and check out South Dakota," Nina said. "You're late. You were supposed to be here yesterday."

"Took my time on the road, is all." Butler gave her a quick kiss and tracked back to his Harley, snapping open saddlebags, unclipping cords, grabbing an empty water bottle, his longish blond hair in his face.

"What the hell are you doing here, Butler?" Jump asked.

I moved forward. "Why don't we take this inside?"

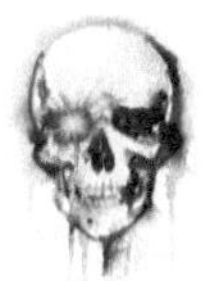

"What I'm trying to lay out for you here is that Notch and his Broken Blades declared war on you months ago in so many small ways, and he's made inroads, even with his sources depleted. We need to deal with it, and, Jump, you don't have the manpower to ante up. I just bumped into one of his boys on the road, and let's just say, he wasn't happy to see me."

"Fuck no," I muttered.

Butler was holding court at the big table. It had only been a year or so since he was last invited to sit with us, but it felt like much longer to me. He was here, he was sober, he was trying to get back in.

He folded his hands, his jaw set. "I had to make sure he understood that fucking with me and the Jacks was not an option."

Kicker, our Vice President, and Dready exchanged glances. Lock and Bear visibly tensed.

Butler leaned in toward Jump. "You think about that."

Jump only dragged his fingers through his gray-streaked beard.

"The Broken Blades have fallen on low times," continued Butler. "They've been making enemies out of old friends, especially the Flames. Their income has tanked, and they've been losing members and chapters."

"At least two that I've heard of have shut down," said Kicker.

"Right, and now Notch, their esteemed president, is desperate to hang on to his club's traditional territory," added Butler.

I lit another cigarette. "Parts of Nebraska and Wyoming."

"Yeah. Doesn't look good," Butler said. "And Notch isn't happy with the circling vultures."

Jump folded his hands on the table. "Notch hasn't been happy for decades. Tell me something new."

Butler dragged on his cigarette. "Now that his club is outnumbered, he's been trying to recruit."

"And who's panting over his territory?" Jump's bulky shoulders rose, making his neck seem shorter than it actually was. "Let me guess. Finger and his Flames of Hell?"

"Makes sense," I said. "They're both in Nebraska, both border each other, and both have different alliances. The Flames could swallow them up real easy and get rid of an adversary."

"And spit out the bones." Jump leaned back in his thick leather chair, his eyes on Butler. "What's this really all about? You want to stay?"

"I want to be a part of this club again. Yes."

"Why should I care about what you want?"

"I'm bringing you new blood to the table."

Jump's huge shoulders rolled again. "How so?"

"I can bring you a connection to one of the largest outlaw clubs in this country," said Butler.

"You been playing in the sandbox with other clubs again, you sneaky fuck?"

"That ain't the way of a nomad, Jump. I only take orders from the Jacks' national prez."

Holding Butler's hard stare, Jump took in a long breath and slowly released it. "Have you now? Well, you know I've never been interested in that sort of connection."

"This way—"

"You mean, *your* way?" spit out Jump.

"I'm talking about an MC network with the Flames of Hell. And no, the Jacks won't be the underdog satellite to a bigger national club or the lackey to some big-city mobsters or a Mexican cartel. We have the opportunity to create a pipeline from the East Coast through the Midwest and the Great Plains with other clubs who share our philosophy."

"The Flames are big, man. They've got plenty of mob ties," said Dready.

"They do, but not to all their businesses or all their territories. It wouldn't have to touch us, not directly. We do our thing out here, keep the trade flowing. They get access to our product, high-quality tried-and-true product, and we get greater and easier distribution."

"Percentages?" asked Kicker.

"Negotiable."

"And what do they want from us in our territory?" I asked.

"Money-laundering to start and slowly introducing their product through our channels out West."

Jump's face tightened.

"It's a form of stability, Jump. An opportunity to form something new. I know about the Blades cutting off your route to Texas. The Colorado Jacks are barely holding on."

"I'm handling it!"

"Are you?"

"You challenging me?"

"No. Stating facts. The Jacks need an ally right now, and the Flames of Hell would be a formidable one. I'm telling you, the Blades' predicament is attracting attention from other MCs that we have historically not gotten along with. If one of them gets a foothold in our neck of the woods, it aint' gonna be good. The time has come to pick and choose, and we need to do so early and choose right."

"Listen to you," Jump let out a dark laugh. "If it hadn't been for your amazing leadership skills, our North Dakota chapter would be solid now. Luckily, Judge has a brain and has worked damn hard to clean up the mess you left behind."

"You think I don't know that? I know that better than you, and it's eating me up inside. I've been out there, Jump. I've visited a lot of clubs. Years ago, you had a chance to work with the Flames of Hell, but you didn't want to. Dig was for it, creating something new and strong in our region, but you blasted that idea out of the water. Then, that opportunity died along with him. Since then, the Flames' reach has gotten even stronger."

"You Finger's number one fan now?"

"I respect the man."

"We've been doing good all these years," Jump said. "If it ain't broke, I don't fix it."

Butler's blue eyes lightened in the sunlight filtering through the one large window that stretched across the side wall. "What do you fix, Jump? Over the years, it's been noticed that you don't fix much."

Heavy silence met that loaded statement. Obviously, the National Jacks weren't happy with Jump.

"And your idea of good only lasts so long," Butler continued. "We need great now."

"Is this why you dragged that bitch out here?" Jump sneered.

Butler pushed his coffee mug to the side. "My old lady happens to be the sister-in-law of the national VP of the Flames of Hell. You'd better watch how you talk and tread."

"And Led is her guard dog, huh? You fuck."

"South Dakota is far away from Ohio. They want to make sure their girl is being taken care of."

"That's up to you, brother, not me." Jump leaned back against his chair. "Unless your cock ain't up for the job. I seem to remember hearing something like that. Is that what Led's here for?"

"Fuck you," Butler spit out.

"Jump, come on, man!" I mashed what was left of my smoke into the ashtray in front of me.

Butler's icy-blue eyes drilled holes into Jump. "My cock gets the job done. Question is, will yours?"

"I don't owe you shit, Butler. You think you can stroll back in here, and I'll hand you the keys to my kingdom?"

"I don't want the keys, and it's not *your* kingdom, is it?" Butler leaned forward. "This needs to go up for a vote."

Jump's eyes hardened. "You still using? Because I can tell you right now, if you stay and get comfy and you fuck up again, I catch you using—just once—you'll be out on your goddamn ass forever."

"I'm not using. Been clean for a year now," said Butler.

"Says you." Jump leaned over on his elbows. "There will be no voting on you coming back or on chitchatting with the Flames until I see how clean or unclean you really are."

"Agreed." Butler slanted his head as he rubbed his hands together. "And another thing—"

"What's that?" A deep chuckle vibrated in Jump's throat. "You and your old lady want the honeymoon suite tonight?"

Butler held Jump's gaze. "I've got Creeper."

Jump's face slackened.

"I know you want him," Butler said. "You need to nail his ass to make your show of strength to everyone out there, to show that our honor's intact. The Flames want him bad after he kidnapped Catch's kid, but I was out there, looking for him, for us."

"He's ours to put into the ground. Ours." Jump rapped his knuckles on the table.

"I agree," said Butler.

Butler's eyes caught mine and then returned to Jump. "Now, I got him, and I'm offering you your moment in the sun."

"You put him there in the first place when you were working with our biggest rival behind our backs. You gave him that power over us, asshole."

"I did. And I regret it. This is me making up for it. But Creeper's mine to give." He settled back in his chair, his jaw firm.

SEVEN

JILL

"SHE'S PRETTY, HUH?" Tania asked as she leaned against the open doorway of Lock's new storage-unit building behind Eagle Wings.

I handed her one of the lemon-and-kale smoothies I had brought from home for the two of us. She'd been here all morning, going through Lock's late brother's shit-ton of collectibles and prized "hoardery." Tania was an art and antiques dealer and all-around collectibles picker who'd offered to help Grace and Lock organize Wreck's vintage treasures since she got home two weeks ago.

"Who?" I raised my hand over my eyes to block out the midday sun and followed Tania's line of sight through the clubhouse yard. "Oh, Nina?"

"Look at her—long blonde hair, big boobs, flat stomach, round ass, tight jeans, long legs, and a fuck-it attitude to go with it."

"You've got a hell of a fuck-it attitude," I said on a laugh.

"After forty, it fully flowers. She's got to be around twenty-five?"

I shrugged. "I guess."

"Not impressed, huh?"

"Tania, she's a lot like the other old ladies I saw while I was with Catch and the Flames of Hell for three years. Same dark roots, same boobs springing out of her too-tight shirt, same resting bitch face, same way of strutting. Only, this one has a different accent. Big whoop."

Tania sucked on the smoothie and made a face. "Must I drink this?"

"Yes, you must. Come on, it's not bad. The lemon and carrot make it tasty."

She swept back her dark hair. "*Tasty* being a very relative term."

We both drew on our straws, our eyes still on Nina going to her car with her bodyguard buddy, Led at her side.

"Grace said Butler's first wife was a tall blonde, too," said Tania.

"Men have their types." I sipped the last of my drink. "I wouldn't call Nina pretty, really, but there's something sexy about her. It's a crass kind of sexy, right? Like, she's up for getting it on any time of day or night."

Tania sucked harder on her straw. "Aren't we up for getting it on any time of day or night?"

"I know I am." I giggled. "You don't like her?"

Tania shrugged. "I don't know her."

"You don't like her."

"I don't have to like her."

I glanced at her. "You don't like her for Butler."

"I first met him a long, long time ago, when he was a prospect for the Jacks. He's a little crazy, but who isn't? After losing his wife and all the crap he's been through, he deserves to be happy again." Tania swished at the remains of her drink with her straw. "Just like the rest of us do."

"Did you hear from your lawyer?" I asked.

"It's all a go. It's just a matter of months until the divorce is final." She raised her smoothie cup and clinked it to mine. "Let's hear it for Wisconsin, the no-fault divorce state."

"I'm glad you're back to stay, Tania. "

"Thanks. I'm all kinds of glad, too."

"Well, if you decide on opening your own store here in town, I think you'll be really happy."

"I was serious about that idea, you know. Meager has really perked up the past few years."

"I think you took Rae by surprise."

Tania let out a laugh. "I always catch my mother by surprise. It's a special talent I have."

I sat down in one of the chairs by the doorway to catch the breeze.

Tania put a hand on my shoulder. "Are you feeling okay?"

"Better, that the nausea has eased up. But now, I have that full, tight feeling everywhere. I can't wait to get a couple of new bras and maternity jeans and shorts today. I should've saved the stuff I had worn when I was pregnant with Becca."

"I wish I could go with you, but I really need to make a dent in this today. It's turned into a much bigger project than I expected."

"No problem, Tan."

As Rae had a couple of friends over for coffee and Penny, Tania's sister, had taken Becca for the day, I'd stopped by the club to see Tania and ask her if she wanted to come to the shopping mall with me in Rapid. I'd gone into the Eagle Wings office to say hello to Grace, but Boner had been there instead. He'd mumbled something about having to pick up a few things in Rapid and offered to take me to the mall.

Tania wiped her hands on a wad of paper towels. "You sure about going with Boner?"

"Yeah, why?" I asked.

"Last thing I remember, you two barely spoke to each other."

"That was in the beginning, when I first came to Meager. Everything's good now. We talk, hang out."

"You do?"

"I mean, if and when I'm around here. We've bumped into each other in town on occasion. He hangs out with Grace a lot so…"

"Right."

"Becca likes him. He's good with her."

"Oh, that's sweet."

"Yeah, it is."

The week before Grace had brought me pink-frosted cupcakes and huge iced cookies that Boner had bought for Becca from the cafe, all of them decorated with a huge *B*. Becca had flipped out with excitement and again later, from the sugar overload.

And just like he'd promised me, he'd sent a prospect over to mow the lawn and deal with the weeds in Rae's backyard. Sy would come over once a week to trim, weed, and check on the watering system. Yesterday, he'd even brought over some fertilizer that Rae had recommended he pick up, and refused to take any money for it.

The first time he'd come over, I'd fed Sy pork chops and scalloped potatoes. Yesterday, I'd sent him back to the club with a chocolate sheet cake with a big fat *B* on it and lots of flowers in yellow frosting that had been designed by Becca.

I'd gotten a phone call and a growly, *"That was good cake, Jill. Really dark chocolate. That's the way I like it."*

"I'm glad you liked it," I'd replied. *"Becca and I made it from scratch."*
"You make good scratch, sweetheart."

I'd felt like I'd been gifted a huge bouquet of red balloons and they'd lifted me up into the air. Positively giddy.

I shook myself from my Boner daydreams and focused on Tania slowly rolling out a large piece of cracked canvas with colorfully painted clowns on it.

"That's amazing. Is that a hand-painted poster?" I asked.

"Yes, it's an old circus poster from the fifties."

"Wreck was really devoted to collecting. It's like an education in Americana, isn't it? Especially local Americana. Bygone era of the West and the Great Plains."

"It is, isn't it?"

A nasally grunt made our heads turn toward the door.

"What the hell is all this junk? You cleaning up for them? Is that your job around here?" Nina stood in the open doorway, her arms folded across her ample chest.

"Hey, Nina," I said.

"I don't work here," replied Tania, her voice as icy as a freezer on a hot summer day. "This belongs to Wreck, one of the members who passed away years ago. He was Lock's brother. I'm going through it for him, organizing it. Some of it might go to my store in town."

Nina's eyes widened. "You have a store?"

"Well, I'm looking into it."

"Awesome. What kind of store?"

"I buy and sell antiques, vintage things. So, I'm hoping—"

"Oh." Nina's dull gaze shifted to me. "Hey, is there a Sephora around here?"

"Yeah, there is *one*—" I started to reply.

Tania shot me a strained look, forcing my laughter back down my throat.

Nina's face lit up. "Thank God! Where?"

"In Sioux Falls."

"Cool." Her eyes flashed. "Wait, where's that?"

"The other end of South Dakota. Almost a five-hour drive, give or take traffic," I said.

"Are you fucking kidding me?"

"Nope, she kids not," Tania said.

"What the hell?" Nina's hands shot to her hips. "Only one? *One* in the entire goddamn state? What kind of place is this? Don't you people have malls?"

"Sure, we people have malls," I said, my native twang lacing my voice. "But the same stores aren't in *every* mall."

Nina rolled her eyes, her mouth hanging open.

"Bummed, huh?" I asked.

"Well, yeah. Shit, this is ridiculous. How do you live here?" She let out a huff of air. "Is there a beauty salon in this friggin' town at least?"

"Yes, indeed-y," I replied. "And many, many more in Rapid City. That's only forty minutes away on a bike and a bit longer in your car."

"Great."

"Alicia could tell you the best places to go," I said. "I'm sure you'd appreciate her opinion more than ours."

"She's a stuck-up bitch, and I don't like her," Nina muttered.

Tania raised her eyebrows. "Alicia is the president's old lady, and you're the new girl on the block."

"I'd show some respect, if I were you," I added.

"You're not me," Nina snapped. Smug as all hell.

"Excuse me?"

Nina stepped toward me, her jaw tight, chest out. "Backwoods bitches."

"Watch your mouth!" Tania spit out. "Back off!"

My hands curled into fists, my arms shook. I wanted to yank her hair. I wanted to push her out the door all the way back to Ohio. I wanted to—

An arm came around my waist, pulling me away. I flinched back into a hard wall of muscle.

"Whoa! What's going on?" Boner's deep voice reverberated through my back, his warm arm pressing into my middle. That intoxicating Boner brew of earthy spice and motor oil embraced me along with the heat of his body.

"Rudeness is what's going on," I said. He pulled me to his side.

Boner aimed his don't-fuck-with-me face at Nina. "I'm taking Jill into Rapid to hit the mall. You want to come along?"

What?

Nina shifted her weight. "Is there a salon in that mall?"

"Two in fact," I replied.

Boner jerked his head to the side. "Get your shit and meet us at my truck in the yard. Three minutes."

Nina flounced off.

I turned to Boner. "Why did you do that?"

"What? Stop the bitch battle?" he said.

"No, invite her."

"You might not like her, but you gotta play nice with the new old lady. She doesn't know her way around yet, and she needs to make a friend. Might relax her tight little ass."

"You like her tight little ass?" Tania asked, her hands on her hips.

"No, I don't. And, thankfully, it ain't my ass to like."

Tania and I laughed.

Boner stared at us. "Are you two done?"

"Fine, fine, you're right." I let out an exhale. "I know what it's like to be the new old lady. She doesn't like it out here very much though. South Dakota must be a shock after Ohio."

"Right, 'cause the Buckeye State is such a fuckin' paradise." Boner's lips pressed together as his gaze followed Nina and her tight little ass striding toward the clubhouse. "She'll get used to it."

EIGHT

JILL

"I WOULD'VE GONE TO Lenore's lingerie shop in town, but she's a little too expensive for me right now. After the baby's born and I lose the extra weight, I'm going to treat myself there."

Every time I was in Boner's presence, I'd ramble. Then, I'd try to explain my rambling, which only led to more rambling. And now I was rambling about stupid bras. *Gah!*

We'd dropped Nina off at the first beauty salon we passed at the mall. Boner had tagged along with me to the maternity store where I found a couple of pairs of shorts and a new pair of jeans. Now, I needed to find bras, and there was only one place to go that had a wide selection of styles, fabrics, and sizes.

Boner's long, shiny dark hair swung as he tracked through the displays and tables at Victoria's Secret, hands shoved in his pockets. I was dazzled by the colorful and flashy displays of undies and nighties and lingerie and makeup and perfume bottles. Happy overstimulation to the extreme. I needed to get out more.

Boner made a strange growly noise that got stuck in the back of his throat.

I grinned. "What is it?" *As if I didn't know.*

His eyes flashed. "What the hell do you think? Why couldn't you do this shit with Nina?"

"She's doing her thing at the salon—hair, mani, pedi, the works. You could've just dropped me off, you know. You didn't have to tag along. I'm not going to get lost, for Pete's sake. There's a bench right outside the store. Go sit down. I'll be out in fifteen minutes. I promise."

He shot me a what-planet-are-you-from look. "I'm not leaving you on your own."

A shiver raced through me from the base of my spine, all the way up my neck, like it did whenever he said those protective declaratory remarks in that insistent tone. But, of course, he said those things because the baby I was carrying was the source of any fascination he had with me. I had to stop assuming that his concern, those intense looks, were about anything else or anything more.

"Fine. Suit yourself."

I grabbed a delicate peach-colored lace demi bra and thong panty set from a display rack and held it against my body.

So pretty. If only…

I turned to face Boner. "What do you think?"

A look of pain flashed across his face. He narrowed his eyes as if the lingerie gave off a glare that was as harsh and bright as direct sunlight.

I walked toward him slowly. "Well?"

His gaze traveled the length of my body from the bra against my chest and down my torso before settling on the delicate panty. His teeth scraped his bottom lip, and heat stabbed my insides.

He shook his head and glared at me.

I leaned in closer to him. "You okay, *Boner*?" I whispered.

His eyes held mine. *Those eyes.*

I liked any opportunity I had to spend time with him. He was always in the back of my mind. When I changed Becca's diaper, I thought about Boner. When I took a shower in the morning, I thought about Boner. I waited for Rae in the doctor's office, and instead of seeing the images I was scrolling through on my Instagram feed (which included many tatted, bearded hotties), I would see those incredible green eyes, that dark face.

"Buy it, and let's go," he said, his voice even, controlled, low.

Those hard green eyes shot their lasers at my lips, and my pulse spiked.

"I'm just kidding, Boner. Bad joke. Sorry. Unfortunately, this isn't what I came here for. I came here for something totally utilitarian—a bigger bra to fit these growing boobers."

His gaze dived to my chest again, and then he swung away from me.

What is wrong with me? Why do I keep provoking him?

I dropped the peach set onto the nearest stand and charged toward the smooth form-fitting support bras in the next room. I plucked three bras a size larger than my normal 34C off the display table.

"I'm going to try these on," I mumbled as I gestured toward the fitting rooms at the back of the store.

He only nodded and folded his arms.

There was no salesgirl around, and I went right in to an open dressing room and closed the door behind me. I tore off my T-shirt and unhooked my bra. I put the straps of the new bra through my arms, hooking it at my back, and then I leaned over the way my mama had taught me, fitting my girls in their place. I rose up and adjusted the cups again as I looked in the mirror.

I tugged on the straps, on the sides of the cups. "Shoot, still small."

I made a face at myself in the mirror as my fingers worked the tiny metal hooks. "Come on. Shit!"

My ringtone went off. "Great." I grabbed my bag and fished out my phone.

"Hello?"

"Jill?" Nina's voice squawked over the line.

"Nina?"

"Listen, I decided to get highlights. So, I'm gonna be another forty-five minutes at least, okay? Will Boner be pissed?"

"That's fine. I'll let him know." My hands went behind my back to jimmy the hook once more.

"You should get over here. They're having a special deal on—"

"I can't right now, Nina. Bye!" I dropped the phone and twisted the bra some more.

"Damn it!"

Snap.

I groaned loudly as the pressure on my breasts finally gave way. My arms eased as the bra popped open, and I tore it off me. "Finally."

The door flew open. "You okay?"

Boner stared at me, those tourmaline eyes taking me in.

All of me.

We stared at each other.

His gaze fell to my bare breasts, and my skin flared with heat.

That now familiar pained expression passed over his dark features. "Jill—"

My insides pulsed at the sound of his rough, raspy voice.

I covered myself with my hands, still holding the bra.

"Fuck, you're beautiful," he breathed. He stood there in the bright pink dressing room, perfectly still, his lips parted.

I could change everything now. Right here, I could veer us off the safe track we'd been on all this time. Sidestepping, smiling politely, laughing at each other's jokes, the lingering glances, heavy looks, and then drifting away, always the drifting away.

I could do this.

My pulse raced as I reached out, taking one of his large hands in mine and putting it over my breast. His heat soaked right through my flesh. His calloused fingers and the coolness of his silver rings on my enflamed skin made my breath audibly snag.

"What are you doing?" His voice was a rough whisper.

"I like you."

"I like you, too, Jill."

My heartbeat stumbled over itself, and I pressed my hand over his. "Good."

"Don't make this harder than it is, sweetheart."

"It doesn't have to be hard, does it?" I took a step closer to him. "Not when it feels this good."

My other hand latched on to his black T-shirt, and I pulled him in to me, the door closing behind him. "Do you like how it feels?"

His answer was a groan, his hand flexing over my breast, his thumb moving, stroking.

"We've been dancing around each other for a while now," I said.

"I like looking out for you." His jaw stiffened as his fingers whispered over my delicate skin, his thumb brushing over my nipple. "For the baby."

My fingers traced over his hand. "Is *this* about the baby?"

A muscle pulsed along his jaw, his head tilted. "You're carrying my little niece or nephew in there. Gotta keep you both safe."

His hand gently kneaded my breast, and liquid heat flooded my chest as my knees weakened.

"I like that about you." My hands clung to his taut sides.

He moved, his lips hovering over mine.

Yes.

My breath stalled as a brush of warmth fell against my lips, skin against skin, a light and gentle press. He paused to look at me, and I reached up and kissed him back, opening my mouth to him, my tongue slowly stroking his, beckoning.

I shamelessly arched my back, begging for more, offering him more.

He pulled away from me. "Christ." He cupped both my breasts and took a nipple in his mouth, gently licking, nuzzling. My head sank back against the wall.

"Yes, yes, yes," I chanted, my skin on fire.

He sucked on the other nipple, his teeth grazing the pebbled point. My pelvis pressed against his. His tongue lashed lazily in between my breasts.

Such a long tongue.

He licked me to a slow death, sending me to his own private underworld.

My knees quivered. "Boner!"

He leaned lower, and a squeak escaped my throat as his tongue found my navel and flicked at my piercing. My nipples hardened even more, if that were possible, and one of his hands palmed me again, roughly this time. He planted kisses all along my belly, and my breath stuttered at the sight. My hips involuntarily twisted toward him, my insides pulsing. Wild need coursed through me.

Use me, take me, drag me to your secret lair.

He rose up, and his teeth grazed the underside of a curve.

I let out a loud gasp.

"We okay in there?" rang out the loud voice of the salesgirl.

My body jolted in his hold, my breath throttled in my lungs. Boner's eyes shot to mine.

My hand flew against the door. "I'm good. Thanks! Be out in a bit!"

"You sure you don't need anything?" she asked beyond the door.

Boner's eyes pierced mine.

Fuck yes, I need, and I'm being taken care of.

"No, no, I'm fine. I'll let you know."

"All righty!" Her footfalls faded over the carpet of the small aisle.

I lunged at Boner, kissing him, smashing my aching bare breasts against his hard chest. He dug his fingers into my hair and deepened the kiss, once more pushing me back against the thin wall, which shuddered.

"Jill…Jill…" he groaned.

I buried my face in his throat and laid kisses against his warm skin. That musky, earthy scent overtook me, a hint of mellow spice and pepper and something else, something almost sweet. I moaned like an untamed creature in his arms. My fingers finally made contact with his smooth skin under his T-shirt. I let out a sigh at the muscles moving at my touch. My fingertips skidded over a long grooved scar indented along his torso. He let out a deep growl and stilled.

His fingers gripped my jaw. "This can't happen," he breathed against my swollen lips.

"What? Why?"

His eyes flashed. "It can't."

My heartbeat screeched to a halt and teetered on a thin wire. *Oh. Mindy.*

How the hell could I have forgotten about his current girlfriend or whatever she was? Shit. Shit. Shit.

I was throwing myself at a taken man. I used to complain about women like me.

Ugh.

I wanted to melt through the floor. "I'm sorry." I wiped my hands over my hot face.

He stood up straight and stepped back, putting distance between us.

"Jesus, you have nothing to be sorry about." He took in a deep breath, his hands on his hips. "Get dressed. Buy whatever the hell you need to buy, and do it fast 'cause I need a cigarette." He scooped up my old bra from the floor and handed it to me. "You need money?"

A chill raced over my skin. I grabbed the bra and put it back on without letting go of his gaze or turning around. His face tightened into thin angles at the sight.

"No, I have money."

He charged out of the dressing room, and I threw on my shirt.

At the display, I quickly snatched up two bras a size larger than the one I had tried on and a couple of colorful panties. I raced toward the cashier where, luckily, there was no line. Boner waited for me by the exit, and we left the store.

I released a breath, my fingers twisting around the handles of my shopping bags. Underwear shopping would never again be the same for me.

Boner slung an arm around my neck and pulled me close, taking the shopping bags from me. "We okay?"

There was that intriguing earthy scent threatening my grip on sanity. There was that protective older brother type of affection again. But this time, that affection was laced with heat that was specific, real, not a fantasy on my part, not a girlish wish.

"Yes, sure. Of course," I blurted. The warm metallic scent of his leather vest made my stomach curl. I'd had that Bonerworld wrapped around me, been inside it, for a brief moment.

Shouldn't I be embarrassed by all this?

I'd put his hands on my naked breasts, inviting him to touch me. I'd done that, but he'd stopped it.

My insides tumbled.

No, I wasn't embarrassed, only disappointed.

Because I want more from him.

That exquisite pleasure had come on like a freight train. I hadn't felt that sort of intensity in God knows how long, if ever. It was deep, huge, blasting.

That tongue, his mouth—he knew how to use them.

His touch, so simple—gentle one moment, intense the next—was everything.

Maybe it was so very exciting because we had been in a public place, and it had been unexpected. Pregnancy hormones had obviously not helped me out there.

Who am I kidding?

I was nuts for him and had been for a long time. Yes, I liked that he cared about me and looked out for me, but I was insanely attracted to him and intrigued by him, too.

I glanced at Boner. He was looking down, his expression almost…sad.

Why?

All of this wouldn't be figured out over a cig break at the mall, that was for sure. Our friendship was very important to me though, and I needed to make sure I wouldn't lose my friend.

I pressed my lips together and slid an arm around his waist. "We're good."

His face relaxed, and he planted a kiss on the top of my head. We strolled in the direction of the nearest exit, his one arm hanging off my shoulder.

He smoked in silence on the edge of a bench by a sand-filled canister while I sat on the bench opposite of him and chewed on a piece of gum. Boner scanned the parking lot as he exhaled a long stream of smoke. I squeezed my thighs together, grinding on my gum, but it did no good. The ache in my chest and the throb between my legs remained.

I couldn't tell what he was thinking. Boner was extremely private. I suspected only Grace had his complete trust, judging by the easy way they were together—the knowing looks they shared and the natural physical affection they showed each other, like a simple touch on the arm, a squeeze of the hand, a quick kiss on the cheek. It was nice, and I liked that about them, their bond, like a real loving brother and sister who were there for each other.

He had a left-of-center dry sense of humor that I really enjoyed. He was smart. He saw odd twists that others didn't see or notice. But there was always an underlying thread of severity, a guarded severity that he seemed to reserve just for me. I reminded him of his best friend's horrible death; there seemed to be no getting past that.

After I had gone through with the surrogacy pregnancy for Grace and gotten pregnant with her and Lock's baby, Boner had looked at me with new eyes. This wasn't the wariness and cool suspicion of when I had first arrived from Nebraska. This was something new. Something that resonated in the depths of my soul.

Was it admiration? Respect?

Whatever it was, it sent a ripple of warmth through me every time.

It's about the baby, what you're doing for his best friends.

He was attracted to me as well though. The madness in the dressing room had just confirmed that. And it was good madness, electric and fiery good. Slow burn combustion.

I crossed my legs and stretched my back in an effort to release the tension in my chest and my too-tight bra.

No use.

My boobs would never be the same.

Ten minutes later, I chewed on a second stick of gum, and Boner was on another two pieces as we strode back down the mall to meet Nina. At the salon, we found her paying the cashier.

She sauntered over to us, her face beaming. "You like it? I look good, right?" She stroked her long mane, thick waves of golden honey. Her nails were painted a dark berry color with tiny skulls applied on the thumbs and shimmery stars on her fingernails. She had a fresh coat of pink lip gloss coating her lips.

"You look great," I said, suddenly feeling like the harried housewife. I needed a makeover and quick.

"What's wrong with you?" Nina made a face, as if she'd spotted a huge spider crawling on me. "Your chest is all blotchy."

"What?" My hand flew to my chest. "No, um…I'm just hot."

"In this air-conditioning?" She smoothed her shiny hair over a shoulder. "You should get a haircut, too, you know? I told you to get down here."

"You done?" Boner asked, his voice clipped.

"I'm set," she murmured.

In the truck, I sat back in the cab this time and leaned my head against the cool window. Boner shoved the truck into gear, his shoulders taut. I didn't think I could bear sitting so close to him just now, like I had on the way over with my body charging with nuclear molecules the entire ride. Now, I hummed with the erotic rocket he had launched inside me almost an hour ago, and there was no way to disengage it.

The truck suddenly veered off the road and pulled in at a drive-through fast-food joint.

"We're getting food now?" asked Nina, fidgeting in her seat.

"Jill should have something to drink. I still have a stop to make before we head home." Boner glanced at me in the rearview mirror.

My chest tightened at the serious tone in his voice, the flash of his eyes.

"Order me a Diet Coke?" Nina asked as she toyed with an app on her phone.

Boner placed the order for three drinks at the speaker stand.

I leaned my head back against the headrest. I didn't even have to ask, and I wouldn't have. I hated asking for people to go out of their way for me. I hated it, and he seemed to know it. He knew. He always knew, and he was so damn thoughtful.

How thoughtful was he with Mindy?

At the service window, he handed over money to the cashier and got our drinks. Our eyes met as he passed me my iced tea, our fingers brushing over the icy cup.

"Thanks," I murmured.

"Yeah." He raised his chin at me.

I settled back into my seat and clutched the cold tall cup to my chest and neck, sipping on it. He pulled out onto Route 44.

"So, are you eating everything in sight these days?" Nina asked.

"No, although I've been having all sorts of strange cravings lately."

"Like what?" she asked.

"Yesterday, I saw a Burger King commercial on television, and this life-and-death urge came over me to have a bacon double cheeseburger. I've never even eaten one of those before."

Nina laughed. "Never? You're kidding! Did you go get one?"

"I grabbed my car keys, but I forced myself to sit on the sofa. I closed my eyes and rocked back and forth as I took deep breaths until it faded. Then, I chugged two glasses of water and chewed on an apple."

She groaned. "Did it work?"

"Sort of. Luckily, there's no Burger King near home, so I couldn't indulge on the fly anyway."

Boner's brows furrowed as he glanced at me through his rearview mirror. "You shouldn't be out on the road in that condition."

"What condition is that? Hungry?" Nina asked.

"Distracted," he replied. "Next time you get one of those overwhelming urges, Jill, call me. I'll bring something over." He shot me a look. "Whatever you want."

Whatever I want?

"Oh, I don't want to bother you. I know you're busy. Anyway, I get lots of urges."

Babble, ramble, shut up!

His eyes shot to mine. "I'll make the time." He returned his attention to the road.

I don't think we're talking about burgers anymore.

"Is there a Wendy's around here? Wendy's is my favorite," said Nina.

Boner's long fingers rubbed his forehead, swept down his beard, and smoothed over his mouth—the mouth that had brought me to my knees thirty-three minutes ago. My eyelids sank a few degrees, and I leaned my head against the cool window again.

"You guys need to try the..." Nina rattled on about her favorite fast-food burgers as I drained my decaf iced tea.

Boner's attention stayed pinned to the road, his long hair a dark curtain between us. He punched the radio on with a quick jab of a finger. Bad Company blared over the speakers, slamming aside my hazy thoughts.

Yep, my sky is burning, all right. I'm on fucking fire.

NINE

BONER

I'D TOUCHED HER.

Naked-ish Jill. She'd stood there like a spooked baby bird, all alone in its nest. Vulnerable. Totally irresistible. That long strawberry-blonde hair falling in waves around her blushing face. Those cushiony lips parted, those tits. Fuck, those perfect full tits. So damned beautiful. She'd taken my hand in hers, and…time had stopped along with my pulse.

Jill had wanted me to touch her. Like a fucking pinup centerfold just for me. She'd wanted me to do it, and I did, and then I couldn't stop. Kissing, licking, stroking. Her tits were just the way I'd imagined they'd feel—soft but firm, totally addictive.

I ran a hand across my chest. Her mouth, her skin, her lips, her tongue still had my blood simmering.

After the mall, I'd dropped Jill off at home, Nina at the club, and headed to my house where I cleaned up, downed a beer, and fell back on my bed, trying to get those images of Jill out of my head. I couldn't let myself go there. Could not. I felt that heaviness in my gut, that clamping in my chest, whenever I was around her.

I know what that is.

I know.

Connection. Need.

My eyelids sank. My breathing deepened as my body gave in to fatigue, but it was a fitful sleep that only brought shrill voices from a lifetime ago, from a broken connection.

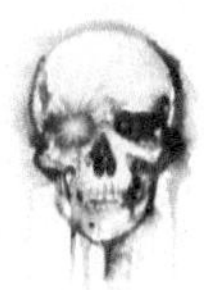

PAST

"Inés, you need to calm down. I told you, we'll leave Denver soon."

"You keep saying we're gonna leave, you keep saying soon, but we're still here. Still here!"

"Things are busy. I haven't—"

She blew out a huff of air, her head swinging to the side, as if she were disgusted by the sight of me. "The Executioners are always busy. You always have the next job and the next job. It never stops. But I need to go to LA. You told me so many times we'd go. We haven't done shit!"

"We need money, Inés, so that once we get to fucking LA, we can eat, find somewhere to stay. You know what that's like, come on."

"Once we get there, I'll get work. I always do. You worry too much. We'll have money coming in."

"We don't know that."

"But I make money now!"

"Inés, your last gig was weeks ago. You spent it all."

Her mouth tensed. Her dark eyes flitted around our tiny one-room apartment, like a trapped moth looking for the light.

She'd promised me she'd save it, but, of course, she hadn't. She'd gotten two modeling jobs in a row and celebrated by buying herself and her friends clothes and trinkets and taking them out to a club. Then, she'd had to have new pictures taken of herself and a fancy portfolio binder to put them in.

Inés hadn't been taking her meds either. She'd been trying cocaine instead. You couldn't get modeling gigs while you were trashed, but she thought she was fucking invincible.

She tugged on her dark hair. Her black-lined eyes blazed with volcanic fire. "This place is killing me. Why can't you see that?"

There was that fragile tone of voice I knew so well, the little girl who'd clung to me for years in that rotten apartment of her father's.

Her dark velvet eyes softened, pleading with me. She was the one who would take my hands in hers whenever I'd finally get home, usually just before sunrise. She'd massage each swollen finger with ointment, wrapping them in bandages, as she murmured sweet words and told me funny stories to help me forget the hell I'd been a part of that night.

The one who believed in me, who trusted *only* me.

But that was changing. I could feel it, sense it, like an animal sensing an earthquake coming on.

"I know, Inés. I know."

She shoved at my chest. "You know, you know? What the fuck do you know?" She sprang to her feet, grabbed her little leather backpack, and ran out the door, her hiss hanging in the hot humid air.

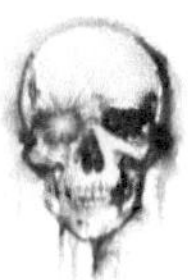

My eyes flew open, and I gasped, a cold sweat prickling my skin. I blew out air, as if it could sweep away that vivid memory.

My phone buzzed and vibrated, its small screen lighting up my dark room.

I rubbed my eyes and reached over, grabbing the phone.

A message from Butler.

Where the fuck r u? Get yr ass over to the Tingle NOW!

I took in a breath. What better way to get Jill's hot little body from burning my retinas and those acid-laced memories from dancing in my brain than by having professional strippers do their thing in front of me?

I threw cold water on my face, changed my shirt, shoved my boots on, got on my bike and sped over to the Tingle.

But I was wrong. Being here only made me testy.

Mindy was working tonight. She spun the hell out of herself on the pole and then got me drinks, one after the other. She sat in my lap, her one arm slung around my shoulders, and flirted with Butler.

I couldn't breathe. Her powdery sweet perfume was a nauseating cloud between us, stifling me. The pounding music hammered through my head.

"I'll be back," Mindy said, hopping off my lap. I stretched my legs.

It was no use. Everywhere I looked, there was Jill, and everywhere I looked, there was no Jill. Something inside me plummeted thirty stories, like a runaway elevator out of control. I slid my hands up and down the slippery sides of my glass of whiskey, and it was *her* smooth skin under my fingers, *her* wet lips under my touch.

We'd crossed several lines that we both knew stretched between us. The I'm-too-old-for-you-and-you're-too-young-for-me line, the don't-be-a-horndog line, the don't-fuck-with-the-single-mom line, the we're-just-friends line, the I'm-fucking-someone-else-and-I-shouldn't-be-wanting-you line.

I was attracted to Jill in a goddamn painful way. Even now, my balls ached, my chest hurt. I was supposed to be looking out for her.

That's what I do.

Not breathing heavily over her, taking advantage of her. She was pregnant with Grace's kid, and I was the next best thing to an uncle that kid would ever have. And there was Mindy. I'd kept forgetting about Mindy.

What the hell was I thinking?

I'm not thinking.

It was up to me to stop it. This was just a fuck-up, a blip, a bad move. It was totally natural. There she'd been, topless, less than a foot away from me. Shit, it was a crazy moment of insane indulgence. *Back to status quo tomorrow.*

I leaned back in my seat. Before I dissolved the memories, I relived holding her in my arms again, her tongue sliding against mine in some sort of discovery journey of tasting, stroking, and fire-branding.

Fuck.

Mindy danced on the smaller side stage. A blond college geek hooted loudly as he stuffed bills in her G-string, and she licked her lips as she rocked her ass at him. It was crude and hot, but it wasn't giving me an erection, like it had weeks ago when we first started fucking. Mindy was a pretty girl with a sleek body who seemed to enjoy whatever I'd dished out.

"Boner."

But it was only Jill's voice I heard begging for more of me. Jill's smooth, silky body coming to life under my touch.

Jill. Jill. Jill.

She'd felt so right in my hands, her heart beating so damn fast in her chest, her body trembling at that first fucking touch. Her full lips had opened for me, her eager tongue had danced with mine, her little moans had come soft and quick. She'd pressed those hips against me, urging me on. I could've fucked her right there in that tiny bright pink dressing room.

And I'd wanted to. God, I'd wanted to.

I could barely stop myself, but it was more than the instinct to fuck, to get off. It was this whole body experience.

And what the hell was that?

I gritted my teeth. I'd wanted to mate with her. Every cell in my body and brain had called out to her, drawing me to her. I had a unique hunger only she could satisfy.

She was some sort of forbidden fruit that I'd built up in my mind.

Me and forbidden fruit.

I drained the whiskey from my glass and signaled for another.

It was wrong. *Wrong.*

Here was a bright and determined girl who was getting a fresh start in life, settling in, carrying Grace's kid. Jill had made that happen. There was something wrong about me lusting after her, jumping on her.

It was just some sort of alpha instinct kicking into overdrive, wasn't it? I hadn't been able to protect Grace, so I'd protect her baby's mommy, like Dig had protected Jill. That was the root of all this. Had to be.

But every time Jill walked into a room, she changed the energy in it, charging it. I could feel it—this bundle of positivity and warmth, this light.

I'd felt a hell of a lot more in that fucking pink dressing room at the mall.

Butler slid an ashtray in front of me. "Hey."

My vision focused on a long column of ash dangling from my fingers. "Thanks." I tossed the butt into the ashtray.

I lit another smoke and sat up straighter in my chair. "So, how are you doing?" I asked Butler.

"It's good to be back," he said. "Good to have a routine again."

"Things with you and Jump any better?"

"Getting there."

"Just keep things clean, man. It'll all be good."

"I've been clean over a year now, and I'm keeping it that way." Butler's bright blue eyes settled on the dancer at the pole on the main stage. "I'm determined not to go backward."

Going backward.

Jill was certainly not going backward. She'd gotten out of a bad relationship. She'd moved on to a good place for her kid and herself, determined to make a better life. And here she was, mine for the picking if I wanted, like an overripe grape dangling on the vine in front of me, begging to be plucked, promising the mellowest pulp, the sweetest juice.

But being with me would be a step backward for her.

What could I offer her that was any different from the bullshit Catch had offered her? I might be older and wiser than Catch, but I was in a groove of my own making that had taken me years to perfect. The lone rider, the team player who faded in the background, the quiet but sturdy cog in the wheel. Jaded, tinged with years of rust, like one of Wreck's vintage collectibles. I was the killer when called upon, the ruthless hound on demand, the one they depended on to clean the mess that had been left behind.

I was the dead end.

Jill needed to be with a guy like that dipshit I'd seen her with at the coffee shop. A guy who could wear a bright blue designer T-shirt with jeans that had been ripped on purpose, and he'd paid extra for the privilege, along with permanently clean high-tops, and a white-toothed smile that came easy all the goddamn time.

That wasn't me. I was backward from all that. Of course, that guy was like the blond geek here, still showering Mindy with bills.

"Hey. You okay?" Butler asked, clinking his bottle of non-alcohol brew against my glass of whiskey.

"Yeah." I wiped a hand across my face. "Sure."

"You look rattled."

"Just distracted."

Butler laughed, his chest shaking. "We're in the right place for that."

"You okay being back here again?" I asked. Last time Butler had been to the Tingle, Grace had ditched him, Jump had beat him up, and then Creeper had shot at him and Dawes on the staircase.

He shrugged. "Yeah, fine."

Ever the Mr. Cool.

"How's it feel to be settled down again?"

"Huh?" Butler's gaze remained on Mindy peeling off her top onstage.

"Your old lady? That going good? It's been a while."

"Yeah, it's good. Nina's good."

"You surprised me with that one. Thought you and me would be the old bachelor crew forever around here."

He only laughed and clapped a hand on my shoulder.

The music segued into another pounding electric beat. Mindy and one other dancer sauntered over to our table.

She stuck her tongue in my ear. "Why don't you come upstairs with me to a room? Let me—"

I winced. "No."

She leaned over me. "You sure? I haven't seen you in a long while. I could give you a nice massage. You seem a little stiff." She rubbed one of my shoulders. "I like getting you *un*-stiff."

"What part of no do you not get?"

Her small eyes flared, her lips pursed. "Are you picking me up after work tonight?"

"No, got shit to do."

"Fine." She flounced off, disappearing into the crowd.

Butler sent off the dancer in his lap with a wink. "Bro, you sure you're okay?"

I shrugged and put out my dying cigarette. I'd thought coming here would take care of my Jill issues.

Obviously not.

I exhaled the last thick gust of smoke. "Business is doing real good here with Kicker running this place, don't you think?"

Butler pushed his empty bottle back and forth between his hands. "He's doing a great job. It's packed on a Wednesday night."

"Business has never been better."

"I wanted to ask you. I've got to find a place to rent. Can't stay in that fucking room at the club much longer. You know of anything in town?"

"Yeah, I might. I'll find out more and let you know tomorrow."

"Thanks."

"Where's Nina tonight?" I asked.

"She's out with Alicia, Grace, Suzi, and Mary Lynn. It's ladies' night at Dead Ringer's."

"Oh, yeah?"

"Yeah. By the way, thanks for taking her out today to the mall. She had a good time with you and Jill."

You and Jill.

I flicked at my lighter and dragged deeply on another cig.

Yeah, me and Jill had a good time, too.

I rubbed a hand over my jaw as Mindy came back out, wearing a different sparkly outfit, tits on full display in a string bikini top. She ignored me while she mingled around the tables until she found the blond geek and his pals. They ordered a round of drinks, and Mindy slid onto his lap, laughing. Another sucker bites the dust.

These past few weeks, it'd been fun, hooking up with Mindy. I liked her fine. Funny, a smart-ass.

But I wasn't nuts for her.

I hadn't been nuts for anyone in a long, long time. I'd always kept nuts at a dry minimum anyway. That shit just un-simplified your life, and I hated drama. I'd had enough of it to last me several lifetimes.

"Let's get out of here and head to Dead Ringer's." I packed my aging dented Zippo in my jacket. "Let's go check out what no good the women are up to."

Butler flashed me that I-got-your-number grin of his. "You don't like watching your girl work, huh?"

I tapped my fingers on the table and shot out of my chair. "She's not my girl."

TEN

BONER

I WIPED MY HANDS and headed for the water cooler. I punched the blue button over the plastic cup, grabbed it, and gulped at the icy water.

I'd been in a snarly mood all morning at work. I'd growled at everything from the coffeemaker to Dawes, who'd only been trying to help me with this old Dyna I'd been working on.

Since Lock opened Eagle Wings, he had me run bike service and repair and oversee special builds. I'd always been satisfied doing repair and leaving it at that, but the kid had insisted. I stepped up and made sure our shop ran like clockwork. I hated backlog, especially when Lock's custom-detailing crew was waiting to get their hands on the bike.

Fuck it.

I was toast. Burnt toast, charred on both sides.

"You need something stronger maybe?" Butler poured himself a cup of water.

I tossed a hand in the air. "The rust on that bike is unbelievable. The idiot should've kept it under a tarp and in good storage, not under a heap of garbage."

"Well, that's what they pay us for."

"Yeah, that they do."

"Speaking of which, is that Dig's Camaro in the new storage shed?"

"Yeah. Why?"

"You still got it."

I pushed at the cold water button again. "'Course I do."

"Can I take a look under the hood? From what I saw, you've kept it in prime shape all these years. There's no reason why—"

"No."

Butler's neck stiffened. "Bro, I'm the one who used to work on it for him when he couldn't. Let's me see if—"

"I said no," my voice snapped.

"Hey, sorry to interrupt," Tania said from the doorway leading to the storage units.

Butler's eyes landed on her. "You're not interrupting."

She glanced at him and took a step back. "I'm in a bit of a bind, and I was hoping someone could help me."

"What do you need?" Butler tossed his cup into the garbage can.

"I have an appointment with someone on Skype in ten minutes, and I can't miss it," she said. "But I forgot to pick up these two prescriptions for my mom at the pharmacy, and she's going to need them in a few hours. My sister's out of town today, and Jill's in Rapid with Becca, and her phone must have died because I can't seem to reach her. Do you think you could send someone to pick up the prescriptions and bring them to the house? I'll call my mom and the pharmacy and let them know. I'll make it up to whoever the lucky dog is with plenty of pizza and beer, I swear."

"Sure thing," said Butler.

I pitched my empty cup in the trash. "I'll take care of it."

"Are you sure?" Tania said. "You're working. I don't want to interrupt—"

"I need a break."

"You're a lifesaver," she said.

"Yeah, that's me." I undid my jumpsuit.

More like addicted, obsessed, crazy, a masochist.

Twenty-five minutes later, I knocked on Rae's door. Jill swung it open, the house phone at the side of her face, her mouth set in a hard line, reddish-blonde curls in her eyes. She waved me inside the house, putting a finger to her lips, and then she pointed to the playpen in the living room. I gently closed the door behind me.

"Yes. Okay." A hostile, seething tone in her low voice caught my attention.

"Okay, I said!" She charged into the kitchen, and she spewed out more tight words. She was pissed.

I snuck a peek into the playpen. Becca was sleeping on her stomach, her mouth open, one hand clutching the baby doll I'd bought for her. A pinch twisted in my chest.

I headed for the kitchen. Jill slammed the phone on the counter, her face screwed up into a knot.

"What's going on?" I asked.

"Oh, the usual."

"What's that exactly?"

"That was Catch on the phone. He hasn't been up here to see Becca or his mom for a long time now, over two months. Personally, I don't mind, but Rae does. He's her son. This is so typical of him, but it really makes me mad after all the crap he laid on me about me leaving him and moving up here and…" She averted her gaze, shaking her head.

"And, what?"

"Me hanging out with the One-Eyed Jacks."

"It's not like you're some groupie, for fuck's sake. You don't even hang out. You drop by or—"

"I know, but he's still all possessive." She crossed her eyes.

"Yeah, okay. I get that."

"Well, I don't get it!" She planted her hands on the counter. "And I'm sick of it. It's okay for him to blow his daughter off, saying she's too young to realize anyhow. He's blowing his mom off, too, when he does that. Boner, the disappointment on her face this morning! Even Tania, Ms. Tough, was disappointed. She plays it like she's accepted his douche bag ways, no big deal, but I know she keeps hoping for the best each time. He's being so unfair. I'm sure he's doing it on purpose to get back at me, but the thing is, I don't give a shit, not for me. *They* care though, *his family,* and they certainly don't deserve it."

"He's an asshole, Jill. Nothing much you can do about it." I touched her arm, and our eyes met.

Yesterday, her grayish-blue eyes had been soft and vulnerable, but now, they were more like steel in the sunlight that was filling the kitchen with early evening gold. It took my breath away.

I raised the small white bag with the Meager Grand Cafe logo on it. "Maybe you need a double creamy mocha thingy to make you feel better?"

"A mocha thingy?" She grinned. I'd made her day. "Decaf?"

"Of course, decaf." I handed her the bag, and she quickly uncurled the top.

"Of course," Jill murmured. She chewed on her lips staring into the bag. "Thank you."

"Rae's prescriptions are here." I tossed two stapled bags from Walgreens on the counter. "Tania had a meeting and got stuck and—"

"Thank you. I was in Rapid at a Mommy and Me class with Becca and my battery died—"

"No problem, and this is for Becca." I put another Walgreens bag on the counter.

One of those huge smiles of hers broke over her face. "What did you get her now?" She opened the bag. "A tea set?" She took it out of the bag and removed the plastic cups, saucers, and teapot from the packaging. "Oh my gosh, she's going to love it. Thank you. I'll wash it and have it ready for her."

I leaned over the counter as she popped a straw through the iced coffee and drew on her liquid paradise. Her pouty lips rolled as she swirled the coffee in that mouth of hers.

"God, that's good." She licked her lips.

I stared at her, my nerves popping off one by one like a well-timed firework display.

Her eyes found mine. "You didn't have to come over, Boner."

Oh, yes, I fucking did.

"I needed a break from work."

"Thank you—for everything." Her hand made a sweeping gesture over the prescriptions and the toys lying on the counter.

"You don't have to thank me."

"You hate it when I say thank you, don't you?" Laughing, she moved next to me and leaned in close, standing on her toes. A haze of coffee and chocolate rose between us. "Thank you. Thank you. Thank you."

She planted a kiss on the side of my face, and I let out a muffled grunt.

She settled back down on her heels, our eyes locked on each other's.

My breathing suddenly hit fifth gear. I liked her close. I wanted her closer.

My fingers cupped her face. *So soft, so—*

"Boner," she breathed, a hand clutching my side.

That urgent whisper, her tugging on my shirt. I grabbed the coffee from her hand, and it hit the counter with a *plonk*. I crashed my mouth onto hers, my tongue invading. Sweet coffee, icy cold and wet hot. Her tongue lashed against mine, and she wrapped her arms around my middle, pressing against me.

Jill.

I devoured, I tasted, I took, and she was the victor.

I lifted her onto the counter, and she let out a tiny gasp. The cotton fabric of her skirt was a pathetic barrier to the storm raging between us.

My forehead slid against hers. "Rae here?" I whispered against her mouth, my fingers smoothing down her throat, across her chest.

Her flesh trembled under my touch.

"She's next door."

My hand tucked under her skirt, sliding up a smooth bare thigh. She immediately parted her legs for me. My fingers brushed past the damp fabric at her center, pulling it out of my way, as her body quivered in my hold.

"Yes," she cried out.

With that cry, she gave me a piece of herself that I didn't want to let go of, only wanted more of.

My knuckles brushed her wet heat once, twice, my pulse spinning out of control. Two of my fingers nestled around the lushness of her clit and stroked.

I groaned. "Fuck."

Clutching my arms, she let out a low moan, and I swallowed it with my mouth as I gently stroked her. Her eyelids sank closed. I gripped her other thigh with my free hand, and she arched her back. Her eyes opened and melted with mine, her fingers digging into my sides.

Those stormy blue eyes begged, pleaded, demanded.

I'll give it to you. Fuck, I'll give it all to you.

My thumb circled her stiff clit, and she let out another moan, which shuddered right through me.

"You like me touching you, Jillee?" I slid two fingers inside her silky heat.

Fuck, yes.

Her body tightened around mine, small cries slipping from her quivering lips.

I nipped her bottom lip with my teeth. "You like me inside your cunt, baby?"

"Ma! Ma! Ma!" Becca shouted from the living room.

We froze. A toy squawked and honked in the distance, and Becca cried out again.

Jill buried her face in my shoulder, her breathing ragged, her body trembling. I held her tight against the painful crash of being denied.

What the fuck are we doing again?

I let go of her and stepped back. She licked her lips, her face blooming in different shades of pink and red.

"I'll get her." I washed my hands at the sink as she smoothed her skirt down over her bare legs.

Those legs.

Those legs wrapping around me while I'm pounding into her. Those legs jacking up over my shoulders while I bury my face in her—

"*Ma!*"

I charged into the living room, and there was Becca—face wet and red, punching her feet into the floor of her playpen, arms stretched ferociously over the railing. I followed her line of sight to where her pony lay on the floor. I picked it up and brought it to her. Her knees bent and popped up as she shook the whole playpen.

"Here he is, Becs. Mr. Pony is back."

Her blue eyes widened like little full moons. Her mother's eyes. Eyes I had just now gotten lost in, melted in for a stolen split moment in time.

Stolen is right.

"Bo-Bo!" She raised her arms at me.

My chest squeezed.

"Bo-Bo!" she repeated, her lips pouting.

"You want me to pick you up? Okay." My hands grabbed on to her sides, and I lifted her high in the air, her legs and arms stretching.

My muscles stiffened as I waited for tears, panic.

She burst out laughing.

I gathered her back into my arms, a hand at her back, another under her rear end. "That's me. I'm your Bo."

She chattered to herself as she fluffed out strands of my hair and tugged on it, wrapping her fists in it. Becca took her other thumb in her mouth, slobber sliding out of the corner, and sank her head against my chest.

"Let's find Mommy, huh?"

We turned around, and there stood Jill, watching us, her cheeks pink, those beautiful eyes of hers soft, hair mussed. I had done that to her, and my chest surged with heat all over again.

Her lips pulled together. "You awake, honeybunch?"

"She threw the pony, and then she wanted it back."

"She does that all the time." Jill tucked a finger in Becca's diaper. "Still dry. You want some juice, sweets? I'll get you some juice, okay?"

Jill went back into the kitchen and came back with a spill proof plastic tumbler with a thick straw sticking out of it. Becca almost launched from my arms at the sight.

"Put her back in the playpen, and I'll give her the sippy cup."

I put Becca back in. She grabbed the brightly colored sippy cup from her mother's hands and drank as she swiveled on her hips. The sweet scent of apple juice rose in the air. Her entire being was about consuming that juice.

Jill's beautiful little girl, who looked just like her, except for her dad's dark hair. Jill, who was pregnant now with Grace's kid. Jill, who I should be looking out for, not fingering her on Rae's kitchen counter or jacking off to her picture on my cell phone in my kitchen and in my own bed.

That was this morning.

"Jill—"

"Let's be friends, right?" Her voice was tight.

My eyes met hers.

"You can't say it, can you?"

I grimaced. "I don't know what to say first."

"I do. We, us? This feels good,"

"Jill, you're my fucking Madonna. Not—"

She let out a laugh. "I'm sure she's done it on a kitchen counter or two." She picked up the baby doll off the floor and a large multicolored velvety worm.

"No, that's not who I'm talking about."

Her face flushed again as she dropped the toys into a straw basket. "You did make me feel 'like a virgin' just now, I have to admit." She sang a line of the infamous lyrics. "That's going way back now. See how I know my pop music?"

"Not *that* Madonna!"

Her brows bunched together. "What are you talking about then?" She stared at me, her jaw slowly slackening. "Oh, oh, you mean—" The blood drained from her face. "Oh."

"I shouldn't be pinning you down in your kitchen. You-you need to be worshipped."

She moved toward me, her blue eyes leveling with mine. Her hand landed on my chest and slowly rubbed up and down. The heat rose up my neck, my face.

"The way you touch me, kiss me, is worship," she whispered. "Believe me, I've never had that before. Ever. I can feel your heart pounding through your mouth, through those fingers. I can only imagine what it would be like when—"

I put my fingers over her lips.

She blinked and clasped my hand, her lips nuzzling my fingertips. "I'm not the Virgin Mary, a divine goddess, or some delicate fairy princess. I'm just me."

Her lips brushed over the thin skin of my wrist where my pulse raged. Something shimmered in my gut at her soft touch, the heat in her eyes.

"You're not just *anything*. Not to me."

"I spread my legs for you just now. I urged you on."

"Yeah, you did." I peeled her hand off me and forced out a laugh. "You need a fuck, little girl?"

Jill punched my chest. "A, I'm thirty-two years old, not a little girl. B, I need *you* to fuck me."

My heart slammed against my ribs, my mouth dried. "We both know—"

"Save it!" She marched into the kitchen.

I stood still, my eyes shutting closed like a castle gate against the cavalry of possibilities of me and Jill rising before me.

A drawer slammed in the kitchen. Her voice rose loudly. "I've been with boys, and I've been with men my age—"

I stood in the doorway of the kitchen, Rae's white-and-blue trimmed kitchen straight out of the pages of *Cozy Country Home Magazine*. I was the interloper, the intruder. I was the fucking, *What doesn't belong in this picture, boys and girls?*

Jill spun around, facing me. "I like you. I want *you*."

"Jill—"

"You're older than me. So what?"

"Over thirteen years older."

"That doesn't matter to me, Boner. I'm not counting. I'm very attracted to you. Plus, I trust you. I know I'm safe with you." A slight tremor unfurled over her lips. "I like that. I need that," she whispered.

I let out a breath as I wiped a lock of hair from her throat.

Yeah, she needed that, especially after what she'd been through. She'd put on that brave face, sporting that breezy attitude left and right, but I knew—*I knew*—there was a gooey center to all of it.

Like there was to mine.

Was she still looking for another biker to come save her? Was that how she'd hooked up with Catch and stayed with him, even after it had gone to shit between them?

I didn't want to be her biker security blanket. I didn't want to be her cardboard-cutout dude whom she'd plant at her side and convince herself that everything would be all right.

I wanted—

My back straightened, I lowered my chin. "I don't have to be your man to protect you. I'm always here for you. You know that, don't you? You need me. I'm here. Right?"

"Right," she said quietly.

"Jill, I've never had an old lady. I don't want one."

Her eyes widened. "I didn't say I wanted to be your old lady." Her neck suddenly elongated. "I mean, I've been an old lady, remember? I don't want to go there again."

Why did that surprise me? My spine stiffened. *Why did that piss me off?*

I folded my arms and eyed her, my pulse springing in my neck. "I'm not Catch the Asshole either."

"Whatever you say," she muttered, her eyes narrowing. "You're seeing Mindy, aren't you?"

The two of us glared at each other. A Mexican standoff without the guns.

"Mindy and I aren't—"

She threw a hand up in my direction. "Right. Whatever." She put the bottle of juice back in the refrigerator and slammed the door shut. "Let's forget this conversation. Totally embarrassing, all of it. You've got Mindy and a bunch of other *chiquitas* wherever you go. I get that. Believe you me, I get that. What do you need me for?

I need to get a grip." She pummeled the door of an open cupboard, whamming it closed. "Thank you for the wake-up call."

"Is that what you think of me? That hooking up with women, one after the other, is all I'm capable of?"

"Isn't that what you just said?"

"No! That's not what I said. I—"

She lunged at me and kissed me deep. Declaration and defiance and desire. Her tongue searched for the answers she wanted in my mouth.

Fuck, if only I could give her what she wanted.

She ended the kiss and swept my hair back from my face, a small hand wrapping around my neck. "I like you. I want to be with you. I don't care that you're older than me. You've got a few gray hairs. News flash: So do I. Only difference is, I cover mine up with a box of hair color once a month." She raised herself on her toes and planted a gentle kiss on my lips. "You're seeing Mindy. She's younger than me. What's the difference?"

"What's the difference?"

"Yeah? What the hell's the difference? Why is it okay that you fuck her, and you can't fuck me?" She froze, her mouth dropping open, her eyes huge. "Oh my God, I can't believe I just said that." She visibly shrank and turned away from me, leaning over the kitchen counter. "Please forget I said that."

"Jill, I like you. I do."

Her head whipped around, and she faced me, her eyes glassy. "What do you like about me?"

"What's not to like? I see you, and I fucking lose all control. Any logic flies out the window."

"Tell me."

I took in air through my nose, my eyes riveted on gray-blue ones. "Your softness. Underneath that sharp-talking mouth are endless curves of creamy soft I could get lost in."

"Go ahead," she whispered. "Get lost."

The heat between us vibrated. Several feet of distance separated us in that kitchen, but I could feel her skin on mine, her breath on me right that very instant. She wasn't going to let this go or let it be, and she needed to. She beckoned me into a new world, *that* world, but I couldn't go there with her. It would blow me apart, and I was already blown apart. Decades' worth of debris.

She took in a deep breath. "I want you. I like you. It's very simple and very real." She searched my eyes, her chin set. "Would this be a problem with Grace? Is that why—"

"No, of course not. It wouldn't bother her."

"Or the club? Because of my history with Catch. Is that why you're—"

I shook my head and moved towards her, my hand reaching out and drifting across the soft skin of her upper chest, so pale next to mine. So delicate. Unmarred.

Her eyes fluttered for a moment. "If you want to keep this a secret, that's fine with me."

"Secrets are poison."

Becca's singsong shouts rang out, and the bump and crash of thick plastic echoed from the living room.

I removed my hand from her silky throat and stepped away from her. "She threw her sippy cup now, huh? Guess she wants a refill."

"She's not the only one," Jill mumbled.

"I gotta get moving anyhow."

Her eyes flashed. "You do that."

"Jesus, Jill." I turned and swung open the screen door, hustling down the narrow steps.

Behind me, the door crashed.

ELEVEN

JILL

"Just one more block, and we'll be home, sweets." I guided Becca's stroller down the last block before Rae's street.

This sleepy neighborhood, in a quiet almost nondescript small town on the edges of the Black Hills, really had become our home in the past four months that we had been here. I was glad I'd jumped on Tania's offer to come to Meager with her. It was so crazy impulsive of me—*oh, what else is new?*—but without a doubt, it was the best impulse I'd had in years, if not ever.

Dusky orange, startling pink, and faded blue illuminated the thin blanket of bumpy clouds in the vast sky over us, yet just as quickly as the colors had surged to life, the brilliant glow began to fade into the sunless, murky shadows of early evening.

I pushed the stroller past the row of boxy houses that were all the same shape and size. It wasn't a very exciting neighborhood really, but there was comfort in the familiar lines, a gracious pleasantness in the clean, well-cared-for exteriors, an ease in the spinning *whir* of water sprinklers filling the air. Each house sported a manicured lawn, trimmed with a variety of flowers and potted plants, and seasonal banners hung by a number of front doors. Only the *ding ding* of an ice cream truck was missing.

"I love our sunset walks, Becca. It's so much nicer here than where we lived before. We're so lucky to be living with Grandma."

My heart squeezed at the thought that I was finally able to give this simple goodness, this kind of no-need-to-freak-out-about-tomorrow contentment to my daughter. Not freaking out about my tomorrows was very unusual for me. I'd been a pro for years now.

But I was freaking out about one thing, one person.

Boner and I hadn't spoken to or seen each other since last week when he'd come over with Rae's prescriptions, and we'd fooled around in the kitchen. No, *fooled around* was a ridiculous phrase. It had been more than that—something positively violent. At least for me.

He'd only touched me, barely entered me with his fingers. He hadn't even had the chance to make me come—well, *almost*, but that didn't matter. It was a beautiful, glorious, hot, and crazy moment, and I couldn't stop daydreaming about it. I couldn't stop fantasizing about what it would be like to have his naked body against mine, demanding surrender and abandon.

But he always stopped it.

I hadn't heard from him or seen him since our finger-fuck that never was. He probably had shut it out of his mind, hitting the Delete key in his memory chip, and that was that.

Boner still saw me as that vulnerable, needy teenager he had shooed off club property a lifetime ago.

I shouldn't have to convince him to pursue anything. He wanted to fuck me, but I was a loaded issue. I wasn't some chick he could just do and dump. No, I was a part of his inner circle now.

The kitchen event was strike two, wasn't it? I really didn't want to suffer the humiliation of a strike three.

Time for me to hit that Delete key, too.

I let out an exhale as I pushed the stroller around a bump in the road where a tree's roots had broken through the asphalt, creating an ugly ruptured mound. We turned the last corner and my breath snagged, my eyes widened.

The alien invasion had landed.

The angry black monster trimmed in dark orange and midnight blue skulked in the driveway behind my car.

That Harley.

His Harley.

My illusion of liberation. The bike I'd ridden on for years, thinking I'd found the man of my dreams. The bike I'd ridden on, feeling the anxiety of not belonging, the tension of being wrong and trying to make it right.

I gulped in a breath, and my heart jumped back to life.

"Becca, your daddy's here."

I gripped the handlebar and guided the stroller up the street toward Rae's driveway. I unlocked the front door, pushed it open, and steered the stroller into the house.

Rae sat in her padded lounge chair, her face drawn, her big dark eyes deceptively calm. "There they are," she said, her voice straining to inject cheer into the room.

Catch's long legs were stretched on the coffee table. His eyes flicked over me.

Yep, still sexy with that lazy slouch he'd perfected, the always mussed brown hair, the twist of indifference on his lips. In concert with his perpetually creased forehead and the opaqueness of his small brown eyes, he could aim a what-the-fuck look at you without any effort at all.

Yep, still relieved to be away from him.

Plastic smile. "Hey. This is a surprise."

His lax expression turned positively acidic, and my pulse sprinted.

Is there something I should be worried about?

Catch rose up from the sofa, his height filling the room, and I stepped back as he approached us. He bent over the stroller.

"There you are, cutie." *Snap click* went the seat belt. "Daddy's here. Look at you, baby girl." He held her in the crook of his arm and planted kisses on her nose, her cheeks. Slowly, I let go of my pent-up breath.

"I'm sorry. Did I miss your call?" I asked.

"No," he replied, his eyes glued on his daughter, who studied his face, a finger in her mouth.

I glanced at Rae. Her hands were flexed stiffly in her lap.

I should have been pleased that he'd come, unannounced or not. This was what I'd wanted, wasn't it? Becca's dad to see her, Rae to reconnect with her son.

"This is a nice surprise, huh, sweets?" I patted my daughter's back. "Would you like some coffee? There's plum cobbler. Rae showed me how to make her recipe this morning. There's ice cream, too. Have you had dinner yet?"

"We have chicken pot pie from yesterday," Rae added.

He ignored us, and turning away from me, carried Becca to the couch.

My scalp prickled. "Well...I need to get Becca her fruit and yogurt. Rae, do you need anything?"

"Just bring me the yogurt. I'll feed her," said Rae, her eyes on her son and granddaughter.

"Okay." I ducked into the kitchen.

I got out the organic vanilla yogurt and an apple and a pear from the refrigerator. I washed my hands, cleaned the fruit, chopped it up, and tossed it into the small food processor. My limbs functioned on automatic. I was a robot performing its tasks.

I guess a ladies' only evening of me and Rae watching that *Magic Mike* DVD that I'd rented for us this afternoon was now out. I'd been looking forward to a laugh and a mindless couple of hours.

I pressed the button on the food processor again to make the fruit pieces smoother, its sharp buzzing noise drilling into me.

He was being strange. I knew him too well. He usually joked and made small talk. My stomach did flip-flops as I mixed the fruit cream with the yogurt. I scooped it into Becca's bowl, grabbed her spoon, several napkins, and her bib, and I flew back into the lion's den.

"Here we go." I set the bowl on the small round table at Rae's side.

Rae wiped her hands with an antibacterial wipe. "Drew, could you bring her high chair from the kitchen?"

"I'll take her," I murmured, approaching Catch.

His dark eyes settled on me as I took Becca from his arms. He tracked into the kitchen, and I shot Rae a questioning look. But what was I expecting? She was his mother. She had to be thrilled to see him.

Rae's lips pressed together, and her eyebrows quirked. Ah, Rae was not feeling the love either. Somehow knowing that she was as suspicious as I was only knotted my stomach tighter.

Catch returned with the high chair and set it at his mother's side.

I slid Becca into the seat and fastened her belt. "There we go. Time for fruity tootie!"

"Apple, Mommy." Becca smacked her lips together, her little fists banging on her tabletop.

"Yes, honey, an apple is in there," I said.

Catch and I stood side by side like awkward preteens at a school dance as Rae fed Becca.

"Drew, get something to eat, son. You cannot come for a visit and not let me feed you."

"I could eat. The cobbler sounds good. Haven't had anything like that in a long time."

Becca's tongue lapped at the yogurt on her face.

I went into the kitchen, and Catch followed me.

"I'll microwave it for you. With the ice cream, it's better warm," I said.

He only nodded.

"It's good to see you." I grabbed the cobbler from the fridge.

"Is it?"

Not really, but what the hell do you want me to say?

"Of course," I replied. "What a great surprise for your mom and Becca." I shoved the plate of cobbler in the microwave and tapped at the keypad.

He leaned back against the counter, his gaze wandering around the kitchen. "Bad surprise for you?"

"What? No. I'm glad you came."

"Where's Tania at?"

"She's out of town, chasing a lead on some antiques just over the border in Wyoming."

"She hanging out at the Jacks'?"

I took out the carton of vanilla ice cream from the freezer. "She spends time with Grace. Tania's been helping her out with a project over there, going through some stuff they've had in storage for a while."

"You helping her with that?"

"No, I help out your mom." I jabbed and scraped at the hard ice cream with the metal scoop.

"You don't go over there?"

Here we go again.

I squared my shoulders. "I've brought my car there for a tune-up and to have my tires replaced. Another time, I dropped off a couple of things for Tania that she'd forgotten at home, and I hung out with Grace in her office and helped her answer a few phone calls before going to a doctor's appointment."

Fuck.

I still hadn't told him I was a gestational surrogate for Grace and Lock. I was almost four months along now, and I needed to tell him. It shouldn't be a big deal. It wasn't like I had met someone else and was getting married and moving to the Philippines and taking Becca with me. But everything having to do with Catch made me anxious. His temper was mercurial, his reactions unexpected. A real Gemini.

His brow creased. "Doctor's appointment for Becca? She okay?"

I got the dish out of the microwave and topped the warm cobbler with the ice cream.

"At her age, there are regular visits, vaccinations—that sort of thing."

"Right."

Great, and the lying begins.

I handed him the dessert. "Here you go."

Catch dragged his spoon through the mound of sweet, creamy homemade goodness. He gouged out a heaping spoonful and shoveled it into his mouth. His brown eyes rested on me while he ate.

"It's good, right? You like it?"

He nodded. "So"—he swallowed—"you like it here?"

"Yes, I do."

"Why?"

"Why?"

"Yeah, Jill." He narrowed his eyes at me. "Why?"

"I really like your mom. She and Becca are great together, and it's the best thing for your mom to have that kind of happy distraction right now. Becca has her grandmother in her life. She'll never know my parents, of course." I took in a tiny breath. It was still hard, still hard to talk about, to say out loud. "Now that Tania has come back to stay, it's been fun."

"Fun, huh?"

"Yeah, we all get along, enjoy each other's company. It's nice."

One of his eyebrows rose as he shoveled in the last spoonful. "A real family." His plum-smeared dish clattered on the counter at his side.

The same spot on the counter where Boner had fingered me to heaven a few days ago.

I cleared my throat. "We're *all* a family, right? Becca misses you. If you had called us, we could've planned—"

"Been real busy lately. Hard to get away."

"Things are good then?"

"Yeah, Finger gave me a few more responsibilities. It's all good."

"That's great. I know that's what you've been wanting."

"Yeah." He shifted his weight, staring at me, studying me.

I took his dish and brought it to the sink. "Rae is doing her exercises, and she actually feels better more often. She learned how to inject herself with her—"

"What are you talking about, inject herself?"

I rinsed his dish and tucked it in the dishwasher. "It's one of the medications for MS, Catch. It's really expensive, too, but luckily, her insurance is covering it—for now at least."

"It took her a while to come to the door and open it. She was using a cane."

"She uses a cane now and a walker."

"It's strange, seeing her have a difficult time moving. She was always a really active, independent person."

"That's what Tania said. We weren't expecting you. Otherwise, I wouldn't have taken Becca out and left Rae to answer the door on her own. If she falls again—"

"We're finished!" Rae called out.

I grabbed the microfiber dishcloth and went and picked up the empty bowl, wiping down the high chair's table top.

"You want me to take the high chair back to the kitchen?" Catch asked at my side.

"Yes, please." I unfastened Becca from the seat, and Catch took the chair.

"Someone was very hungry!" Rae laughed.

"You ate everything, didn't you?" I said to my daughter.

She murmured something to me, her fingers in her mouth.

"Rae, I need to take a shower, and I can get that done before she needs a diaper change, which should be pretty soon. Is that okay?"

"Yes. You go on. Take your shower." Rae shooed me with a hand.

"I got her," Catch muttered, taking Becca in his lap.

I tossed her lilac and pink ponies onto the sofa next to him. Becca grabbed on to the lilac one right away, brandishing it in her dad's face.

"I'll be back in a bit." I charged down the hallway toward the bathroom.

"Take your time, honey," said Rae.

I closed the door behind me and took in a deep breath. *Okay, so far, so good.*

He was a bit cranky but seemed to actually want to be here to see Becca and his mom. He hadn't called first, which still made me nervous, but he was here. He was here, and that was a good thing, a step in the right direction. He was probably tired, which was making him moody. Nothing new there.

I tore off my sneakers, socks, shorts, oversized T-shirt, and underwear. I tossed the clothes into the wicker basket and got in the shower, more relaxed than I'd been when I first entered the house.

Ten minutes later, I was in my bathrobe, heading back to my room, rubbing a towel through my wet hair. After applying my body and facial moisturizers, I tugged on a pair of cropped yoga pants and my new bra and panties. I found my favorite pale pink T-shirt in my drawer.

Dizziness swirled in my head, and I held on to the edge of my dresser as I took in a breath. The T-shirt fell from my feeble grasp.

"Hey, where are the diapers? Ma said you had more in here. We gotta talk, too."

I pivoted toward Catch's loud voice.

He stood in the doorway, his eyes trained on my body. His head jerked back, nostrils flaring. "What the fuck?"

"What?" I leaned over and grabbed my shirt. The dizziness surged inside me again, and I teetered and stumbled back against the bed.

He charged into my room and grabbed my arm, pulling me up from the bed.

"Ow! What the hell are you doing? Let go!"

But he wouldn't let go. His grip on me tightened, and he shook me.

"Stop it, Catch! You're hurting me!"

"You've been here a few months, and you're already knocked up with some other guy?"

Oh dear God.

"You did it with me, and now, you're doing it again?" His voice shook.

"What? I never did anything on purpose! You were the one who didn't want to use anything, remember? You wouldn't listen to me."

"Now what? You just got knocked up again to get with somebody? I don't even have to ask whose it is. I've had eyes on you, you fucking slut, and sure enough, my point has been proven."

"You've had me watched?"

"You are such a fucking joke! You ran off from me, all accusing and a total fucking bitch about me and other women and how you were being treated. Then, you come here, and bam, you hook up with a One-Eyed Jack. You're such a fucking train wreck."

"Shut up! Your mother—"

"Yeah, you came up here to take care of my ma, to make a family for our daughter. What are you doin'? Skipping out in the middle of the night to fuck your Jack? Or maybe you're letting him in here to fuck your brains out while our kid is in her crib in the next room? This was my room, growing up. My bed!" He pointed to the bed I slept in. "Jesus!"

"That's not how it is. It's not what you think!"

"You think I'm an idiot?"

"No. No, of course not. But it's not—"

"Are you pregnant or not?"

"Catch—"

"Answer the motherfucking question."

"Will you lower your voice? Please—"

His eyes seethed. "Answer me!"

My stomach curled. "Yes, I'm pregnant."

He gripped my chin, his fingers digging into my jaw. "Is that what you do? Go from man to man, club to club, getting knocked up?"

I shoved at his chest. "Fuck you!"

"What are you, his mistake, and he's out, partying with his bros?"

"'Cause that's the way you did it, didn't you?" I scooped up my T-shirt and tugged it over my head.

"What we had was different. I used to think it was. You used to say—"

"I used to say a lot of things," I spit out. "Things that fell on your deaf ears."

"My sister whoring herself out to them, too?"

"You are such an asshole."

He smacked me, and I fell back on my hands on the bed. My face burned, tears sprang in my eyes.

He towered over me. "What I gave you wasn't enough?" His voice was low, controlled, yet full of fervor. "I need to remind you?" His fingers went to his belt.

My hand shot up, my legs coming up against my tummy. "Please, please don't do this! God, please—"

His hand lashed at my face again, and I fell further back on the bed, the wind knocked out of me. His fingers dug into my hair and pulled. My scalp screamed. I choked on a breath.

"You're not worth my dick, bitch. I knew it would happen, was waiting for it, but not this." He shoved me onto my back, his eyes smoldering over me. "The Jacks think they can fuck with me? With the Flames? What did they promise you, huh? You been telling them shit about me? About my club?"

"They've never asked me a thing. And I've never said anything to anybody."

"You think you're the shit, don't you? So smart. Instead, you got yourself pregnant, like some idiot teenager who didn't know any better. They're just using you to get to me."

He yanked at me and gripped my arm. His large hand clamped over my shoulder, steering me, shuffling me out of my room, pushing me down the hall.

"Ma, me and Jill are gonna go out and grab a drink." He swung open the front door. "We got stuff to talk about."

The cool night air rushed over my skin. I managed to shove my feet in the flip-flops I kept by the front door.

"What's going on? Drew! You leave that girl alone! Drew!" Rae's voice echoed behind us as he pulled me down the driveway toward his bike.

"Catch, please, we can't leave your mom and Becca alone. Please!"

"They'll be fine. Get the fuck on, and don't fall off, baby."

"I'm not even wearing real shoes!"

"Shut the fuck up, and get on the goddamn bike."

TWELVE

BONER

"Gimme another, man."

Dawes handed me another bottle of brew. "You okay?"

Nothing a club party couldn't fix, right?

Butler was officially being welcomed back into the fold. Over two months had gone by since he first arrived, and he'd been a very good boy. Jump had finally called a meeting, and we'd taken a vote and reinstated Butler as a fully patched-in member once again. He and Nina had rented a small place in town, and he'd been helping at the Tingle.

The club courtyard was jamming with loud music and brothers I hadn't seen in a while up from Colorado, North Dakota, Montana, Iowa along with plenty of good food and plenty of sexy women.

Yet I couldn't wipe the frown from my face or the glower in my soul.

I spotted Grace laughing with her friend Lenore, who owned a shop in town. Yeah, the lingerie shop Jill had been talking about.

Lingerie and Jill.

Jill in lingerie.

Jill out of lingerie.

Jill naked.

Ah, shit.

"Yo! Shut it! Speech!" rang out over the crowd from all corners of the yard.

Jump stood up on a table, his hands in the air. "As president of this club, I want to say a big welcome back to our brother Butler as a fully patched member here in Meager." He held up Butler's battered leather vest with his club patches, his colors, the South Dakota rocker back where it belonged. "Everyone, give it up for Butler and his old lady, Nina. Welcome home!"

Everyone hooted and clapped, whistles tearing through the courtyard. Nina and Butler stood together, a huge grin lighting up his face. He lifted his chin, a fist raised high. Nina's smile was blinding. She soaked up her moment in the limelight.

I remembered the night Butler had gotten patched in the first time. It was the same night Dig had claimed Grace as his old lady. That night was pure amazing. The world had been ours. Nothing ahead but blue skies and endless road. I squeezed my eyes shut. Now, Dig was gone, and Grace was married to someone else. But she had a shot at more of that amazing, at another baby, thanks to Jill.

Jill, Jill, Jill.

The memory of her squirming on her kitchen counter, my fingers sliding inside her, made me suck in a breath.

Dawes handed me a fresh bottle of beer, and I gulped half of it down as I watched Butler shaking hands and hugging brothers from our Colorado chapter.

Once upon a time, he used to be a king. He had risen to president of our North Dakota chapter. He'd made good. Then, his own wife had gotten killed in a freak accident, and shit had gone downhill from there for him. Booze, women, drugs. And the ultimate twist on his road to hell—skimming off the top of his own club and helping out a rival MC. After Jump had forced Grace to spy on him, a shit-ton of crappy truth had come out in a whirlwind of blood and disappointments. Butler had resigned and taken off on his own.

I'd been in touch with him off and on, more often in the past few months. He was a bro from the old days, and I couldn't turn my back on him. He'd needed a friend encouraging him to get clean, stay clean, and keep on keeping on. Yeah, he'd fucked up big, but he still had a good heart down inside. He'd just had to find it again.

It'd be swell if I could take my own advice.

"I'd also like to welcome two members of the Flames of Hell from Ohio, who came out here to party with us. Brothers!" Jump raised his beer bottle in the air.

More cheers and howls.

Nina planted a kiss on Butler's mouth, clutching onto his upper arm. Butler and his younger woman. He had himself an old lady again after all these years. He was settling down, settling in.

What was I doing?

I was here, where I'd always been. Comfortable. No, I didn't function by considering my level of comfort. I was free from hardship, unhurried. That was how I set my calibration. That was what I considered success.

Yeah, I was good.

I swiped at the beer on the edge of my mouth as I leaned back against the bar.

"Hey, sexy on a stick."

That was a creative come-on since I was the thinnest of all my bros. A redhead stood in front of me, her tube top of a dress leaving nothing to the imagination. That was always convenient— you knew what you were getting, all of it easy, accessible.

"I'm Shelley Anne. Mindy told me all about you. Said I should introduce myself. So, I'm introducing myself." She licked her overly-lined lips and held out her hand. "Hi."

I stared at her.

She swept her hair to the side, posed her legs at an angle, and smiled huge at me, her cheeks puffing with the action, like she was on the runway at a beauty contest.

Was she waiting for me to pass judgment and give her a score? Yay or nay to get between my legs?

Her shoulders dropped. "You're Boner, right?"

"Yeah."

"Oh, good. Can I get you another drink, Boner?"

"Just got one."

Her lips tipped up. "Something to eat maybe?"

"Nah."

She leaned into me, her hands against the bar. "I auditioned today at the Tingle. I've never danced professionally before, but I've been taking classes. And I just got these." She arched her back and thrust out her full hard tits.

Sure, suck my cock, and I'll get you a job.

What else do you need from me? What else can I get out of this deal?

Because it was a deal, a bargain, an enterprise, a game. A game that gave me what I wanted in return for some spare change. A game I never minded.

Button pushed.

I minded today.

"How old are you, Shelley Anne?"

"I just turned twenty."

I'd figured as much. No desire to touch her flared over me. No desire to flirt or toss a few ridiculous dirty jokes came over me.

She grinned at me, and in that grin, I saw what I was to girls like her. So many girls.

"Sexy on a stick."

"Bone me, Boner."

"Is that boner for me?"

"Have I got a lady boner for you, baby."

"I can make that boner better."

"You got any pot? Your pot is famous all over the Wild West. Just like your cock."

"I love the way your bike roars. You can put your metal between my legs anytime."

"You met Shelley Anne, babe?" Mindy, her brown hair curled into long coils, plenty of makeup glittering on her face, flashed me a tight grin. Expectant, almost daring.

I leveled my gaze at her. "Says you sent her over."

"I did." Mindy planted a long kiss with a hint of tongue on my lips, her eyes on mine, a hand lingering on my chest. "I thought you'd like to meet her. She and I have been spending some time together, and we wanted to hang out with you tonight. Make it a memorable night." Mindy's heavily made up eyes seemed to dance in the lights shining down on us.

Shelley Anne giggled.

Fuck no.

Grace's laugh rang out, and my body snapped at that sound. That was real, that was…

I drained my beer in one long swallow, clapped it on the bar, and charged in that direction.

"Hey! Wait up!" Shelley Anne's voice piped up from behind me.

Grace and Lock were kissing hard. Lenore stood with them. Today, Lenore's hair was pink and the bottom half dyed a sea blue that matched her huge eyes. The woman was covered in ink and constantly changing her hair color. Something was up with that. She scanned the crowd, her posture rigid.

"Lenore."

Her eyes landed on me, and she visibly relaxed. "Hey, Boner. How are you?"

"I'm good. You seen Jill? Is she here?"

"No, I haven't seen her."

"Jill's home, watching a movie with Rae," said Grace, Lock holding her from behind.

Lock whispered something in her ear, and they both laughed.

"I don't need to watch that movie when I have you," she said to him.

A hand shoved itself in my back pocket, and I jerked to the side.

Shelley Anne.

"Found you," she said on an eager giggle.

Lenore grinned and winked at me, and I untucked Shelley Anne's hand from my pocket.

"You gonna show me your bike?" she asked, her voice high.

"No. And, sweetheart, I don't hire dancers for the Tingle. All the best to you."

"Oh. Okay. But, um, don't you want to hang out or something?"

"No."

"But Mindy said—"

I strode back inside the clubhouse, got behind the bar in the lounge, and poured myself a whiskey.

Mindy leaned over the bar. "Something wrong?"

"What the fuck are you doing?"

"Thought you'd enjoy mixing it up a little. She's game for anything. Trust me, not to be missed."

"I'll miss." I knocked back my drink.

"Seriously?" She let out a hard laugh. "Well, something sure has you in a mood. What could that be?"

"What's he doing?" a woman's voice shrieked in the distance.

Hollering rumbled from outside. A chaos of voices and bikes clamored though the dark courtyard. One man yelled above the others.

I tracked down the hall and out into the courtyard.

"Where the fuck is he?" bellowed that male voice.

My instincts caught fire, and I looked over the sea of heads. A circle had been formed around a tall guy with dark hair. A guy pulling on something.

"Don't do this! Let me go, asshole!" a woman's voice rang out.

My heart stopped. My blood rushed through every vein.

"Shut off the music!" I barked out.

The music cut off.

"Oh my God!" Grace's voice. Full of pain, shock.

A razor scraped up my neck and around my throat.

"It's a fucking Flame, man!" Tricky shouted from where he stood on top of an old wooden table. "It's Catch."

I gestured at Tricky with one hand, and he hopped down from the bar, Dawes alongside him, their guns drawn.

Venom filled my blood, feeding me, as I charged forward, pushing women and men out of my way. My insides boiled and roared, my heart steamed. I was going to kill him.

I searched for Lock in the crowd. His stillness gave him away. He caught my gaze and nodded once. He moved seamlessly through the opposite end of the throng, toward Catch.

"Put her down! What the hell are you doing?" Grace said, her voice loud, firm, diving off the edge of frantic. "Let her go, Drew. Now!"

Grace had known Catch since they were kids. He was her best friend's younger brother. She was trying to talk him down any way she could, using his real name was either a panicked reflex or a ploy.

Jill pulled on Catch's hold with both her hands, but he only yanked on her hair. She gasped loudly, stumbling. A purple bruise swelled on her face.

My blood roared. *Motherfucker.*

"How did you let this happen, you stupid bitch?" Catch yelled at Grace.

Butler yanked Grace back, but she only pushed against his arm, her face red.

"Catch! Don't do this!" Grace said.

"Catch, let Jill go," Butler said. "You got a problem? Let's talk about it inside. But you let the girl go."

"Was this part of your sweet little plan all along, Butler?" Catch said. "What else you got up your sleeve, huh?"

I slowed my pace down, slinking through the people craning to see, all my senses tuned to the joker holding court.

"What the hell is your problem?" Grace asked, her voice sharp.

He shoved Jill in front of himself, her rounded belly sticking out of her pink T-shirt. "She's fucking pregnant!" he growled. "I let her come up here with you and my sister. You're supposed to be watching out for her and my kid. You fucking promised. And this is what happens?"

"You have no idea what you're talking about." Grace's eyes flared. "Let her go now! You're hurting her!"

I remained still as I followed Lock's progress.

"I told you. I warned you, warned you both. She's got my kid up here, and she's been fucking a Jack the whole time while she's in my house, in my bed?" He pushed at Jill's rear with his knee and aimed his gun at her belly. "Didn't take long, did it?"

Butler pulled Grace behind his body. "Put the gun down, man. Not on a woman."

"No!" Grace jumped in between Butler and Catch, her arms outstretched over Jill.

"Fuck off!" spit out Catch, twisting Jill away. "You think I haven't been watching her? I've seen them together. Where is he? He too much of a pussy to show his face? Is he partying without her tonight? He got himself another whore here at his club while this one's at home?"

"What the hell is going on?" Mindy grabbed at me.

"Get back," I said on a hiss, shoving her away.

I snaked in between the men and women. They parted for me. I slid the safety on my 9mm, the clicking sound of the metal making me high.

Here I am, motherfucker.

Catch's wild eyes found mine. Eyes of a rabid dog, eyes I'd seen so many times before on men and women who thought they had the upper hand on me, eyes that I quickly drained of their arrogance with a look, a shot, a slice, a slam.

I aimed my gun at his face.

"There he is!" He shook Jill in his grip. "Did you forget your whore tonight?"

"Let her go. Now." My voice pierced the night air.

A venomous grin split his face.

"Catch, it's not Jill's baby!" Grace said.

"You know how stupid you sound right now, Grace? You smoking the special house weed, drinking their juju juice?"

"It's *my* baby," Grace replied.

"What?" Catch's face twisted.

Grace stood still in front of him, Butler's hand gripping her arm. "Jill's my surrogate. She's carrying *my* baby *for me*. Now, let her go!"

Leaning into Jill, Catch slanted his gun toward Grace. "What the fuck, babe? You sold yourself to them?"

Jill cringed and shrank in his hold.

"You doing this shit for money? You—"

Catch's head jerked back in one hard swift motion, his eyes popping open wide like a spooked horse. Lock angled his long knife at the fucker's throat, his other hand thrusting in Catch's hair, yanking his head back further.

"Drop the gun, let her go, and get on your knees. NOW!" Lock's voice boomed, his black eyes glinting.

Gasps and a needling jittery silence reigned. Adrenaline rapid-fired through me, all my senses focusing on Catch's face still in my range.

Butler let out a hiss as he twisted the gun from Catch's hand. I moved forward and peeled the fucker's grip off of Jill, and she fell into my arms.

I pulled her behind me and pressed my gun into Catch's forehead. "You do not touch my woman ever again. "

Catch staggered. "*Your* woman?"

"And you do not spy on her, motherfucker," I continued. "Ever. You hear?"

Lock pulled on Catch's arms, pinning them behind his back, and Catch grunted, stumbling.

I tilted my head back, eyeing him. "Jill is mine."

Mine.

Jill shuddered, clutching at me, pressing into my back. Her tremors jolted my heart into overdrive, into my new millennium. Her arms wrapped tightly around my middle.

"You need to respect the mother of your kid, and you need to respect my old lady," I continued. "Basic principles in life, which are obviously still beyond you." I twisted the gun against his head, grinding it into his skull. "I think you need a lesson."

"Your old lady?" He struggled against Lock's hold.

"My old lady."

There. I'd fucking said those words for the first time.

My heart banged against my ribs, as if I'd snorted too much blow. But there wasn't any coke in my system. There was only Jill.

Me holding on to Jill and Jill holding on to me. My body surged with the rush, the high intense.

"Jill? Jill!" Catch shouted, straining toward her.

Jill stepped to my side, an arm still around me, wiping at her face as she straightened her head. "I'm with Boner." Her voice was steel, her gaze hard. "And I'm carrying Grace and Lock's baby."

Catch bucked off of Lock with a grunt, but Lock snatched him back in, shaking him like a marionette on strings, muttering threats in his ear.

I pushed Jill toward Grace and Lenore, and the three of them scrambled out of the way.

"He here on his own?" I asked Lock, my eyes and gun remaining on the trash at hand.

"Looks that way," Lock replied, still holding the blade at Catch's throat.

"I'm here, and he's a brother. What the fuck?" muttered Led.

Nina stood beside her bodyguard from home. Led was a fucking Flame brother to Catch, albeit from another chapter. The two other Flames from Ohio stood at Led's side.

"We got a few personal issues we need to iron out here, Led," Butler said. "Gotta be dealt with."

"The fuck you say."

"Shit's gotta be dealt with," Butler said, raising his voice. "No more, no less than what he deserves."

"Enough of this fucking chitchat." I gestured at Tricky and Dawes. "Cellar."

"Let go of me! Fucking Jacks!" shouted Catch.

Lock kicked Catch, and he sprawled to the ground.

Butler stood before Catch. "You fucking idiot. Such an idiot." Butler jerked his head at Dawes and then in the direction of the clubhouse.

Tricky and Dawes grabbed Catch's arms and hoisted him upright. They dragged the asshole through the courtyard and inside the building with Led and the other two Flames behind them.

I lowered my gun and sucked in air as I turned to Jill. Gripping her by the neck, I planted a kiss on her mouth, thick curls of her hair tickling my face. "You're staying with me here tonight."

"Okay," she breathed, her eyes lifting to mine.

Yes, mine. All fucking mine.

"Did he hurt you?"

"No, no—"

"What's this then?" I held her chin, my eyes glued to the purplish-red mark on her cheek.

"He slapped me."

"He's gonna pay."

"Boner—" Her fingers dug into my shirt.

I pressed my forehead into hers. "I'm not gonna kill him—not tonight. But he's gonna learn his lesson." My gaze skimmed down her body. Short leggings, T-shirt, flip flops. "Jesus, he dragged you out here like this? On his bike?"

She only nodded, her breath choppy.

"Motherfucker—"

Her hands cupped my face, and she kissed me.

Was it to shut me up, stop my rage? Or was it for her own relief and reassurance?

I had to control my shit and give her that reassurance now. That was what she needed.

Fuck, I need it, too.

I kissed her hard taking her in my arms, pressing her against me, warming her. "Stay with Grace until I get back, okay?" I forced my voice to come out gentle.

"I need to call Rae, make sure she and Becca are okay," she said hoarsely.

"Jill, let's go inside and call them," said Grace, touching her arm.

I shot Grace a look. "Take her to my room, stay with her." I brushed Jill's forehead with my lips and stalked off toward the clubhouse.

"Your old lady?" Mindy caught up with me, matching my long strides, her eyes flaring. "Since fucking when? If I'd known that, I—"

I kept moving. "Get the fuck out of my way."

THIRTEEN

BONER

HIS BLOOD SOAKED MY SHIRT and stained my knuckles.

And I fucking loved it. But I always loved this.

A rush of white heat surged through my veins and filled my pumping heart to the edge of erupting. I nicked his neck with my knife, my other hand yanking his head back.

Eye-to-eye.

The tension in the room was absolutely mouthwatering.

"Say it again, motherfucker."

"Jill is yours." Blood spilled out of his nostrils. Blood tinted his teeth, seeped over his broken lips. "Jill ain't mine. She's…she's your woman. All yours."

"You fucking touched her. You hit her, you cocksucker." I seized his middle finger and bent it all the way back.

Catch howled, his body flinching. The loud pop and snap filled my ears as a loud moan broke from his throat. I twisted the loose digit and then shook it.

His skin drained of all color, his lips loose, his sweat and blood splattering at my feet. Warmth spread through me, and the room slowly came back into focus. Butler against a wall, Kicker and Dready against the door. Lock at my side.

Lock punched him, and Catch collapsed with a satisfying *crunch* to the floor.

Jump approached the douche bag. "Now that we've all made our points real clear"—he shot me a look, and I pushed back from Catch's heaving body, my hand flicking out in a take-it-away-Prez gesture—"why don't you tell us what this is really all about? This has to be about more than pussy."

Catch coughed and spit on the floor. "Tell me you all haven't sweet-talked her into telling you shit."

"Like what?" asked Jump.

"'Bout the Flames of Hell."

"We don't strong-arm chicks unless we really have to. And, as far as I know, shit between our clubs is good. Isn't it? Or maybe you got cause for what I see as this fucking out-of-control paranoia?"

"The Broken Blades have been shitting on us lately. We've had deals and agreements in place for years. Suddenly, they're reneging on 'em. That shit with Creeper kidnapping my kid a few months ago was only the beginning. He thinks I owe him more than what I paid him for doing some side work for us. Then, he goes over to the Blades and does shit for them, too. Bottom line, Creeper was a Jack once upon a time. What do you want me to think? Jill—"

"Eh!" Kicker shoved the point of his cowboy boot into Catch's ribs.

Catch choked. "I mean, Boner's old lady." He coughed and swallowed hard. "She comes up here, gets cozy with you, and it would be the obvious choice for the Blades or you to get to me."

"Finger okay this bullshit you pulled tonight?"

"He only knows I came to see my kid. When I saw—"

"Boner's old lady is a good girl," Jump said. "She's real special to us. Last thing we'd want to do is put her on the spot, make things uncomfortable for her. We don't do that to one of our own."

Lock made a noise in the back of his throat, and I threw him a glance. I had to agree. Jump could twist shit when and how he liked. He'd done it with all of us at one point or another, most recently Grace. The mark of a fine leader.

"The Blades have been assholes for a long while now. Sounds like we have a few things to talk about. But I ain't in the mood now, for some reason." Jump moved toward the door, followed by Lock and Kicker.

Catch's head sank back on the floor. "You should make the time."

Jump slanted his head. "Oh, yeah?"

"You ever heard of the Calderas Group?"

"New tacos from Mexico?" muttered Jump.

"No, asshole."

Dready shoved his boot into Catch's side. I lit a cigarette.

Catch coughed up blood, and a gob of red slobber fell from his mouth. "They're from Denver. Gangbangers gone upscale. Been playing footsie with the Blades, and Notch has been licking their brown dicks. Finger ain't happy. You should check 'em out and then come lick my dick."

Dready punched Catch hard across the jaw, and his head fell to the side, his eyes snagging on mine. I spit on his face.

"Who's running their show?" I asked.

Catch jerked his head at the sharp sound of my voice. "This 'Spic. Calderón. Alejandro Calderón."

My breathing suspended for a split second at the sound of that name. My muscles locked, my head stiffly drawing back.

I motioned at Dawes and Tricky, and they picked up Catch and dragged him from the cellar, through the kitchen, out the lounge, down the hall, and out the door. They dragged him across the dirt and gravel, past the gate that lay open just for him. The boys dumped him on the road, and Led crouched over him.

I tossed my cigarette by his sorry ass. "You have a good night."

I charged back into the clubhouse and poured myself a whiskey. I stretched my arms against the bar and struggled for air.

"Bro, you okay?" Dawes asked.

"Go away."

"You sure?"

My body shook. "Go!"

A running soundtrack of screaming voices and spurting blood and cracking bones filled my ears.

Promises broken.

Oaths sworn.

Curses invoked.

Dreams destroyed.

Alejandro's fucking voice jumped in my head. *"One day, I'm going to come for you, and I'm going to take it all away."*

Then, I'd had no dreams left, my dreams had petered out, drained away.

Once I became a Jack, my only focus had become survival and a good time doing it.

But now I had a dream.

Now, I had Jill.

My hands dug in my hair as a wave of nausea surged up my throat and yanked on my insides. All the reasons not to be together with Jill, not to make a life with *anyone*, reared their ugly heads and laughed at me.

I had put hundreds of miles of road between me and the Calderóns. I had changed my name, kept away, laid low.

It didn't matter, though, did it? Hearing Catch say his name just now proved that.

But tonight—*tonight*—I had finally given into the temptation, to the promise of *her*. I'd tasted that rightness singing in my blood, filling my arms. I had found the one thing I had always wanted but had refused myself for fear it would be threatened, taken away.

How can I go back to being that man again? How can I go back to being without? To being without her?

I couldn't. No fucking way.

I would protect her with every ounce of whatever strength and cunning was left in me.

I would hold on to what I had claimed.

To Jill.

To my own life.

Hold on for as long as I could, for as long as it would last.

FOURTEEN

JILL

"YOU ARE THE BEST FOOT AND LEG MASSAGER EVER."

"I learned from the best," said Grace.

"Lock?"

She grinned. "Mmhmm. He spoils me rotten."

"You're spoiling me rotten now."

Grace and Lenore had taken me to Boner's room and given me a ginger ale to drink. I'd insisted on taking a shower, and then Grace had handed me a T-shirt of Boner's to wear. Lenore had left soon after.

Tears clouded my eyes. "I'm sorry about all this."

Grace glanced up at me. "What do you have to be sorry about?" She rubbed her thumbs into the sides of my calf muscles.

"Catch and our never-ending drama. I should've told him sooner. I kept putting it off. I knew he'd freak out. I—"

"Jill, he chose to lose it. He chose to drag you here and stake some sort of Neanderthal claim where there is no claim for him to make. Even if the baby you're carrying were yours and not mine, he'd have had no right to behave the way he did. Yeah, they're his crazy emotions, and Catch has always been a fireball since he was a kid, but he's not a kid anymore. He put your life in danger, even his own with the way he came out here and the shit he said."

Her hands traveled down to my feet again, her thumbs focusing on my arches.

"They're teaching him a lesson now, aren't they?" I asked.

"I think you know the answer to that." She released my feet and rubbed her hands together, the light, clean fragrance of her moisturizer lingering between us. "Are you feeling guilty about that?"

I dropped my head back against the headboard and stared at the ceiling. "No, I can't say that I am."

"Good."

I took her hand in mine. "Thank you."

"You're very welcome. Do you want some more ginger ale? Lenore brought this bottle of water, too."

"I'm all set."

"You okay with staying here tonight?"

"Better, now that we spoke with Rae, and I know that she and Becca are okay."

"Thank God for Martha the neighbor, huh? She kept things calm and got them both in bed for the evening."

"She's such a good person."

Meager was a good town with good people. But I had brought the bad. The bad to Rae, the bad to my daughter, and now, the bad to Grace.

My chest caved in, my lungs squeezed.

"Jill? Honey, look at me." Grace's voice got woozy. "Breathe with me. Come on. Listen to my voice. Let's count, okay?"

My throat tightened, my skin prickling. "You do that, too?" I gasped for a breath.

"For years now. Count with me. Here we go. Breathe in slowly. That's it."

"One, two, three, four."

"Hold. One, two, three—"

I held my breath and heard my voice join Grace's. "Four."

"Release."

"One, two, three, four."

All my focus went into my breathing, my counting. I stared at Grace's hand firmly on mine. Her beautiful diamond eternity bands were all lined up on her ring finger.

Yes, the diamonds.

I held them in my line of sight and gave them my spinning emotions. My fear, my panic, twisted out of me and headed for the diamonds.

Mole tied me up to the bed, the headboard rattled and banged against the wall.

The rope burned into my wrists.

His gleeful sweaty face above me.

His sour breath steaming over me.

"Breathe," came Grace's steady voice, breaking through the images.

Give it all to the diamonds.

"One, two, three, four," I intoned.

"I'm gonna fuck you like a train, bitch, and you're gonna love it! Choo-choo!"

That "beloved" flashback played out against the back of my eyes like a movie.

"You gimme the pizzas for free, and I'll let you play with her. Just don't fuck her pussy. That's all for me."

My chest squeezed.

It's just a flashback, images, a memory. It can't hurt me. I am more than a memory. I am more than a memory.

"Hold."

"I've never fucked a pair of titties before. Can I do that?"

"As long as I get to watch while I eat those pizzas you got."

My neck went limp.

I'm here on Boner's bed, in Boner's room, at the One-Eyed Jacks in Meager, South Dakota. Becca is safe with her grandma. I am not alone. I'm with Grace.

With Grace.

With Grace.

Spin away. Spin away.

"Release—"

"One, two, three, four."

My shoulders slumped, an opened water bottle was before me, and I took it and drank slowly as Grace's fingers wiped the hair back from my face.

"Lie down. I'm right here, and I'm not going anywhere until Boner gets back, okay?"

"Okay," I whispered hoarsely, lying back down on the bed.

"And don't worry. I changed the sheets when you were taking a shower."

"You did?"

"I didn't look too closely, but I wanted you to be comfortable. I have this thing about clean sheets. It comes with age. You'll see."

We laughed together, and that lightness felt good.

Grace shut off the light in the room, and I curled myself around a pillow and let out a breath.

There was still more to give to the diamonds.

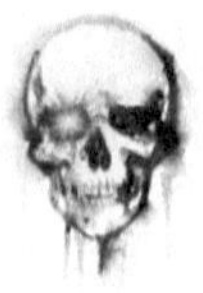

A light tickle skipped up and down my neck, and I arched away from it. "Hmm."

An arm wrapped around my middle, settling on my belly. "Jill." *His voice.*

I opened my eyes.

"You okay?" Boner asked.

I turned in his arms and nestled in his hold. "Are you okay?" I murmured against his throat, savoring the mild creamy soap scent of his damp skin.

"He ain't coming near you again. He gets to come see Becca and his mom and Tania, and that's it. You don't ever have to be in the same room with him." His hand stroked up and down my back. The hand that probably, moments ago, had been punching Catch, smacking him, throttling his neck, making him bleed.

For me.

I curled up in Boner's arms, my one hand sliding in his wet long hair, so cool and lush against my fingertips. "Thank you."

"You're not scared, are you? Being here with me?" His voice was low, tentative.

"No. No, not at all."

"Grace and Lock are spending the night here, too."

"Good."

A heavy sigh escaped his lips. He was worried. My hand smoothed up and down his tense back.

"He scared you, threw you on a bike, half-dressed. All this in front of his ma and Becca?"

"Yes."

"Such a motherfucker."

I planted a long kiss on his tense shoulder. "It's over."

"He fucking hurt you. You got nothing to say?"

"I thought I'd never see Becca again. I thought I'd lose this baby."

He gently kissed the side of my face over my bruise. "Fucker," he whispered.

"Or you. I thought I'd never see you again." I melted against him, my lips brushing his chest.

He sucked in a tiny breath. "You okay with this? Us together?"

"Are you?"

"You said you didn't want to be an old lady again. I get that."

"And you said you didn't want an old lady."

"We can do this until the baby is born. Then, you're free of me, of all this."

Free of him?

A heaviness seeped through my middle. He had claimed me to protect the baby. Of course he had.

I didn't want to be an old lady though. I didn't want that role. I wanted…*damn it,* I didn't know what I wanted. I only knew that, right now, it felt good, so good, to be in his arms, in his bed.

I got what I had told him I wanted, didn't I?

"Right, exactly. For the baby," I said. "I can pretend to be your old lady until then."

Boner coming to my rescue had been grand and valiant, impulsive and smart. But still, I didn't think Catch would let this go so easily. He liked to prove all his points, and he always had to have the last word. The Jacks might have gotten their licks in tonight and made the boundaries clear, but Catch wasn't done. I was sure of it.

I tangled my legs in Boner's. The T-shirt I wore suddenly felt thick and rough between us. I yanked it off me.

"Jillee."

I threw the shirt on the floor. "I need to feel you." I lay down on top of him. "Hold me," I whispered.

Boner took in a slight breath. His hand slid over my ass, and a shiver zipped up my spine as he stroked my rear, his other hand diving into my hair. His cool skin against my heat left me breathless. I was hyperaware of every part of me touching every part of him—our feet, our legs, his huge erection hard under his boxer briefs, his heaving chest under mine.

I needed this blunt honesty to ground me right now.

His minty breath was hot against my skin, and I swept his sensational long, thick hair back from his face.

His brows tensed together in a dark knot for a moment and then released, as if he didn't understand the mystery before him but realized that it didn't matter. It was simply better to admire it.

I felt small within his unyielding firm embrace. He rubbed my scalp, and sighing, I relaxed under the power of his gifted fingertips. I glanced up at him. His tender touch and intense gaze had me under a spell.

"I had to make sure he understood," he whispered, his heart beating steadily underneath me.

"I know. You don't have to explain."

He was concerned about my feelings. *Holy shit.*

"I had to," he said.

My core swirled with heat at the dangerous low tone of his voice.

Was it fucked up of me to be turned on by it, by his harsh grip on my flesh, the violence he implied?

I brushed his jaw with my lips, and my fingers stroked over his upper chest. "Did you punch him?"

"Yeah." His thumb slid inside my mouth for a heart-stopping moment and then dragged across my bottom lip. His eyes gleamed in the shadows. He was high. On blood, on making his move, leaving his mark. On me.

"Did you cut him?" I asked.

"Yes."

His hand slid under my panty, cupping my ass firmly, and I let out a whimper.

My hand ran across his chest and down alongside his body. "Did you make him bleed?" I whispered.

"Fuck yes. And I broke a bone. Just one."

I kissed his shoulder, licking over the hard contours of his upper arm. "Did you like it?"

He sucked in a quick breath. "I didn't want to stop."

I crushed my mouth to his, and my fingers brushed over the long scar along his middle, and he pushed my hand away.

"How did you get this?" I asked.

His head sank to the side. "War wound, long time ago."

"Were you in the Army?"

"No." His body tensed. "Another kind of war."

This wild mark forever lashed on his body was proof of the violent life he led, and although it made me uneasy, it also sent fiery sparks shimmering through me. My leg slid higher in between his, and I followed the trail of crisp hair down his abs. My hand tucked under his waistband and wrapped around his stiff cock.

I stroked his rigid length, and my tongue created wet swirls over his smooth chest. A groan escaped his throat as my tongue flicked around a nipple and over a pec. In a flash of movement, I was underneath him, my back to the mattress, his lips sucking on a breast. His torso pressed against me, and I let out a gasp at the exquisite surge of sensation between my legs.

"I want to make you feel good," he rasped, a hand stroking over my hips to my ass.

"Boner—"

His eyes glinted in the dark. "I want to make my old lady feel good."

My whole being glowed at his words. His lips skidded down my middle, and I shuddered as he moved south, ripping off my panty.

My hands dug into his hair. "Boner—"

His eyes found mine. "Let me give this to you. I want to give this to you, baby. I need to," he breathed, a hand on my breast.

Suddenly, both his hands were under my ass, lifting up my lower body, and his mouth sank over my pussy.

"Boner!"

His moans met mine in the air above us. His tongue swirled gently, then ferociously, and then gently again. He pushed my legs further apart and angled his mouth to discover more of me, take in more of me, tease me, consume me. My head rolled back on the pillow.

My old lady.

I gasped loudly, both my hands fisted tightly in his thick glorious hair. My hips shamelessly rocked against his face. "Don't stop. God, don't stop. Bone—oh, Bone!"

His silky hair brushed my thighs, and my lungs squeezed painfully as he sucked on me, his shoulders surging with the effort, his rhapsody of grunts and groans propelling me into a fantastic unknown.

I crashed and soared all at once, right there, in his mouth. I trembled under the intense force of the sweet glory he'd given me.

Boner lifted up over me, taking me in his arms. He turned us to our sides on the bed, his choppy breathing filling my ear. "You call that doctor of yours first thing tomorrow, and you confirm that you can have sex. All kinds of fucking sex. Hard, fast, slow, front, back—ask her about everything. So, we're sure."

"Upside down sex, too?" I kissed him and then laughed as I pressed into his chest, enjoying my taste on his lips.

"Not funny."

"I'm going tomorrow morning. Grace called her, and we got in for a visit, first thing."

"I'm taking you."

His fingers slid in between my ass cheeks, pressing against my entrance, and I let out a small cry at the tremor of sensation.

"And don't forget about your ass. You want me in your ass, baby?"

I laughed out loud, but he swallowed the laugh in a hungry kiss. "I'm not joking," he said against my lips.

"I know you're not joking."

Boner pushed me onto my back, and his teeth nipped across my jaw, down my throat. He sucked on my breasts, going from one to the other, roughly stroking them, his insistent wet tongue flicking at my sensitive nipples, and I squirmed under his weight.

I hooked both my legs around his torso, locking him to me, his head bent over me. My hands smoothed down his dark hair to his back, a waterfall of heavy silk, and it was mine, all mine, to enjoy. I bloomed under his hungry kisses, his gentle sucks, his stinging licks, his harsh grip.

"These tits are gonna fucking kill me," he said in between kisses.

I let out a stream of lazy laughter.

His thumb rubbed back and forth over a nipple. "I love your laugh." He pressed closer against me. "Never lose that laugh. I need to hear it."

I basked in the thousand sparks shimmering across my skin from his touch, from his raw voice in the shadows. But something sad lingered in the air from his tone, his silence.

"Are you okay?" I whispered.

"Yeah. You know, you never answered my question."

"Which one?"

He chuckled, his hair falling across his face, tickling my skin. He settled his head on my chest. "Do you want me in your ass?"

I kissed his forehead. "I want you everywhere."

FIFTEEN

BONER

"WHAT A MESS!"

My head lurched off my pillow, and my eyes unglued in the semidarkness. A girl stood, facing the mirror opposite my bed, her light-colored hair, hair the color of dawn, fell past her shoulders.

Jill.

I let out an exhale and fell back against my pillow again. For a second there, I'd thought…*no, impossible.* That was another fucking lifetime.

The first of many fucking messes.

I sat up in the bed. "What did you say?"

"My face is a mess," replied Jill. "I'm all puffy."

I rubbed a hand down my chest. "You're fucking beautiful. You just didn't get enough sleep."

"Sorry. Did I wake you up?" She leaned over me, her fingers tracing a line up my chest.

I clasped her wrist and brought her hand to my mouth, kissing it. "You're beautiful, Jillee."

"Stop."

"You are, baby." My thumb glided over the edge of the bruise that motherfucker had left on her cheek. "You are."

She tangled her fingers in mine. "We should leave soon, so I can see Becca and Rae, change my clothes, and then we can get to the doctor on time. Grace called me earlier."

"Oh, yeah?"

"She's going to meet us at the doctor's."

"Good."

I pulled her down and kissed her. Her small moans and soft giggles made something warm ripple through my chest.

Jill's tongue, Jill's breathy moans, Jill's taste.

Jill. Not black-eyed creatures from the past.

"How do you feel?" I asked.

She pushed my hair away from my face, a pink color rising on her cheeks. "Let's just say, you made me feel like a million bucks last night," she said softly.

I chuckled as I wrapped a hand around her upper thigh. "You tasted better than a million bucks. You coming on my mouth? Even better." I grinned at her as she squirmed on the edge of the bed.

My hand stroked over her belly, and she covered my hand with hers. "I'm looking forward to seeing the ultrasound, making sure everything's okay with our Super-baby. Grace was so upset. I hated seeing her like that."

I kissed her shoulder. "I know, babe. We were all upset."

"I should've told Catch sooner. I could've had Tania and Grace with me to make it easier. That would have been a no-brainer. Me and twenty-twenty hindsight." Her eyes got watery.

"Hey, this ain't your fault." I sat up, holding on to her hands. "That motherfucker did this all on his own. He didn't have to react that way. He chose to threaten your life and the baby's. He chose to put you on his bike and drag you over here to make a statement. Then, he goes and pulls a gun on you and Grace. Why? 'Cause he was jealous, pissed off? You two have been over for months. Guy's a dick, Jill. Needs to grow up."

"I could've been mature about it instead of avoiding it and putting off telling him. I knew that he'd have some sort of reaction, just not so thermonuclear." She let go of my hands and pulled on the hem of her T-shirt. "And now, my pathetic drama created problems for your clubs."

"Listen to me, this shit is not on you. Get that out of your head right now. And nothing about you is pathetic."

I wrapped a hand around her neck, pulling her close, and took her mouth, slowly kissing her.

"Minty girl. You found my toothbrush?"

She nodded. "That okay? Or does that gross you out?"

"It takes a hell of a lot more to gross me out, baby."

She let out that priceless small laugh again.

"How are you really doing though? Hmm?" I tugged at her lower lip with my thumb. An odd warmth burrowed through my insides at the sight of her cheeks flushing, her eyes shining back at me.

This is temporary. Temporary.

"I'm fine. No cramping or twinges or—"

"No, I mean, getting taken like that must have set off a few alarm bells for you, huh?"

"I guess. Yeah. A few."

"A man you trusted, the father of your kid, turned on you. Can't ignore that shit, Jill."

"It's over now." She moved away and went back to the mirror, combing her fingers through her hair.

"You need to talk it out. You can talk to me about anything. I'm a good listener."

She grinned. A greedy grin, like a kid who had gotten a huge ice cream sundae and refused to share. "You're good at a hell of a lot of things."

I jacked up from the bed and swatted her on the ass. "And don't you forget it."

"I don't think I ever will." Her eyes held mine through the mirror.

I stretched out behind her, and her gaze fell to my chest and then lower to my hard cock. I winked at her. "I'll be ready in five."

She smiled at me, and that heat inside me only burrowed deeper.

Fuck, everything was worth that smile.

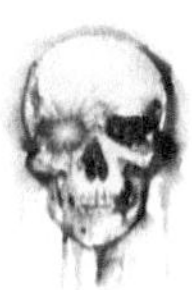

I got dressed, and grabbed Jill a banana and a yogurt from the kitchen for a quick breakfast in my truck. We stopped at Rae's, so she could change, see her daughter, and reassure Rae that she was fine.

At the doctor's office in Rapid, Grace was waiting for us in the parking lot. Once we all got upstairs, the receptionist ushered Jill in right away with Grace at her side.

I sat in the waiting room and stretched my legs, my shades still on. I didn't have to remove them. They adjusted in the light into a groovy purply tone. It also kept people away. I didn't like people in general. Most bikers I knew didn't either.

A woman in a very tight suit with a briefcase at her side lifted her head from her cell phone and stared at me, a thin eyebrow poking up her forehead. I glared at her, and she went back to tapping on her phone. A pregnant woman was reading a picture book to her young son who was eating a chocolate bar. He looked up at me, and I gave him a tight grin.

I flipped through a parenting magazine and skimmed an article on prepping for the baby's arrival. I tossed it and shuffled through the other magazines on the table at my side. Celebrity gossip rags, health and exercise rags, pregnancy and delivery—

Ugh, no, thanks.

I'd been to a lot of places, but a gyno's office was not one of them.

"Oh, Brent, honey, let me clean your hands and mouth," said the mom, putting down the storybook. "What a mess!" She wiped down his hands with a wet wipe.

A mess.

Gets messy.

"Very messy."

I took in a breath and leaned over, my elbows on my knees.

I was fifteen years old at the genesis of my big mess.

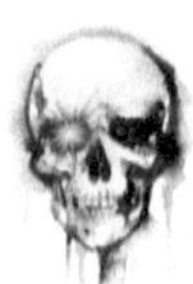

PAST

Spanish curses, slaps, and a woman's squeaks and breathy shouts echoed through the thin walls of the apartment.

"He'll be done soon. Come here."

Inés shivered, her teeth chattering, as she wrapped her slim body up in mine.

"I hate it when he does this," she whispered.

"I know. Me, too."

The sounds of my Uncle Johnny screwing some *puta*, as he called the women he brought home, from his room next to ours was a frequent ritual. His Spanish only came to life when he was mad, drunk, or screwing women, which was most of the time.

This was home for the last five years.

It was Inés's home though, not mine. Inés and I had shared a bed since I'd first come to live with them, but now, I was fifteen going on sixteen and she was fourteen. It was hard for me— emphasis on *hard*—when she would curl up against me in the middle of the night or cuddle up in my arms after a nightmare, which was pretty frequently. She had turned into this pretty, curvy girl all of a sudden. Just like the girls at school I liked to stare at.

Inés had lost her mom in a car accident long before I had lost mine, and her dad had turned into a freak show.

She had me, and we had each other. We cooked, shopped for food with whatever money he'd left for us, did our laundry at the crap Laundromat down the street, and managed to get our homework done.

Uncle Johnny's grunting grew more intense, and the woman started letting out more of those weird squeaking noises.

Inés's fingers traced a lazy trail across my chest and down my middle.

"Don't."

"Ticklish?"

"It's not that."

"Then, what?" she asked, her fingers still stroking me.

"Just—don't."

I was too embarrassed to tell her, but it was painfully obvious and getting more and more painful all the time.

"I know."

I blew out a breath of air. "What do you know?"

"It's this, isn't it?" Her hand stroked over my huge erection.

"Stop it!" I clamped a hand on her wrist.

She planted a kiss on my chest and kept stroking me.

"Shit, stop it," I breathed, my hips moving.

"I don't want to," she whispered.

Her palm cupped my balls over the thin cotton of my boxer briefs, and my body jerked. I choked on a moan.

"Does it feel good?"

"Yes," I said through my gritted teeth.

She lightly stroked me up and down, up and down. "Have you done it before? With Lucy?"

Lucy, a girl who liked me at school. She'd only let me cop a feel of her tits so far.

"No."

A noise rolled in the back of Inés's throat as her hand kept moving over me. My muscles were on fire. I was on fire. *Should I let myself react?* It was too difficult not to react, so difficult to hold it back.

"Oh," fell out of my lips.

The pear scent of the shampoo we both used floated through me as her head shifted over my chest.

Her hand slid under the waistband of my worn-out boxers.

"Ah, Inés!"

"Is that good?" she whispered. "I've heard you when you do it to yourself. You always think I'm sleeping. I want to do it to you."

My fingers dug into her shoulder, my other hand curled into the sheets at my side, fisting the nubby material. My lungs hurt from holding air in. I was too afraid I'd explode, and then Uncle Dickwad might hear us.

Would I get loud like he did?

If he caught us, he'd throw me out on the street, kill me. He hated having me around, another mouth to feed. But he'd grown to like the fact that I now looked out for his daughter. He didn't have anything restraining him from his daily or nightly activities—women, drugs, gambling, stealing.

I clamped my jaw down tight against the strain.

She kissed the side of my face and nuzzled my throat as her strokes grew harder.

My feelings for Inés were a secret wish I'd kept locked up in my twisted heart. I barely understood these feelings myself. She was my first cousin, as good as a sister.

We can't. It's wrong. So wrong.

But with every stroke of her hand, those feelings exploded like tiny hot-air balloons all through me. It felt good…so good. The wrong made it even better.

"Shit!" My cock throbbed and pulsed, my hips tensed.

A string of Spanish curses and loud drawn-out groans coming from Uncle Johnny and his *puta* were the soundtrack for my very first orgasm at the hands of a girl.

I blew, my cum spurting.

Her body jolted. "Oh!"

Both our gazes went to my dick in her hand. She blinked up at me. Waves of euphoria flooded through me.

"That felt so good," I whispered.

She smiled against my skin and crashed her mouth against mine. She gave me her tongue, and my stomach flipped. I swirled in a kaleidoscope of color and distorted sensations.

This was what kissing should be like.

This wasn't what I should be doing with Inés. This was for other girls…for Lucy…

This was bad. This was wrong.

Fuck it. Ah, fuck it.

I took her in my arms and kissed her deep.

She pulled away, giggling, her dark eyes huge, and sparks went off in my chest. I hadn't heard that sweet tiny laugh of hers or seen such an effortless smile on her face in ages.

"Gosh, my hand is…full of you. This gets messy, huh?"

I dropped to her side and pulled her in close to me. "Very messy."

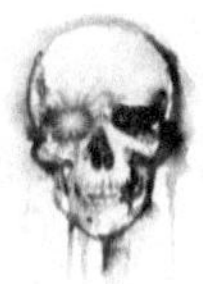

"Hi."

A child's voice sliced through my fog, bringing me back to the doctor's waiting room. Two big brown eyes with long lashes stared up at me.

I sat up straight, my eyes focusing on that small face. It was the little boy whose mother had been reading to him.

"Hey there," I replied, clearing my throat, pushing my hair away from my face.

"Brent, come back here." The mom gestured at her son. "Don't bother the man. I'm sorry."

"It's all right. Hi, Brent."

He tilted his head at me.

I gestured at the book his mother held in her hands. "You like your book?"

Brent nodded.

"I like books, too."

Brent stared at me, as if he'd finally met Darth Vader. A mix of fascination, awe, and excitement sprinkled with dread.

I pointed to his T-shirt that had dancing carrot and broccoli figures on it. "You, uh…eat your vegetables? You like broccoli?"

He only made a nasty face, and I laughed.

"How about cucumbers?"

Brent shrugged his shoulders.

"I like cucumbers," I said. "They're really fresh and…refreshing. You got to try 'em. They're green, too, but they're tasty. You gonna try 'em?"

Brent nodded. He reached out and touched my silver rings, his fingers landing on my One-Eyed Jacks skull.

"Honey, don't touch the man!" The mom's face tightened. "I'm so sorry." She moved to stand up.

I held my free hand up at her. "It's fine. Please."

Brent's tiny lips parted as his index finger traced the round, smooth head of the skull. "You like that one, huh?" I asked him. "Me, too. That's my favorite. You like this one?" I pointed to the fanged snake ring.

His eyes widened, his lips twitching as he nodded again.

"You're a lucky boy to have a mommy who reads to you."

"Does your mommy read to you?" he asked.

"Uh, yeah, she did when I was like you." I slid up in my seat, lifting my sunglasses off my face. "She was real busy though, so she didn't have a lot of time to read to me. But I liked it a lot when she did." I glanced over at the book his mother held in her hands. A lion, a zebra, and a giraffe decorated the cover. "You like animal stories?"

His eyes lit up, and he smiled.

I smiled back. "Me, too. I liked jaguars the best."

"Jag-oo-ars?"

"Yeah, they're big cats that run very, very fast. Like tigers, sort of, but they have spots instead of stripes. They're beautiful."

"Ja-jag-oo-ars!" Brent said.

I'd loved tigers, lions, jaguars, cheetahs, leopards, panthers at Brent's age. My mom would bring home small picture books for me, and we'd sometimes go to the library and search for more. We would both try to sketch the animals, and I'd color while she cleaned our tiny apartment. We'd plaster the kitchen and our bedroom walls with our creations. Our homemade wallpaper would hide the cracks in the walls, the old stains that she had desperately tried to wash off with bleach but would never come out.

"Mi cachorro, *you are so good at coloring. You stay within the lines, and you make the colors so bold, so alive.* Muy bueno. "

"Let's find a jaguar." I took out my cell phone, got online, and looked up pictures of jaguars for Brent. I clicked on one of a jaguar crouching, about to spring into action. "Here's one." I tilted my phone toward him. "What do you think?"

Brent leaned over my arm, his thirsty gaze gulping down the animal's photo on my screen. He bobbed up and down on his toes, his fingers digging into my forearm. "Ja-goo-ar!"

"Ja-goo-ar!" I roared, and he laughed loudly, hopping on his toes.

"Mrs. Landon?" the nurse called through the glass window.

Brent's mom slowly pushed up from her seat, a hand over her huge belly.

"Come on, Brent, honey, it's our turn," she said. She turned to me, her face softening. "Thank you. He doesn't usually talk to strangers at all. You obviously made quite an impression. All the best to you."

"Yeah, thanks," I said as Brent shuffled back over to her. "Bye, Brent."

Brent took his mother's hand, but his eyes remained on me as she pulled him through the open door.

I rubbed my thumb over the jaguar on my phone's screen.

Mi cachorro.

My mother always had a variety of sweet names for me. She'd said she was going to use them all whenever she could because, one day, I'd be grown up, and I wasn't going to let her say them anymore or let her hold my hand or kiss me on the cheek.

She was wrong.

What I wouldn't give to hear her voice call me "my puppy" in that gorgeous Argentinian Spanish of hers once again.

"Mi flaco."

I'd been her skinny boy all right.

I wiped a hand over my mouth and took in a short breath.

The door clicked open, and Grace and Jill swept into the waiting room, both of them beaming. I sprang to my feet.

"Super-baby is fine. We saw and heard the heartbeat. Here, look." Jill handed me a photo of a mass of gray and black blobs. "She or he is doing great."

"Great news." I held her gaze. "How are you doing?"

"Oh, wait! I forgot to ask the doctor something." She brushed past me and Grace and talked to the receptionist, who gestured her back through the open door again. I handed Grace the photo, and she studied it, probably for the hundredth time.

A few minutes later, Jill reappeared and slid her hand in mine. "All set. Let's go. I'm starving."

"What did you forget? Is everything okay?" asked Grace.

"You know me. I had a couple of questions about food and calorie intake. Now that I'm in the second trimester, I want to make sure I'm on the right track."

"You're so good about that." Grace breezed through the front door and hit the elevator button. "Woman of steel."

Jill squeezed my hand, her face pink.

We waved at Grace as she drove out of the parking lot, and I got Jill in the truck. I swung in and started her up.

"She said yes," Jill said.

"Who?"

"My doctor, just now."

I turned out onto the street. "Yes? About what?"

"She said yes about the sex."

I tore my eyes away from the road and shot her a glance. "She did?"

"She did. Yes to everything."

"Everything?"

"Yes!" She laughed. "I didn't want to ask in front of Grace. It felt…weird. Is that silly?"

"No, sweetheart."

I squeezed her thigh, and her hand clapped over mine.

"My first trimester went well, and now that I'm in the second, I'm good to go." She waggled her eyebrows. "But we should use a condom and lots of lube—water-based lube only, she said—if we're going to have anal sex."

"Ah." Images of Jill naked and on all fours in front of me, her luscious ass squirming back against my cock jumped in my head. I adjusted myself in my seat.

"I'm in the mood for a huge breakfast now—waffles with lots of butter and syrup, eggs, bacon, the works."

"Oh, yeah? What about all those calories you were talking about before?"

She leaned back against the headrest, a relaxed smile on her face, both her hands pressing mine. "I think I can afford the indulgence. I'm going to need the extra calories now. Don't you think?"

"Baby, I'm still stuck on the way you said 'lots of lube.'"

"Boner, focus. I want waffles. Really good waffles."

"There's only one place then. It's in Pine Needle."

"Two towns over from Meager, right? I've never been."

"Not much to see, except for this great little cafe."

Her hand stroked mine. "Is there a drugstore there, too?"

SIXTEEN

JILL

WE FINISHED OUR TERRIFIC, terrifically huge, breakfast at the small cafe in Pine Needle, and Boner brought me home. I was so relaxed, so full of food, so happy that the baby was fine and that Grace was relieved.

We stepped into Rae's house and were met with quiet. A text from Penny when we'd left the cafe had told me that she had taken Becca to her house for the morning as Rae was tired and would bring her back around noon. I peeked into Rae's room where the door was ajar. She was asleep.

"Poor thing. Last night must have really stressed her out. She never usually takes naps this early in the day."

"This shit's gotta be hard on her."

"It is. She's a tough lady, but your son is your son—not to mention, your only granddaughter. I'm so thirsty. That bacon did a number on me."

I went into the kitchen, got a glass from the cabinet, and filled it with water from the faucet. Boner came up behind me as I drank, a hand moving around my middle. He swept my hair to the side and gently bit my neck, and a shiver raced over my skin.

My head fell back against his chest. "Bone."

"Can't get enough of you." His hot breath fanned my neck. "But gotta get back to the club."

"No time for a quickie?" I leaned over the counter and pushed back against him. I couldn't help myself.

A groan and a long string of curses flew from his mouth as his hands rubbed my hips and down my ass. He ground himself against me. My one arm flew back and went around his neck.

His hand went under my skirt, between my legs.

"Bone, God—"

"Jill, honey, are you here?" came Rae's tired voice from within the house.

I jerked like a live wire, and Boner's body stiffened against me.

"I'm in the kitchen, Rae!" I called out. "Just cleaning up. Be there in a minute."

Boner moved again, his erection grinding up against my ass.

"Take your time. Did they say if it's going to rain today, honey?" asked Rae from her bedroom as the voices of chirpy morning news reporters flared from her television set.

Boner pulled my skirt up further, and his hands ran up my bare thighs.

"I-I'm not sure!" I said.

He tore down my panties to my knees.

I sucked in air, my hands clinging to the edge of the counter. "Would you like a cup of tea, Rae?" My voice strained.

"Sounds perfect," she replied.

I leaned over on a groan and filled the electric kettle with water. I jammed it in its base and flipped the switch on it.

He kneaded my ass, tightly squeezing the flesh. I moaned as his fingers teased my rear entrance, slid down into my wetness. My skin heated with the promise of more.

His teeth sank into my ass cheek, and I let out a groan. I lifted myself up on my toes as he licked me, his fingers working me. This was something off the charts, something that satisfied another part of me, not just getting to the big O. I gasped at the torrent of pleasure thundering through me, my body a mass of electricity.

The kettle beeped, and as if on cue, I came.

He released his grip on me. His warm tongue snaked over the curve of my ass, lavishing the bite mark he'd undoubtedly left behind. That mouth then made a trail up my lower back. I held myself up at the sink, my legs wobbling, the room spinning at his sudden gentleness.

He chuckled, his face in my neck, and inhaled deeply, as if he were committing my scent to memory, feeding some sort of essential hunger. He let go of me, washed his hands at the sink, and splashed water over his face. I handed him a couple of paper towels, and he rubbed his face dry as I fixed my skirt.

"You going?" I was in a haze.

"Yeah, baby, I got to get to work." He grinned. Devilish and playful all at once. "And you have tea to make."

Right, the tea.

Boner let out a laugh and planted a kiss on my forehead. He headed out the back door.

"Wait!" I lunged at him, throwing my arms around his neck.

His eyes met mine, his hands pressing in at my sides. A slow smile lit up his face. He was surprised.

So was I.

I brushed his lips with mine. "Have a good day at the office, dear."

His body shook with laughter.

SEVENTEEN

JILL

JIMMY FALLON TAPPED through a song-and-dance routine with a celebrity who was promoting his new movie.

Click.

A Republican senator defended his harsh comments against the Democratic governor of his state.

Click.

Ugly gold hoop earrings with diamond chips were bargain-priced on a home shopping channel.

Click.

A hard-rock music video from the '80s. The drummer shook his head so hard that all his crimped long hair rippled in his face as he banged on the drums, his sweaty arms shining in the colored lights swirling over him.

"Whoa."

My cell phone buzzed, and I absently reached over and grabbed it off the nightstand. My journal and pen fell, thudding on the carpet.

"Hello?" I crunched on ice from my glass of water.

"Jill?"

My body jumped at the sound of Boner's voice, and my glass tipped, spilling cold water on my camisole top.

"Hi. How are you?" I sat up in bed and put the glass on my nightstand, wiping down the water from my cami.

"That's what I wanted to ask you."

"Me?" I banged on the remote to mute the volume. "I-I'm good." I pulled on the wet cotton fabric, flapping it against my chest.

"I couldn't stop thinking about you all day." His voice was soft but intent without a trace of awkwardness. Blunt sincerity.

I closed my eyes and let his words, the supple tone of his voice, sink in, and they did. They penetrated like a wave of sound through every layer of skin, muscle, and bone and settled in my thumping heart.

"Me either." I folded my legs under me.

Moments lapsed in charged silence.

He blew out a breath. "Shit, did I wake you up? I just noticed the time."

"No, no, you didn't wake me up. I'm in bed, flipping channels on the television. What are you doing? Are you at the club?"

The thought of him taking the time to call me, only to go jump Mindy or some club skank once we got off the phone, made my stomach harden. I was his old lady, but come on.

"No, I'm home."

My chest relaxed, as if a thousand needles that had threatened to jab me suddenly disappeared.

"I just finished working out," he continued. "But I couldn't concentrate. Had to talk to you."

"Why couldn't you concentrate?"

"I still feel you on me."

My eyes sank shut, a breath shooting out of me.

"Jillee?"

"Yeah?" I managed.

"Did you like it? Feeling me on you?"

Heat flooded my chest. "Very much. Very, very much."

"I didn't expect it," he said.

"What didn't you expect?"

"Feeling connected to you."

My chest tightened. *Me, too.*

"You reminded me that there's still magic," he whispered roughly. "That there are things of wonder still left to experience."

The air knocked out of me at his confession.

"I'm guessing you liked feeling connected to me?"

A low chuckle erupted over the phone. "I liked it, Firefly. A lot. A hell of a lot."

"What did you call me?"

"You're like a firefly, Jill. You glow bright in my night."

"You go chasing them regularly?"

"No. Not at all." He took in a long breath. "Just once, when I was little. One summer, my mom and I stayed out in the mountains for a week. It was the first time I'd seen fireflies. I would stay up every night and watch them, dance around the field, trying to catch them. My mom got me this huge jar, and we managed to catch a lot of them. It was magic. The best magic ever."

My heart hammered in my chest. There was plenty of magic between us. Fairy-tale firefly-in-the-night magic. Magic I had hoped for but hadn't expected. Yet here it was, buzzing and glowing between us.

"But when we had to leave and go home, I had to let the fireflies go free," he said. "I was really upset, but my mother told me it wasn't right. They had to be free in the wild or maybe they would stop glowing. I wanted to keep them forever, hoard their magic for myself. But some things, really beautiful things, you can't hold on to forever, can you?"

An ache twisted inside me at the resigned tone of his quiet voice.

"I wish you were here with me right now, holding me," I whispered.

"Want to hold on to you, Firefly. Keep you just for me."

I swallowed hard past the lump of yearning lodged in my throat. "I'm right here." A compulsion to keep him on the phone and listen to his voice grabbed ahold of me. "Talk to me. Tell me anything."

"What do you want to hear?" He let out a soft laugh. "About the rebuild I worked on today? What I had for dinner?"

I giggled. "Yes. Yes, all of it."

He told me about the bike he was fixing for a new client, how the rust had made it so difficult, and how the parts had been taking forever to be shipped because it was a foreign "pretentious piece of shit." How he had been teaching Sy how to use a knife. How he hated the beef burritos Dawes ate almost every day for lunch because they smelled so greasy.

I tugged on my wet camisole. "Hold on a sec," I mumbled into the phone.

"Why?"

"I have to take off my top."

"You have to, what?" his voice sprang over the line.

"I spilled water on it before, and it's more wet than I thought. It's bugging me so—"

"What are you gonna change into?"

"A red lace nightie with a high slit up the sides," I replied.

He made a growly noise in the back of his throat. "What are you wearing, Jill?"

"*Tsk*. How could you tell I was fibbing?"

He chuckled. "Red lace sounded a bit extreme."

"Extreme for me? Great."

"Firefly, tell me what you're wearing."

"A blue cotton camisole with matching shorts." I let out a sigh. "How exciting."

"How soft, you mean. Wet cotton plastered over your tits? The best. Panties underneath?"

"No, I never go to sleep with underwear on."

"Me neither."

"Really?"

"Gotta let your privates breathe. Shouldn't keep 'em covered up all the time. Isn't natural."

"Exactly. Although—"

"What?"

"I bet you go commando all the time."

He only laughed.

"You do, don't you?"

"Wouldn't you like to know?"

I most certainly would.

"What are you wearing now?" I asked.

"I'm in a pair of sweaty shorts. Nothin' else."

"Sweaty, huh? From working out or thinking about me?"

"Both. You were ruining my session."

"And what kind of session was that exactly?"

"Meditation and then tai chi. Then, I said fuck it and hit the punching bag. Better but still no use."

My eyes closed, picturing him in still poses, totally focused in careful concentration, and then later exploding in rapid-fire movements against a bag.

Yes, perfect. Perfect. Perfect. Perfect.

"Then, it's my obligation to help you get over it," I said. "Make up for the disturbance I caused you tonight."

"*Disturbance* is the word, Firefly."

My stomach dipped at the sound of his low voice almost sighing out his nickname for me.

"If you were here with me, I'd lick that sweat right off your chest," I said.

A groan.

I leaned back onto my mattress. "I'd lick you all the way down to your navel and then tug those very, very sweaty shorts down those hips and—"

"Jill—"

"I'd rub my face in you."

"Ah, fuck." He let out a muffled groan. "Did you take off your shirt yet?"

"No."

"Do it." Exasperation, urgency laced his voice and made me drop my phone.

I tugged off my camisole and fell back on the bed, picking up the phone again. "I did it."

"Are your nipples hard?"

"Very hard. Hard—as in, I'm listening to your voice, to the sound of your breath, and it's making me crazy hard."

"Squeeze your tits for me."

I squeezed a breast and let out a soft moan at the sensation, at the sensation of him waiting and listening. "How do you want me to touch you, Bone? Tell me what you like."

Another groan.

"Tell me," I repeated, his heavy silence driving me insane with anticipation, with need.

"Your hand on my balls first, then rubbing all the way up my cock."

I clenched my legs together. "I'd rub you gently then hard."

"Yeah." His breathing grew heavier over the phone.

"I'd kiss the top of your cock long and slow. Then, I'd suck once, twice—"

"You fucking tease."

I licked my lips. "Hmm. Then, I'd—"

"Dip into that beautiful pussy for me," he said on a hiss.

I did as he said and let out a soft moan as my clit pulsed underneath my swirling fingers.

"You wet, Firefly?"

"Very wet." My breathing grew sharp.

"Wet for me?"

"Only for you."

"I want to kiss you on the inside of your thighs. Up one and then down the other. Lay a trail with my tongue on your white skin. Make you dirty for me."

I let out a moan. "I want to be your dirty girl."

I gripped the phone, my head grinding back into my pillow, my hips circling as he told me how he wanted me to touch myself. I let his deep voice wash over me as I imagined his piercing green eyes beaming their approval, making my insides flutter, singeing my skin with their fierce heat. My breasts ached for his attention. I closed my eyes and stopped thinking. I only listened to him and did as he'd told me.

I felt the kiss of his magnificent hair splayed over my abdomen like heavy satin ribbons. I tugged on that thick hair, held on to it, as his long skillful tongue flicked over my flesh. His words were raw, his voice rough. I stroked myself faster. I came hard, muffling my sharp cries into the phone.

"Damn it, Jill—fuck." He muttered a string of curses, grunting as he came.

My legs strangled a pillow, my body doubled over another one. "Could we make this a regular nightly thing? I'll give up watching Jimmy Fallon. That's huge for me. I get insomnia now all the time, you know. It'd be really helpful."

His low chuckle settled inside me. He left me with a raspy whisper, "Get some sleep, Firefly."

EIGHTEEN

BONER

I HATED LOOSE ENDS.

I parked my bike in the back of the Tingle. I had to get this done.

"Hey, Cassandra." I greeted the manager of the strip club.

An attractive African American woman, Cassandra had had the job for years now, taking over where Jump's old lady, Alicia, had left off, managing the girls and running the place under the Jacks's supervision.

Under Cassandra's precise direction, the Tingle had undergone an overhaul—a renovation of the building and the decor and across-the-board firing and hiring of staff and dancers. The investment had been big, but the payoff had been bigger. The club attracted men from all backgrounds and social strata and plenty of women, too. There'd been talk of putting together a ladies' night with male strippers at some point. That would be fucking popular, for sure. Business was good.

"Hey, you." Cassandra slanted her head at me, a tablet in her hands. She gestured down the hall. "Kicker's in his office, if you're looking for him."

"I'm looking for Mindy. Saw her car in the lot."

"She's out front, working with the new girl."

"Thanks."

I headed down the hall, toward the main room of the club. Under the glare of the bright house lights, there was no mystery, no drama, no sensation, no theater. The rows of empty tables and chairs were stark against the black floor and walls, like layers of lifeless bugs. The lighting fixtures seemed excessive and awkward, the stage a narrow glamour-less runway fitted with poles. All of it seemed ordinary. Or maybe I was just too used to it, desensitized.

All this ordinary would transform once the place opened tonight, the specially designed colored lights creating their finely-tuned magic along with the pounding music and the throb of sexual anticipation. A mesmerizing playground of greed, indulgence, and lies.

Mindy was sitting on a table, her feet planted on a chair, watching Shelley Anne perform her routine to some pop tune. She glanced at me, her eyebrows shooting up.

"Got something to say."

Her attention returned to Shelley Anne. "I'm busy."

"Just for a minute."

"That's what I'm worth to you, huh? A minute of your time. Such a prick."

I leaned back against the table, and we both watched her new protégé twist around the pole on lethal heels.

"I have an old lady."

"Yeah, it's fascinating how that happened. No one else seemed to know about her before. And *her*? Jesus."

"Watch it."

She glared at me. "We've been screwing for over a month now—"

"I haven't been marking my calendar."

She clamped her mouth shut.

"We both knew what we were doing, Mindy, what it was about."

Her back straightened. "I got that you saw other women. I'm not stupid. I was seeing other guys, too."

"So, what's the problem? Why you got a stick up your ass?"

"I guess none of it counted for anything, huh?"

"Like what?"

She let out a dark laugh. "Should I be impressed that you came here to explain?"

I pushed up from the table. "I didn't come here to explain nothing. I came here so that you're clear on what's going on and what isn't."

"Yes, sir, I'm clear." Mindy ran a hand through her long ponytail and returned her attention to Shelley Anne, who was crawling on all fours on the floor of the stage, trying to imitate a cat in heat. "I'm very clear."

NINETEEN

JILL

PIPES ROARED BEHIND ME. I looked over my shoulder as I strapped Becca into her car seat. Boner, on his bike with those purplish shades, pulled in right next to me on Clay Street in the center of Meager. A little sting went through me at the sight of his dark splendor on his vintage Harley, at the memory of his voice in my ear last night.

"Make you dirty for me."

"Bo!" Becca clapped. "Mommy, Bo!"

I grinned at him. "Hey, Bo."

He grinned back. Wicked, knowing, pleased.

"Rae told me where I'd find you," he said, shutting off his engine.

"You called Rae?"

"Yeah, I wanted to surprise you for lunch. You haven't eaten yet, have you?"

"No, but I made a tuna salad for us at home before I left."

"No tuna. Buffalo."

"Buffalo salad?"

"Buffalo burger, hon." He laughed. "Bacon-double-cheeseburger kind of buffalo."

My eyes popped open.

"Yeah, that's what I thought. You said you've never had one, right? This one is top of the line."

"Seriously?"

"I don't kid about burgers. It's one of my essential food groups. Can't have you missing out, especially when it's a local specialty."

Sexy times and good food. Who would have thought a fake relationship would be such a pleasure?

"Follow me."

"I should check on Rae first."

"Rae's digging into that tuna salad and French bread with Martha, as we speak."

"She told you about the French bread?"

"And the Greek olives."

"And Martha came over?"

"The lady from next door, yeah."

"Oh, geez. You got it all covered."

"On most days, I do. Get in your car, key in the ignition, and follow me."

"Anything else?" I asked.

"Double-check Becs. Make sure she's strapped in tight and put your own seat belt on."

"Unbe-freaking-lievable."

Boner shot me a you're-loving-this-as-much-as-I-am grin.

He willed his engine to make that insane uproar once again. I stood there, motionless, mesmerized by the sight of him in a very worn-out leather jacket, a blinding white V-neck T-shirt with a silver chain with a snake charm hanging from it, and dark blue jeans that must have been new because there were no rips in them. His silver rings glinted in the sunlight.

"Jill. Car."

"You don't like me gawking at you?"

I was openly gawking. What did it matter?

After the mall, the kitchen counter—episodes one and two— his room at the club, and last night's little phone sexscapade, and not to mention, now that we had official Old Man/Old Lady status, I could do it openly for a change, couldn't I?

"Oh, I like it, Firefly, but I'm a man on an empty stomach. I might bite."

Promises, promises.

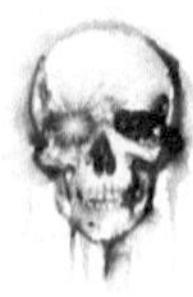

"Jill, you going to eat it or just keep staring at it?"

"I don't know how or where to begin. It's huge."

"At least Becs knows how to eat. You like it, Becs?"

Becca grinned with a mouthful of buffalo burger, clutching a thick sweet potato fry.

I stroked her tiny hand. "Slowly, honey, okay?"

She nodded as she chewed.

I raised my knife. "I'm going to have to cut this in half."

"Aw, Jill. For shame," he said, laughing as I cut the massive burger in two.

"And now I'm going to eat it all." I took a shameless huge bite of the juicy beast in my hands. The smoky rich flavor of the grilled meat, the luscious combination of the cheese, the bacon, the—

"Oh my God," I managed between chews.

Both Boner and Becca stared at me.

I swallowed. "This is a religious experience."

Boner grinned at me as he took a swig from a bottle of local craft beer, and Becca chomped on another fry.

My phone buzzed in my bag. I wiped my hands and fished it out.

Catch.

Ugh. Great timing. It was tempting to ignore his call, but he'd only keep trying and accuse me of avoiding him.

"Hello?"

"You think I'm going to let this go, you are dead wrong," Catch snarled over the phone.

I wiped my hands on my napkin, avoiding Boner's laser gaze. "What's up?"

"They tried to humiliate me."

"What did you think was going to happen?"

"I knew you and Boner had been hanging out, but his old lady? What did you go and do that for? You need committed dick in you?"

I shot up from the table, and Boner's eyes narrowed at me.

"Be right back. Got to take this." I charged toward the restrooms in the back of the restaurant. "You're disgusting."

"Yeah, we know I'm disgusting. But you? How long is it gonna take till you drive the man insane with your bullshit?"

"Shut up, Catch. What do you care?"

"We were good for a while there, but you're the one who fucked it up."

"I remember it differently." I leaned back against a wall by the ladies' restroom.

"Yeah, sure you do. But you started it, with your suspicions and insecurities. You did that. All your uptight crap made us a mess."

"Yes, I did go overboard, and I regret that. But you sure did something about it, didn't you?"

"That's right. All the shit you were always accusing me of, I finally did it. And you know what? I enjoyed myself."

"I have no doubt."

"And I have no doubt you're still a miserable little girl who takes out her shit on everybody else. Gotta say, I'm concerned you're gonna be doing that to our daughter. I don't want her to be messed up in the head like you."

"You're concerned, did you say? Well, *Daddy,* seeing as how she's already been the victim of a kidnapping before she even hit two years of age, things are not looking too good on that score."

"That was a royal fuck-up. Won't ever happen again."

"News flash, Catch—me being with my old man is not about you. It's about me. Nothing I do is about you, but everything is about our daughter. I do put her first, unlike you, and I trust my old man and the One-Eyed Jacks."

"My old man." Sweet hell, listen to me.

"Your daughter is a Flame first. Just because you're warming a Jack's bed, don't mean my kid, my own flesh and blood, has got to be subjected to 'em."

"Subjected? As far as I know, the Jacks and the Flames are not enemies, are they? Oh, I get it now. You'd be happy if I were with an accountant or the stock boy at the local supermarket, so you could be the big macho dick in the room?"

"Shut the fuck up, Jill, and listen. You can't be straight with me if you tried. My kid is not growing up around another club, you hear? And the Jacks are not gonna tell me what to do and how to do it. That's my kid we're talking about. You should show a little more gratitude that I let you leave Nebraska in the first place."

"Are you forgetting that I came to Meager with *your sister* to live with *your mother* and help her now that she's weak and frail?"

"They could've hired a professional to do what you're doing, but my sister managed to sucker you into it."

"Have you even offered to help your sisters financially with your mother's care, by the way? Your mother has good days and bad days. They come and go. And, thankfully, while the going is still good, your daughter is getting to know her very special, very wonderful grandmother. Doesn't that mean anything to you?"

"It does, but meanwhile, you're sucking Jack cock in the background. So, this is how it's gonna go. We aren't goin' through lawyers, for obvious reasons, so we're gonna do this my way."

My heart skipped a beat. "Do what?"

"You're gonna give me custody of Becca."

"What?"

"You're her ma. I get that. So, you can have her every other couple of weeks."

"What are you talking about, Catch? You're being totally unfair. This is bullshit."

"You're gonna do as I say, and you know why?"

"Why, asshole?"

He laughed. "'Cause if you don't, your old man is gonna pay for it. All it takes is for me to give the word to Mishap, and you know what's gonna happen, don't you?"

My blood froze.

Mishap was the Flames of Hell assassin-on-demand. A former Army sharpshooter, his services were legendary. Hired not only by his own club nationwide, but also contracted by other clubs and even Mafia from all over the country for his particular skill set. Murder for hire. At long range, under the cover of night, in the blinking light of day—either way, quiet, untraceable, unmistakable.

"Catch, please. Please. Are you totally insane?"

"Not totally. You do as I say, and there will be no insane mishaps, baby." His low chuckle rumbled through the phone. "Maybe I'll start off small, just for kicks, so you get that I'm serious about this."

"You always have to have your kicks, don't you?"

"This is real simple, Jill. You stay with your old man, but I get my kid the way I want my kid. You do not tell him, my mother, or my sisters about this conversation. This is club business, and you know what that means. I taught you well, didn't I?"

"Yes. Yes, you did." My voice cracked.

One night, Catch had made me watch Finger shoot a man, point-blank, in the face with a rifle. A prospect who had snitched to an undercover cop about business. Catch had wanted me to understand how important keeping secrets was, now that I was a part of a new way of life. He'd told me I needed to wrap my head around it and stay committed to it. I'd gotten it all right, in flying blood and chunk spattered Technicolor.

Afterward, he'd fucked me against the chain-link fence of the compound as the party roared on around us. He'd fucked me until I stopped feeling numb, and my incessant shuddering had been transformed into another kind of shuddering by the quick, harsh orgasm he gave me. His loud grunts, enthusiastic filthy monologue, and the sharp gleam in his dark eyes as he'd hammered into me had told me that it had been exciting for him to share that slice of his life with me. He'd been buzzing with it. I'd been a crazy mixture of terrified, stupefied, and needy, all the while realizing how wholly dependent on Catch I was for my sanity and survival at the Flames of Hell.

After the orgasm had faded, the numb had quickly returned. What had I gotten myself into once again? Way too much.

I'd thought I'd finally gotten myself out of it when I took our daughter and left him and Nebraska behind.

I gripped my phone tighter, my stomach gnarled into knots, as I watched Boner cutting pieces of burger for Becca from where I stood. "Don't do this to Becca, please. Come see her whenever you want. Whenever. But she's too young right now for you to take her from me and have her on your own. The last time you did, you handed her over to some club women, and she ended up getting kidnapped by that lunatic."

"I want my kid down here with me. I'm her father. Me. Not some One-Eyed Jack."

The line went dead.

Fuck. Fuck. Fuck. Fuck. Fuck.

My hand flew to my mouth, and I choked back the screechy sob rising in my throat. I took in a breath and made my way back to our table.

Boner's eyes followed me as I sat down. "You okay?"

"Fine. That was the billing department from the rehab where Rae was a few months ago. There's an issue with a Medicare payment that hasn't gone through yet. I couldn't hear what she was saying, so I…" I gestured toward the hall where I'd gone to take the call. "It's always something with health insurance."

The abrupt change in tone and spirit from Catch's phone call to this domestic bliss of me, Boner, and Becca eating a meal together was nothing short of whiplash. I settled back in my seat and gulped at my ice water.

During those few years with Catch, my normal had been this very same all-systems-at-high-hell adrenaline level which was shooting through me right now. It was a shock after all this time. I couldn't come down *and* lie about it right this very second.

How can I tell Boner right now, here in a crowded restaurant and in front of Becca?

No, I had to keep it together until I could think about this later when I was alone in my room. Later, yes.

Under the table, my feet rose, and my toes ground into the floor.

Boner drained his beer, his eyes on me, and set the bottle back on the table with a clunk. "Becca decided she loves sweet potatoes now."

My shoulders fell. "Really? Wonderful, sweetie." I kissed my daughter's greasy hand. "We'll have to buy some for home."

I forced myself to eat my burger.

"Everything okay?" he asked after we'd finished.

"Huh? Oh, yeah. Thank you for this. I really loved it."

He wiped at his mouth with a napkin and pushed a lock of hair behind his ear.

Make conversation. Say anything. He's the Sergeant at Arms of an MC. The man's life is all about deciphering suspicious behavior and clues. Damn it, where's your ramble now?

I got out the mini packet of baby wipes from my handbag and wiped down Becca's face and hands. "Did you and Dig come here?"

His brow furrowed. "What?"

"Did you two come here and eat burgers in the old days? Did he like them as much as you? You never talk about him, you know. I'd love to hear a few stories."

His head tilted. "Would you?"

"Sure I would."

His teeth dragged across his bottom lip. "Yeah, we used to come here. Back then, it was a dump though, a real hole-in-the-wall, and the burgers were dirt cheap. It was about all we could afford on a good night. Times have changed, as you can see."

The small space was crowded and noisy, and the oversized vintage counters trimmed in chrome gleamed, as if they were new. The restaurant had been featured in several travel magazines, judging from the framed articles on the walls. People sporting suits and ties, probably all the way from Rapid, were sitting at the small square cloth-covered tables alongside local ranchers and farmers. Times had changed. Local, home-grown was "in" and in demand.

He stuck a toothpick in his mouth and signaled for the check. "You think Becs has room for ice cream?" He nudged my leg under the table with his own.

My head ached, my chest felt like a lead weight was pressing on it. Boner was expecting things from me, Catch was expecting things from me...*Catch was terrorizing me.*

I zipped up my handbag. "I should get Becca home. It's coming up on nap time. She only takes one a day now. And she's had a big day. Boy, do I miss that second nap."

"I'll bet. What's wrong?"

"Nothing." *Plastic smile.* "Thank you for this, but you don't have to—"

"Take you to eat?"

"I mean, if it's part of the Old Man/Old Lady show, I get it."

He quirked a dark eyebrow. "Jill, you're trying to tell me something, but I'm not getting it."

I unzipped my handbag, tugged on another baby wipe, and wiped down my own fingers. "You don't need to entertain me."

"You gonna tell me what I need now?" His tone was brittle, slicing.

I shot him a look. "Maybe all you needed was to save me."

He tossed the toothpick onto his empty dish. "And maybe all you ever needed was to be saved."

Boner was right.

But I didn't want to be saved this time. I wanted to handle things on my own. I needed to be able to do that.

I unbuckled Becca from the restaurant high chair.

I would give Catch a day or two to cool off, and then I'd call him. Offer him a compromise. Something. Something that did not involve the Jacks and the Flames.

TWENTY

BONER

"WHO THE HELL knew babies needed so much shit?"

Grace's eyes blazed at me from across the stroller department of the baby store in Rapid. A young couple shuffled out of my way.

"A lot of *stuff*. They certainly need a lot of stuff," I said, lowering my voice.

"It seems to get worse every time," Grace said. "My nephew was born almost seven years ago, and I really don't remember my sister needing half of this"—she glanced at me—"*stuff*."

"See what I mean?"

"I can order the stroller for you." The petite salesgirl returned from the stockroom. "We should have it within two weeks."

"That would be great. Thank you," Grace replied.

"I have your information on file. We'll give you a call."

Grace slid her arm through mine and led me to the other end of the store. "Let me show you the crib we picked out."

"We're not shopping, are we?"

She elbowed me. "We already bought it. I just want to show it to you."

"Fine. Show it to me."

"So, how are things with your old lady?"

"How long have you been waiting to ask that question?"

"I've been trying to fit it in since we got on your bike at the club."

"Grace."

"I don't want to put you on the spot, but I want to know." She squeezed my arm.

"I ever get involved in your drama?"

"No."

"Okay, so?"

"You've never had an old lady before, and you jumping in and saving the day at the party was all sorts of amazing and wonderful, but I'm just concerned about how it's been for you because—"

"Because?"

"Because I think you really like her—like, really, really like her. And I really, really like Jill. I'd like my baby's mommy to have a happy, fulfilling, and satisfying pregnancy. And I love you. So, I have a vested interest in the two of you working out."

"Jesus."

"You know better than to play it cool with me. Let's hear it."

We stopped in an aisle lined with Baby Einstein CDs. *What the hell was that?*

"Earth to Boner."

I met her gaze. "I like her."

"I know that."

"But this relationship thing is just until the baby's born."

"What?"

"It'll keep Catch away from her now that the line's been drawn."

"Right."

I slapped at a ladybug mobile, and it spun awkwardly.

"You're full of crap," Grace said. "The way you came at Catch, I figured it went deeper than the everyday concern or attraction."

"Just doing the right thing."

"Oh, shut up!"

"Are we done here?"

"Mr. Denial? Hello?"

I twisted a heel into the floor. "I'm dealing with it."

Her eyebrows jumped. "Dealing with it? What does that mean?"

"I mean, I feel shit for her."

She led me down another aisle filled with night lights and glow in the dark crap. "Good shit?"

"Yes. Very good, good shit. But she just got out of a relationship with that asswipe, and she told me a while back that she wasn't looking to be anyone's old lady. We're hanging out, and it's…good between us."

"Oh, good."

I rubbed the back of my neck. "I know she likes me. She hasn't been shy about that, but I keep thinking, maybe it isn't about me, maybe—"

"It's about Dig?"

"Yeah. It's just a voice in the back of my head. But, yeah, maybe it's her vicarious hero worship of my dead best friend who saved her life when she was a teenager."

"Have you asked her?"

"No, I haven't asked her."

"You've got to find out. If you really like her and want to pursue the relationship for real, you need to be straight-up with each other. Are you being straight-up with her?"

"Yeah, sure."

She twisted her lips. "You need to be, so there aren't any crazy, stupid misunderstandings and all sorts of petty bullshit."

"You're so damn smart."

Grace pinched my side.

"Ow, woman!"

"What did you tell me a few months ago when my first surrogate miscarried, and I was flailing? You remember? You said, 'Deal with your shit before it deals with you.' You also told me to let Miller in, to let him really be there in my heart and not let go. How are you and Jill going to work if you're only letting her part of the way in, and you're not sure if she's all in either?"

"You think I don't know this?"

"Boner, if you have feelings for the girl, you should pursue it and live those feelings. Enjoy them. My sister only had a few years with her husband and her son, but she enjoyed that time, appreciated that kind of happiness. You deserve that kind of happiness too. You so deserve it, honey." She stopped walking and pressed her lips together, sucking in a short breath through her nose, her eyes watering. "You've been alone for way too long, and I don't know why that is."

I shrugged. "I've never been normal. So what?"

She leaned into me. "You're very, very special to me. I know there's plenty you haven't shared with me. Maybe you can't because it's just too painful. I respect that. Whatever it is though, please don't let it get in the way of you and Jill, if you really want to be with her."

I stared at my boots and took in a breath.

"Boner?"

"I've never had this before, babe," I whispered. "This sort of good through and through."

"And you're not sure what to do with it? Is that it?"

"No, I know what to do with it, and before you ask, I'm not afraid of it either. I want to soak myself in it, in *her*. I just don't want it to get taken away, like everything and everybody else."

"I know. But we don't have control over that, do we?"

I might.

Her hazel eyes searched mine. "You've got to let that go. Otherwise, there's no room for anything else. That's what I had to do. You do it, too. Let it go, and soak in it." She hugged me, planting a kiss on my cheek. "I'm so happy for you. Please, please, Boner, be happy, too. This isn't a burden. It's a new kind of freedom."

Freedom? Not for me.

"Boner, you okay?"

"Yeah." I picked up a bag of spongy bath toys that had fallen on the floor and put it back on the shelf with the others. "It's fun between me and Jill. No pressure. Plus, she's thinking about what she wants to do with her life. She's had to deal with a lot of shit from her past, and that sucks. We know how that feels, and I don't want that for her. I just…"

"What?"

"I just wonder if she sees me as one of her new possibilities or if I'm just good enough for now."

Grace didn't say a word. We both stood still, right there in the middle of baby car seats, her hands gripping my jacket.

We both knew too well the cost of tiny hopes and the pang of wanting to feel those hopes grow and survive, but not sure if they ever would. For years Grace and I both yearned to live that *other life* that was always just beyond our fingertips. Convinced we weren't worthy, we rarely—if ever—reached toward it. We had avoided it, surrounding ourselves in the bland, the tasteless, the dull, the stale. But, there came a time when you recognized it, and wanted it more than your next breath, when you'd do anything—just fucking anything—to taste it, to have it for yourself.

And you reached.

Grace and Lock had finally reached, and they had it now.

Grace let go of my jacket and wiped at her eyes. Her gaze snagged on something over my shoulder.

"Oh, nice." She moved toward a row of plush rocking chairs beckoning to her from across the aisle. She glided her hands over the deep back cushion of an oak-stained one, a small smile blooming on her face.

Something shifted in my chest.

Grace was smiling over baby furniture.

I crossed the aisle and joined her. She sat in the chair and smiled again as she rocked. Fuck, this was a hell of a difference from over seventeen years ago—when she had been lying in a hospital bed, wanting to end her life, after she'd lost her first love and their unborn baby and had been told she'd never be able to carry another one after the emergency surgery she had to have.

Grace had begged me for a way to end it, so I brought her the pills. I didn't want her to suffer anymore. I only wanted to give her what she wanted. Grace was the one who held us together, and I'd never seen her like that before—no anchor, tossed on the sea, blind, drowning, no will to lift her head up, to even take her next breath.

I was tempted to end it with her that black night of a hundred horrors. She took the pills I'd brought her, and she made me leave.

Butler's wife, who ended up staying with her that night, figured it out though. The doctors pumped Grace's stomach, and thank God, she made it.

It was her choice, but I'd made it happen for her. And the unsuccessful attempt only made her more miserable than before, if that were at all possible. I hated myself for it even more, and we could barely face each other after that night.

A month later, without a word, she left South Dakota and all of us behind. All I knew was, with Dig dead, their baby lost, and Grace gone, too, I'd lost everything that meant something to me all over again. Yeah, I still had the club, my brothers, but the meaning of it had been ripped away, broken.

Just like it had been in the aftermath of Hurricane Inés.

Months had gone by after Grace had left without a word, but I had to know, I had to see her, and I was real determined. I'd kept tabs on her sister and stolen her mail a couple of times. I'd finally found a card from a post office box in Dallas under their mother's name.

I went down there and waited for Grace. One day, she showed up to check her mail—thin, spooked, blank. I followed her home to this tiny studio apartment, and I broke in, not wanting to take a chance that she wouldn't open the door if I rang the bell like a normal visitor. She was actually glad to see me once she'd gotten over the shock. We got wasted, strung out on booze, weed, and regret—talking, talking, talking—and we ended up kissing. We stopped it and fell asleep on the sofa, holding on to each other.

When I woke up the next morning, she was gone.

I was destroyed, stranded. Again.

But I knew she was right for leaving. We'd only called the ghosts back up that night. It hadn't been comforting. It had been haunting, and it'd sliced deep and hurt in new, fresh ways.

It had been dangerous to see each other again.

If I brought her back to Meager or stayed with her, we would have only clung to each other, making us something we weren't, something we weren't meant to be, and it would have been out of our pain and loneliness, not something whole but something made up of missing.

She had been right to cut us off and cut us up into pieces, but it sucked all the same. It hurt deep.

At some point though, I had to crawl out from under the grief. We both did.

I didn't see her or hear from her for over fifteen years, not until the night she strode back into the clubhouse last year and asked me to pour her a whiskey.

One of the best moments of my life.

When she told me she'd stayed away because a club out west, a rival MC, forced her to, that had made me crazy all over again. Why hadn't I seen that? Why hadn't I figured that out? I could've stopped it, helped her, unraveled it for her. It was what I did, what I'd always done.

But when my emotions were wrapped up in someone, I couldn't see straight. I didn't read the usual signs.

Inés had proven that to be true.

I suppose there were times when only we could extricate ourselves from our own ravel in order to make it stick.

Now, here at a baby store, of all places, all these years later, I got to bear witness to Grace's renewal, this turning over of her soil. All her fragmented ends and splintered edges had been smoothed, her smoldering cinders doused with cool water. Hers and Lock's. All of that was in this smile of hers because of a piece of furniture, and my heart swelled at the sight of it.

I sniffed in a breath. "You're into this nesting thing now, aren't you?"

She eyed me. "How the hell do you know about nesting?"

"I saw an article about it at the doctor's office when I went with you and Jill."

"Nesting is real, and it's here to stay. Miller's eyes now glaze over when I start with how many blankets the baby might or might not need, which bottle warmer is more efficient, blah, blah, blah-di-blah-blah."

"On that note, where's the crib?"

She rolled her eyes. "They're over here."

We moved through the rocking chairs into the crib area.

"We saw this one online and really liked it." Her fingers curled over the rail of a dark wood sleigh bed–style crib. Blue-and-yellow fluffy bedding accented the piece, which was trimmed with a matching quilted panel all around. A small stuffed gray elephant and a brown velvety dachshund stuffed animal had their arms around each other in one corner.

Something crimped in my chest.

Jill would be giving this baby life. And after it was born, that baby would be in this crib in Grace and Lock's house. *What was that going to be like for Jill?*

My gut clenched. I wanted to be there for her. I wanted to share that with her, make it better—whatever *it* was going to feel like. It might not be all good. Who the fuck knew?

"Boner, you like it?"

"What?"

"The crib, hon. We don't know if it's going to be a boy or a girl, so I figure, this design is a good neutral, not feminine but not too plain."

"You don't want to know yet, do you?"

"There are so few true surprises in life anymore, and that is surely one of them—if not, the best. We want that surprise." The edges of her lips quivered slightly. "We need it."

I slung my arm around her shoulders and kissed the side of her head. "I know you do." I gripped the wooden rail of the crib. "I like it. It's a good crib."

I wanted that kind of surprise, too.

I wanted to feel Jill's hand in mine, to go to sleep with the sound of her even breathing in my ear and the weight of her relaxed body in my arms. I wanted to hear her laughter ring within the walls of my house, to eat good food with her, to have Becca throw her toys around my living room and make a mess and hear her cry or laugh down the hallway.

What would that feel like, look like on an everyday basis? I didn't know, and I fucking wanted to know.

I wanted to feel it in every corner of my house, in every corner of my soul.

An urge to see Jill overtook me.

Spending time with her, just the two of us, had been proving to be a challenge. She had to live at Rae's house and take care of her. Plus, she had Becca. With Tania working late hours of the day and night to get her potential store organized while also going through Wreck's shit, Tania's availability to Becca-sit and Rae-sit had been rare the past couple of weeks. Then, I was working at the shop, going on runs through North Dakota and Wyoming, checking in on our operations.

Jill and I had been a bunch of stolen moments.

And still, those stolen moments had been better than any random fucking where me and whoever it was would get off. I'd zip up, she'd clean up, and we'd eventually stumble our separate ways.

Each and every time Jill and I had been together, I was filled with a new hunger, a new desire, a more urgent need demanding to be satisfied again and again and again. It wasn't only a release, a consumer necessity.

Shit, Jill and I hadn't even had sex yet—like real-fucking-penetration-of-prime-body-parts sex.

I fucking needed to fuck my woman already, for fuck's sake.

"Grace, I need your help with something."

"Ohhhhh, really? Must be important for you to actually ask me for a favor."

"Very fucking important."

"Will you stop cursing in here?"

"Are you gonna fucking help me?"

"Boner!" She pinched me again.

"Cut that out!"

TWENTY-ONE

BONER

"Delivery!"

I knocked on Rae's kitchen screen door.

Jill was crouched in front of a kitchen cabinet, scrubbing it with a small towel. She swiveled around, gasping, her body jerking back against the cabinet, a wide-eyed look on her face.

"Babe, it's me. You okay?" I pushed at the door handle, but the door was locked.

She let out a deep breath, clutching the towel in her grip, her shoulders tense. "Sorry!" She took in a gulp of air and stood up, a hand over her chest. "You just spooked me. Come in."

"Screen door's locked."

"Oh, right." She bit her lip and tossed the towel on the counter. Her face flushed, she came to the door and unlocked it, swinging it open.

"What's wrong?" I entered the kitchen, and she closed the door firmly behind us.

"Nothing." She pushed the hair from her face. "I was just daydreaming, and I didn't hear you."

"You didn't hear me pull up on my bike?"

Her gaze darted to the full plastic bag in my hand. "What's this?"

"I heard you had a craving for Chinese food."

"I do?"

"Sure you do."

"You're a nut."

"Should I take my nut and my Chinese food and get out of here?"

Her eyes flared. "Hell no. Give me that bag!"

"Give me a kiss first."

She pressed her lips against mine. My heartbeat clanged like a bell bonging in my chest.

I tracked into Rae's gleaming kitchen. The food brought in a harsh smell in contrast with the lemony-lavender fragrance that filled the space. Clean and inviting. *Jill.*

I plopped the full-to-bursting plastic bag on the counter. She rifled through it as if it was a gift bag from a fancy jewelry store. I was claiming my opportunity today. If your planets don't align, you need to make it happen for yourself.

Jill faced the counter, her back to me, as she went through the food boxes. "Sesame chicken, pork lo mein…"

"I wasn't sure what you liked, so I got a selection."

She glanced at me over her shoulder. "Shrimp and broccoli."

"I saw Becca heading home with Auntie Grace. She said Rae went to the movies with a friend?"

"Yeah, they just left. It was very last minute. Ah, Mongolian beef."

"Lose the shirt."

Her fingers gripped the white food container in midair. She turned and stared at me.

My head slanted. "Do it."

Jill put down the small white box of food and ripped off her blouse, exposing her full round breasts in a pink bra.

My lungs squeezed. Her eyes transfixed on my gaze caressing her tits, her breathing deepening.

I raised my chin. "Go through the food. Tell me what you find."

She swallowed and turned back to the food on the counter. "Chicken and cashews." Her voice was suddenly breathy.

I stood behind her and leaned over, taking in the warmth of her skin, nuzzling the tousle of her freshly-shampooed hair. Flowers and sunlight.

My lips brushed the curve of her shoulder. "Take off the shorts."

The swift *rip* of her zipper set off a fireball in my veins. My dick pulsed at the sight of her pushing the denim over the curve of her hips. Her shorts thudded to the floor, and I kicked them away. Her plump, firm ass peeked out from a delicate pink thong.

"Dumplings." She let out a laugh.

I laughed, too.

I pulled on the thong string along her ass crack, applying pressure on her pussy, and she let out a whimper.

"Keep going," I said. "There should be..."

"Sesame noodles."

"That's the one." I snapped the thong back against her ass, and she let out a gasp. My fingers skimmed her skin until they reached her bra strap and unhooked it. Goose bumps rose over flesh. "Take this off."

She twisted the bra off her body and tossed it to the side. I cupped her full tits and pressed against her. She let out a cry, her ass moving back against my cock.

Both my hands sank into her silky wetness. "There's my girl. Fuck yeah."

We both groaned, and she leaned her head back against my chest. "Bone..."

"Grab the sesame noodles," I whispered in her ear. Releasing her pussy from my grip, I nipped at her earlobe.

She grabbed the container, and I led her by the hand to the round table Rae had in the middle of the kitchen where I lifted her up onto it, laying her on her back. Her lips parted as she stared at me.

Full anticipation. Just the way I wanted her.

"This is my favorite," I murmured.

I scooped up a strand of noodles slathered in the spicy sauce with my finger and tucked it in my mouth. Her forehead bunched, her heavy gaze fixed on me.

I sucked on my fingers, the spicy mixing with her tang on my tongue. "Sesame Jill."

She let out a low moan and squirmed on the table, her legs falling open, her head sinking back.

I held out a noodle and laced it over a breast, around the nipple. "What should I do now, baby?"

"I think you should eat."

"I think I should, too, but ladies first."

I held another noodle over her mouth, and she opened wide, her tongue stretching to meet it.

My pulse pounded at the sight, my balls seizing in my jeans. "You hungry?"

I touched the noodle to her tongue and then pulled it away. Her back arched, her tits jiggling with the movement.

"Take it." My voice caught in my throat as I dropped the noodle in her mouth.

She savored it as if it were a rare, exotic delicacy, her eyes on me.

"You like it, huh?" I asked, my fingers trailing down her middle to her pussy.

She nodded, licking her shiny lips.

I gently circled her clit over the fabric of her panty. "I'm fucking hungry, too. So fucking hungry."

Removing my hand from between her legs, I leaned over her chest. My tongue swirled around a pebbled nipple, and she moaned loudly, her body jerking at the contact. I traced wet circles over her and finally sucked on the noodle, nuzzling her skin. I lapped at the spots of spicy sauce on her tit, kneading it hard, getting it in my mouth.

My other hand pressed between her legs, rubbing over the slippery fabric. Her pelvis rocked, desperate for more friction. The satiny material under my fingertips grew wetter and wetter, and Jill shuddered on Rae's old kitchen table.

She was at my mercy, aching for what I could give her, adoring my touch, relishing my desecration of her absolute perfection.

No, I'm making her more perfect.

My fingers stroked the unbelievable softness between her breasts. "I just want to sink my teeth into you."

Her brows jumped, a wicked smile sweeping her lips. "Do it," she whispered.

My middle finger brushed over a rough bump. "What's this?"

"What?" She raised her head, her eyes squinting at the spot where I was rubbing over her skin. Her head fell back. "An old scar. It's nothing."

"Here, on your perfect tits? How'd that happen?"

"Feed me some more. I'm starving."

"Jill? Tell me."

"Please." Her fingers flexed and curled into fists at her sides. "Not now. Not now."

"Jillee?" I gently cupped a breast. "You can tell me anything, baby. Anything."

Her head sank back against the table. "The jerk who took me years ago. I don't even want to say his name."

I closed my eyes. *Mole.* The fucker who'd kidnapped Jill and kept her tied up on a motel bed for two days. The fucker whose body I had destroyed and gotten rid of. If I had known then that I'd be feeling this mess of emotions that I was feeling for Jill right now, I would've taken more time and much more pleasure in dealing with his corpse.

"Boner—"

"Nobody will ever hurt you again. I promise you," I breathed against her warm skin before planting gentle kisses over the white bumpy scars. "You hear me, Firefly? I want you to forget that fucker and every goddamn evil thing he did to you."

"I don't want to forget."

"Why the fuck not?"

Her hand came to my beard, her fingers running through it. "The details have dulled over the years, and I don't dwell on them like I used to. But I do remember that there is such a hell out there. It makes the good in my life so much sharper and in focus. Becca, Rae and Tania, Grace and her baby. And you. You're so clear to me. And I want you all to stay that way."

There it was again. That strength, that shining vitality that would blow me away each and every time she wielded it like a lightsaber in a dark galaxy.

A slight smile swept over her gorgeous lips. "Either feed me or fuck me until Rae comes home from the movies. She might get tired and come home early, and before she does, I want *you* to come inside me."

I stared at her as the endless possibilities, the anticipation, were eating me up. I'd won the lottery and couldn't decide how to spend my winnings.

"Help me up."

I scooped her off the table and set her down on her feet. Her hair was mussed, her eyes dewy, lips red and swollen.

I can't wait. No fucking way.

I turned her in my arms and leaned her forward. I grabbed one thigh and propped it up on the table, opening her up to me.

Fuck, what a sight.

Her cunt inviting me in, her full ass curving before me. My brain cells popped as I ran my fingers through her wet heat.

"Bone?" she whimpered.

"Need you now, Firefly. Right the fuck now." I squeezed the soft flesh of her ass. "Like this."

She only let out another whimper, her back and shoulders relaxing, her fingers curling around the edge of the table. "God, yes…"

I undid my jeans and shoved them down my hips. I grabbed her hair and pulled her head to the side, nipping and nuzzling her damp skin. Goose bumps spread over her shoulders and her arms. I held my cock steady against her slit, my heart pounding through my chest, and I slid inside her wetness.

She let out a low moan, her forehead sinking on the table. I dug my fingers into her hips, slowly pulling out and rocking back inside her even deeper. My cock throbbed in approval.

"I went and got tested. Got the all-clear to go bare." My brain cells bended and waved like flags obeying the force of the wind. "Oh shit, Jill. Shit, I can feel you on me, babe. So good, so fucking good." I thrust into her tightness, an epic explosion building inside me.

Her breathing grew quick and choppy, her palms gripping the table. Her ass had me in a trance as I plowed into her, over and over again, watching my cock thrust in and out of that pussy, watching that pussy sucking me in. My pulse fired like a thousand rockets going off, one by one.

I drilled deeper, and she pushed back against me, shuddering in my hands. I couldn't hold back any longer.

Sweetest fucking torture ever.

Everything faded. Everything melted away, except for this— me moving inside her, her all over me, taking me in and moaning for more, the table shaking and rocking, her cries getting louder. I exploded, my cum bursting inside Jill. I held her gorgeous body on mine, her sweat a sheen of gold on her pale back.

I leaned forward and licked a trail up her salty spine, my hands finding her incredible tits. "Which way to your room?" I pinched a nipple.

"Wh-what?"

I was a man on a mission.

A Fuck Mission.

A Come Until You Can Come No More Mission.

"Your room."

She let out a groan—or was it a laugh? "I don't think I can walk."

"Walking ain't required."

I pulled out of her and grinned as she sank down on the table with a moan, her arms bent at her sides. I yanked up my jeans and lifted her in my arms. Her eyes met mine. Her lips fell open. Innocence and satisfied woman all in one.

Yeah, I was on a Melt with Jill Mission.

"Last room on the right," she said, her hand wrapping around my neck, as I carried her down the hallway. "Bone, when you licked me in the kitchen that time, I almost…" she whispered, out of breath. "Could you do that again?"

A Make Jill Beg for Mercy Mission.

"I'm gonna lick you all over, Firefly."

I kicked her fucking door open.

TWENTY-TWO

BONER

"WHAT DO YOU GOT FOR US, BUTLER?" Jump ran a hand through his silvery-black beard. The Jump signal for, *Let's hear your spiel. This had better be good.*

All eyes in the meeting room turned to Butler.

Butler planted his hands on the great table. "The Calderas Group that Catch told us about is based in Denver. Salvadoran mob parading around as a Latin American import-export business—coffee, wines. They play it real highbrow, but they're actually far from that."

"What does that mean?" Jump's eyes narrowed.

"They're gangbangers from way back in the eighties."

"No shit," muttered Kicker.

"They got tired of being told what to do by the white-collared dons in town and of being pushed around by every new gang on the block, and there were many. In the mid-'90s, they got their shit organized. They managed to control the low-level crap—robberies, assaults, murders—that had gotten them unwanted attention and their members in jail," said Butler.

"They've risen above where they started, which was the gutter. Under the radar of their fancy big-money legit enterprise—the Calderas Group—they've managed to retain their ties with one major player from Mexico. Which means, they're still heavy into crack, cocaine, weapons, like they used to be in their youth but doing it now wearing suits and ties and hanging out in better restaurants and clubs."

After I'd left Denver, I hadn't stepped foot there again, avoiding it at all costs. In my early years as a Jack, I'd told our then prez that there were warrants for my arrest, that I couldn't chance it, which was partly true.

My fingers pressed into the smooth surface of the table. "Which gang from Denver in the eighties?"

Butler leaned back in his chair. "The Executioners."

My eyes lifted to his.

"Did you know them?" he asked.

"I knew who they were, yeah," I managed.

"They got control of choice routes out of the old country through New Mexico to Colorado. But since Colorado legalized marijuana, the Feds have been raiding pot businesses all over the state, so the Executioners or the Calderas Group has taken some hits over the years. They're looking to shift their reach, and it looks like the Broken Blades snagged their attention in little ole Nebraska."

I reached for a smoke and lit up. "The Blades have that old underground warehouse and meth factory somewhere in the boonies in their territory. Everyone's had their eyes on it. Why not them?"

"Good point," said Butler. "Plus, with the Blades making our life difficult in Colorado and down through Texas, if this Calderas Group works with the Blades, and they use that warehouse and factory as a new hub of operations, they'll have us by the balls—as in, slicing our *cojones* clean off on our Southern routes."

"Which will, of course, make them think they can take more and more and more as they go," added Kicker.

I stopped listening. The weight of centuries old failures still stuck in my chest, still crushing. That burn sliced right through me again after all these years. A warning.

"You got a plan?" Kicker asked Butler.

Jump grimaced, making a smacking noise with his lips, his gaze bearing down on Butler. "Why don't you go ask your friend Finger all about it? If we're gonna move ahead on this new cooperation with them, no better time than the present. Get organized with the Flames, and keep watch on the Blades and that Calderas Group. 'Cause if those spics come up with some sort of formal agreement with the Blades, we've got to be ready."

The fucking plague was in the next village, spreading its poison, and it was only a matter of time until it arrived at our gates.

TWENTY-THREE

JILL

MINDY GLARED AT ME from her stool at the bar at Pete's Tavern in town. Even though she was with a sexy blond guy in pressed jeans and a Western-style shirt, who slid a huge pink cocktail in front of her, her sour scrutiny remained on me.

Here we go.

It was nothing I hadn't seen before, nothing I hadn't dealt with before, but I hated it.

Boner handed me a tall glass of a berry colored beverage with a wedge of lime. "How's that?" He sat in the chair next to me.

"Looks great. What is it?

"Cranberry and club soda with lime."

"Oh, yum. Thank you."

He grinned and brushed the side of my face with his lips as I sipped on my surprise drink.

Lenore and Tricky sat close together across from us at a table talking and laughing. They'd been seeing each other off and on for a while now. Older woman, younger man.

You rock, Lenore!

Grace and Lock hustled over and settled into the two remaining chairs.

"We didn't miss Allen's first set, did we?" asked Grace, hanging her handbag from her chair.

"No, but you cut it close," replied Lenore, sipping on her beer. "What happened?"

Lock's smug grin was our answer, and we all laughed.

Grace blushed. "Can I help it if I'm married to a demanding, bossy man?"

Lock let out a deep laugh. "I'm the demanding one?" Grace shoved at his chest.

It was great to be out on a couples' evening to hear local musicians at the town watering hole. However, Mindy continuing to glare at me was not only deflating my buzz but also twisting the knot in my stomach that had formed with Catch's phone call.

I sipped on my cool drink, hoping it would provide me with calm, confidence, mettle.

Ha.

I still hadn't told Boner about Catch's phone call. I didn't like keeping anything from him, but I really didn't want to start more problems.

Finger would never agree to something like that. Maybe Catch was just mouthing off, maybe he was just—

"You good?" Boner stroked my back.

"Huh? Oh, very good."

Boner pressed his lips together, his arm slinging around my neck. "I talked to her. She won't be a problem." He tilted his head toward the bar.

"You talked to Mindy?"

"Of course I did."

"You broke it off with her?"

"There was nothing to break off. We were just a hook-up."

I shifted on my suddenly uncomfortable wooden chair.

"I wanted her to know from me that it wasn't gonna happen again, that it was done," he said.

I leveled my gaze at him. "That's what you want?"

His forehead furrowed. "Are you kidding me?"

I swept a lock of hair from my face. "I'm just asking."

"Look at me." Boner's sharp eyes studied me, green beams of laser seeking truth not to be denied. He leaned in closer to me. "We fucked the other day, or did you forget? Did you forget the way it was?"

How could I forget?

I was still sore, sore and warm everywhere. Even my nipples now zinged into stones just from the sound of him saying *fucked* in that rough, harsh tone.

"No, no, I haven't forgotten."

He cocked an eyebrow. "Then, what? What is it?"

I took in a small breath. "I feel like I've disrupted your life, and I don't want that. I don't want you to feel like I'm holding you back."

"And again, are you fucking kidding me? I'm with you. I *chose* to be with you."

"Because you felt like you had to, because you're a stand-up guy. Because circumstances—"

"Because I'm selfish when it comes to you."

I blinked.

"Get this straight in your head, Jill. I don't want anyone else. I don't want to be with anyone else. I don't want to be *inside* anyone else. This whole discussion is pissing me off because this tells me that the way I was with you in bed, in the kitchen, on the kitchen table, on the floor has not proven this to you or made it clear."

His eyes flashed, and the bottom dropped out of me under their force. Even my clit pulsed.

I pressed my legs together. "I-I didn't mean *that.*"

"So, I'm wrong in assuming—"

"Yes."

"I don't need to make any adjustments then?" he asked.

"Adjustments?"

"In bed, in the kitchen, on the—"

Hell no.

He was a sexual powerhouse—stamina, passion, attention to detail, tender and raw, generous and communicative. We'd even tried anal sex, which I'd done before, but never really enjoyed much. With Boner taking his time with me and being gentle, encouraging, and even funny, I'd relaxed and enjoyed it a hell of a lot.

"No. No adjustments needed." I touched his face, my fingers dragging through his newly trimmed beard. *I need to touch him.* He raised his chin and lowered his eyelids at the contact. "Boner, my point is, I don't want you to feel restricted."

"Restricted?"

"You've been a free agent since forever. And now—"

Music flared from the small stage, and the lights dimmed. One of the musicians began playing a ballad on his acoustic guitar as his bandmates got organized. The din of the crowd settled. The bar was thick with people, every table filled, and the staff hustled with drink orders.

Boner's eyes flickered over me. His body hardened against mine. "Something wrong? You feeling stuck? Restricted?"

"Me?"

"Yeah, you."

"I wouldn't call it restricted."

"What would you call it?"

"Overwhelmed," I blurted.

A shadow passed over his face, giving his hollow cheeks an even sharper appearance. He cupped the back of my head. "Jillee, I know I get intense. If it's bothering you—"

"No." I pressed a hand onto his chest and rubbed over a pronounced pec. "I like your intensity. A lot."

My face was very hot, and I was sure my skin was a thousand shades of pink and cherry red.

He took my hand in his and kissed it. "So, this is the good kind of overwhelming?"

"Yeah," I breathed, staring at my hand nestled in his larger one. "I just thought that, since this arrangement is a temporary thing, I don't want it to be a confusing one, too. I'm trying hard not to be overwhelmed, which might only lead to more confusion, which might then make you feel uncomfortable and restricted."

He shot me that now familiar but still jarring what-planet-are-you-from look.

"Because here I am," I continued, "the ex of your new hostile enemy, and now, I'm suddenly your old lady. I'm the new commitment, which you've never had before, and I don't want to be a burden."

His hand wrapped around my neck and pulled me close, his mouth crashing on mine, taking, declaring, giving. Everything spun on that kiss.

"I've wanted you for a long time, Jill. A long fucking time," he said, our faces mere degrees apart, his beautiful eyes boring into mine. "I had to make a move. I made it. I didn't do it 'cause I felt sorry for you or felt bad. I did it because it was right. Right for me, for you, for Catch. Yeah, and for Super-baby over here."

He rubbed a hand across my belly.

"Firefly, every which way you turn this Magic Eight Ball, there's only one message that floats up to the top, and that message is, *Yes*."

I laughed, and he planted a quick kiss on my lips.

"So, yeah, your douche bag ex might have tipped my hand," he continued, "but I'm glad he did. I like sleeping with you and waking up with you whenever we can. I like your kid. I like your cooking. I fantasize about your body and your mouth all the fucking time. I like being close to you. And after the baby's born, I'm gonna have you tied to my bed and strapped around me on the back of my bike, and then you'll know the meaning of the word *overwhelmed*."

My heart stuttered.

"Neither of us wanted a commitment in the beginning, Firefly, but you know what? I'm liking it, and I think you do, too. So, relax, and let yourself like it. What the fuck?" He dipped his head and whispered in my ear, "I want you overwhelmed."

I held him close, drinking in his scent, savoring the hard wall that was his chest, the silken brush of his hair against my skin. My eyes shut, and I pressed against him.

He was my thrill. My high. He was my castle fortress against the evil eyes of Mindy and Catch and whatever other dark clouds were rising in the horizon because they always were.

To hell with all of them.

"I think I get it," he whispered.

"Get what?"

"You're jealous."

"Jealous?"

He cast a quick glance toward Mindy at the bar.

I averted my gaze and let out a huff of air. "Well, just a little, *little* bit."

He kissed the side of my face, laughing. "Jillee, you got pieces of me no one's ever had."

My heart banged against my ribs, and I buried my face in his throat and hugged him.

The guitarist ended his ballad, his imploring voice still hanging in the air. Applause and cheers thundered through the old bar. The spotlight shone on Allen, the bassist Grace knew.

Boner's arm settled over my shoulders, and I curled into him. Happy aches spun through me, fresh shivers, deeper heat.

After all those months of circling each other, even now that we'd had sex, those feelings of wanting him, of liking him, had only intensified, not abated.

At the outset, I had thought that my crush on Boner was a fascination born of simple physical attraction and deeply engraved insecurities.

But I was wrong.

A need had grown inside me and taken hold, taken root, a need for him that was more like a calling. And his confidence in an *us* only pitched propane at that fire.

I brushed his cheek with my lips.

Overwhelming.

TWENTY-FOUR

JILL

"I DON'T THINK I've ever liked popcorn this much. This is actually tasty." Boner held the huge stainless steel bowl in his lap and shoved fluffy kernels in his mouth. We lounged on Rae's living room sofa, watching television.

"It's air-popped organic with butter and sea salt."

His hand stilled over the bowl, a dark eyebrow raised. "I love it when you talk gourmet."

I let out a laugh and handed him a fresh beer. "It's hardly gourmet."

"It's light-years better than that microwave crap."

"That microwave crap will kill you."

He glanced at me, munching. "Have you always been into food?"

"My mom loved to cook, and that used to be our thing together, cooking and baking." I tucked my legs underneath me and sank onto the sofa next to him. "And Rae is an amazing cook. She can't stand over the stove for too long anymore, so she sits and gives me directions. She's taught me a lot of her family recipes, and I like that, it's important. I enjoy it. It's a creative way to unwind and spend time with someone, and in the end, you're left with something yummy to eat."

Our attention went back to the television.

He stroked my thigh. "I like binge-watching TV with you."

"Because I feed you?"

"Yeah, that, too, but it's nice. Just hanging here—calm and quiet, you and me. Rae and Becs in the next room all snug. Tania somewhere else."

I giggled.

"See? You like it, too, Firefly."

"I never would've thought that you would enjoy this sort of thing—watching television with a girl on a couch with her kid *and* a parental figure in the next room."

"Baby, going out with the boys and doing what we usually do gets to be just that—the usual—after a while."

"You've had girlfriends you've spent time with though, right?"

"Yeah, but—"

"But not like this?"

My mind went to Mindy at the coffee shop, Mindy at Pete's. Perfect body, super confident, stripper pole-pro Mindy. She'd probably invite Boner over to her house and open the door, naked and slathered with whipped cream and strawberry syrup. She wouldn't have made him popcorn and snuggled up to him on the sofa to watch an entire season of *The Red Road*.

He tossed more popcorn into his mouth. "Not like this, no."

And there you go.

I shifted on the sofa, unbuckling my legs, pressing my bare feet into the edge of the coffee table. Of course, *this* was different for him. This was nice plus comfy plus easy plus no frills, which equaled boring.

He pressed into me, a hand wrapping around my thigh. "I like this. This is way better. Spending time with my woman like this, in the comforts of home."

Great, he'd sown his wild oats, and now, he was with me—the *comforts of home.*

That was me all right. Here, in my casual light-blue sundress and flip-flops, my hair up in a ponytail, a dash of mascara and whatever had been left of my eyeliner pencil I'd rushed to apply just before he'd arrived two hours ago.

I wiggled my dark purple–painted toes on the coffee table. At least I'd gotten a manicure, a pedicure, and had my eyebrows threaded with Grace and Tania this morning. That was saying something. I'd been so proud of getting my ass in gear for that, so together.

Oh, brother.

Mindy probably had a regular weekly appointment with her mani-pedi-waxing lady.

I knew what the Mindys of the world were like up close. I'd been with Catch as his old lady for almost three years. I'd lived with the club girls, the hanger-on chicks, the other old ladies. You had to be on your A game at all times to hold on to your man and keep the wolves at bay. Being with Catch—rather, trying to be with Catch—had taught me that.

Yes, Boner was different—older, more mature (mature, period!), definitely wiser, incredibly sexy but in a darker way than Catch. But like Catch, he was a very, very attractive man with power at his MC.

Although Boner was a man in his mid-forties and a senior member of his club, he was definitely not some old coot drinking in the corner twenty-four hours a day and riding only when he absolutely had to and only if his arthritis wasn't acting up. Something must be in the water in Meager because even Willy, the eldest member of the club, was incredibly fit, a carpenter by trade who kept up his own business on the side. He'd consistently join in on runs, and he always had a younger woman on his lap.

I needed to step things up.

Comfortable and cozy was not *hot* or *amazing* or *addictive*. It was…comfortable and cozy. I was Boner's old lady now, and I knew he genuinely liked me and wanted me. We certainly had a hefty dose of chemistry between us, but how long would that last now that we were actually together? Would the fascination, the zing between us fade, like it usually did in the other few relationships I'd had?

I didn't want him to regret the decision to claim me as his old lady that he'd made in a blaze of testosterone. But I also didn't want him to treat me like some girl on a pedestal and then sneak off with some biker groupie to let loose and feel free.

"Jill, should we lower the TV? You think it's too loud, and Rae and Becs might wake up?"

Rae and Becca had fallen asleep together on a *Dora the Explorer* television marathon in Rae's bedroom.

"I already lowered it. Stop worrying. They're out for the rest of the night," I said. "Anyway, I put the baby monitor in Rae's room, just in case, so we'll hear them if they wake up."

He winked at me, a sly grin lighting his face. "Smart move, Firefly." He drained his beer.

I let out a laugh. "God, I feel like we're teenagers."

He adjusted my legs over his. "What do you mean?"

"You know, the girl and her boyfriend are watching TV while the mom and dad are in the other room. And they're holding hands—"

"The mom and the dad?"

"No, Bone, the boy and girl. They're holding hands, or he has his arm around her shoulder, and they can't help themselves. Slowly, slowly, they start touching, exploring body parts, kissing, sucking on each other's tongues, sneaking hands into shirts and fingers down pants, holding in their groans and moans, desperately trying to stay quiet. You know…"

His eyes squinted. His forehead puckered. He needed a translation but didn't know how to ask for one.

"You've never done that?" I asked.

"No. But right now, I'm kinda stuck on the way you said 'sucking.'" He grinned as he fed me a couple of kernels of buttery popcorn.

Of course he hadn't ever done that. From what little I knew of his past, he had always been on his own and out in the big, bad world. He'd probably never dated, never went to a girl's house and got introduced to the mom and dad and dealt with that horrifying and mystical combination of sexual tension coated with a hard shell of parental disapproval and apprehension. No, he'd always gotten what he wanted, when he wanted, charged in and took it, or it landed into his lap with no doubts and no holds barred.

I licked the salt off my lips. "You never went out on dates in high school?"

"Never went on dates." He kissed the side of my mouth. "Never finished high school."

"Oh, I'm sorry."

"Don't be."

"Did something happen that you didn't finish high school?"

He returned his attention to the TV and tossed more popcorn into his mouth. "I had a job." He stared straight ahead, his teeth grinding on some small hard kernel of corn.

"Was it a good job then?" I asked.

"Pay was real good."

"I don't mean to force you into telling me about yourself." I took a handful of popcorn from the bowl. "The past is the past. I know that better than most."

"I don't talk about it. Ever. With anyone. We're together now though. You should be able to ask me what you want to ask me."

"Okay. Well, I don't know what your real name is, and I'd like to."

He held my gaze, a pained look passing over his face, as if he were the President of the United States, about to deliver heavy news to the nation.

"Santiago."

Light filtered through the cracks in my heart. A strain of guitar strings roused me.

"Santiago," I said, enjoying the unexpected exotic sounds tumbling from my lips. "That's beautiful. Spanish?"

"My parents were from Argentina."

"Argentina? Is Giddon your real last name?"

He shook his head. "Arana."

"Santiago Arana," I whispered.

"My parents had just gotten married, and my mom's brother brought them to Denver where he lived, so they could chase their piece of the American dream."

"Where did Boner come from? I'm assuming it's because of your very generous—"

He let out a small grunt. "I was thin as a kid, and whenever I got a hard-on, which was pretty often, it would be way fucking obvious." His tongue swiped at his lower lip, his eyes shifting away. "That's what I tell people." His voice was low, his eyes almost pleading with me.

Or were they testing the waters of my reaction?

I reached out past the pleading look and into the unsure sea of green, the choppy waters being held at bay.

"That's the funny story, the easy one, right?" I asked, my voice just above a whisper. "But it's not the real story?"

He only shook his head.

My throat stung. "Tell me the real story."

A shadow passed over those eyes, his hair fell forward, covering half of his face.

"Does this tattoo have anything to do with it?" My fingers traced the snake twisted over his left forearm.

"Dig and I got these together. I got my snake on my arm. He got his around his waist. 'Strike first, attack before you get attacked.'"

My fingers traced over the snake's vicious face. "He has three bones in his mouth. It's hard to tell with those huge fangs. You've got to look closely."

My eyes caught on his. The green was startling, shining glass that took my breath away. He was ready to tell me something yet ready to choke it back down at the very same time.

I took the popcorn bowl away and entwined our fingers together, rubbing my other hand over the inked snake. "Tell me."

"After my parents got to the States and I was born, my dad ditched my mom for some other woman and took off for California. Never saw him again. My mom worked hard, cleaning people's houses or their shops after-hours, anything she could find. One morning, she didn't wake up, died of a brain aneurysm in her sleep."

"How old were you?"

"I was ten. I went to live with her brother—my uncle—and my cousin, Inés. My uncle got into gambling as we hit our teens, and we pretty much took care of ourselves. He owed money." He took in a breath. "Big money."

"Oh."

"He had me working after school doing drop-offs for these Salvadoran drug dealers who were pals of his bookie's. That's when he took her, when I wasn't home."

"He took Inés?"

"Yeah. When they finally came home that night, she was like a different person. She stopped talking, just stared at the wall. Wouldn't even look at me. Wasn't too hard to figure out that he'd pimped her for his debt."

"Oh my God."

"She was fourteen." Boner averted his blank gaze. "I freaked out. Really freaked out. I knew the only way out of it was to get away from him. So, one morning, instead of going to school, we took off. But he caught us. He punched me, slapped her, threw shit at us, threatened to send her back to the bookie. I knew I had to make it stop." He held my gaze. "There was only one way to make it stop."

My pulse pounded in my neck, and I squeezed his cold fingers with my own.

"He was talking shit to Inés, slapping her, and she was crying and shaking. That's when I grabbed the crowbar he always kept by the back door. I hit him with it. I hit him across his back. I hit his knees, his legs, his arms, his head. I kept smashing, smashing, blood flying everywhere, his bones cracking." He sucked in a breath. "And I fucking enjoyed it."

"I bet you did."

"I grabbed Inés and the crowbar, and we took off. I had just turned sixteen. I started running odd jobs—collecting payments, threatening and killing with that crowbar for this gang I knew through the drug dealer I'd worked for. I kept us alive—on the street but alive. It was hard for Inés, but she hung on. I promised her things would get better, and she kept believing they would. She kept believing in me."

"Of course she believed in you."

He rubbed our hands together. "I didn't even think about it when I was bashing my uncle. I just hit and hit and hit him. I'd hit him to stop him from hurting her anymore and to start a better life for us. There was no good versus evil, wrong or right. There was only that iron in my hands. My hate, my love, my fear, my wishing—it all went into that crowbar. But we got shit-all anyway." His hands slid from mine. "Smashing bones turned into a high-paying job though. It became my trademark. I was real popular in certain circles."

From boy to vicious killer in one night.

My stomach hardened. "So, Boner comes from breaking bones?"

"It earned me a nickname. *El Hueso.* The Bone." He studied my face. "That scare you?"

"No, it doesn't." I took his hands back in mine. "I'm glad you broke his bones. Thank you for being honest with me, for trusting me."

A shiver razored around my neck as he studied me. "I do trust you."

I kissed his hands. The hands that had broken so many bodies. The very same hands that had protected me, adored me.

He cleared his throat. "I wanna do the teenager thing with you."

"Oh. We can do that. We kind of are already."

"How should I sit or whatever?" he asked, pulling himself up.

I couldn't contain my grin. "Just sit back against the sofa."

We adjusted ourselves.

"I'll shut off all the lights." I leaned over and switched off the lamp on the end table at my side.

We were engulfed in darkness, save for the glow from the television screen.

"Put your arm over my shoulder."

He did.

"Good. Now, I'll sit back, and we'll keep pressing closer together while we watch TV. Then, you can start going for a little bit more."

"Like, go for a titty instead of dipping into the popcorn bowl?"

I shoved him with my shoulder. "Yeah, something like that."

"Okay."

"Okay." I settled back against his outstretched arm. His hand hung low over my shoulder, and his other hand slid over my thigh. I squirmed appropriately and let out a dramatic sigh, my attention glued to Jason Momoa on the television, but my stomach fluttered and flipped over what Boner might be planning.

His lips hovered over the side of my face. His hand came up and brushed my hair away, a fingertip trailing down my neck. He leaned in, his warm breath fanning over my skin as he took my hand in his.

Every cell in my body braced for his whisper, his words. Something sexy, something hot, something—

He shoved my hand between his legs. "You gonna suck my cock?"

"Boner!"

"What?" He laughed.

"Not like that!"

He laughed harder, his chest shaking. "A teenage guy would so say that."

"Really?"

"He would *think* it."

"Forget it."

"I was kidding," he said. "Let's do it again."

Shaking my head, I leaned forward and grabbed some popcorn from the bowl on the table.

"I can do this," he said, pulling on the back of my dress. "I want to do this. Come on, work with me."

I leaned into him once more and crossed my arms in front of my chest. His thigh pressed against mine as his nose trailed along the underside of my jaw.

"You smell good. I like your perfume," he said.

"Thanks." My eyes remained glued on the television.

He turned toward me, his one hand running slowly through the back of my hair and down my neck, leaving delicious shivers in its wake. Featherlight kisses whispered across my neck, my jaw, my cheek. My pulse pounded in my veins, but I still didn't budge.

His fingers slid underneath the edge of my cotton sundress, lighting a trail of fire over my bare thigh. I held my breath as he got closer and closer until those long fingers touched my pulsating center ever so gently, ever so delicately. A veil of pleasure had me in its delicate net.

His fingers finally sank over the right place and stroked. "There you are," he breathed.

A low moan escaped my throat.

"Shh. Mommy might hear us."

He bit on my lower lip just as his fingertip edged under my panty and dipped inside me. His eyes were hooded, his lips parted. Our mouths were only degrees apart.

"Jillee."

My breath shortened, and I angled my hips as more of his hand sank between my legs.

He nuzzled my ear. "I need your tits, baby."

Fire zipped through my blood at the demand, at the raw ache in his voice. I leaned back against him and pushed the spaghetti straps off my shoulders, tugging the tube top of the dress down. My aching breasts spilled over the edge of the material.

"Play with 'em."

I squeezed my breasts, kneading them, as his gaze burned over me in the harsh white glow of the TV.

"Fuck, you're gorgeous, Firefly. Gorgeous."

His fingers curled inside me, stroking my inner wall, and I gasped.

"Fuck my fingers, baby."

I moved my hips against his hand, moaning as we both found the precise fantastic angle and rhythm together.

He kissed a breast, licking and nuzzling, his hair sweeping over the sensitive skin. "Fuck. I liked waking up with you when you spent the night with me at the club, those tits pressed into my back, waiting for me to suck on whenever I wanted."

"Me, too."

"You need to stay here though, huh?"

"I do."

"I can't stay here though," he said.

"No."

"Maybe I could stay and then sneak out the window?"

"That does fit right in with the—*ah!*—angst-teen theme we've got going on."

"Shit…"

I rocked harder against him. "Could be fun."

"Just watching you…I'm gonna fucking explode," he said on a grunt. Bending his head, he licked the underside of a breast like a wildcat.

"I'd rather have you exploding inside me."

"Want to do that, yeah, but I want to make you explode on my fingers first." His fingers slowly dragged out and then dived back in, thrusting faster.

"Oh shit." I gasped.

"So tight, baby."

Every muscle in my body tensed and vibrated. My hips ground against his hand as his two fingers urged me toward higher ground, toward infinity. His thumb stroked over my clit, and wings fluttered inside me, creatures taking flight to a place I never knew existed and plunging me deep into an abyss. All of me hovered on the edge with them, with him, as they soared, lifting me higher.

He pushed one of my hands away, and his hot wet mouth sucked on the other breast. Suddenly, his hand left my body, and he dropped to the floor, his mouth between my legs. I cried out, my back arching, as he spread my legs wider, a hand around my thigh. He sucked on me with a needy hunger, and my hands clung to his hair. I shattered in that swirl of color and heat.

"Santiago!"

He stilled. My trembling body squeezed around his immobile form. My eyes fluttered open and snagged on his. Hard glass, impenetrable. Not windows to the soul. Opaque barriers.

His hands released their grip on me, and he slid away. He sat back on the sofa, his gaze averted. A slicing ache replaced the fullness.

Shit. Shit. What just happened?

I wasn't sure, but it was as if a switch had been turned off. An alarm had sounded, and he was on edge, upset even.

I sat up, pulling my skirt down and lifting my top over my bare chest. "Bone?"

The barrier had seeped from his eyes and hardened down his face. The ridge of his dark brows was tight, giving him a forbidding severity. The playfulness, the raw sensuality were gone.

"Boner, did I—"

"It's nothing." He wiped at the edge of his mouth with his thumb and planted a kiss on my forehead. "I should go. I've got a run tomorrow to the chapter in North Dakota anyway. Got an early start."

He rose from the sofa, kernels of popcorn tumbling down his leg. "I'll be spending the night up there. I'll call you." He brushed my cheek with his hand as he headed for the front door.

"Boner, wait—" I followed him.

His long strides and heavy footfalls pounded out an unmistakable beat—*reject, retreat, get me the fuck out of here.*

He left.

I locked the door after him and peeked through the side curtain. He didn't glance up at the house as he swung on his bike. He took off, and his powerful engine droned right through my shaky heart, leaving only acrid fumes behind.

TWENTY-FIVE

BONER

"WHAT THE FUCK?"

The case was empty. It was gone.

Dig's Python .357 was missing.

The cherry wood case with the glass top I'd picked out myself was splayed out like a plundered treasure chest in a corner of the meeting room where a number of knives, skull sculptures, local awards, framed photos, and other club memorabilia were on display.

"We had the Howl last night, and people were roaming everywhere," muttered Kicker. "Could've been anybody."

I'd been at our North Dakota chapter the past two days, and I'd stayed an extra night. I hadn't wanted to be back here for the Full Moon Howl, as we'd tagged the party years ago. After the last time I'd seen Jill, I'd needed…fuck, I wasn't sure what I'd needed. But a club party was no answer.

My heart thundered against my ribs at the sight of the empty case.

It was exactly that—a treasure plundered.

Dig's favorite gun since he'd first won it in a knife fight with a drunk cocksucker on a winter run to Daytona in the early '90s.

The gun he'd used to kill Jill's kidnapper.

The gun Grace had used to shoot his killer.

Fucking gone.

After his death, that gun had become a symbol of the man who'd dedicated his life and energy to the One-Eyed Jacks, who'd striven to move the club forward and make it strong.

My eyes darted to a photo of us hanging on the wall. Dig and me and Wreck exhausted on the side of a highway after Jump had wiped out on the way to Idaho. Another one of Dig flashing the finger, his face full of cocky bravado, as he sped off on his '67 Panhead.

Sour bile rose in the back of my throat.

That gun was fucking sacred, holy.

I gnashed my teeth. "Who the fuck took it?"

"Someone who's got balls. Someone who knows how to hit where it hurts when he wants to make a point," rose Kicker's voice behind me.

"How the hell—?" My voice roared, and I reined it in. "How did this happen?"

Here, in our meeting room, where our traditions were observed and celebrated, our decisions made, secrets shared, and ambitions forged. Here, under the witness of photographs of our chapter's members, past and present. Here, under our very roof, under our fucking noses.

"I don't know, man," Kicker muttered.

"You'd better work on changing that answer. This door's always locked during a party," I said.

"Well, yeah."

"What the fuck does that mean?"

Kicker shifted his weight. "Jump was in here."

"'Course he was. He's the goddamn prez."

"I mean, with women. Alicia's been gone for over a week now, visiting family in Texas."

I rubbed a hand across my chin.

"I'm not sayin' that—"

"I get it. Contact all our pawnshop buddies—and I mean, all of them—and not by email. Get them on the phone, personally, and put them on the lookout for the Python. This includes all our other friends in the gun trade—on and off the grid."

"Right. On it."

"Hey, you finally back?" Butler stood in the open doorway, his jawline a harsh, blunt edge. "What the hell is going on?"

"Somebody stole Dig's Python. Broke the case."

"What the fuck?" He strode into the room, filling it with a wave of emotion. "Anything else gone?"

"So far, no," I replied.

He held my gaze. "That piece ain't worth shit to anyone else. Yeah, it's a collectible. It's worth a few bills, but—"

"But it's priceless to us, and whoever took it knew that. They're making a point. A fucking ballsy point. I'm gonna get it back and then cut his fucking balls off." I eyed him. "Led knew about this gun. Now he's gone."

"Yeah. Him and those two other Flames from Ohio came back here for the Howl," said Butler.

"I thought they'd all left together a while back?"

"They did. All three of them took off to do the usual touristy shit—Mount Rushmore and Crazy Horse, Sturgis. But they all came back last night for the Howl, partied, and then left for Ohio first thing this morning."

My pulse throbbed in my neck. I hoped to hell it was Catch and the Flames jerking our chain. The alternative sent an icy claw ripping up my spine.

Alejandro's threat from years ago remained fresh in my mind: *"I will find you, wherever you go, and you will suffer. I will find ways to make you pay...One day, I will take it all away from you. I promise you."*

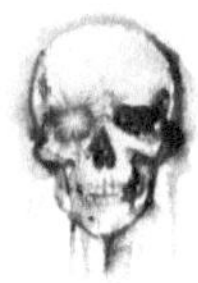

PAST

I was losing my mind.

Inés had disappeared without a word after we'd fought about going to LA. My friend Julio told me he'd heard she was with the Calderón brothers, our fucking bosses.

Julio and I were two of their many soldiers. We rarely actually saw them though. The Calderóns would come to you. You didn't find them. I'd usually get my orders through a fine line of other worker bees unless it was a special assignment, those they handed down personally. And there were plenty of special assignments for me.

After a success, I'd be invited to hang with them at one of their infamous parties. I was their prized discovery, their exceptional apprentice in the dark arts of vengeance and terror, and I enjoyed being singled out. I'd drink from their wine. I'd eat from their table. I'd take Inés, and we'd have ourselves a taste of the good life, their high life.

The fucking crazy life.

Big mistake.

Over two weeks after she'd taken off, I caught them at our place. I noticed their shiny hot rod double-parked outside our building that afternoon. No one double-parked in my neighborhood and lived to tell about it.

The moment I opened the door, I heard the moaning and the low guttural Spanish, the seething tone of a male voice. Slaps and hard smacks on flesh and heavy panting. My hand released my knife from my lower leg, and I prowled silently through the dark narrow hallway of our shabby apartment, my pulse racing.

I reached the end of the hall, and my brain stuttered. My eyes burned.

Inés was on all fours on the rug on the floor, sucking off Felipe Calderón, while his brother, Alejandro, held her hips up high in a tight grip and drilled his dick inside her. Inés's small tits jiggled, her whole body bouncing with the force of Alejandro's fucking.

I bit down on my lip, and the metallic flow of blood filled my mouth. My heart pumped so hard that I thought it would explode, yet an eerie cold oil slimed through my veins.

They were saying ugly things to her and to each other, and it drove them faster, harder. Their faces were scrunched in intense concentration. They were blitzed on an acid high. The large muscles of the brothers' legs, their arms, their asses bulged and bunched up under the strain.

Felipe's pelvis thrust in her face, his long dick plunging in and out of her mouth. She stared up at him like he was a god who held all the secret answers to her life. Both his hands were fisted in her mass of dark hair, keeping her facing up at him. Moans warbled from her throat, saliva dripping from her lips. He came with a loud growl, and she swallowed.

Felipe pulled his wet dick out of her mouth. "You like that, don't you, *mi perla negra?*"

Black pearl? What the fuck? He already had a pet name for her?

"I love it," Inés replied. "I love you."

Obviously inspired, Alejandro fucked her harder from behind. Felipe held onto her, muttering to her in Spanish, swatting at her tits.

Inés was their possession, their slave, their drug, and they were addicted.

And so was she.

That tiny room reeked of sweat and sex and betrayal, choking me, flattening me. The blue-and-pink Indian rug we'd found in a flea market together, the huge beaded pillows she insisted on keeping on the floor, the shimmering curtains we'd created out of brightly colored fabric samples and scarves—everything now defiled, everything foul, everything melded with the shadows.

You are ours. You are nothing. They had told me as much from the beginning, and it was true, wasn't it?

I slid and stumbled back down the hallway and out the door, vomiting the minute I rounded the building, my head spinning.

I waited and waited, sweat running down my enflamed chest. Laughter, muffled words, and the *roll, scrape,* and *bump-bump* of a suitcase burst out the door and down the broken cement steps.

She was leaving—with them.

I was a raging bull, nostrils flaring with smoke and fire. My neck craned toward them.

"What are you doing, motherfuckers?" I yelled.

Both Felipe and Alejandro stopped and turned, throwing me a casual glance, as they put the suitcase into the trunk of their hopped-up Dodge Coronet.

Felipe's black cat eyes narrowed. "She's ours now." His voice was so fucking relaxed, so fucking confident.

"The fuck you say! Inés! What the hell are you doing?"

She only glared at me from a curtain of straightened glossy hair, her face still flushed. "I've had enough. Okay?"

"Okay?" I shouted. "Okay?" I stalked toward her, my limbs made of molten iron. I would singe her, burn her, make smoke and ash of her.

Smash her.

Hands shoved me back. "Hey, hey, hey." Alejandro towered over me. "Stand down, *hermano.* She came to us, wanted to be our bitch straight off. Felipe and I have what she needs." He palmed his crotch over his loose low-slung jeans, his tatted arm taut with the action, his jaw jutting out. "How can you compare yourself to the two of us?" He shoved his fingers in my face, grinning. "No way, boy, you can't."

But Alejandro was wrong.

Inés wasn't just my hole, just the girl I shared a crib with, had on my arm at parties, or hung with around the hood. She was my mission. She was a part of me.

"She's with us now. You understand what that means?" Alejandro said, his head slanting, dark eyes glinting.

Felipe leaned over and licked Inés's willing lips with a disgusting flutter of his tongue as Alejandro wrapped a hand around her ass and rubbed.

"Time for you to try a *gringa*, *El Hueso*. I'm telling you, they come to us like flies." Alejandro winked. "Wild side, *papi*."

I stared at the three of them, my heart chugging in my chest.

Felipe's eyes narrowed as he threw an arm around my neck. "She's your cousin, man. You're not supposed to be fucking your cousin. We saved your soul from *purgatorio*, for sure, eh?"

They both laughed, but Inés stood still, her hands gripping a leather handbag I didn't recognize.

I pushed Felipe off me. "You know she's barely sixteen, right?" I spit out.

Felipe only glared at me, his jaw rigid. But the gleam in Alejandro's eyes was unmistakable, his tongue dipping against his lower lip. "Sweetest pussy ever."

Inés raised a well-groomed eyebrow as she leaned her body into his.

The weeks of worrying about her, wondering what she was up to, who she was with, if she had lost it and was wandering the streets or had gotten raped and was trapped somewhere, her head chopped off, or…

But this? With them?

Felipe and Alejandro constantly dangled the carrots of more money, more responsibility, more advancement, more prestige, yet never delivered because they would hoard it all for themselves and enjoy the power of denial they lorded over the rest of us.

Inés was throwing me away for a joyride with these two? This was what she needed, what made her happy?

What about us?

All the bloodletting, all the beatings, the burning, the carvings, the cleaning—I'd done it all for them. The smell of acid, bleach, and charred flesh filled my nostrils as I gulped for air. *All for her, for us.* At the end of every single cliff I'd hung from every day, I'd clung to her.

White light exploded in my eyes, and a rush of adrenaline surged from my feet through my middle, boiling in my chest, pounding in my head. I charged through the air, screaming, yelling. Blows of pain shot through me, the smash of cement against my back, a sudden blinding, throbbing sting all through my middle. I gasped for air, and my eyes flared open.

Everything stopped.

Inés leaned over me, her knife in her hand—the one I had bought her, the one I had taught her how to use.

Now, it had my blood on it.

My bleary eyes drowned in her dark pools looming over me.

"Look what you've done, Santi! Leave me alone! Why can't you just leave me alone?"

The blare of sirens rose down the street. Inés pulled her lips together and wiped her knife clean on my ripped shirt. Clutching the blade to her chest, she tumbled into the Calderóns' car, a figure pressing in after her.

A pointy boot end kicked me hard in the ribs, and I coughed up blood and vomit on the pavement, my body coiling at the pain shooting through me. Another boot jammed into my lower back, and my head knocked against the cement.

Suddenly, my body was jerked up, and Alejandro's voice thundered in my ear. "Don't you dare come near her again, or I'll kill you. You will fucking regret the day you were born. I will find you, wherever you go, and you will suffer. I will find ways to make you pay."

My body slammed into the cement once again, flopping open like a tossed puppet.

Car doors banged, an engine roared, rubber screeched.

A whirlpool of glaring sun and stifling heat enflamed the reek of garbage on the cement where I lay. My blood simmered on the pavement before me. My arms were heavy and wet, glued to my body.

I tried to focus through the daze.

My hands fell from my stomach, and a long slash of torn flesh branded my middle, blood everywhere.

Inés had left her mark on me.
Nothing came out of my mouth, but I screamed.

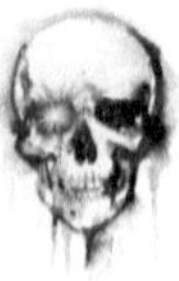

"Hey, Boner."

Butler's voice brought me back to Earth, to the club meeting room, to the empty gun case.

"What do you want to do about this?"

I rubbed a hand across my prickly scar. "Need to find out who took it and why," I replied.

I have to be sure.

"Let's do it."

"Get ready. I got to go home, change clothes, change bikes, then I'll meet you back here in an hour. We're gonna pay the Flames in Nebraska a visit."

Butler's blue eyes flashed at me. "Right behind you, brother."

TWENTY-SIX

BONER

"Hi." Jill was perched on my front steps, halfway up and halfway down. Her eyes skidded over me, and my stomach clenched. I'd done that—planted that hesitation, that doubt in her.

"Hey."

"Um, I'm not bothering you, am I?" Jill gestured back to her car. "I can go—"

"No, you're not bothering me. I just got out of the shower." I rubbed a hand down my bare chest, and her eyes followed the movement. Her cheeks flushed, and she quickly averted her gaze.

She wouldn't have done that before. Before, she would've grinned at me and made a flirtatious comment or made a move on me. Now, this fence of fucking propriety had shot up between us. I didn't like it. I didn't like a barrier between me and Jill, especially one I couldn't see or climb or tear down with my hands.

"Get in here." I held open my door for her.

She climbed up the last steps and shrank through the doorway, as if she were entering a portal to the dreaded realm of the unknown.

Her gaze spun over my living room furniture, the U-shaped open kitchen, the huge front bay window I had fixed up with a custom cushioned seat that doubled as storage. Her eyes finally landed over the fireplace on Lock's huge charcoal drawing of me on my Harley. The piece was a blur of movement, thrill, and self-determination that he and Grace had framed for me last Christmas.

"That's you, isn't it?" she asked.

"Yeah, Lock drew it."

"He's so talented."

"He is."

Jill licked her lips. "You said you'd be back from North Dakota this morning, and I just dropped Becca off at her Aunt Penny's, so I thought I'd stop by."

"Glad you did."

"I like your house," she said, rooted to her spot in the middle of the entry way.

"Thanks. Got it on a foreclosure about seven years ago. Been fixing it up here and there."

She took in the polished wood, her eyes widening, as if she'd suddenly realized she was stuck in the center of an iced-over lake. "It's beautiful. You don't see this much anymore."

"I finally refinished the floors. I'm a traditionalist at heart."

She peered into my living room. "It seems big for someone on his own."

"I like open space. My own, especially."

She only nodded.

"What is it?" I asked.

"I completely understand. I haven't had my own space in a long, long time."

"You'll get there."

She raised her head and let loose a small smile. I captured that sunbeam in my chest and felt its heat diffuse in my system. But the distance between us remained like a cold slab of stone separating us.

"Jill, come here."

Her posture straightened. "I came over to apologize for the other night and tell you that we don't have to keep this charade going." She let out a breath she'd seemed to be holding on to forever.

"What charade?"

Her eyebrows lifted. "I thought after the other night on the couch—"

"Jill, I wouldn't have had you in my bed that first night at the club if I didn't mean it, if I didn't want you there."

She fidgeted, one hand rubbing up and down her opposite forearm.

"Firefly." I reached out my hand toward her.

She stared at it, and my throat burned.

"Jillee, please, baby."

She took three steps toward me and laid her hand in mine. Cool, soft.

I brought it to my lips. "I'm sorry for getting up and leaving the way I did that night."

"No, I'm sorry. I went overboard. I usually do. Not that I usually…you know…" She blushed. "What I mean is, I'm sorry I brought up all those difficult memories for you and made you uncomfortable, then I only made it worse when I said your name."

I pulled her in close, and she finally pressed into my chest.

All the tension I'd been carrying in my shoulders and back released. "Stop. You didn't do nothing wrong. I overreacted."

"But if that's the way you feel, Boner, that's the way it is."

"I've never shared my past with anyone before. Only Dig." I smoothed the soft waves of her hair from her face. "But I couldn't stop myself from telling you the truth. I wanted you to know. But when I heard you say my name—"

"You see her in me, don't you? Your cousin, Inés?" Her face reddened, and she shifted her weight. "The wanting to keep me safe, like you kept her safe. I get that."

Jesus Christ. Nothing could be further from the truth, but I couldn't tell her that now, I couldn't tell her the whole horrible tale. I couldn't.

I swallowed hard. "It's not about her. This, what we have, is about you."

Her eyes searched mine.

"When I lost Dig and Grace, that old futility came washing back over me, chaining me. I lost everything all over again. Couldn't save anybody. But you—you'd survived your shit. You survived, Jill. I knew you would."

"What do you mean?"

"I ran you off club property—at least, what? Twice?"

She nodded.

"I watched over you for a year after that, making sure none of them found you. Making sure you hadn't told and that other assholes weren't taking advantage of you. I made sure."

"You watched me?"

"Going to school. Going to church. Youth group meetings. Going to football games with your girlfriends. Going on dates. To your therapist. I watched you."

She stiffened in my hold. "I saw Dready off and on, but then he stopped showing up."

"I came up a few times after I'd told Dready to stop. Until I was sure you had settled back into normal."

"Normal? Nothing was ever normal after *that*!"

"The last time I'd come up, was when you had just gotten your Honda. I was on my way to Montana, but I stopped at Ellston and trailed you from school. You'd left alone that afternoon and headed for this strip mall in the next town. I parked my bike across the street and followed you into one of the offices."

I closed my eyes for a moment and could still picture that big black plastic plaque on the door with the doctor's name on it.

"You were getting help," I said. "It was a year after your abduction, but good times at Ellston High and a bi-weekly serving of God hadn't been enough to keep the boogie man at bay. You were there at a therapist's on your own, maybe your parents and your friends knew about these visits, maybe they didn't. But either way, fuck, you were getting the help you needed, doing something about your pain, facing it, wrestling with it in order to move on."

"Dr. Linda Hoskins," she whispered. "Specializing in children and adolescents and issues related to family conflict, sexual abuse and neglect."

"Yeah." I studied her face, a faraway look in her eyes.

I had rubbed my gloved hand over the engraved letters of the doctor's name on that plaque in front of her office. "*Help her,*" I'd whispered to them.

Jill's anguished voice from that first night at the club had come back to me as I stood in front of that therapist's office: *"Just a girl. Just a stupid girl."*

"*You fucking are not,*" I'd muttered to myself.

Dready and I hadn't seen the usual signs of a teenager acting out in Jill—smoking, wearing skanky clothes, or heavy makeup, anything obvious that from an otherwise normal kid would have said *"I'm flipping the fucking bird at you, world."* And there she was getting professional help.

I'd gotten back on my bike and ripped down Route 90 toward Montana. Toward business. Back to my day to day.

Away from Jill forever.

"You followed me back then? You?" she asked, her soft voice bringing me back to the present.

"Lots of times, and I'm glad I did. Watching you, I'd thought to myself, 'there's one less fucked up person in the world.' Two parents who gave a shit and showed it, school, friends, therapist, a system that worked. You'd gotten into college, had a boyfriend. You were golden. If any of us had a shot at normal it was you. After about a year I stopped. You didn't need me no more, for whatever it was worth."

Her fingers pressed into my flesh. "It was worth a lot. I didn't even know."

"I needed to make sure."

"You did that for me?" She whispered. "Why?"

"You were worth it."

"Boner."

"I didn't want you collapsing in on yourself—like I had, like Inés had done. You were around the same age as she was when shit went south for her."

"Bone—"

"I figured I could believe in a little bit of good for a change after seeing you do well."

"Boner!" She gripped my arms. "My parents got killed the following year."

"What?"

"They were driving back from a cousin's wedding in Oklahoma, and there was a tornado. The motel they were at, it—"

"No."

"Yes. I had to quit school. I lost their house, lost the boyfriend, got a job and then another."

"Baby—"

"Plenty of not-so-great boyfriends and not-so-great jobs. I bounced around the area, every time thinking a new place, a new town would make the difference. But it didn't. Not when you had the same lessons to learn and still refused to, not when you sank yourself into a dark place and couldn't find the way to climb out. Then, I met Catch, and I thought I found my answer, but that didn't work out so great, but it gave me Becca." She sucked in a breath. "I named her for my mom, Rebecca."

"It's a beautiful name."

"It is."

"If I'd known, I would've—"

"Offered me a job as a stripper?" she said, a crooked grin on her face.

"No. No, I don't know."

"We met again anyway."

"We did."

We held each other's gazes.

"Yeah, we did," I repeated.

Her eyes filled with water.

"Jillee, what is it?"

"It's just that, all this time, I thought you and Dready and whoever else you'd sent up to check on me were doing it to intimidate me only."

"Well, yeah, that was part of it."

"Part of it. Not all of it?"

"I had to make sure—"

She put her hand on my arm. "It means a lot to me. Look, I'm sorry I made you uncomfortable when I said your name."

"It surprised me, is all."

Her watery eyes shot up at me and held mine with that steely confidence. "It made you sad. I don't ever want to make you sad. I care about you, and I don't want whatever we have to make you sad."

"Firefly," I whispered, my heart twisting in my chest.

My thumb rubbed over her lips. "You took my breath away, coming on my tongue. I did that to you, and it was so beautiful to watch, to *feel*. And then you said my name, and I lost it. You do that to me, Jillee. Every time we're together. Every time I think of you." I leaned my forehead against hers. "You."

What had she said to me?

"Get lost."

She'd dared me.

I am lost, baby.

Lost in you.

Lost without you.

Fucking lost.

But I couldn't afford to get lost.

I took in a breath. "I have to get dressed. I've got some business to take care of with Butler. Should be back tonight."

"Okay."

"Do me a favor. Stay home today. You got appointments and stuff?"

"Yeah, actually, I do."

"What is it?"

Her eyes widened. "Just something quick in town with Nina."

"I'll call Sy and have him tag along."

"What's wrong? Is something going on?"

"Just being cautious. With me out of town, I want to make sure you're safe." I eyed her. "It's an Old Man/Old Lady thing."

She laughed.

My heart thumped in my chest like an excited horse's hooves on dry earth. *This girl.* "Need a kiss, Firefly."

She pressed herself in my arms and kissed me, completely opening up to me, taking, sharing, giving me her warmth.

So unlike Inés.

Jill's fingertips skimmed my scar, and I let out a hiss of air.

Inés had folded and blasted our house of cards with a cruel grin on her face. She'd turned into someone I didn't know.

And so did I.

But this was the opposite of all that.

"Boner," Jill's breathy voice and warm hands on my skin brought me back to my fucking spectacular present.

She ripped the towel from my waist and flung it on the floor.

There's my Firefly.

TWENTY-SEVEN

JILL

HE RAISED ME IN HIS ARMS and pushed me back against the front door, growling, grinding his erection into me. The creamy soap scent of his freshly washed skin and the press of his taut bare muscles made me rabid.

He tore off my T-shirt.

His green eyes electrified. "Is that the bra that—"

I had gone back and bought that peach bra and panty set that I'd teased him with when we first walked into the store at the mall.

"It makes me feel pretty, sexy, like you see me. I think of you on me when I wear it."

His face softened, and he let out a groan as his fingers stroked my skin. They worked quickly, unsnapping the hook at my back, releasing my breasts, and I let out a gasp. He wrapped the bra around my wrists, raised my hands above my head, and attached the bra up on the empty coat hook on the back of the door. His hands smoothed down my wrists, my arms, in between my breasts, my tummy, around my hips. He shoved my straight cotton skirt down over my hips, down my thighs.

He was on his knees, looking up at me. I was on display for him, hanging on the door. I squirmed as his tongue nudged at my clit over the thin satin of my panties, wetting the fabric, his burning heat penetrating my seismic center.

My pulse jumped as he peeled down my panty, sliding it down my legs, stopping mid thigh. All I wanted to do was thrash and smash my body into his mouth, but my legs didn't have freedom of movement with the panty and the skirt bound around them.

"Ah, fuck," he murmured as his thumb slowly stroked up and down my strip of curls, tantalizing every nerve ending. The dark god coaxing me to enter his sensual underground.

I didn't need persuading.

My grip on sanity loosened as his thumb sank over my throbbing clit, his focus riveted on my pussy.

"Oh!" My back arched.

He let out a groan as his nose gently nudged at my center, the invasion of its hard edge causing explosions along every bunched nerve in my body. My eyes rolled in the back of my head, my fingers gripping the bra at my wrists. His hands clutched my bare ass as his hot wet tongue explored my pussy, the tense tip swirling up and down, teasing my slit.

"Oh, Bone."

His tongue lapped at me in long, slow licks. I was going to die of pure sin and pure pleasure. Die here, hanging on the back of his front door. His fierce eyes locked on mine as he teased me, adored me. His lips latched on to my clit and sucked. I was bolted to the fucking door by his mouth.

Pure sin, pure pleasure.

I shuddered, my brain jamming, my body his desperate prisoner. His teeth lightly grazed me, and I cried out.

His eyes grew heavy, a devious slant to them. "You like that?"

"Yes," I whimpered. "Shit, I knew it. I knew it."

"What did you know?" He licked my pussy again.

"I can feel your heart pounding through your mouth," I said. "Just like I told you." My head sank back as my hips arched toward him. "Just like I told you…"

He sucked with intention. I didn't know which end was up any longer. I didn't know where I began and if I ended.

"Let it go." His voice rose over my burning skin. "Don't hold on to it. I'm gonna give you plenty more."

Boner buried his face between my legs, two fingers toying with my ass.

I let it go and burst like a ripe berry in his mouth, my body jerking in his hands, helpless, on fire. He kept on kissing, sucking, nuzzling as I came down, his eyes on me. That intense fervor pulsating through me made me limp in his hold. I was a gaping wound, an overflowing rushing river of emotions and feelings. I was high, laid bare on Boner's altar of sensation.

And I loved it.

He slowly wiped his mouth on my thigh, kissing it, nipping it with his teeth. He tugged my skirt and then my wet and twisted peach thong down my legs, pulling them off my feet. I let out a moan as his hands lightly swept up my legs, my middle, and over my swollen breasts. His fingers tickled up the underside of my arms and unhooked them from the wall, tossing the bra to the floor.

Eau de Jill lingered on him, and something wild and savage overtook me.

I kissed him hard, my hand digging into his hair, then down to his waist, over his hard ass, and around to his thick, very thick, very hard cock.

Glory be to all that is holy.

I wrapped my fingers around his warm flesh and stroked him up and down, my hand twisting over his stiff length.

"Ah, fuck me," he rasped, his mouth hanging open. The gleam of his bared teeth sent a shiver razoring through me.

Hungry black wolf and his willing mate.

Yes, that was what I wanted, to mate with him like the untamed creature he'd turned me into.

He pulled me to the edge of the long burgundy sofa as my heart hammered in my chest. "Lie back."

I did as I was told and brought my legs up. On the sofa, he sat on his knees in front of me with his hands gripping me, and slid inside me with one smooth, slow thrust.

I struggled for air. So full, so full, and he wasn't even all the way in yet.

He let out a deep groan. *"Fuck."*

I rocked my hips toward his, and he gripped them tighter, holding me closer to him.

"Oh, yeah." My hands pressed into the ridged fabric on the sofa. It was velvet to me, it was satin. I was suspended in air, in sensation, in his beautiful eyes.

He burrowed his way deeper into me. "Fuck, you're like silk."

We moved together, desperate to find one another, more of each other, to make a precious and hidden small dream come true. We wanted to touch it, touch the light it gave off with every hot breath, every grunt and gasp, every slide of our bodies.

"Tell me if I'm hurting you. Tell me. Damn it, Jill…"

He slowly thrust out of me, and a long cry escaped my throat.

I pushed my hands against the arm of the sofa behind me. "You're not hurting me. Keep going. Don't stop."

He drove inside me once more, angling his hips a few degrees to the side. "You feel so good. Fuck, I missed you."

His face looked pained as he finally buried himself deep. I felt the pounding of it through my heart, my lungs, my throat.

"You like my cock, Jillee? You want more of me?"

"I love your cock. So damn perfect. I need it."

He pumped into me in steady strokes, and I relished the stinging sensation of his tight grip on my flesh, the burn of his thickness moving inside me, demanding its place. Yes, demanding, and I willingly surrendered.

All I wanted was to feel him, feel everything about him, the good and the bad, the dark and the shadowy, and feel it all over me.

I was blowing apart into little bits and never coming back the same.

My one hand went between us and stroked my clit and the other squeezed a breast. I was greedy.

He sucked in a hiss of air. "My fucking dirty girl."

"That's not so dirty."

"Baby, on you, it fucking is. Trust me."

My head fell back. "I want to be dirty for you."

Boner's jaw tightened as his beautiful lean body worked its glorious magic over me. His long dark hair hid part of his face from view, but I could see his brilliant eyes. They smoldered a hole through my heart, a hole that I knew only he could fill.

Only him.

His shoulders bunched with every intense movement. My insides surged as the drumming pulse of our shared pleasure overwhelmed me, echoing through every vein and every hollow in my soul.

TWENTY-EIGHT

JILL

"YOU NEED HIGHLIGHTS, LAYERS, THE WORKS. You've got such great color, Jill, but you haven't touched it in a while, and it needs something. How about a dark red color along the bottom half?"

"No, I'm not into that ombré look. Anyway, Nina, when you're pregnant, you can't go dying your hair with the usual crap, you know."

Nina had insisted on taking me to the beauty salon in Meager, and I'd let her because I really wanted some kind of makeover. I was gaining the inevitable baby weight, and now that Boner and I were together, I wanted to be the best I could be—and maybe surprise him in good ways, too.

He had this wicked smile that blew holes through my heart. Actually, Boner had two sorts of smiles—sweet wicked and bad wicked. Either one would do a dangerous number on my insides, like it had earlier at his house when I'd ripped his towel off him.

I'd gone over to see him to apologize for having made him uncomfortable by talking about his past. I had also planned on finally telling him about Catch's threat, but amazing sex had gotten in the way of that conversation. It was stupid to keep it from him, plus it was eating me up inside. Catch would always be a part of my life, and I had to trust Boner to handle him wisely or there was no moving forward in this new relationship of ours.

"This is the salon where Alicia comes, right?" Nina asked.

"She only comes here. Grace, too. I got a mani-pedi here with Grace and Tania not too long ago. Very nice. It was called Danielle's Beauty Shop, before. They just changed the name."

"When Boner gets back from his little trip out of town, he's gonna be thrilled," Nina said as we walked through the door of the new Danielle's Day Spa.

Sy, the prospect, leaned against his bike, drinking a soda, right outside the door.

"Why did Sy have to come with us today? What's going on at the club? Boner didn't say."

"This gun got stolen from the club meeting room. It belonged to someone called Dig, Butler said. They'd kept it in a locked display case and everything."

My stomach hardened. "It got stolen?"

That was Dig's gun, the one he'd used when he rescued me.

"Yep, it's gone." Nina shrugged. "They were really upset about it."

You have no idea.

"The men might have a lead," she continued. "That's probably why they took off today."

"Welcome, ladies," said the receptionist at the front desk, interrupting the flow of ice through my system.

"We have an appointment for highlights and a cut and style for my friend. Also, a bikini wax for both of us," said Nina.

"Okay." She scanned her appointment book. "Right on time. Follow me." The woman gestured toward the interior of the salon. "Waxing first. Sorry about the temporary rooms. Our renovation is taking longer than we expected."

"No problem," I said.

Nina leaned into me. "Remember, take it all off. All of it. Make him speechless. Works every time. Speechless is real good."

Nina left me in the curtained off room.

The waxing technician washed her hands and then turned and smiled at me. "Hi, I'm Trina. Why don't you get undressed and lie down and let me see what we have. Are we taking it all off today?"

"I'm not sure. My boyfriend likes my landing strip. A lot."

"My boyfriend" sounded so lame coming out of my mouth. He was something more.

I got undressed, got on the therapy table, and she inspected me. My toes curled.

"Why don't we give him a really pretty strip?" asked Trina.

"I'd like that."

Trina carefully performed her torturous craft, and I held my breath and grimaced as she did so.

"What do you think?" she said as she patted baby powder over me.

A delicate and very thin strip of short blondish-red curls remained between my legs. The rest of me was perfectly clean and bare. "I love it. I really do."

"Good." Trina smiled as she cleaned up her tools.

Another waxing session was going on in the adjoining temporary room, separated from mine only by curtains.

"I'll let you get dressed, so you can come back out and head to your haircut."

"Great. Thanks, Trina."

"You're welcome. I hope he likes it!" She left the room.

I slowly pushed up from the table and reached for my yoga pants. The thin fabric felt cool and smooth against my skin. No underwear necessary until the irritation eased. I slid my flip-flops on.

"That is some hickey! And bite marks right up your thighs. Tell me you came like a freight train? Please! Who was this animal?"

My head turned toward the shrill female voice rising from behind the curtain to the next therapy room.

"A very *hungry* animal!" said another female.

A burst of loud laughter.

"His mouth was just awesome."

"Lucky!"

"And he was an old guy, too. I know it sounds crazy, but he had this freaking gleam in his eyes from the get-go. I'm telling you, the man knew how to appreciate the female body."

More giggles.

I rolled my eyes as I glanced at the mirror and smoothed my hair back.

"He laid me out on this huge wooden table. He's the president, after all. He can do whatever he wants, you know?"

"Yeah, and he did you!"

"Oh my gosh, he was sucking on me. I mean, *really* sucking on me. Mindy was giving him head."

At the sound of that name, my ears pricked up like a jungle animal's listening for prey.

"I keep telling you, Stace, you gotta try a threesome," the girl continued. "It's so freaking hot. With me and Mindy, there's this trust and it's just fun. You should come with me next time there's a party. You need to get out more anyway."

"Yeah, I need to get a life. Maybe a party at the One-Eyed Jacks would be just the ticket."

Spikes of ice raced over my skin. This was Mindy's new dancer friend whom Nina had mentioned when she'd told me about the doings at the Full Moon Howl earlier in the car.

They had fucked Jump in the club meeting room?

"You guys are wild. I don't know if I could do that, Shell."

"Never know until you try it. That's it. Next time, I'm bringing you with us."

"I'm not a dancer like you and Mindy. My body—"

"Oh, they just want good pussy that can give as good as it gets. Wear something super hot, and they'll be all over you in no time, like bees to honey. You're having a dry spell, Stace, and this is how to end it."

The curtain on the other side of my room flew open.

"Hey, how'd it go?" Nina's lips curled into a grin. "Let me see."

I touched my fingers to my lips, my head tilting toward the next curtain. The women's voices rose again, and Nina's face clouded.

"There are lots of hot guys at that club, Stace. A few of them are taken, but for the most part, that's not an issue. Mindy was sleeping with this other older one. Now, he's hot! You should see this guy—long, long dark hair, big green eyes. Too thin for me, but he had some hot tats on his arms."

My pulse ratcheted up a couple of hundred notches. Nina held my gaze, her eyebrows springing up her forehead.

"At this other party we'd gone to at the club, me and Mindy were gonna do him together, but he didn't want to. Weird, huh?"

Something snapped inside me. They were talking about my man, his body, like he was a piece of fucking meat. He was meat to them. Some sort of prize to be seized and devoured, then the carcass tossed away.

My man. My beautiful, sweet, savage—

"Anyway, she said he was just okay, so I guess I didn't miss much. Whatever."

Nina charged across the small room. She ripped open the curtain to the other room.

"Hey, orgasm queen, that's my friend's old man you're talking about," Nina spit out.

The color drained from both Stacey's and Shelley Anne's faces.

"Uh…oh," managed Shelley Anne from her lying down position where she was having her legs waxed. She quickly sat up. "Sorry, sorry! It was meant as a compliment. I didn't mean nothing by it. Just that—"

"Just that, what?" I asked.

"He's really good-looking and you're a super lucky lady." She smiled, as if she'd just gotten caught eating the last cookie in the jar and was denying it with crumbs all over her face.

"She is super lucky, and so am I," said Nina. "My old man is a member of the Jacks, too. And I'm gonna make sure that you and your little friends don't come around the club anymore. That kind of kiss-and-tell bullshit is a serious no-no where I come from."

Stacey's gaze bounced from Nina to me and back to Nina again.

Shelley Anne raised her hands in the air. "I'm sorry. You're right. That wasn't cool."

"You want to have girl talk about great sex you had? Terrific," I said. "But you don't talk about the club or its members or what goes on behind closed doors. Ever."

"You're right. Totally," said Shelley Anne. "I'm sorry. Um, listen, I just got a job dancing at the Tingle. I like my job a lot, and I really, really need it. Please, please don't tell them. I promise, it won't happen again. I won't ever come over and party or sleep with any of—"

Nina let out a dark laugh. "Aw, you promise, huh?"

Shelley Anne and Mindy doing Jump.

"You"—I pointed at Stacey—"out. And not a word."

Stacey nodded and ran out of the room.

"Now"—I faced Shelley Anne, who was visibly shrinking inch by inch every second that passed under my glare—"here's the deal." I softened my voice. "If you're helpful to me, I'll be helpful to you. Tell me what I need to know, and I'll help you keep your job. If not…"

She pressed her bare legs together. "Anything, please. Anything. What is it?"

"You were with Mindy at the clubhouse at the Full Moon Howl party last night?"

"Right."

"And you and Mindy had sex with Jump?"

"Yeah."

"Where did you have sex?"

"It started in his office, but then Mindy had this idea for all of us to get on that big, long table so that he could—"

"So, it was Mindy's idea to move your private party into the meeting room?" I asked and glanced at Nina. Her eyes widened at me.

"Yeah, he unlocked the doors and then locked them behind us. And we…you know."

"Were you and Mindy both working him at the same time, or you took turns?"

"What? I mean, why do you—"

"Ticktock, ticktock," said Nina.

Shelley Anne bit her lip. "Okay, at first, all three of us were going at it together on the table and stuff. You wanna know what exactly we were doing?"

I made a face as if a bad smell had seeped into the room. "Not really, but I need to, so yeah, keep going."

"Then, Mindy decided I should get on all fours on the table, so Jump could fuck me from behind."

"Mindy decided?" said Nina.

"Yeah, and she covered my eyes with a scarf she'd had on. Then she put the bandanna Jump had been wearing on his head, over his eyes. He got pissed at first, but then he liked it." Shelley Anne shrugged her shoulders. "He laughed."

"So, Jump was fucking you blind?"

"Yeah. You know, I read about that in a book once. It really enhances—"

"Right. So, what was Mindy doing when you were getting it up the ass?" asked Nina.

"Oh, no. Later, he did my ass. Then, he was—"

"Shelley Anne," I said, letting out a sigh. "What was Mindy doing while you were getting it, doggy style?"

"I-I don't know."

"You don't know?" asked Nina.

"At first, she was playing with me—you know, with my tits, and—"

"And then she wasn't?" I said.

"Yeah. I figured she was tea-bagging Jump or something."

"Oh, the visuals," murmured Nina.

"Anyway, she'd blindfolded me, so I'm not sure. I was coming so hard. Seriously, Jump's awesome, you guys."

Nina bit her lip, tamping down her laughter. I shot her a look and focused on Shelley Anne once more.

"When you were done and you took the scarf off, where was Mindy?" I asked.

"She was kissing Jump, and then they started doing stuff together."

I toed one of my flip-flops. "By the way, did you guys have your handbags with you?"

"Not me. I hate taking a handbag to parties. I had my money and ID and my phone in my pockets. Mindy had my keys though. She always carries this big Coach bag."

"Oh, I like Coach bags," said Nina, grinning like an overzealous infomercial hostess.

Shelley Anne's eyes lit up. "Me, too! I love them. They're amazing, right?"

"Did Mindy have her Coach bag with her in the meeting room when you guys were in there with Jump?" I asked.

"Of course she did. You can't go leaving your shit around at a biker party, right?"

"Oh, absolutely," I replied.

"Truth," murmured Nina.

Mindy, Mindy, Mindy.

"Okay, we're done here. Remember, Shelley Anne, you don't say a word about our conversation to anyone, especially not Mindy, or I promise you, you'll be history. And we will find out if you've opened your trap. We always do."

The color drained from Shelley Anne's thin face. "No, I won't. I promise. I swear."

"For future reference," I said, "Jump's wife comes here to Danielle's all the time, and she's a very respected citizen of this small town of ours. Trust me when I say, you do not want her to find out about you and her old man."

Nina shook her head. "Damn, if she found out..." The unmentionable hung in the air.

I glanced at Nina, exhaling heavily. "I know, right?"

Shelley Anne's eyes widened, her mouth falling open, her face reddening.

Nina and I moved to leave the therapy room, but I had one more thing I needed to say to Miss Shelley Anne.

I turned and faced her once again. "Just so you know, your BFF, Mindy lied to you. You missed out big time." I winked at her. "My old man is absolutely amazing in the sack. Fucking fantastic."

TWENTY-NINE

JILL

NINA AND I HURTLED toward the club in her RAV4, Sy zooming ahead of us.

"We're going to find that bitch!"

I glanced at her. "*We* are?"

"Hell yes, we are! She stole that gun from the clubhouse!"

"And what the hell is she doing with it? Did she do it to get back at Boner? To sit back and have a laugh while the men scrambled to find it? That's just nuts!"

"Obviously, she is fucking nuts," replied Nina.

My head sank against the headrest. "Maybe..."

"Maybe I'll start off small, just for kicks, so you get that I'm serious about this."

I slid back up in my seat. "Holy shit."

It was a perfect Catch move, wasn't it? Audacious, unexpected, an unforgiving sharp cut deep to the bone.

"Shit, shit, shit," I muttered under my breath.

It had to be some kind of setup. Catch was taunting me with his threat and fucking with the Jacks, all in one go.

Had his club sanctioned this?

Getting Mindy to do his dirty work was certainly a sparkly touch.

Was this a trap he was setting up for Boner? I mentally kicked my ass for not telling Boner about Catch's threats to take Becca away from me and do him harm.

My jaw clenched. I had to *do* something.

During my first trimester of pregnancy with Becca, I'd found a club woman giving Catch a blow job in a bathroom at the Flames clubhouse. I'd sputtered and stumbled as I backed away. She was one of the older women they'd had around for many years. I'd seen her get into fights with other women at parties, and it was never pretty. She'd heard me come into the room and glared at me, his dick twisting in her mouth. In that moment, I'd been upset and revolted and utterly petrified.

Krystal, another Flames old lady, had found me in the hallway. Her eyes had flared at me as she grabbed a beer bottle and clocked the woman on my behalf. A bleary-eyed drunk Catch had stood there, his wet cock hanging out of his pants, while all my chained fury and emotion had vibrated in my veins. I had stood there shaking, unable to speak.

"That's the way to do it, honey. You got it in you, or don't you?"

Krystal had tossed what was left of the bottle on the floor, shaken her head at me, and stridden back to the party, as if nothing out of the ordinary had happened.

Her obvious disappointment had burned through me. I had been unworthy of the Old Lady title.

I'd envied Krystal's instinct for wild action without a second thought, that instinct to stand up and fight for herself, her sisters, and what she believed was right. Obviously, I'd had the instinct for flight.

Unworthy is right. Not this time.

You got it in you, or don't you?

I got out my phone and dialed up Penny. "Pen? Hi, I have a couple of more errands I need to run with Nina." I raised my heels as the lie escaped my lips, Nina glancing over at me. "Could you keep Rae and Becca until tonight? I'm sorry this is last minute."

"Sure, Jill. Roy and the boys went to a softball game, so it's just us girls. We were going to call you to have dinner with us."

"I wish I could. Becca okay? Did she eat enough?" Becca had started going through a picky eater phase. At least, I hoped it was only a temporary phase.

"She did fine. She ate every pea in her bowl, one at a time and by hand, but she ate every last one. I think it's because she loves the taste of melted butter so much."

"That's so exciting! Oh my gosh. Thanks, honey."

"Sure. I took pictures, I'll show you later."

"Okay. Bye." I clicked off the call.

I turned to Nina. "Let's do this."

She whooped loudly, smacking her hands on the wheel of her Toyota.

A few minutes later, we pulled into the club. Alicia's blue Cherokee was parked in her usual spot.

"Oh shitters!" Nina pulled in alongside it. "Alicia's back from Texas?"

"Perfect timing," I said.

"She's going to blow a gasket."

"Not just a gasket. This is good. We'll take care of Mindy and get the men the info they need."

We hustled from the car and charged into the clubhouse.

Nina stopped Dawes, who was hauling a box of files from Jump's office into the meeting room. "Have you heard from Butler? He's not answering his cell."

"Nope. He and Boner haven't come back yet. Anything up?"

"Jill and I have a lead on how the Python disappeared. We wanted to let the guys know."

"They had an idea, too, and headed south to go deal with it." Dawes cast a pointed glance at me.

Catch, of course.

Alicia strode into the room. "Hey, girls."

I grinned. "Hey, Alicia. Welcome home. Could we talk to you for a minute?"

Nina raised her chin at Dawes. "Get my old man on the phone, would you? It's a nine-one-one."

He stared at us.

Nina waved a hand in his face. "Old Lady powwow."

He rolled his eyes and ambled off.

Alicia raised an already arched eyebrow at us. "What the hell's going on?"

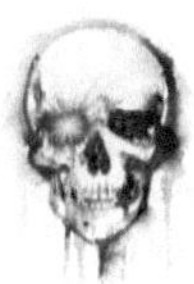

The three of us headed for the Tingle in Nina's car. Alicia had called Cassandra, the manager of the nightclub and confirmed that Mindy was there rehearsing. On the drive over, I explained my Catch suspicions to Nina and Alicia.

"You see, Mindy did all this to get back at Boner for being with me."

"Using my old man to do it," Alicia said. "And colluding with another club to steal from us at the same time. That goes above and beyond."

"Above and so fucking beyond," I agreed. "And so very fucking low."

"And Catch is not taking Becca away from you, Jill. You told Boner about him threatening you, right?" Alicia asked.

"No, I haven't told him yet."

"Why the hell not?" Her throaty voice got louder.

I bit my lip. "I didn't want to make things worse between the clubs. And now this happened."

"Things are already worse, and he needs to know, Jill. You don't keep secrets like that from your old man. That's not protecting anybody. You're not in this alone anymore, hon."

"Thank you. That means a lot to me."

"It's the truth," Alicia replied.

We swerved into the Tingle parking lot.

Alicia turned to me. "You stay back. You and the baby are more important than this bullshit."

"Yeah, but this bullshit has to be dealt with," I replied.

"Damn straight," she replied. "And it will be."

Suddenly, the back door of the night club swung open, and a movement blurred before us.

"That's her. Somebody tipped her off!" shouted Alicia.

She and Nina ran toward Mindy, who was opening the door of her car.

I charged after them. Nina got Mindy facedown against her car, her arms twisted behind her.

"Get the fuck off me!" Mindy yelled.

"Shelley Anne told us all about it," Alicia said.

"All about me fucking your old man?" Mindy wrestled with Nina's steady grip. "He was as horny as a teenager. You don't feed the beast, do you? He even found me again later on, hungry for more, and I fed him good and plenty. Don't you worry."

Alicia viciously dug her hands into Mindy's long brown hair, yanking it to the side. Mindy screeched.

"Boner didn't want you for his old lady? Tough fucking shit, little girl," Alicia said.

Mindy glared at me, her breath ragged.

"Anyone force you to do this?" I asked.

"No!" Mindy struggled for air, her neck craning.

"I think you'd better apologize to our president's old lady," I said.

"Fuck you! I will not—"

Nina twisted her arms further and kicked a leg between Mindy's.

I rested my hands on my hips. "The men know that it was you. Jump and Boner know. Twist a guy's dick. He's going to twist back. They're coming for you next. Did you take the gun from the case?"

Mindy's hands tightened into fists.

"Did you give it to someone else?" I pushed.

No answer.

I stepped closer to her, my voice softening. "Catch has a nice circle of hellfire on the front and back of his leather jacket, doesn't he?"

A choked noise escaped Mindy's mouth, her eyes flaring, her body jerking in Nina's hold.

"Ding, ding, we have a winner," I said.

"Fuck you," Mindy spit out.

"Really? Well, I tried this the nice way. Now, we're going to have to do this the *Alicia* way."

Long icy-blonde hair flew in my vision. With a grunt, Alicia punched Mindy in the face, knocking her out. Blood spattered on the hood of Mindy's silver car.

"Well, since heavy lifting is out for me," I said, taking Nina's car keys from the back pocket of her jeans. "How about I do the driving?"

THIRTY

BONER

BUTLER AND I HAD ARRIVED at the Flames of Hell property about two hours south of Meager, in the vicinity of Elk, Nebraska, south of Chadron. All around the property, the high chain-link fence was trimmed with barbed wire and dotted with cameras. Butler did all the talking and got us in through the heavily guarded gate. I didn't trust myself to speak just yet.

Catch rolled into the yard as we swung off our bikes, and I knew. I knew he was responsible by the slant of his head and the crooked grin splitting his face as we followed him inside their clubhouse.

He started out by denying it. I let him run his mouth, but then I cut him off and got to the point.

"I get that Jill was your piece of good for a while there, and she gave you the miracle that is your daughter. But you didn't take care of all that amazing when you had it, and now, Jill is my woman. And nothing about her, except for the kid you share, comes under your jurisdiction. You need to accept that and move on. I didn't take away anything that was yours. I only claimed what was mine."

"Fuck Jill."

My pulse flared. "Say again?"

Catch pulled the Python from his back. "This gun? I like this gun."

"Do you now?" murmured Butler.

"Oh, yeah. I appreciate a good firearm, especially one with history."

"Then, you'll appreciate that you wouldn't have Becca if it wasn't for that gun, the man who owned it, and his perfect aim," I spit out.

"So I've heard."

"Put the gun down, Catch." Finger stood in the doorway, his distinctive sandpaper voice making Catch do a double take.

Finger folded his arms across his chest. "I'm gone two days, and you managed to bust out your balls again, bro?"

"Did what needed to be done," muttered Catch.

"Not with that gun," Finger interjected. "That belongs with the Jacks. You respect the weapon of a good man, a good brother. I don't take that lightly. I admire your play, but *this*? This isn't right." Finger's eyes rested on me. "It's disrespect to a man I knew and admired."

Catch leaned over and raked a hand through his hair, as if that would juggle a few brain cells to help him better grasp the logic of his prez's argument.

"Catch," Finger said, his throaty voice low.

Catch stuck out the revolver. The bullying boy in the schoolyard had finally been caught red-handed by the principal.

"Come give it to me," I said on a snarl.

Catch moved forward, got in my face, eyebrows raised, and dropped the revolver as my hand reached out and caught it.

Little shit.

"Party's over," said Catch. "I'd invite y'all to stay, but I don't think that's a good idea."

"Ah, no thanks," I replied. "I've heard the beds around here suck."

"You mother—" Catch lunged at me.

Two Flames dragged him back.

"How we gonna get past this shit now? You wanna tell me?" Butler's voice thundered.

"I'm gonna need an apology," I said, eyes going from Catch to Finger. "Then, the Jacks are gonna require a sweet form of payback for this heavy transgression. But first, I wanna know how you did it, Catch. Who'd you use to get it? Are you that much smarter than I took you for?"

"Your woman did it for me. Didn't take much to convince her either. Heart of flames, that one."

I saw red. "Son of a bitch!" My hands clamped around his neck and squeezed.

"Boner!" Butler yelled.

Hands shoved me back, my hair flying in my face. "You lying piece of shit! Jill would never—"

Catch choked and coughed, his face different shades of red, his hands shoving at my chest, curling in my shirt. "Yeah, Jill *would never* a hell of a lot of things, but with me, she sure as fuck did. Goes to show you."

I pounced on him, my fist landing on his jaw, and he fell back, grunting. Another Flame moved toward me, but Finger stopped him with a hand on his chest.

"Catch more than deserved that," Finger said.

A loud *ting* sliced the air. Butler untucked his phone from a pocket and glanced at it. "Fuck." He tapped the phone and put it to his ear. "What the hell's going on?" His eyes flicked up at me. "You and Jill did what?"

I grabbed the phone from him.

"We realized it was Mindy who stole the Python for Catch," Nina said.

Mindy. Of course. Fucking Mindy.

I tossed the phone back at Butler.

"We're on our way back. Don't do anything else." Butler shut down his phone.

My eyes pinned on Catch. "You been watching me, you knew about me and Mindy and you got her to do your dirty work, you slick scumbag?"

He let out a laugh. "Aw, you thought I was talking about your old lady before, huh? Nah. This other bitch, she was more than willing."

Teasing, lying piece of shit.

Butler moved next to me. "Let's get out of here." He cast a dark glance at Finger. "Compensation needs to hit the table."

We got on our bikes and waited for the compound gate to open. And that was when I saw him.

Across the street, a dark-suited figure, wearing black sunglasses, leaned against a silver Cadillac Escalade.

His hair, shorter now, was still that shock of shiny black. His round face was more swollen than when I'd last seen him, but that acidic expression etched on his mouth was the same.

He slanted his head.

Butler spoke with the Flame at the gate, but my eyes were riveted on Alejandro Calderón, my hands gripping my handlebars. The edges of his lips curved as his hand went to his temple, and he saluted me with two fingers. Another well-dressed man opened the back door for him. Alejandro climbed in, his eyes never leaving me. He watched me from his window, that twist still on his mouth. His driver started up the Escalade, and they sped off.

My wait was over.

THIRTY-ONE

BONER

I STRODE INTO THE MAIN HALL, and those gray-blue eyes flashed up at me from the sofa. With a quirky grin on her face, Jill held a huge margarita glass with a frozen green drink in it. She might as well have been having a cocktail at an upscale beach bar, not stretched out on the faded blue corduroy couch of the One-Eyed Jacks MC clubhouse lounge.

She put down her drink and wiped at the edge of her mouth. I dived at her and took that mouth. Apple and icy vegetables shivered over my tongue.

"What the hell are you drinking?"

"It's a smoothie I just made. The ladies added vodka to theirs." Her face was flushed. "Do you like it?"

My girl-woman. I raked my fingers through her hair, tugging her head back. "No, but I'll take it."

I kissed her again, our tongues making fresh declarations.

Her arms wrapped around my middle. "You got the gun back?"

"Yeah."

"Good." She buried her face in my throat. "Good."

"You want to tell me what the hell happened around here?"

"Nina and I bumped into Mindy's gal pal Shelley Anne at the beauty salon in town, and we overheard her bragging about partying with Mindy and Jump at the Full Moon Howl."

"Jump?"

"Yeah, Jump had himself a good ole time with both lovely ladies. By the way, Alicia came home from her trip to Texas today, too."

"Ah, fuck." I leaned back against the sofa.

"Big fuck. She wasn't too surprised, but that sort of humiliation truly sucks." She leaned over and took another swallow of that green frozen crap.

"And what did you and Nina do?"

"We had our girl's back, of course. Old-lady code and all."

I eyed her. "Old-lady code?"

Jill shrugged. "It's a minefield out there."

She went into detail about how Mindy had gotten the gun out of the clubhouse.

I rubbed a hand down my face. "Shit. Have you seen Jump?"

"He's making himself scarce. Alicia went ballistic, and the three of us headed for the Tingle where we found Mindy. There was a bit of a smackdown in the parking lot."

"Jill, did you—"

"Not me. I did use my verbal skills to let Mindy know how I felt about what she'd done."

I raised an eyebrow. "I bet you did."

She took another swallow of her frothy green cocktail. "Mindy's downstairs in the cellar. Your woman scorned awaits."

I wrapped her hand in mine. "You're all jazzed up now, aren't you?"

She squeezed my hand. "I got angry, but this time I focused and did something about it. It felt good to stand up, fight back."

My woman had fought back.

In that fight, do we splinter like bone or stand tall, as if we were hard and made of iron? Our bodies were made of bone, but there was iron to be found within, and each of us had to find it.

I brushed her cheek with a quick kiss. "Standing tall, baby."

She pursed her lips. "I hate that Catch did this. I really hate it."

"He tried to make me believe that you had done it for him."

Her eyes shot up at me.

"I didn't believe him, not for a second."

Jill's hand twisted in mine. "He called me and threatened me, saying he'd take Becca."

"When?"

"When we were at the burger place."

"Why didn't you say anything?"

She didn't answer.

"There's more, isn't there?"

She pressed her lips together.

"Say it, Jill. It ain't gonna be nothing I haven't heard before."

Her wet eyes met mine. "He threatened your life if I didn't do what he wanted. He said he'd get to you any way he could. Would start out small, like he did today, and then—"

"He ain't going to touch me or have anyone else do it. Finger was not happy with him either. You should've told me. Your life and safety do not get threatened, and me and the club don't know about it. You hear me? No matter what kind of hold he has over you."

"He doesn't have a hold over me."

I tilted my head at her, my hand smoothing across her jaw. Her gaze was steady, emotional but steady. I rubbed a thumb across her cheek.

My woman.

I had to protect her with everything I had, for as long as we had.

"Are you going to the cellar now?" she asked. "Do your judge-and-jury thing?"

"No, I don't want to see that bitch. That's for Jump to deal with, his mess to clean up and save face if he can. I did what had to get done. Now, I want time with my old lady. You got to get back to Rae's?"

"Actually, Grace and Tania are having a girls' sleepover with Becca and Rae at the house. Doesn't that sound nice?"

"I could think of a few other choice words for it."

She let out a soft laugh and pressed her face into my chest.

THIRTY-TWO

JILL

BACK AT RAE'S, I quickly packed an overnight bag, chatted with Tania and Rae, and gave my daughter a big hug and kiss where I got my hair covered in homemade play dough.

I followed Boner back to his house. He parked his bike at the end of the long driveway and immediately grabbed my bag from the car.

"We got a whole night, huh?"

I smoothed my hair back, checking for more dough bits. "A whole night."

I glanced up at the massive stone chimney rising over the cedar siding–paneled house, which was nestled on a green hilly slope, the hill joining the low mountains farther in the distance. A deep porch wrapped around the front, and that incredible bay window was prominent in the center.

Boner unlocked the thick wooden door and pushed it open. He took my hand and brought me inside where he punched a series of numbers into a security-alarm panel on the side of the door.

"I need to get in the shower. I'll take your bag up. You relax. Be back down in a few."

"Okay."

He planted a kiss on my mouth, his fingers lingering at the side of my jaw. "So good to have you here all to myself. Finally," he said quietly.

He toed off his boots and climbed the stairs, my bag in his hand, his dusty leathers creaking as he moved, the wood steps groaning in his wake.

I stepped into the living room. Spare and uncluttered, except for the stone fireplace with a slab of dark wood for a mantel and the wood trim along the edges of the ceiling. Matching dark wood shutter blinds lined the great bay window, and the thick navy blue cushions dressing the window seat were inviting. A single burgundy-colored sofa faced the hearth.

Did he ever have the guys over to watch a game on the TV and have a few beers?

My gaze skipped around the stark room. He didn't have a television.

He had a turntable, receiver and speakers though, and lots of music albums. Actual vinyl albums lined the built-in shelves on one side of the fireplace. I shuffled through the records. The Allman Brothers, Jimi Hendrix, Velvet Underground. Early Rolling Stones, late Beatles. Grateful Dead, Led Zeppelin, Eric Clapton, even Cream, the collected works of Johnny Cash. The classics, baby.

A number of books filled the set of shelves on the other side of the fireplace. I ran my fingers over the worn spines of the paperbacks. Henry Miller, Charles Bukowski, Dostoyevsky, Joseph Conrad.

Pablo Neruda. Oh, I'd enjoyed his poems years ago, and I hadn't seen a book of his since the one I'd discovered in the library at college my freshman year.

I pulled out the slim volume and flipped open the pages. A piece of scrap paper fluttered out at me—a palm-sized square with ripped edges, as if the original piece of paper had been torn into quarters for scrap paper. I unfolded it. Two lines were scribbled in blue pen.

I reached out for you
And destroyed you instead

I blinked. It was Boner's handwriting. I recognized it from notes he'd left for Grace on her desk. I leafed through the Neruda. Another paper had been tucked in the last quarter of the book. I opened it, my heart thumping.

I want to remember the sound of your breath
When I said no
No to the smoky secrets
No to the thick lies
But I couldn't say no to the mystery inside

You laughed
And pulled me closer
And I kissed you
I kissed you
And it was like fire
A fire of absolutes
A fire in the dark
A fire in my heart
A fire that left only ashes behind
Ashes
Ashes
We all fall down

Same handwriting. These were little poems. Clips of heart-heavy emotions. Passion.

Boner wrote these. *Who were they about?*

I put the two poems back where I'd found them and went through more books, pulling out volumes, checking the insides. Nothing. I took in a small breath. I needed to stop. His poems were an exciting discovery, but it was as if I'd stumbled onto his journal, and I was reading it. Bad, very bad.

I wanted more.

Last book, I promised myself.

Selected Poems of Rainer Maria Rilke. I opened the tall paperback, and there it was—another paper. I unfolded it.

You raised my hopes
When I wasn't looking
I wasn't sure before
And now I'm the one who wants more
But you're missing
I can touch you, I can kiss you
You can hold me in your arms
But you won't let me see you
You're missing

You bolted tight your doors
Jammed your windows
Locked your drawers
I can't remain in the cold anymore
You want me, but you push me away
You fill me up and drain me away
You seek me out and then leave me in doubt
You hold me tight and then let go
You let go
You're slipping away
Making a mess
Separated by your sadness
A sadness that has no name
A sadness you can't explain
You won't tell me
You're missing
Remember when the laughter came easy
And sweet words and kisses had meaning?
You're bound in a box
And I can't cut the strings
You're missing
You want me, but push me away
You fill me up and drain me away
You seek me out yet leave me in doubt
You hold me tight
And then you let go
You're missing

My body swayed. I gripped the book tightly. *Beautiful. So sad. So...*

I gnawed on my lip and took in a breath. No, no. *I'm eavesdropping on his heart. How would I feel if he'd cracked open one of my crazy-ass journals?* I wouldn't like it. I'd be mortified, embarrassed. My journals were my safe place, my refuge. I needed to write in them to make sense of my world and my emotions that were usually waging a battle inside my head.

The battle to stay sane.

Maybe this was Boner's way of staying sane.

I tucked the poem back into the Rilke and slid the book into its gaping slot on the bookshelf.

I'd wanted answers, but I only got more questions.

The need to hold him and make it better overtook me. But this was no scraped knee that a kiss on the skin and some antibiotic cream would make all better.

I hiked up the stairs, my fingertips skimming along the smooth polished dark wood banister. The doors to two rooms were open, and one was closed. I peeked into the first open room, which had a simple pine double bed in it and a pine dresser with a small brass lamp on it. A framed crisp black-and-white poster of a mountain range was hanging on the wall.

I passed the closed door and went on to the next room. Boner's bedroom. The queen-size bed was made with a royal-blue-and-black-trimmed quilt. Matching curtains hung across the long bank of windows. I drew them open, and my breath caught. The view was pretty damn spectacular.

The Black Hills stretched out beyond, pink-and-dusky-blue-sky rolled overhead, as the sun began its descent, touching the tree-furrowed low-lying mountains. It was quite unlike the country suburbia of Meager where Rae lived. Here, on the outskirts of town, was a magical hush, a quiet grandeur.

My gaze swept over his bedroom again. Orderly and simple.

A large round mirror sat on top of the dresser, and an unmarked dark purple glass bottle stood sentry before it. I picked up the small bottle and sniffed. That unique blaze of warmth that Boner's scent inspired in me every time flared through my veins. I took in another whiff. Wood, black pepper, amber, maybe a hint of chocolate, too.

Glorious. Boner had custom-made cologne? Man of hipster mystery.

I would have expected a no-frills guy like Boner to just grab whatever man products he saw by the cash register at Walgreens—*if* it occurred to him that he should have them—whenever he popped in to pick up a new pack of cigarettes or gum or condoms.

But no, here was something handmade-to-order just for him. My fingers lingered on the glass bottle's decorative grooves.

I touched a tiny knob on one of the small cube-like drawers at the wooden base of the vintage-style vanity mirror. *What would he put in these? Cuff links? Not likely. A watch maybe? His rings? Extra condoms?*

I tugged the drawer open. Two rolled up balls of paper tumbled forward in the drawer. A third was open and very wrinkled. I spread it out on top of the dresser.

> If I could be with you where rules didn't apply
> I'd live for the moment
> Without asking why
> If I could be with you

I unrolled the next paper.

> Embraces that mean a thousand things
> Glances that hang on strings
> I let go of your hand
> Is it forever?
> And years from now
> Will you even remember?
> I want to remember
> I want to remember it all

My pulse pounded in my neck, blocking my air. I unraveled the other balled up paper.

> Who did I cut myself into pieces for?
> The man in the moon
> Or the ghost in my living room?
> I'm nothing but cold inside
> Am I supposed to tremble at your threats, at your dark
> visions?

I don't have many tears left
Let me slash the rope gouging my throat
I'm to blame
Yet I don't get the rules of this game
I hate you
And you hate me
I don't get the rules of this game
When did it become a game?
When did we become nothing but pain?

The water in the shower stopped running, and fumbling sounds came from the master bathroom. I stuffed all the papers back into the small drawer, shutting it with a loud *thunk*, and I stood there, staring at that tiny drawer.

He wrote. He wrote poems. Boner wrote. And not in a notebook but on slips of scrap paper bundled and hidden probably all over this house.

Why not have a notebook? Where would I find more? Under the bathroom sink? With the forks and knives?

He had surrounded himself with these jagged pieces of heartbreak tucked away all over his organized, simple house.

How old were these poems anyway? I planted my hands on the edge of the dresser, and my stomach clenched. *Were they all about the same woman?*

He'd told me he never had an old lady. Grace had said he'd barely ever had a serious relationship before, just very short-term serial monogamy or he played the biker field. He'd tended to keep things with women casual and light.

Until me.

"I don't want anyone else. I don't want to be with anyone else. I don't want to be inside anyone else."

So, who were these tortured words about? An epic first love?

"There's my impatient Firefly."

I pivoted, and there he stood, the naked pirate home after a hard day's pillaging. A sheen of water on his skin glistened in the light from the bathroom as he toweled off, a grin on his face, his cock at fantastic attention.

"Missed me?"

I was unable to suppress a smile. "I did."

He planted a kiss on the side of my face and went to a drawer next to me. He pulled out a pair of warm-up pants and then a plain black T-shirt from another drawer. He tossed the towel at me and tugged on the pants.

"I explored your house a little. You don't have a television, do you?"

"Is that going to be a problem?" He let out a laugh. "A deal breaker?"

"No, I'm just curious."

He stretched the T-shirt over his head. "There's lots of noise everywhere I go—the club, the shop, the bars. When I actually get to be here, in my own place, I want it quiet. The noise is fun, the noise is what I know, but this is apart from that. I need it."

I tore my eyes away from his molten gaze, hugging the towel to my chest. "This purple bottle is interesting. Is that your cologne?"

"You like it?"

"Very much."

"It's an oil blend. Lenore started to make her own fragrances from natural oils and flowers and spices and whatever else. She made me a couple to test out. This one's my favorite. She's coming out with a line at her store. They're unisex. It's the new thing, she told me."

"It smells great on you, but I love the way you smell."

"You mean, the oil?"

"You *and* the oil."

A low chuckle erupted from his throat. "That's good." He took the towel from me and brought it back to the bathroom. "I've got a surprise for you. Come here." He took my hand in his.

"Surprise? I like surprises!" I shoved his tormented poetry out of my mind and gripped his hand. He led me out of his bedroom and across the hall to the closed door.

Oh boy, the secret room.

He pushed the door open.

My breath caught. "What have you done?"

THIRTY-THREE

JILL

I FROZE.

"You like it?" Boner asked.

My gaze fell on a white crib decorated with a pink-and-green quilt and quilted paneling. A matching white dresser stood proudly to its right.

He threw an arm around my shoulders. "I like the minty green with the pink crap. What do you think?"

"Boner, you didn't have to do this."

He only stared at me, the soft ease sliding from his face, like water down a windshield, leaving stiff, harsh angles behind.

"I mean, this must have been so expensive," I added.

"I wanted to do it for you and Becs. Whenever you stay here, the two of you will be comfortable. She'll be safe in a crib, and you'll be relaxed, knowing she's safe in a crib and in her own room for a change. This turns into a toddler bed, too."

"I don't know what to say."

He removed his arm from my shoulders and shifted his weight. "Say anything. Anything else but, *What have you done?*, or, *You didn't have to do this*, or, *I don't know what to say.*"

"I'm sorry."

"Or, *I'm sorry.*"

My hands smoothed over the polished slick wood of the crib. So solid. "It's just that—"

"Jill! What the fuck?"

He was spending money, making plans, looking ahead.

"I can't live with you."

His nostrils flared. "Why not?"

"I can't leave Rae. I take care of her and her house. It's a paying job."

"I know all that. We all know that. But there are times, like tonight, when you have a night off or a day or a few hours, and we can be together. And this way, Becca can be here, too, with us."

I nodded, chewing my lower lip.

"All this would make that situation easier on everybody. You don't have to coordinate babysitters on top of caregivers or whatever the fuck." His head slanted. "But you like it the way it is now, don't you? The *not easy*, the *having to steal time here and there*. Yeah, you like the *not easy* because it's easier for you. *That's* convenient for you, isn't it? This here"—he gestured with his thumb at the crib, the dresser—"spells complicated, doesn't it?"

My face heated.

"Because what's convenient for you is not having to commit to anything with me. You're in. You're out. Bits and pieces. You get horny, you come find me, you call me."

"That's not true. You know that's not true."

"No, I don't. I honestly don't. What are your plans after the baby's born? You haven't said a thing. You staying with Rae? Moving out? Moving out of Meager? Leaving South Dakota? The United States? Which is it?"

"I'm not sure yet."

He lifted his chin. "So, you are thinking of leaving?"

"Initially, that was the plan." I swallowed past the sawdust in my throat. "Have the baby, find a real job, school part-time. Move to Rapid at least."

"And go on nice dates to coffee shops with Matt."

My head snapped up. "What? No…"

His fingers gripped the the handrail of the crib, his knuckles whitening.

"I'm not sure what I'm going to do. I love Rae, and she and Becca need each other. They should have time together. I really don't want to ruin that, but I also need to do what I need to do."

"And I don't fit into that category?"

"What category?"

"Need."

"For God's sake! You know what I mean!"

The green light in his eyes dimmed, his jaw set. "Jill, I don't think you know what you mean. Am I holding you back? Or you're pushing back, so you don't get too far in it?"

"I don't know." I averted my gaze. "I care about you and—"

"And?"

"Bone, I lived the life for almost three years, and I didn't particularly enjoy it."

"I'm not Catch."

"I know. Oh, I know."

"Have things been bad for you at my club since you became my old lady?"

"No. Not at all."

"Then, what the fuck is the problem?" His voice spiked.

"Coming here to Meager—just ripping up and taking off to a new place, trusting people I didn't even know—was a gamble that paid off beautifully. It was a huge step for me. But this was supposed to be my time. For me. For me to finally stand up on my own two feet and forge my future or whatever. And instead…"

"Instead what?"

My heart sloshed heavily back and forth in the sour muck filling my chest. "Instead, I'm attaching myself to another man again."

"You're attaching yourself to me—to *me*—not just some other guy."

"To you, yes." I held his hard gaze, which seared right through my middle. "And maybe Catch was right—to another bike club. The problem is…"

"There's a problem?" He gritted his teeth.

"Let me finish, please. The problem is, I don't want to live a life where I just let things happen to me. I want to do things, make things happen."

"You made this pregnancy happen. You're changing lives. You did that."

"Yes."

"You changed your daughter's life and Rae's by leaving Catch and Nebraska. And today, you got the club its piece of justice by nailing Mindy and her friend. Don't you see that?"

I only nodded, my lips pressed together. My face tightened as I tried to force down the lid on an unrelenting jack-in-the-box of emotions.

"It's something else. What is it?"

"It's just that, after the baby's born, it might be hard for me to be here. Maybe Grace won't want me here. I don't know. I've never done this before. I don't know what the *after* will be like." My throat stung, my eyes welled with water. "I know it's not my baby. I'm just carrying it, but I still love it and care about what happens to it. After I give birth, maybe things will be strange between all of us, and it would just be better for everyone if I left. Cleaner." I wiped at my eyes. "I don't know. I don't know what it's going to be like."

"Look at me."

I met his raw gaze, and my chest hurt.

"You don't have to burn your bridges, Jill. You don't have to cut all of us off, let us go."

"I don't want to," I breathed. "I don't want to." My vision turned watery again.

"Don't." He grabbed me, his lips taking mine, his tongue invading, his taste swirling with my salty tears.

His forehead slid against mine. "You feel that? That's real, Firefly. Trust me when I tell you, *that* is being alive and free. Do what you got to do, follow your dreams, make your plans, but you don't have to walk away from us—from me—to do it."

I clutched at his waist, our eyes locking.

Dreams, plans—I had clung to them so tightly when I first got to Meager. But dreams evolved, didn't they? They transformed into different dreams, new ones, better ones.

Both the baby I was carrying and Boner had made one of my dreams come true for me—a home, surrounded by good people who had become good friends. No, more than that, they had already become family to me.

"Thank you for Becca's room. This is an incredible surprise and such a wonderful gift. No one's ever done something like this for me. I'm sorry I reacted the way I did. I didn't mean to be ungrateful or freak out on you, but I did freak out. Forgive me."

He brushed my hair away from my wet face. "You're welcome."

I hated that I'd hurt his feelings. I hated the things I'd said. "Boner—"

He rubbed his hand across my throat, gripping it, collaring it. "I'm right here, baby. But you've got to want this, too. You've got to choose it."

We made a quick stir-fry with strips of pork, red peppers, and carrots, along with a romaine lettuce salad on the side. I had fully expected to find only cans of beer and maybe an empty egg carton in his refrigerator. But no, Boner actually had a few real food supplies.

We ate at his square kitchen table, me telling him stories about Becca when she was younger, him telling me a few funny stories about when he had been a prospect.

We cleaned up, and he took my hand and led me up the stairs to his room. Butterflies fluttered in my belly, and it wasn't the baby. I felt like the proverbial virgin on her wedding night.

I had packed something special in my overnight bag for this evening, even though I'd almost talked myself out of it at the last minute. Now, I was glad that I had bought it just in case we ever had a whole night to ourselves. I went into his bathroom to change.

The sting of guilt from seeing the disappointment in his eyes earlier over my reaction to him setting up a nursery for Becca still hadn't worn off. I was determined to make it up to him.

I swung open the bathroom door and entered his bedroom.

"Fuck me. What are you wearing?"

"It's called a baby-doll nightie."

"Baby-doll?"

"Mmhmm…" I shifted my hips and toyed with the pink satin ribbon between my breasts that held together the ivory sheer open front apron-style robe that just brushed over my hips. A pale pink thong completed the look.

"Are you trying to kill me?" he said from the bed where he was lying down.

"I wanted to turn you on."

He groaned, a hand rubbing across his forehead.

"Do you like it?" I hummed that Madonna song as I straddled his body on the bed.

"Jill." His voice was a warning. His hands rushed up my bare thighs, and he ground his erection against me.

My fingers ran up his chest. "I'm sensing you like this look."

His thumb grazed the patch of delicate fabric between my legs, and heat uncoiled inside me.

"Do you like wearing it for me?" His voice was husky, low. His thumb circled, applying more pressure.

My breath got shorter, and my hips rocked gently against his. "Hell yes."

"You want me, Jillee?" Two of his fingers slid underneath the satin fabric of the panty and dipped up and down over my wetness. "'Cause I want every inch of you, Firefly."

My lids hooded my eyes. I couldn't form words.

His free hand pulled on the elastic of my thong. "I like that you did this for me, but you don't have to hook me, Firefly. I'm already hooked."

He took his fingers away, and the stretchy fabric snapped against my skin. I let out a whimper at the mild sting.

"It's icing on my already frosted cake." He sucked on his fingers.

"G-good." My voice shook.

He ripped off his shirt, and I helped him pull down his pants, tossing them to the floor. Sheer, blissful nakedness. His natural state. I loved his body. Lean and muscular, angrily inked, taut, and ready.

"Get back on me and turn around. I want to enjoy my present."

Still kneeling on the bed, I turned around and straddled him again, shimmying my tush at him.

He muttered a few choice expletives under his breath, a hand gripping my ass cheek.

I peeked over my shoulder. He stroked himself with one hand. I took in the sight of him, his jaw slack, the muscles of his chest and arms straining as he rubbed his thick length, his eyes on me. My knees weakened, my heart beating wildly in my chest.

"Back up over me. Get close."

I turned around again and inched back over his chest, my ass in the air. His fingertips traced patterns over my skin.

He let out a low moan. "What did you do down here?" A fingertip grazed through my little line of curls. "Fuck," he growled, his hand cupping me.

Score for the airstrip.

Two of his fingers slid inside me, curving just where they should, stroking rhythmically. I cried out in return, the ability to form words beyond me as his fingers explored and beat out a rhythm, calling me to a primal ritual. I leaned over and nuzzled his stiff balls.

"Give me that pussy," he said, his voice rough.

I moved further up the bed, and his tongue lapped at me. I jerked in his hold, my head falling forward, and I cried out at the lavish, sensual caress of his lips, the pressure and suck of his mouth. The pleasure was so delicate and so intense, all at once. Suddenly, his mouth turned savage, and I gasped loudly, my hands curling in the sheets, my body on fire. His hands held me in an urgent, painful grip, my breasts brushing the coarse hair on his legs. I felt shameless and wild and vulnerable all at once.

His fingers left me and rubbed my throbbing clit, punishing me with a fierce wall of pleasure. "Want my cock in you now."

There was that savage impatience. A buzz of adrenaline shot through me.

I lifted off him, turned, and straddled him again, sliding his cock inside my wetness. "Yes!" I rolled my hips over him again and again, my hands planted on his chest.

I held his burning eyes as I found my rhythm, steadying myself on his chest. His hands slid over my undulating ass, keeping us close and tight together.

"Fuck me, Jill. Fuck me good, sweetheart." His voice was hoarse.

"I want to…make you…come…hard," I said on several gasp-filled breaths.

"Always do for you, Firefly. Only you, only you."

His one hand grabbed ahold of the tie of my sheer lingerie and tugged on it. The material fell open, exposing my swaying breasts. He took one in his palm, roughly kneading it. I moved faster over him, the sensations leading me on, his hungry gaze chasing after me.

"Firefly," he breathed, his corded neck straining. "Baby."

I was lost in my rhythm, lost in the force of my body's response.

The fingers of his one hand went into my mouth, and, grabbing his arm, I sucked on them for dear life. Their salty taste, the thick skin made my need more sharp, more fervent, more desperate.

He thrust into me harder. "Fly, baby."

I flew, and all the bright pieces that were me were his to throw across his night sky and capture whenever he wanted.

THIRTY-FOUR

BONER

"Arvin hides this shit, Willy. I'm telling you. I have never seen this kind of range of early Indian and Harley parts. Fucking unbelievable." I opened up the back of my truck.

A knowing grin lit up Willy's face. "The man certainly has a very particular supply."

"I think he only likes to sell to Willy," Butler said, laughing. "I bet he hides it from everybody else."

"There is that, too," Willy said, settling on his bike, putting on his gloves. "He sure doesn't give us any discounts, but I'm still grateful."

"So am I." I shoved a box of vintage headlamps into the truck. Butler and I loaded my truck with the rest of the engine parts and the rusted frame we'd just bought from Arvin Hooper, an Army veteran buddy of Willy's who lived outside of Spearfish.

We were working on a special made-to-order bike and had contacted Arvin. Sure enough, he'd had a few prime parts we were after. We'd also found some specialty items Lock and I had wanted for the shop.

Willy adjusted his goggles, his lid fitted over his thick gray hair brushing down his neck. "Let's get on home."

I stared at him as he gunned his engine.

In my first years as a Jack, Willy and Wreck used to say that very same phrase when we'd be on the last leg of a long run. To me, it had always been a throwaway saying, old-fashioned, a cliché. I'd be exhausted from hours in the saddle, from too much partying, only wanting a couple of beers to knock me out and a real bed to collapse on. I'd roll my eyes and groan when I'd hear it come out of their mouths.

Looking back on it, it was the *way* those two used to say that phrase along with a quick, purposeful glance at each other, each and every time. It was as if they had known something the rest of us didn't.

Those words had never sounded so good to me.

I raised my chin at Butler. "Let's get on home."

Butler got into the passenger side and slammed the door shut.

My phone rang. *Dawes.* "Hey, we're just leaving."

His sharp intake of breath over the line made me still. My hand clutched the door of my truck. "Dawes?"

"You gotta get back quick, man."

"What is it?"

"Mindy. It's Mindy." His voice was low, almost choking.

"What about her? She causing problems again?"

"No. Someone shut her mouth for her."

"What?"

"We found her this morning on the back gate off the track."

"What are you talking about?"

"We found her body hanging off the old gate. There was a crowbar on the ground, covered in blood and—fuck, it's bad, man. It's bad." His voice shook. "Jump is freaking out."

My eyes squeezed shut. "Where do you have her now?"

He cleared his throat, sniffing in air. "Dealing with it. What the fuck is going on, Boner?" Dawes whispered hoarsely.

"Do what you got to do. We're just leaving now."

"Okay, okay."

I got us back to Meager in record time.

"Holy fuck," muttered Butler at the photo Dawes had taken of Mindy's body hanging off the fence. An unwanted doll ditched in the garbage teetering on the edge of the can.

Her face was unrecognizable, her long brown hair matted with blood, and her clothes were ripped and soaked in red, her body broken.

I deleted the photo.

"This isn't Catch. He's crazy, but he isn't vicious like this," Butler said. "This is just fucking over the top. You're gonna have to work hard to convince me this is him."

"It's not him," I said.

"Well, it's a fucking message. Someone's watching us. Are they fucking with Jump? The whole thing with Alicia put Mindy on the map."

"She was leaving town," said Dawes, his arms wrapped around his middle. "One of the girls said Mindy had already packed up her shit at her apartment and was planning on leaving this weekend. Just like she had been told to do. What the fuck?"

I stared at the crowbar at my feet in the grass, my eyes following the long line, the curve of its head. I recognized the incisions, the notches on the lower left edge. My hands flexed on instinct.

It was my crowbar.

My piece of iron was covered in so much blood and bone—and not just Mindy's. Etched with marks from my many early successes. I had left it behind in Denver, a wild, stupid gesture. A fuck-you to Inés. A fuck-you to Alejandro Calderón.

And now, he was fucking me right back.

THIRTY-FIVE

JILL

"Perfect," I murmured to myself.

Six new T-shirts for Boner, washed and ready to be worn. Three black and three charcoal-gray T-shirts, each one bearing a different graphic design—discreet, hip, nothing too crazy trendy. One had Johnny Cash's name and guitar on it in a faded print. Two of them sported Harley-Davidson graphics that I'd picked up from the store in Rapid. One was from his favorite local craft brewery. The other two were simple V-necks that were a fitted cut, close to the torso, a little sexier than the usual boxy, loose fit. I folded them, smoothing out the fabric on each one, and made a neat square pile on his bed.

Boner had given me a key to his house so that I could drop off a few things, if I wanted, to make life easier for us. Being able to spend time together was a last-minute thing usually. I'd brought over a small package of diapers, a toothbrush, underwear, the baby-doll nightie, and a pair of comfy leggings and a T-shirt to keep handy here in his room.

I went through the drawer with his T-shirts and took out the really old, faded, and worn ones. At least ten of them. I planned on putting these in a corner of another drawer, just in case he didn't want to part with them. I knew better than to dictate fashion to a man like Boner who seemed only comfortable in a certain zone. I wanted him to find the new ones in the morning when he went to get dressed, and hopefully, he'd enjoy the surprise.

On the whole, his clothes were arranged neatly. It was pretty darn impressive. I kept all the things I'd brought over tucked in a tote bag in his closet. I didn't want to make any sort of mess or create visual disorder in here.

Something hard slid against the wood of the drawer, and I peeked over the edge of it. A small photograph in a simple brass frame. A woman and a boy with very short hair. *Oh, those eyes.* They both had the same incredible large, luminescent green eyes.

Boner and his mother. It had to be.

She was beautiful. Dark hair, slender face, pale skin. She stood behind him, her arms wrapped over his chest, her face pressed against his. Same heart-stopping, sincere smile. A huge smile. Boner's arms were raised and wrapped around his mother's neck. Eager for her touch, delighting in her affection. He was gloriously happy.

My ribs squeezed. What had happened to this boy?

It wasn't that Boner didn't smile or laugh or enjoy himself, he did. Outwardly, he seemed very content with his life, but this sort of beaming, excited joy was not the man I knew. The man I knew was careful, guarded, his soul reined in, not on display. Here, the joy was positively electric.

I chewed on my lip. I was supposed to be putting clothes in his drawers, not inspecting his personal items.

I put the frame back in the bottom of the drawer, and my fingertips brushed soft suede. I pushed back the shirts, and pulled out a black suede pouch with small round bead-like shapes inside it. I tugged opened the silken drawstrings on the pouch and drew out a long necklace with a series of dark red stones. I held it up, and two chains dangled in the air before me. It was broken. This was a Roman Catholic rosary. But there was no cross pendant hanging from it. The cross was missing.

I fingered the end of the rosary. *Was it his mother's?*

There was a violence in the missing cross and the broken chain. My imagination was running away with me. Maybe this was just some trinket he'd picked up somewhere?

But no. I'd seen his house. There were no frivolous or sentimental objects, no decorations anywhere. Boner wore jewelry, but it was always silver chains or leather cords with small charms like a snake or his One-Eyed Jack skull. This was an authentic rosary, too, not one of those trendy-necklace type ones.

I tucked the rosary back into the pouch.

"What are you doing?"

I pivoted at the sound of his voice, my lungs pinching in my chest.

"Oh! I was—I did some laundry, and I was just putting it away for you."

He filled the doorway, staring at me, his hair full around his face ending just past his shoulders, his dark brows forming a ridge over those green eyes, his lips pursed under his mustache.

Heart-stoppingly beautiful. Heart-stoppingly threatening.

"Laundry?" His deep voice snapped at me. "I don't want you doing my laundry. You don't have to do that shit for me. Been doing it all my life. Don't have to have a woman do it for me."

"Actually, I, uh, went shopping, and I got you a few new T-shirts. I washed them, and I was just putting them away for you. I wanted you to be surprised when you got dressed."

"Oh. " His lips twisted, his jaw set. "Thanks."

"You're welcome."

"What's in your hand, Jill?"

Shit. The suede pouch was in my grip. I held it up. "I found this. I'm sorry. I didn't mean to—"

He quickly closed the distance between us and plucked the pouch from my hands.

"I'm sorry."

"It's fine."

"Bone, it's obviously not fine. You're—"

"I'm, what?"

"Is it your mother's?" I asked. "The rosary?"

His face darkened. "Yeah, it was hers."

"It's missing the cross."

His eyes leveled with mine, and I braced. "I ripped it off her hands in her coffin, and the cross got torn off."

My breath caught.

That sharp-edged honesty, that unmistakable frankness was as an iron bell clanging loudly. An ugly, jarring sound, but it was truth, and it had to be told.

"The stones are lovely. Are they garnets?" I asked.

"Yeah, garnets." His shoulders dropped. "She loved that deep red color. It was her favorite." He tucked the pouch in the drawer and slammed it closed.

"What was your mother's name?"

"María Angélica," he said slowly.

The slight lilt in his pronunciation skipped through me.

"That's beautiful."

"It is. She was beautiful, too."

For a moment, his face had a faraway look to it, his tired gaze drifting before returning to me. The need to wash the sorrow off him came over me.

But how?

His face remained grim. I'd pissed him off with my questions. I shouldn't have been such a Curious George.

He shifted his weight. "I was on my way to see you. Sy and Bear are gonna be watching over you. I'd put you on lockdown, but that isn't going to work too well with Tania being out of town again. No daycare or classes for Becca for a while. You don't do any driving. The boys will. You need to take Rae somewhere or go to the supermarket, call Alicia. She'll organize something with the old ladies."

"What is it? What's wrong?"

"Just do as I said." His voice was firm, cold.

"I will." My lungs contracted. "But—"

"You need to trust me."

THIRTY-SIX

JILL

"YOU'RE NOT HUNGRY?" I stared at his full bowl of black bean chili I'd made for us. It was untouched, the melted grated cheddar cheese on top looking more like melted plastic.

"Huh?" Boner turned to me.

"Since when are you not hungry?" I put my empty bowl on the small table to my side of the log bench where we sat on the front porch of his house the following day. The red-orange sun sank on the horizon in the distance.

"I drank too much coffee today. Bothered me." Boner rubbed a hand back and forth across his stomach, right over his scar.

We had managed to get another night to ourselves to spend at his house, and this time Becca had come with me. She was already asleep in her new crib upstairs. We'd managed to get her to sleep without a problem even though I'd thought that, since she was in a new environment, maybe she'd be anxious about it. She'd had an active enough day, exploring the house, enjoying the staircase a bit too much for my liking, and coloring nonstop.

"Becca loves that room."

"That's good 'cause it's hers."

"I think she liked the stuffed baby elephant most of all," I said. "Pony must be very jealous and lonely tonight on the floor by himself."

He let out a sigh. "Yeah, poor Pony."

Boner remained distracted this evening, even distant.

"Are you okay?" I asked, lightly touching his thigh.

He took my hand in his and squeezed. "Enjoying the quiet with you."

His other hand smoothed down over the new T-shirt he wore, one of the tighter cut ones I had bought for him. A few dark springs of hair peeked over the V-necked opening on his chest. I wanted to slide onto his lap and kiss him there, but something in his mood was different, and a sudden sense of awkwardness stopped me from making such an impulsive move.

"How early do you have to leave for your run tomorrow?" I asked.

"Before six." His thumb rubbed over my hand.

"How long will you be gone for this time?"

"Few days. Depends."

"Is there something you're not telling me?"

His gaze settled on me like a heavy snowfall. "Plenty."

Forthright, yet oblique! Gah.

"I don't mean club business. I feel like something's upset you. Was it me finding the rosary?"

"No."

"Well, you're keeping something from me."

He took in a breath and released it. "I don't keep shit from you."

"Okay." I swallowed the old insecurities down my throat like thick cough syrup. "Except for one thing."

It's now or never. "Who is she?" I asked.

"What? Who?"

"I'll show you."

I let go of his hand and headed inside to the bookcase, Boner following me. I grabbed the Neruda and held out the scraps of poetry to him.

His face visibly hardened.

"I found more," I said. "All over the house. Tortured verses— *beautiful* tortured verses about a woman. A woman you're still clinging to." My voice barely above a whisper, I said, "She's everywhere, Bone. You've surrounded yourself with her."

"I haven't written in a long time." He brought his palms to his forehead and took in a breath. "Those are…fuck."

"Tell me. Why can't you tell me?"

His hands dropped from his face. "It's Inés."

"Your cousin?" I spluttered.

"Yeah, my cousin." His voice was heavy, caustic.

I held his dark emerald gaze, my heart shrinking. "Oh."

His tongue swiped at his lip.

"Tell me," I breathed.

"After I killed her dad, Inés and I took off, but we had nowhere to turn but the drug dealers I'd been working for. I had no choice. We would've gone into foster care or a home, detention center, something. Us getting separated—there was no way that was going to happen. The dealers helped us lay low, even planted evidence to get the heat off of us in the murder investigation.

"We camped out in people's basements, in warehouses, and trailers for weeks on end. We finally got our own place, this tiny shit-box. We were working, bringing money in." He stared into the distance, his jaw set. "I thought we were so lucky."

It slammed into me like a brutal January wind on the plains. "You were in love with her," I said.

"Yes."

"You—"

His eyes flared. "She was my first cousin and my best friend, but being together was the only thing that made sense to us and the only thing that kept us whole—at least for a while. There was no wrong or right. We never discussed it. It was the way it was. It was a given." He let out a deep exhale. "It was fucked up, and we both knew it in the back of our minds, but there was no stopping it."

"You loved her."

"I loved her." He pressed his lips together.

A simple statement of powerful fact, undeniable.

"But she was sick," he said, his voice dropping.

"Sick?"

"Bipolar. She used to have these dramatic, unpredictable mood swings. Ridiculously happy and excited about life one day and then sad and anxious the next. She'd be making grand plans for us at all hours—not eating, not sleeping. Then, the next day or the day after, it would crush her. She suddenly couldn't make a decision about anything, not even something simple like if she should close her closet door or leave it slightly open. One day, smiling, and later on, a crying jag, distant, irritated with the world, irritated with me. She wouldn't eat and wouldn't take her meds most days. I got her what I could, tried to keep her on some sort of schedule, but that never worked, and that wasn't good. Then, she started using."

His shoulders scrunched up, and in that fleeting movement, the strain of the burden he'd been carrying pressed in on me.

"What happened to her?"

"Men were always noticing her, thinking she was older than she actually was. She was pretty and real tall. She used to do some modeling."

My stomach rolled at the controlled tone of his voice.

"Depending on her mood," he continued, "she'd either hate their attention or want more of it. Same went for me. She'd either push me away or couldn't get enough of me. It made me insane. My not being around too much because of work only made things worse.

"She started doing crazy shit. Once, I caught her fucking a guy from our neighborhood at our apartment. We got into a fight, and she left with him. Then, she came crawling back a couple of days later, begging for my forgiveness. I was furious but more relieved that she was okay. It got to the point where I just didn't care about much else, other than if she was okay.

"A few months later, it happened again, but this time, she was fucking the dealers I worked for. They ran a gang, and I owed them for everything, for covering my killing my uncle, for making me the man I'd become. She packed up her stuff and took off with them. She was done with me. I got into a fight with them over her in the street." He rubbed over his middle, my eyes following the sudden movement. "She knifed me, and they took off. I ended up getting arrested on a trumped up assault charge, and I got thrown into juvie."

"How old were you?"

"Seventeen."

"Seventeen?" My stomach churned. "Did you ever see her again?"

"Yeah. Dig and I met in juvie. We broke out together and found her. But she didn't want to be found by me." He raked a hand through his hair, bunching it in his grip. "We had it out, but she wouldn't leave with me. She wanted to stay.

"Me and Dig got out of Denver that night. That was when we got these tats." His fingers grazed over his twisted fanged snake. "I didn't care where we went, as long as we went somewhere. Eventually, we ended up here.

"Are you still in love with her?" I whispered. "That's why you—"

"I hate her." His voice jolted through me like an electrical current, his eyes stony. "I hate her for giving up, for giving in. I kept fighting for both of us in any way I could. I killed for us, stole, destroyed people, but none of it mattered in the end. She gave it all away."

"She was sick. Maybe she couldn't—"

"Yeah, but she made lousy choices over and over again. She could've fought for herself, for us. Taken a stand, made a commitment. Why not? I did. Every fucking day, I did." His voice was harsh, loud. "You did!"

I cradled his face with my hands. "Baby—"

"I killed my uncle—my mother's only brother—and I became an animal. And then I was groomed to become a higher grade of animal. I only got us deeper into the filth, and there was no way out, but I'd never abandoned her. No matter how shitty things got, how rough, how ugly, I never did. But she made her play, and she abandoned me."

"Have you talked to her or seen her since?"

He pulled away from me, his head jerking back, his hair covering a flaring green eye. "No."

The savage wild child.

Yes, just like the young boy I'd once read about who had been discovered in a French forest in the eighteenth century. Deprived of human contact all his life, living alone, he'd become a wild animal. But after being taken in by a man who cared for him and patiently taught him language, gave him the affection and tenderness he'd never known before, the wild child had proven to be an ordinary boy—not deaf, not mute, not mentally handicapped, not a savage as everyone had initially assumed.

Simply a boy.

Santiago.

I threw my arms around him and pressed my face to his chest. "Don't hate her anymore. Don't. It's been long enough. God, enough."

His chest heaved under me, and he dug his hands in my hair, yanking my head back. "You fight. Over and over again. You fought for yourself to get over your hell. You're still looking for a better way, a good day." His wet sea-green eyes loomed over me, taking my breath away. "You don't complain. You fall, you pick yourself up, you go on, and then you give to those around you—to your kid, to Rae, to Grace, the baby you're carrying."

"It's not easy," I said.

"That's right. It's not." He let out a rough breath. "You're bright, Jill, so fucking bright to me."

"I have to live in that bright, or I'm going to break." Tears spilled down my face, his grip on me tightening.

I had to stop him from slipping back into the emotional hell of his past that he'd been clinging to, to that futility.

"I want you there with me," I whispered. "With me and Becca."

He let go of me and pressed his fists into the sides of his head. "I keep trying to fix it in my head, but it won't fix."

"You are not these pieces, Bone. They are a part of you, yes, but *you* are not these fragments, these pieces of scrap paper crumpled, rolled into a ball, shoved in between books, and stuffed into drawers or forgotten pockets."

I held up the one poem.

"You write because your heart is aching. It's full. It needs to deal with all that rage, all that broken love. You're in pieces, and you can't bear it."

"Stop it."

"It doesn't have to be this way."

Tears spilled down his face. "It's always been this way."

His broken voice shattered me. Despair, shame, hopelessness.

My muscles tightened. "You are a good person. You take care of your friends, your brothers. Mr. Dependable. You being the eccentric one works for you, doesn't it? You lay low. No one worries about Boner, do they? *Boner—he's a fun guy, a little strange, but you can count on him when you need the nastiest job done right. You don't want to get on his bad side though. He might pull a knife on you, flip out at a moment's notice. That's just the kind of crazy he is.*"

"I am crazy," he rasped.

I leaned in closer to him. "Your heart is so full that you keep it close to your ribs and only share it with a chosen few. I'm proud to be one of those few. I've told you before, and I'll say it again. I can feel that heart of yours, baby—in your hands, in your mouth, in those eyes, in your words. And I love what I feel."

"Jill—"

"Inés was the last one to call you Santiago, wasn't she? That's why you had that reaction when I said your name that night on the sofa."

His eyes flashed. "Yes."

My heart ached.

"I love your name. It's beautiful," I said, my voice shaky.

I stroked the side of his face with my hand, and his eyes fluttered closed.

"I wish I could make it better for you. I wish I could call you by the name your mother gave you and make you happy to hear it again. But if it's nothing but pain for you, I won't. Ever. I promise."

His eyes opened and held mine. Green fire. "Say it."

A chill raced down my spine as his fingers dug into my upper arms.

"Say it."

I stood on my toes and gently brushed his lips with mine, my eyes never leaving his. "Santiago," I whispered. I kissed him again on the corner of his mouth. "Santiago." Another kiss. "Santiago." I swept my tongue over the seam of his full lips, and they parted, a ragged sigh escaping his mouth.

"Santiago."

Absolution in the utterance, the declaration, the kiss of his name.

"I won't let you go, Santiago. I won't. Hold onto me and don't let me go."

He buried his face in my neck and held me tight. My fingers brushed over the light trail of hair down his abs under his shirt, and I moved to the floor between his legs. I pulled down his sweatpants and took them off his legs.

His form went rigid. "Jill—"

I wrapped my fingers around his stiff cock and stroked his hard length. "I want to make you feel good."

"Firefly."

"I want to make my old man feel good."

His chest rose on an intake of breath. His head falling back, he let out a small groan. My lips nuzzled his lean middle and his tight wall of muscles, which shuddered under my touch.

"Baby—"

I took his cock into my mouth and sucked long and deep and slow. My one hand stroked his base, the other curling around his rigid thigh.

Wash the sorrow from him.

His hips rocked toward me as he let out a long hiss of air. "Fuck, Jill."

I let out a moan as I took him in quicker. I wanted him to explode in my mouth. I wanted to swallow him whole, shake him to his core, claim every last drop of him.

His hands dug into my hair and twisted as his pelvis moved. "Fuck! Yes. Ah, shit. Shit, Jill! Your fucking mouth." He gasped, as if he were in pain, an unrelenting delicious pain—of which, he only wanted more. "Suck it harder. Don't fucking stop. Oh…oh, fuck. Jill, Jill. Oh, yeah…"

He chanted my name over and over again as he watched me, his breaths ragged. My mouth ached, my neck stiffened, my knees hurt, but I didn't give a shit. I wanted him to come, to come big, and I wanted to swallow it all. All my admiration and thrill for him went into my lips and tongue and throat, taking him in, taking him higher.

I worshipped, I revered, I venerated.

His glorious thick cock throbbed and pulsed against the back of my throat. My one hand stroked and rubbed his balls with my spit as both his hands fisted tightly in my hair. He grunted loudly, his eyes glinting at me.

"Fuck, look at you. You're taking me all the way in, aren't you, Firefly? Ah, shit, all the way. So good. So fucking good."

My heart soared, and my fingers dug into his hard rear as I took him all in.

"I'm coming, Firefly. I'm coming for you."

His body suddenly stiffened against me, and thick warm spurts filled my throat as he groaned. I sucked and swallowed until he went limp in my mouth. He lifted me up his sweaty body and held me, his choppy breathing filling my ear.

He took me upstairs to his bed where he peeled my clothes off. His mouth explored every curve of my enflamed body until I trembled. This was need. This was aching for something greater, higher, fuller. I ached for *him*—not just a high or a release, but for this man. His every touch had significance. His every kiss was a promise.

A tremor surged through me. "Take me, take me."

Boner entered me with one long, slow thrust. He made love to me, our breaths mingling, as we clung to each other. He laid a trail of kisses across my throat as he moved inside me.

Surging over me, he pressed his mouth against my ear, his choked groans filling my soul.

"You have me. That feeling in there?" His hand pressed into my chest. "That's me wrapped around your heart, squeezing. I love you, Firefly."

He thrust deep inside me, and I came, my hands digging into his hair, relishing the thick ropes of silk between my fingers as my heart exploded.

He let out a low moan. "If that bright life could come true, I'd want it with you."

THIRTY-SEVEN

JILL

BONER WOKE ME UP the next morning with his fingers between my legs, his mouth at my neck. Groaning softly in my ear, he slid into me from behind, and I gripped his hand at my breast, pushing back against him. His hair cascaded over my shoulder, like a silk shawl. He took us to a sweet, sweet place, sweeping us over a rich, tender crest of sensation.

After, I watched him dress in the darkness, hiding half of my face in the pillows. "What time is it?"

"Five," he replied.

He soundlessly moved about the bedroom in the dark, like a creature of the night. Fingers skidded across my shoulders. My hair was pushed off to the side, and his lips brushed my skin.

"Can I make you coffee before you go? Breakfast?"

"I'll grab something at the clubhouse. Go back to sleep." He stroked the side of my face, his hair creating a light drape around us.

"Be careful. Please."

"Always am." He leaned over and planted a kiss on my belly.

"Be extra careful now." I reached for him and pulled him to me, kissing him. His mouth tasted minty. "Extra, extra careful, okay? For me."

His eyes pulled together, and he drew his index finger down over my lips.

"All for you, Jillee."

And then he was gone.

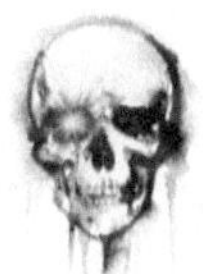

Soon after I'd gotten out of bed, Becca had woken up, and I changed her and then got her and myself dressed. I made her a cream cheese and strawberry jam sandwich, and she nibbled at it while she colored at the kitchen table.

I wandered around the house, holding my cup of tea, my free hand tracing over the wainscoting in the hallway.

The slight chill in the air had me invading Boner's closet, where I'd found a faded black hoodie on a shelf with about five other similar hoodies. I brushed my cheek against the worn smooth cotton as I curled up in a corner of the sofa and sipped on my tea. The soft pink-orange glow of dawn was now a stronger yellow filtering through the bay window, and I smiled to myself.

I glanced at the impressive fireplace and the high wall of stone over it.

This house was Boner's quiet castle of solitude away from the uproar of the clubhouse, but wasn't it big for a man alone? A man who had been an adamant bachelor all his adult life? Why invest money in it, work on it, if he wasn't planning on filling it with his own family one day?

My toes curled into the sofa cushion as I pretended for a second that this was my house, and I could wander around in it and feel completely comfortable in it.

But I already do feel comfortable in it.

There I was, like a teenager with my out-of-wedlock kid living in my ex-boyfriend's childhood room. Camped out and cramped with all of my and Becca's earthly possessions, but we did enjoy living with Rae and Tania. I liked living with women who had positive energy. I hadn't had that in a long while.

I belonged and would always belong, thanks to my daughter.

And here was Boner, all alone in this roomy house. Clean, organized, able to be filled, yet he kept it empty.

We were on opposite ends of the spectrum.

My gaze lingered on the open kitchen with its sleek tiled countertop, dark wood floors, and black-and-stainless steel appliances. Maybe he didn't want to be alone. Maybe in the back of his mind he was hoping, preparing, wishing for another kind of future.

I moved to put my mug on the coffee table. A big piece of paper lay there with *Firefly* written in big letters in Boner's handwriting. Writing was visible on the other side of it, and I turned the paper over.

A poem.

A new poem.

A poem about a firefly.

He wrote a poem for me.

For me.

For me.

For me.

He'd said he hadn't written anything in a long while, and all the others had been about her.

But now, there was me.

Me and Boner.

A shiver raced over my neck, and warmth flooded my insides at the memory of our lovemaking last night. His lips at my ear, his shaky voice uttering incendiary words just for me.

And now this gorgeous poem. I pressed the paper against my chest, my eyes closing.

My man, my lover, my heartbeat.

My phone pinged with a text. I grabbed it from the coffee table.

Grace.

Where's your old man? LOL Is he avoiding me?

I laughed and tapped the button to call her.

"Good morning," I said.

"Oh, geez. Did I wake you? I didn't realize it was so early. I'm sorry."

"No, not at all. I'm sitting here in Boner's house, drinking herbal tea, and Becca's coloring."

"Oh shoot! That explains it then."

"What's that?" I asked.

"I've been trying to reach him since last night, but he hasn't been answering. I intruded on your special night together. I'm sorry."

"He didn't say that you'd called, and I didn't hear his phone ring at all."

"He actually shut his ringer off? Wow, he never does that. Good for him. I hope it was a really, really special night then. Is he still asleep?"

"Grace, he's not here. He left first thing this morning with the guys."

"He did?"

"They went on a run somewhere. He said he was meeting everyone at the club and taking off."

"Really? Wait, hang on."

Grace asked Lock about a run, and his deep voice was muffled in the background over the line. Lock usually didn't go on runs, with Eagle Wings being so busy.

"Honey, there's no run anywhere. In fact, everyone's been told to stay put," said Grace, her voice thinner than before.

The hairs on the back of my neck stood at attention. "But Boner made it sound like he would be with Butler and Kicker."

"No, Jill, nobody left."

Something cold and hard coated my chest. "But he left first thing, just after five."

"Did he tell you where?"

"No, he just said…"

"If that bright life could come true, baby, I'd want it with you."

If.

If?

He'd told me he loved me, said good-bye, and left me a poem, a testament of his soul.

I clutched the phone tighter. "Grace, he's been acting a little strange lately. Moody, withdrawn, emotional."

"Honey, none of those things are strange for him."

"True, but he's been different the past couple of days. I've felt it. Last night, he told me about his life in Denver—before the One-Eyed Jacks."

"He did?" The surprised tone in her voice was unmistakable.

"Do you know anything about what happened, why exactly he left Denver? He said he'd never shared it with anyone—just with Dig, of course—but I was wondering if you had any insight because…" I took in a breath to squash the wave of emotion that threatened to crash over me.

"Jill, what is it?"

"I think he went back to Denver today, and it may not be a good thing," I whispered.

"Oh, shit."

My stomach hardened. "What is it? What do you know?"

She let out a heavy exhale. "The only thing Dig ever told me was that, back in Denver, right before they'd left, he had helped Boner kill someone."

"Who? Who was it?"

"Some local drug dealer, a gang-leader type who was Boner's boss."

"Boner killed him?"

"Yes. Because of a girl."

I squeezed my eyes shut. *Inés.*

"Dig only told me because it was the first time he'd ever witnessed a kill like that. They were teenagers back then. It had blown him away. It was that awful."

"What do you mean?"

"Boner used an iron crowbar."

"Smashing bones turned into a high-paying job though. It became my trademark. I was real popular in certain circles."

"They ran, they left Denver that night. Boner's never been back since, he always said he couldn't go back."

My stomach clenched, my head swirled, a sour brew boiled in the back of my throat.

"Jill, Boner doesn't know that I know that. I've never brought it up, and he's never shared. Jill? Jill? Are you there?"

THIRTY-EIGHT

BONER

AFTER ALMOST SIX HOURS ON THE ROAD, I entered the Denver city limits on I-25. I flexed my gloved fingers on my handlebars and stretched my back as I lowered my speed in traffic.

I had returned to do what I had to do.

Here I was, running toward the very thing that had threatened me for so long, toward what had kept me running all these years.

And even though it filled me with dread, a lightness seeped through my chest, and a slight grin stole over my lips. I hadn't realized it earlier, but I now knew with conviction that the running in my heart and soul had finally ended.

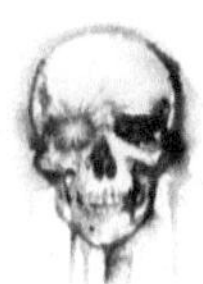

PAST

The cops were the ones who picked me up off the pavement after the Calderóns had taken off with Inés. Following a trip to the ER to sew me up, I got hauled off to jail on assault and attempted robbery charges. Some guy had been paid to play the victim, saying he'd slashed me in self-defense. It wasn't difficult to find witnesses on the street who were more than willing to tell the Calderóns' well-paid version of the God's honest truth.

I knew it was only a matter of time until I got implicated in my uncle's death, if not any of the many, many other deaths and assaults for which I was responsible. I'd be in prison all my life or on death row in no time.

Fuck no.

Not for them.

Not for her.

I ended up in a juvie detention center. I got into plenty of fights, starting most of them myself, but one guy didn't take the bait. Only one—Jake Pence, who would later become the One-Eyed Jacks' Dig Quillen.

"Relax your ass already," he said to me after dragging me out of yet another confrontation. "Lay low for fuck's sake. Use it when it counts."

He had a mop of dirty-blond hair and a get-the-fuck-out-of-my-face glower permanently engraved on his pretty-boy anglo features.

Jake sure as hell didn't look like he belonged in juvie with the rest of us. Juvie wasn't about making friends, but we'd gravitated toward each other. He was like me—couldn't sit still, burning to get out, burning to be free of other people's power over him. I saw it in his cold sand-colored eyes, in the set of his jaw, in the way he didn't talk to anyone.

Anyone but me.

We hung out, made a plan, bided our time. One night, it all clicked into place, and we ran. We made it onto the roof and jumped over and down into a dumpster where we waited in the muck until the truck came to haul it away hours later.

We were free.

"You still want to find her?" Jake asked as we sat on a curb, devouring half-eaten burritos we'd found in a garbage can.

"I have to."

"True love sure is one fucked up proposition," he muttered wiping his fingers on his dirty jeans.

"I gotta talk sense into her."

"If that's what you want, but we need to get the hell out of here."

A group of young boys kicked around a soccer ball in the street in front of us. They looked about the same age I'd been when my mother died.

"I can't imagine my life without her, man. She's always been there for me, and I can't just leave her behind. Bottom line, before we go, I need to make sure she's okay."

Jake shrugged. "Let's get this over with."

Two days later we found her. She was shopping at this small pricey boutique.

"Inés."

Her tense eyes met mine. They swam in something I had no part of, like a strange liquor or a strong expensive perfume.

Was she afraid of me, as if I were some sort of stranger?

She had lots of makeup on, new clothes. She was someone else.

I blurted out my speech about how I forgave her, how everything would be better from now on. We'd finally leave Denver and it would be the two of us again, the way it was meant to be, the way it had always been; all we'd ever known.

"Santiago, I can't come with you. I don't want to."

"They've got you confused. Don't you see? You're their prisoner. For what? For their money? Their attention?"

"They're good to me."

"Good to you? No. They're not good at all." I grabbed her arm. "Let's go, Inés. Come on."

"Stop it. Let go of me."

"I can't!" I spit out, shuddering. "I can't."

"Yes you can. You have to!"

"No."

"I'm pregnant."

A punch landed in my chest. My head spun. "What?"

"I said, I'm pregnant."

I grabbed her hands to steady myself, to feel that connection to her again, especially now. But her hands were cold, and she yanked them from my grip.

I stumbled. "Is it mine? I mean, it could be mine, right?"

"I don't know, Santiago!" She raised her voice, her face a bitter sneer.

I'd asked her an odious, vile question that she never wanted to answer. I was annoying her.

Fuck her.

"You don't know?" I repeated, my soul getting sucked out of me, my heart thundering in my chest, blood rushing in my ears. "You don't know? You don't know! Why don't you know?"

The salesgirl in the store backed away from us, her face pale.

Tears filled Inés's eyes, her head fell to the side. "I don't know!"

"We gotta go, man. Just take her, and let's go!" Jake yelled from the doorway.

"I'm not going anywhere." Her face tightened, and she folded her arms.

Clack, clack, clack went her high heels on the polished floor of the boutique as she stepped away from me.

I shook from the inside out. My body swayed.

I tore my shirt up. The angry red scar hadn't healed. It still sizzled on my skin. "This is what you did to me. Look at me! You cut me. Why? Why?"

"No, no." She shook her head, her hands stretched out. "I didn't. I couldn't. No."

"You did this to me." My voice seethed. "You. What have they done to you?"

Her back straightened, she blinked. "You don't understand, Santiago. You never will because you're a boy. They're men. People listen to them. People look up to them."

"People are afraid of them, you little fool."

She raised her chin. "I'm not afraid of them. I love them, and I don't want to leave."

Love. The word we'd used together, for each other. Now, it wasn't ours anymore. Not anymore. She had tipped a cauldron of molten tar over me with that goddamn word.

"We've got to go!" Jake yelled.

"Go, Santi. Please go." Inés said, her voice suddenly soft, pleading, her hands twisting at her sides. "If they find you here, they'll kill you."

"You already did," I breathed.

Jake grabbed me by the arm, and we tore out of the back of the shop and down the street to the corner.

The fucking Coronet glided to a halt in front of the store.

That night, I got my crowbar from its hiding place in the basement of my old rathole building. "You in?" I glanced over at

Jake as I pulled the iron bar from behind the brick shelf, my limbs lightening at the familiar weight in my hands. "I get it if you ain't."

"I'm in. Sure as fuck," he said, those odd light-brown eyes of his gleaming like tarnished gold coins in the glare of the flashlight he held for me.

"You take this." I tossed him my 9mm.

I slid the plastic baggie with my mother's rosary and the photograph of us out of its hiding place behind a loose brick and tucked it in my jacket pocket.

We found Julio, and he suggested a junkyard that was one of the Executioner's new domains. Felipe was lingering there at about four in the morning with a flunky who was out taking a piss.

Jake got the bodyguard from behind with a knife to his side as I garroted him with a wire cord. His thrashing in our hold, his struggling, his helplessness made me high. Grunting, we finally dropped his lifeless body to the ground.

I approached Felipe, and I didn't even have to say a word. He raised his gun at me, and Jake shot it out of his hand. The crowbar was alive in my grip, conforming to my palm like the soft and unbending iron it was for me. The weeks away hadn't changed that. It propelled me forward—again and again and again through Felipe's howls, through the splintering cracks, through the thuds. The force of my hate and the fury of my rage empowered me. The authority of my anger was so loud, it made me wild.

Inés's voice saying *"love"* fueling me.

"Enough!" Jake dragged me away. "Jesus!"

I hurled that fucking iron crowbar on Felipe's broken, mangled body.

I was covered in blood, bone, gunk, sweat, and grief.

So much grief.

Jake and I ran, becoming a part of the shifting shapes of the darkness. He got us out of Denver, out of Colorado. He had thought ahead, had made detailed plans for us, and I followed, grateful he'd taken on that burden.

I was burnt from the inside out.

We ended up heading for Utah in the back of a truck crammed with fertilizer.

"We're never going back," Jake muttered. His head sank onto his knees, his body shuddering.

Poor kid. All that adrenaline had finally run its course, and all that blood and gore had shaken him up. He'd never killed anyone before this.

I leaned my head back against a crate, the stench of manure unbearable.

"Thank you," I whispered into the shadows between us.

I couldn't remember when I'd last said those words, and I meant them now. It was a relief, it was the truth. He could have called me insane and taken off, but he hadn't. Jake had seen this through with me. He'd had my back. No one had had my back for such a long time.

A long, long time.

"You don't have to thank me." Jake wiped at his eyes. "That felt good. Freaked me the fuck out, but it was good." He sat up straight. "You know shit. You know shit I want to learn, and you're going to teach me. 'Cause that's the only way from here on in. The only way."

I raised my head and was met with hard eyes. Eyes blazing with determination.

What had burned me, had lit him on fire.

What had drained me, had breathed new life into him.

Ah, here were demons. But were his real or were they ghosts?

"You sure? That's what you want?" I asked.

"That's what I want."

"Okay."

"Okay, good." He grinned. Brittle hope and brutal confidence.

"You ever used a gun before today?" I asked.

"Nope."

"Well, you got good aim. Got a bright future ahead of you."

He laughed.

I got him to tell me his whole fucking story, and I told him mine. Oh, his demons were real, all right. Real and bloody and unavenged.

But my fight was done.

He leaned forward. "Plenty of places for us to go. Plenty. We'll change our names, too."

"Jake, I—"

"I'll take care of everything. Don't worry about a thing. You've been through enough lately." He reached out a hand, wrapped it around my neck and squeezed. "We're in this together now."

Jake was a believer in a better day, a blacker one, but it would be a day of our own making. That was something I could believe in, that was something I could hold onto.

He lifted his chin. "You and me, Santiago."

"You and me."

A new fucking era was born for Jake Pence and Santiago Arana that night in the back of a foul smelling truck hurtling down I-70.

"Never goin' back," I murmured.

"Never," he agreed. "And never letting anybody have that power over us again."

Yeah, never sounded real good.

Never was a plan.

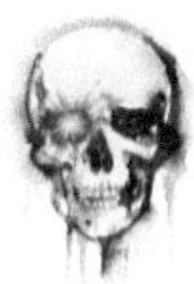

I weaved through the traffic in downtown Denver and willed those bitter images away from my vision.

That tingling numbness just beyond the scar tissue flared across my middle, reminding me of my willingness to believe over and over again. I had known it was tempting fate to have something good for myself, to have Jill. The gods of vengeance were angry at my arrogance.

At least, Alejandro Calderón was.

I steadied myself on the memory of making love to Jill last night and this morning. On the fragrance of my scented oil that she'd dabbed on her chest before we'd finally fallen asleep. On Becca's voice piping up across the hallway in the darkness—a soft babble of words, non-words, and sighs that filled my empty house.

My chest swelled.

I had achieved what I had always known I shouldn't, what Alejandro would never allow.

The last time Alejandro and I had spoken was a few weeks after Dig and I had left Denver. I had made the mistake of calling Julio, and Alejandro had answered his phone.

His voice had smoldered over the line. *"You killed my brother and now she lost my baby, you motherfucker. I will never allow you to have what you've taken away from me. Never. That's a promise."*

Yes, never.

And never was today.

THIRTY-NINE

BONER

I BELIEVED THAT HATE remains buried in our marrow. Does it ever soften? Does its power over us fade? Maybe. Maybe if you were able to forgive.

The glacial dark eyes of Alejandro Calderón told me different. His was a hate born of passion, full of fire.

A security guard had patted me down in the private elevator up to his penthouse high above Denver. The ceiling had to be over twenty feet high. The floor-to-ceiling windows wrapped around the living and dining rooms, offering a massive view of the city and the mountains beyond. Artwork crowded the walls, furniture and carpeting stifled the space.

He stared at me standing in his royal domain. He was pleased to see me. He was pleased with himself.

I nodded at him. "Look at you—a suit, a pressed shirt, five-hundred-dollar shoes, and a palace to go with it."

"The shoes cost a grand, but I wouldn't expect you to know these things, Santiago. Look at you—a piece-of-shit white-trash biker in the wilderness, speeding around in your own little Wild West rodeo."

I only lifted an eyebrow.

"I've grown up, *ese*. While you? You're stuck in the camouflage grunge of our younger days." His fingers waggled in the air, two gold rings glinting in the sunlight coming from the wall of windows. "You could have been at my side, like you were from the very beginning."

"At your side? I was your drudge, not your partner."

"You did good work, my friend. So dependable. You always went above and beyond the call of duty. You were so very responsible, too. A very unique quality. I needed you, and I took care of you. And what did you do to repay me? You killed my brother.

"Even though you were just a kid, you were the best, so focused, so vicious. You wanted to excel, and you did. No gratitude though, *El Hueso*. None. Without Felipe and me, where would you both have gone? What would you have done?"

"You wanted me to pay for that for a lifetime."

He tilted his head and made a sucking sound with his tongue behind his teeth. He held my gaze, but I gave him nothing.

"You took her, Alejandro. You used her, lied to her, made her candy-sweet promises."

His eyes lit into me, his voice puncturing my veins. "Lied to her? You never understood this, but she came to us, Santiago. She wanted us. You couldn't accept that, could you? I admit, at first, she was a new, pretty acquisition. Fun. But Felipe and I adored her. We loved her. It had been going on for weeks before she finally left you. I know, in some ways, she was…delicate, but she was always intriguing, a surprise." He took in a breath. "Our *perla negra.*"

"All this was her idea," he continued. "Us getting off the streets, leaving the bullshit pissing contests behind. The companies, the moving forward into something better than our"—he gestured at me with a flick of his tan hand—"grunge. It was hard and very bloody, but with her at my side, it was all worth it."

Inés—The face that had launched our thousand ships.

"The one horror was that you'd killed my brother like the little savage you were. That devestated her and me both, but Inés made me promise not to hurt you. She felt guilty about what she had done to you. You were family, after all."

Family. My eyes shut tight. Family didn't burn you, throw you away, leave you bleeding to die on the side of the road like an animal.

"So, I kept my word." His voice was hushed, slow. "I let you go. Thankfully, you left Denver and never came back. At least you respected me in that way. At least. But you destroyed my *Perla* in the end."

My eyes snapped open. "What are you talking about?"

"After you'd killed Felipe, she'd started doing blow regularly and had that first miscarriage. We'd gotten married, two more miscarriages, more coke, a bit of smack, eh. Sometimes, she would talk to you in her little hazes. Babbling on about some childhood nonsense or other, crying."

I clenched my jaw and looked away.

"For years she'd go on and off the medication she was supposed to be taking. 'Lithium gets in the way of the good things,' she'd say. A month ago, one night she was home alone at our country house and threw herself off our bedroom balcony."

I held his black gaze. "She killed herself?"

Alejandro lit a cigarette, some foreign brand I'd never seen before. He blew a long thick stream of smoke from his lips. "She was flying on heroin at the time. I tried to keep it away from her, but my little crazy thing, she liked it, like she liked two cocks in her. When she got emotional, there was no controlling her.

"Over the years, she would often disappoint me with the things she did or said, but she was young. The things she'd do afterward to make up for it…ah." He sucked on his cigarette, a grin searing his face. "And I loved her all the more for it. My wife was everything to me."

He offered me a cigarette, and I shook my head.

"Your girlfriend—she's a cute nugget, eh?" He tossed the pack of smokes on his desk. "Banal though." He slid his fingers down his blue silk tie. "Ah, well, they're all banal after you've had the one you know you'll never find again. Am I right?" He took a deep drag and crushed his cigarette into a huge red crystal ashtray that looked like some sort of sea creature, his eyes piercing mine through the smoke. "My *tigresa* wanted her master's blood smeared on her tits, not just my cum."

His lips moved, sound came out, but the two remained detached, separate. I wasn't registering words, thoughts, ideas. Only his fingers stroking that fucking tie was real to me. The old familiar tats around his neck crept over his smooth starched ivory collar.

Yeah, there was an elegance about him now, a refinement, so different from what I remembered of him. Back then, he had been a whip, snapping for attention, and he would revel in the sting singing in the air above him. He had once been a primitive, sadistic little beast, sporting a long mustache, with built arms and a huge chest that I was sure he'd pound like some sort of inner-city fucking Tarzan.

Now, that beast was all dressed up and speaking slowly, carefully, but the same glint was in those dark eyes. The predator. The demon. The fiend.

"Why did you wait so long, Alejandro? Why? You could've found me sooner."

"I did find you." He plucked at the stiff cuff of his shirtsleeve. "But I was waiting until you had something of worth that I could take from you. Inés made me promise not to hunt you down. She made me promise to stay away from you. She would even check to make sure I kept my promise. But she's dead now, and so is that promise."

Alejandro took in a breath of air through his nose. "Your girlfriend is pregnant. Why should you have what I didn't? You took Felipe from us, and in the end, all that *miseria* you created took my children and my woman."

"You seem to forget that you took her from me, *ese*," I said. "You took what you wanted and left me on the street to bleed. You won it all a long time ago. If it didn't end up good for you, that's on you, no one else, not me."

Alejandro grunted loudly and grabbed the red ashtray, throwing it against a wall. A shower of glinting shards and ash shattered over the rug.

"You want my life for theirs?" My voice boomed through the vast space. "Is that what you want?"

He raised that sculpted chin of his, his jaw jutting out. "Yes."

"Then take it. Take it and let them live."

FORTY

JILL

I TRIED TO GET CONTROL of my breathing, but it was nearly impossible. My hand rubbed over my chest as I counted. I should go to the clubhouse and tell the Jacks everything I knew, everything I thought might be going on.

My eyes went to the basket tray by Boner's front door. Empty.

Shit, where are my car keys?

I plowed through my handbag, my stomach twisting into those familiar knots. Nothing.

"Damn it!"

I shoved my hand under the sofa cushions, I checked under the skirt of the sofa, along the floor. Nothing.

"Unbe-freaking-lievable," I muttered. "Becca, have you been playing with Mommy's keys again?"

Becca looked up at me from coloring at the kitchen table, her lips pursed, a stubby black crayon in her hand. I went to the table piled high with her coloring books and sheets and crayons. I shuffled through the heap, pushing the jumbo box of crayons out of the way.

My keys were splayed out at the bottom of the pile. "Thank God."

Becca went back to coloring and singing to herself. My gaze landed on the coloring page she was working on, one of the many that Boner had printed out for her last night. My heart skipped as crayons rolled across the table.

There they were.

Snow White and the Prince.

She was waking up from her death slumber, and he was over the moon, taking her hand in his. My girl had colored both characters in black—Snow White's hair, her dress, her coffin, the flowers, and the Prince's hair, outfit, and boots. Becca would often get obsessed with one color and only use that particular one for everything she colored the entire day. Today, it was black.

The black prince and his black princess.

The crayons spilled over the side of the table.

"Someday, my…"

But *my* prince had come.

My prince was outlined in black and was full of dark passions and poetry, jagged heartbeats and raw whispers in the night, and he was mine. It didn't matter that he was another biker. It didn't matter that he was over a decade older than me. It didn't matter that he did not sport a cap with a feather in it or a cape along with a dashing, eager smile on his face.

My prince carried knives, guns, and brass knuckles, and he wore dirty dusty leathers, heavy boots, and faded black T-shirts and jeans. He tore through the wind on a powerful metal machine, not an elegantly appointed horse. And the smile he wore for me did not only please me, but alternatively scared me, thrilled me, and gave me a burning rush like nothing else.

My heart slammed against my ribs. I caught my reflection in the leather-framed mirror by the front door.

Magic mirror on the wall, who's the scared-est of them all?

Me.

I was the scared girl behind the polite thank-you/no-thank-you smile, who was always running to the next great idea, the next sure thing in an effort to forget, to let go, to leave the gloom, the sorrow, the insecurities behind me. I'd done it over and over again, yet each and every time, I'd bailed and moved on.

Becca had changed all that for me. She had become my new center, my joy. Providing for her, making her laugh while I fed her or read to her, hearing the ringing of that laughter as we sang goofy songs in the car, and then her sleeping peacefully at my side at the end of every day—it had grounded me in a surprising, wholly new way.

Finally finding Grace, being able to help her on her quest for motherhood, being a part of Rae's life—all of it had given me a renewed sense of family and belonging that I relished.

My hand instinctively went to my round tummy.

I was grateful, content, happy.

And Boner?

"I love you, Firefly."

My dark prince had kissed me awake in so many deep, real ways.

I needed to wake up.

Once Snow White had woken up, she hadn't hesitated for one second, had she? The moment she'd opened her eyes and seen the prince, she had known, and she had been ecstatic. She'd immediately thrown her arms out and embraced the Prince—no holding back, no wondering, no second-guessing—gotten on the back of his horse and they both went off to their own kingdom.

My dark prince had made my bright fairy tale come true.

Embrace him.

"Our bright life can come true, Bone," I whispered out loud to my reflection.

I couldn't wait. I had to find him now, and I'd need the big guns to do it. Not just the Jacks.

Finger.

Finger had connections everywhere—or at least, it seemed that way to me. He wasn't just the prez of any old MC. His Flames of Hell wielded power and influence throughout the country. People bowed down to him, licked his boots—literally.

I had witnessed that ritual one night, too, hadn't I?

My breath caught at the memory. Yes, another Catch lesson in Don't Fuck with the Flames. You Know Who's Boss, Baby.

Maybe Finger might respect the fact that I was going to him myself.

Finger never struck me as the impulsive type, not like Catch of the strike-now-pay-the-consequences-whenever-and-who-really-gives-a-fuck-anyhow-as-long-as-I-make-my-point life philosophy. Finger might give me a chance to talk to him. He might listen to what I had to say.

My stomach took a dive. I was persona non grata at the Flames. Would they even let me see Finger once I got there? Would they even let me in?

Screw it. I have to try.

Time for the Flame's Old Lady network. I dialed Krystal's number. Her old man was now Finger's Vice President. Luckily, I hadn't deleted her number from my Contacts list, like I had been tempted to do after I left Nebraska behind.

"Girlie, is that really you?"

"Hey, Krystal. Sorry it's been so long."

"I get it. How are you? Heard your news." She let out a throaty laugh. "Way to bounce back."

"Krystal, something fucked up is going on, and I need to talk to Finger. Is he at the clubhouse? I need to see him. I'm ready to get in my car now and come down."

"Seriously?"

"Very. Is he there?"

"He's here, honey, but I don't know if you're gonna be able to see him."

"This is life and death, Krystal. I have to try."

"Is it Becca? Is she okay?"

"Becca's good. This is about my old man."

She sucked in a breath. "If you're willing to try, I'll see what I can do."

"Okay."

"*Okay*, you're coming? Or *okay*, maybe you're gonna fuck with me?"

"I'm coming. My old man's life depends on it."

"Huh. That's my girl."

I tossed my phone into my bag.

"Look, Mommy! For you."

I turned around. Becca held up her black prince and princess masterpiece.

I smiled at my daughter. "It's perfect. I love it, honey. Bo will, too. Come on, sweets. We've got to go."

I swept all of Becca's coloring books, papers, and crayons into her Hello Kitty tote. She dashed over to the sofa and grabbed her elephant and baby doll, while I got her diaper bag. We put our shoes on, and I took her hand.

We flew out the door.

FORTY-ONE

JILL

"What are you doing here?" Catch walked up alongside me in the Flames clubhouse lounge.

His hand cupped Becca's cheek while I held her fast on my hip.

"Take your daughter." I placed her in his arms.

"Jill?"

"Someone's been following me the whole way from Meager. Black Ford Explorer. Two men in the front seat."

His face furrowed. "Den!" Catch shouted, his arms tightening around Becca.

"Yo!" Den raised his head from behind a computer screen at the long center table.

"Black Ford Explorer's been on Jill since she left Meager. Check it."

The Flames were diligent about their security. They had hidden cameras all over town.

"On it." The *clip-clat, clip-clat* of Den's fingers powering over his keyboard filled the air.

"They have Colorado plates," I said.

"Ah, fuck," said Catch.

"They're still in view," Den muttered. "Got him. Running the plate."

Catch's attention snapped back to me. "What the hell is going on? Why are you here?"

"Boner's missing. And I think he's in Denver."

His lips pressed together.

"I called Butler when I stopped for gas. The Jacks can't find him. He told me about the Calderóns."

Krystal appeared behind Catch. She put a hand on his back and kissed Becca on the cheek. "Hey, beautiful girl! You got so big, Becca! You remember your Aunt Krystal?"

Catch shifted his weight, adjusting Becca on his hip. "Jill—"

Krystal's gaze leveled with mine. "Come on back, babe."

I kissed Becca's hand that was reaching out to me and held Catch's gaze. "Take care of our daughter. I took the risk bringing her here, because I want to trust that she'll be safe with her father and his club. I know you and your brothers wouldn't let anything happen to her, especially after the last time."

He raised his head high. An acknowledgement of my act of trust, of faith in him and his club. I followed Krystal to the end of the common room to Finger's office.

Krystal knocked once and opened the door to the president's office. In the three years that I had been a part of the Flames, I had never once stepped into this room. I took in a breath as Krystal closed the door behind me.

Finger's hard eyes followed me as I approached his desk, studying me from top to toe. It was a subtle flick, taking in every detail. His lips rolled, as if he were chewing on something, and with the motion, the brutal "F" scars on both sides of his face deepened. The smell of tobacco and cedar was strong. He gestured for me to sit, and I did. His two missing middle fingers were a harsh reminder of the life he'd lived and now ruled over.

"Jill," said that familiar scratchy voice.

"Thank you for seeing me. I appreciate you taking the time." I sat up straight in the chair. "I came to see you because Boner's gone missing. I think he went to see this...businessman in Denver who he used to work for a long time ago, before he was a One-Eyed Jack. He has a bloody history with him. Alejandro Calderón."

Finger leaned back in his chair, his features blank, his plaid shirt opening wider at the chest, his dark hair in a low ponytail. "Why didn't you go to your own president? To the Jacks?"

"I spoke with Butler. They know he's missing, and they're in gear as we speak. But I felt strongly that I had to make sure everything possible was being done. Maybe my coming here is wrong and against the rules, and I'll get punished for it by the Jacks and you, but I had to try. I had to. I love Boner, he's a good man. I know, from the years I spent with the Flames, that if anyone could do something to save him, it would be you. I know Dig respected you, and Boner and Butler do, too. All of that makes this a really good idea to me, whatever the consequences."

Finger's eyes narrowed slightly. "You and Catch dealing with your shit? You letting him see his kid?"

"Actually, the last time he and I spoke, he threatened to sic Mishap on Boner if I didn't do what he wanted, which was to give him Becca. I'm willing to chalk that up to a father's desperation to be a part of his daughter's life and not some stupid, egotistical, reckless pissing contest that would only create unnecessary problems between good men and good clubs." I took in a breath. "Finger, I brought my daughter here today to see her dad and her other family as a show of good faith. I want to believe that all the bullshit can be wiped clean. I want to believe that we can start fresh and be fair, for all our sakes and for the good of our clubs."

The deep lines of his face eased. "I owe Boner one."

"You do?"

"That bullshit with the Python."

"Right. Well, maybe Mishap could be given a new target?"

Something resembling a glimmer flashed across his eyes.

A hard knock and the door swinging open had me turning in my seat. Catch stood in the doorway. "Finger, two of Calderón's men followed Jill here from Meager."

Finger slowly leaned back in his seat. "I got calls to make."

I shot up from the chair. "Thank you for seeing me."

I left his office, but I couldn't help glancing back at him. Finger stared after me, and I met that severe metallic gaze as the door closed behind me.

FORTY-TWO

BONER

"It's the new thing—free-trade coffee beans."

I dragged the heels of my boots across the marble floor of his office at the penthouse. I couldn't listen to Alejandro going on about the wine he was importing from Chile and Argentina or the coffee beans from El Salvador or how his numbers had doubled in just less than ten years. I supposed I was impressed that his talent for accounting had finally found a better focus than tallying up meth and crack production and their rates of distribution.

But he needed me to be impressed. *I am, motherfucker. I am.*

My eyes landed on a silver-framed photo of him and Inés that stood on his desk. My throat tightened.

The photo had to be recent, judging from his appearance. She had aged well, but the drug use had worn out her edges, her face really thin, her cheekbones jutting out. She beamed a brittle smile under her dramatic makeup. Her skinny body, wrapped in a sparkly tight dress was pressed against his. Her dark hair was cut below the chin at some strange angle, diamonds on her ears, her arm thrown around Alejandro's neck. All glamour, all glitz. The fucking red carpet.

There were several other photos of the two of them, some casual others formal, a number of portraits of her. Lots of portraits of her.

She had made her choice.

"Que en paz descanse," I said under my breath. I hoped she was at peace now.

Had she been happy, really happy? Who the fuck knew?

I didn't think she'd even known, but she'd certainly chosen a different ride from the one I'd offered. Calderón had loved her, and judging from the photos, she'd seemed to enjoy it while it lasted.

She'd made a life for herself.

Had I?

Or was I only pieces patched together by a leather vest?

My focus remained on the first photo, but her sultry dark eyes faded in my line of sight, and there were only Jill's eyes.

Jill's exuberance over simple things—finding the right brand at the supermarket, enjoying the flavor of a cheeseburger, singing along to a rock tune in my truck, laughing at a stupid television commercial, or tearing up when Becca would try a new food she had previously resisted and actually liked it. Yeah, *exuberance* when she watched me swinging off my bike, when she watched me going down on her—that was fucking real.

"*I love you,*" I'd told her.

Even though she hadn't said it back, I knew she felt it, too, but hers was buried under a pile of *should-do*s, *would-do*s, *hoped-to*s, *maybe one-days.*

I didn't have that jungle of vines blocking my way. Since I'd arrived in South Dakota and become a Jack, I'd always been about the now.

I had told her I loved her, and I was proud of that. If that were the one thing I'd left her with, wouldn't that somehow ease the sting for her? It did for me. It did. No fucking regrets.

My Firefly.

"*But some things, really beautiful things, you can't hold on to forever, can you?*"

No, you can't.

It was time for me to open the lid on that jar.

Be free, baby. Fly.

I knew, by the end of this day, there was a bullet just for me. Would it be in the forehead? The neck? In my stomach so that I could suffer, just for old times' sake? Or a clean one to the heart?

But my heart was full with something other than blood, something not even a bullet could drain.

Not even a fucking bullet.

Alejandro's personal bodyguard handcuffed me, took me down to the underground parking lot, and threw me in the back of a van, my face smashed into a scuzzy rubber mat. Another smaller man bent over me and shot me up with something to knock me out. I caught sight of my bike in the parking garage, standing tall in the distance, as the van doors slammed shut on me.

The van doors unhinged, swinging open, and my eyes unglued. We weren't in Denver anymore. Nothing but flat, dry earth. I'd been out for hours, judging from the sun.

"What did you bring him here for?" Notch, the president of the Broken Blades, studied me, his lips curled into a snarl.

Two Blades lifted me out of the van and threw me onto the ground.

Should I kiss Nebraska soil? *Nah.*

"Listen to me, eh?" Alejandro's eyebrows hopped up and down, his eyes twitching.

Being the *grande* head-honcho must be stressful.

"We're going to do this here. I can't afford to get caught with a dead body and blood on my cuffs right now. Things are tight in Denver."

"Oh, yeah?" Notch took a deep drag on his cigarette.

"Here, you and I can have some fun with him."

Notch sucked on his teeth. "What kind of fun?"

"Set him free on this God awful prairie to run like a wild turkey, and shoot at him. I like that idea. I need to be entertained. It's been a long drive."

Two Blades pulled me up on my feet, and I staggered, still woozy from whatever shit they had given me in the van. I licked at my dry lips, but it didn't help. The nuzzle of a gun poked at my back, and I flinched away from it, my body stiffening, my joints sore. The sun beat down on me. Pain prickled my eyes as I tried to focus on the open, flat stretch of land before me, but the ground only wobbled in the haze.

Notch snorted as he glanced at me and then back at Alejandro. "You really want to do this?"

He pressed his lips together. "You're the one who wanted the One-Eyed Jacks and the Flames of Hell to understand that you and I mean business, big business. Two birds, one stone, my friend. For both of us. I told you I'd provide for your needs."

Notch exhaled a cloud of smoke and signaled to two of his brothers. Fists flew at me, slamming into my middle. One landed on my scar, the stinging throb shooting through me. A blow to my side had me doubled over, crashing to the ground. Pain exploded in my skull.

"I wanna see the Jack crawl." Notch laughed.

I raised myself up but got kicked down. And again. My muscles strained and shuddered. I rolled over, the sun needling my eyes. I pushed up, but a jab to my lower back had me sprawled in the earth. Dirt and dust scoured my dry mouth.

A large hand pulled me up from the ground and shoved me forward.

"Go. Run like a hen. Run!" Alejandro's voice pierced my ears.

"Yeah, give him a head start. Make this more fun," came Notch's lazy voice behind me.

My blurry eyes fell on my snake coiled tight over my arm, his damn ugly face glaring at me, fangs at the ready, broken bones in his mouth.

The bones I'd broken.

Alejandro's bodyguard at my back shoved me again.

"Never again, never go back."

I spun, bashing my handcuffed fists into his throat. He croaked and wheezed, crumpling to the ground. I spotted his gun and propelled myself forward, lunging for the weapon just beyond his feet. I grabbed the handle, but my useless fingers were numb. The fucking gun tumbled from my grasp.

"Shit!"

My head reeled. I forced my eyes to focus.

Shots rang out, yelling split the air. The peal of a semiautomatic ripped around me. I smashed my face into the hard ground.

"No!"

My eyes sprang up at the sound of his voice.

Alejandro trained a sleek, shiny weapon at me. *Was it engraved?*

"You're mine! Mine!" he hissed.

Crack. Crack.

He snapped back as if by an invisible force, disappearing from view.

I crawled to the side and reached for the gun again, my hands sweaty, my fingers sticking to the handle. I rolled onto my back and pulled myself up, pain lashing through me like tongues of fire.

I had to be ready for him. *Have to be ready.*

I stretched my arms, the gun shaking in my hands.

A roar exploded in the back of my skull. A blur of black battered me, and the gun was ripped from my grasp.

"Fuck!"

A Blade pounded my jaw, my chest, the blows hammering through me.

"Son of a bitch!" I rammed my feet into his middle, and again to his crotch. He howled.

Thick pops went off in the air, and his body flinched and seemed to stop in midair, blood spurting over me. I spotted the glint on his belt and snatched his gun as his lifeless hulk heaved on top of me. With a grunt, I shoved him off me, raising myself up again.

And there he was.

Alejandro's huge dark eyes glared at me like flags in the distance. His mouth opened wide in an ugly yell as he pointed his weapon at me.

I aimed through the haze, my shoulders shuddering. Alejandro collapsed like a puppet whose strings had been cut. His jaw loose, his hand wavering over the dried grass, like a useless last-minute flag of surrender, and then it flopped down. I blinked, crawling backwards.

The shot to his head had come from behind him.

What the fuck was going on?

Black dots appeared over the horizon, dots moving, a swarm of dots. The ground rose up, and my eyes hit dirt, my skull thudding on the hard surface.

I trembled, my fingers digging in the earth. Using the surge of adrenaline flying through me, I pushed myself over and fell on my back. A breeze tripped over my face, and I opened my mouth to take in a gulp. I blinked, my eyes straining in the sunlight. Bulky clouds briskly slid across the streaky blue sky.

How do those fuckers move so fast? So silently?

"Bro!"

Butler.

Hands lifted me up. "Fuck, he's bleeding."

"We gotta go, man. Feds are on the way."

Catch's and Dready's voices buzzed somewhere over me. Shuffling, thudding, stamping pounded all around me.

"Get him up. He can't move. Let's go!"

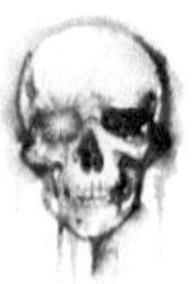

"You're safe, Bone. Don't worry. I'm here with you. Right here."

A soft hand brushed over my forehead, easing the cold that had seeped through my flesh and the shuddering in my veins.

A light kiss on my lips.

Jill.

"Thanks for coming, Doc," a hoarse male voice said in the distance.

More voices, footsteps.

"The doctor said you're going to be fine, Bone. Thank God." Another kiss on my hand.

Her eyes hovered over me, her wavy hair tickling my face.

My fingers uncurled in her hand. "Jill." Needles pricked my throat.

"Right here. We're at the Flames' clubhouse. Their doctor just cleaned you up. It's all good."

"Jill, what—"

"I'll go get Butler for you. I'll be right back."

I pulled on her, my one hand bringing her within inches of my face. "What the hell did you do?"

She blinked. "I chose love. Love, not fear."

I locked on those gray-blue eyes of hers, my lungs pinching in my chest. *Iron in her bones.*

She let go of my hand, and my back sank onto the table I was lying on.

Moments later, Butler dug a hand in my hair. "Fuck, you scared the shit out of me."

"Tell me—"

He leaned over me. "Seems the Feds have been on the Blades' asses for a while. Finger tipped off his contact inside, and the Feds trailed Alejandro from Denver into Nebraska, straight to the Blades' weapons stash, that old bunker you'd mentioned. Turns out, they've been after that location for a while now like everybody else. Not to mention, a crack at the Calderas Group. Huge win for them. Huge win for us. Feds were grateful, and we got you free and clear out of the deal."

"You went to Finger?"

"Not me. Jill. She's the one who figured out you had gone to Denver. She ran down here, talked to Finger herself. Didn't waste any time doing it."

"Jesus." I swallowed. "And Calderón?"

"Fucker's dead." Butler slanted his head. "What the hell were you thinking, bro?"

My chest squeezed painfully—and not from being beaten and bruised and shot at. I fisted a hand in Butler's shirt. "He was coming for me, was gonna get to Jill. Eventually him and Notch would have come for the club. I had to keep Jill and the baby safe. Had to—"

"All right." Butler heaved a sigh, his blue eyes clouding, his hand sliding over my forehead. "I know, man. I know."

FORTY-THREE

JILL

We were home.

Becca and I were staying with Boner at his house for a few days.

Boner's bruises and cuts were healing, and he was getting his energy back, but he remained sullen and quiet. Earlier this morning when he'd seen his bike standing in his driveway again, he actually smiled, but then he went back to his melancholy.

I brought our tea in the living room. Becca was still sleeping, and I was glad. I had something special to give to him.

He wiped his hands on his jeans and stood back from the fireplace, studying the orange flames licking high in the hearth.

"You got to promise me something, Jill. Don't you ever take off like that again without telling anyone where you're going, especially when it's to another club."

"I made an executive decision."

He turned to me. "Jesus. Between Grace, Lock, and you, by the time this kid is born, he or she is gonna be hell on wheels."

"Most likely."

I handed him a faded blue antique tin box, which was decorated with a hand-painted eagle holding an American flag in its claws.

"What's this?"

"A gift for you. I have another one, too, but this first."

He held up the small antique cigar box, inspecting the eagle. "You collecting antiques now, like Tania?"

"No. Grace gave that to me. It was Wreck's."

Wreck was Lock's older brother, who had died years ago. He had brought Boner and Dig into the club and had been their mentor.

"Tania found it while going through his stuff," I added. "It was perfect for what I had in mind, and Lock wanted you to have it, too."

He laid his hand on top of the box, a quiet, solemn gesture. "Wreck and his eagles."

"Open it."

He pushed open the top of the old box, and the tin creaked. A stack of creased papers was folded inside. "What's all this?" He picked through them.

His face lifted, and his eyes met mine. Eyes that questioned, eyes that brimmed with tension.

"Jillee—"

"Those poems are a part of you. A part of you I think you kept trying to trash or hide from view, but you couldn't. They're beautiful and awful, and they're yours. They should be shown some honor and allowed to rest in a special place in your house. You need to come to peace with them. With her."

"It helped, writing them."

"Yes, it does help. I keep journals. Have for a long time."

He licked his bottom lip, his Adam's apple bobbing in his throat as he swallowed. "This fire would come up, and I'd get it out. Then, I'd stuff them wherever." His shoulders jerked up and fell. "Bad memories, unanswered questions."

"You kept them as pieces, shedding as you went."

He nodded, his lips a firm line. "Pieces."

"Are you still asking her why?"

"No. Not anymore." His clear eyes met mine. "Not anymore."

"I'm sorry I read them. I feel like I intruded on your privacy. The last thing I want to do is to make you feel uncomfortable."

"I'm glad you read them."

I pressed a kiss on his cheek. "I'm proud of the bones you smashed. I don't care if that's bad or wrong or foul. I don't think it is. You took your revenge. You exacted your price of justice. You made your mark and torched it into the earth. In all that darkness, you did good things—for you, for Inés, for Dig, Grace, for me. For your club."

"It's not all good." His voice shook.

Tears spilled down my face. "I know, baby. It never is."

We held each other, our choppy breaths mingling, as we wiped at each other's tear-stained faces with our lips.

He released me, took the poems from the box, and tossed them into the fire. "I don't want them. Don't need to hold on to them," he said, staring at the blackened papers curling in the flames. He placed the tin box on the mantel and led me to the sofa.

I touched his leg. "I have something else for you."

"Don't get up—"

"Wait." I went to the front door where I'd left my handbag. I pulled out the suede pouch and gave it to him.

His jaw tensed as he loosened the tie of the small black bag. The rosary fell into his hands.

"I had it fixed," I said.

"Fixed?"

"It was broken. I know the cross can never be replaced. Frankly, I didn't think it should be. Its cross was unique, and it's with your mom. It's hers."

He held up the rosary, and the new pendant I'd found for it swung at the end. His hand went around it, holding it up.

"It's a new cross," I whispered. "For you."

A silver cross made up of swords accented with bones and a skull at the top of it. My heart beat faster every second he remained silent, his eyes glued on the piece.

"This is your cross, made of swords and bones," I said. "You're always ready to defend me, protect me, always ready to put yourself on the line for who you love. No hesitation, ever. You live what you feel. You feel what you live, and you take no prisoners. It's a beautiful, powerful thing, and I'm in awe of you. You helped me see that I can bear the weight of an iron sword that I have to use to protect myself, to protect my child, to protect you. You gave me that.

"Too many of us try to deny all the ugliness, to push it away. You don't, Santiago. You stare it in the face. You always have. You break its bones with your iron sword when you have to. Yes, you destroyed lives with your crowbar. But now, you wield your sword with purpose. You wield it with a full heart and a strong arm, baby, and I love you."

"Firefly." He crushed me to his chest and kissed the top of my head, pulling me onto his lap. "You always believe."

"I do, and I believe in you." I pressed against him. "When I look at you, I don't see some sort of guardian angel, and I don't see gratitude or obligation. I see a man who needs me, like I need him.

I see a man who's brave and strong and extreme in how he feels and looks at the world. A man who loves fierce and hard and unforgiving. And in the very center of his big heart, there's a fire burning." I rubbed my hand over his heart and planted a kiss there. "And I want to be in there, burning and alive."

I wiped my eyes and took the rosary from his hand and put it over his head, moving his hair out of the way. I kissed the cross of swords against his chest, and with a groan, he took my face in his hands and crushed his mouth against mine.

"I need you," he whispered roughly.

We peeled our clothing back, pushing it away, kicking it off. He moaned as he entered me in one long move. His hair teased over my skin, and his cross settled on my chest, stroking me, as he slowly thrust inside me, filling me with his sorrows, his hopes, filling me with his love. He planted himself deep, and I ground up toward him.

"I love you, Santiago."

He drove inside me, joining with me. We were one. It was raw and honest and merciless, and there was purity in that, a purity that I had never known before.

"I broke that bastard who hurt you," he grunted in my ear as he moved inside me. "I did it. Broke his bones. Did it for Dig. Did it for you." His one hand splayed across the curve of my belly against the baby. "You're a fucking gift, a fucking gift."

He raised himself up and stroked my clit in short tense pulses, and my body gave in to his binding grip, to his harsh rhythm.

"Fucking gift," he growled.

We were one creature, surging with one need.

An explosion of cries and sensations shuddered through both of us, melding us together.

His arms tightened around me as he leaned over me. "Love you, Jillee," he whispered against my skin.

We lay there, naked on the sofa, my fingers tracing lines over his chest, over the cross. I moved down and laid kisses on the scar across his abdomen. I knew I couldn't put his pieces back together again, the pieces Inés had ripped apart, the parts of him that so much of his life had made brittle, disconnected. But I could hold him, love him, give him the warmth and hope of us, while he tried his best.

"I got lost in you," his voice whispered in the shadows. "Just like you dared me to. You remember when you said that to me in Rae's kitchen?"

"Yes."

"I got lost, and I found things I'd never expected to find again—powerful, colorful, precious things."

His eyes met mine in the shadows seeping through the room, and I settled back onto his chest. Sheeting rain pelted the windows, hailstones battered the roof and the sides of the house. One of those sudden, unpredictable Dakota storms. It would be over quickly. Its startling, ugly, jarring violence would pass.

FORTY-FOUR

JILL

"I NEED TO COME WITH YOU." I wiped the hair back from my face.

"What?"

"I need to see Creeper. I need to—"

Boner's frown deepened. "You sure?"

"I'm sure."

I knew Butler and the men were going to bring Creeper into the club later this morning, and I wanted to be there. I had dropped Becca off at daycare and went straight to the club and found Boner.

I had to face Creeper and look him in the eyes. This man had stolen my daughter months ago, treating her and us like she was a worthless commodity for his greedy bargaining and blackmail.

In an act of both the Flames and the Jacks moving forward in a new spirit of cooperation, Butler had invited Catch in on finally putting Creeper into the ground. Butler had intended on making this move sooner to bring the clubs closer, but when Catch had taken Dig's gun, that had blown up that plan in its tracks. Now it was back on.

By helping the Jacks rescue Boner, the Flames had achieved what they'd wanted: severely weakening the Broken Blades and getting rid of the Calderas Group. The single bullet that had killed Alejandro Calderón couldn't be traced. Assassin unknown.

Compensation to the One-Eyed Jacks for Catch's dishonorable robbery of Dig's revolver had been fulfilled.

There was satisfaction and excitement in the Jacks' clubhouse. Butler was pleased that his plan for cooperating with the Flames was back on track. The Blades had been crippled, their property frozen by the Feds, their president in a rage. Only Jump didn't share in the excitement, and the tension between him and Butler had intensified. Not to mention the awful tension between Jump and Alicia.

Catch had stopped over to see Rae and Becca this morning, and from what little he'd told me, I'd figured out where he was headed after he visited with his daughter and mother. His anticipation was obvious.

"He's gonna pay, Jill. I got this," he'd told me as he started his bike at the end of Rae's driveway.

Creeper had taken a piece of me when he'd kidnapped Becca. I hadn't known what he was doing to her, if she was crying out for me. *Was she hungry? Was her diaper a mess? Was he hurting her? Was she scared? Did she miss me?*

I had become that sobbing helpless girl again, like I had been when Mole had taken me. Tied up, terrified, desperate, demented. Screaming on the inside, weeping silently, and shuddering on the outside. When Becca was missing, I'd been raked raw, and then I'd finally exploded in a rage. It was as if Creeper had tied me up to Mole's fucking motel bed all over again.

I had to do this.

I held Boner's hard gaze.

"I'm very sure," I repeated.

He took my hand and led me into the clubhouse to the kitchen, through a short hallway to the left of it, and down a well-lit stairwell, our boots making noise against the metal steps.

Bear stood in the open doorway, his arms folded. In the room beyond, Dready and Lock tied Creeper facedown on a long table, his arms over his head. Butler, Dawes, and Tricky stood to the side watching. Catch's eyes narrowed at me.

But I only had eyes for Creeper. That bitter rage I knew so well coursed through me now, like acid instead of blood. That sour swell rose in my chest, buckling my veins. It compelled me forward into that stifling room. I hungered to smell Creeper's blood, his fear, his helplessness, his desperation.

Boner squeezed my hand, and I squeezed it back.

He brought me to the table where Creeper lay bound. The men stopped what they were doing around the table and stared at me. Boner let go of my hand and ripped Creeper's shirt, exposing his back, exposing the great tattoo of the glint-eyed skull of the One-Eyed Jacks. Disgrace, dishonor, shame would all be paid for at last.

Creeper's battered eyes blinked up at me and slackened.

"You took my girl," I said to him. "You were going to rape Tania and Grace."

Knives had been planted on the edge of the table, alongside his torso, like weeds in a junkyard. I took a knife in my grip and yanked it from the old wood table.

Catch darted forward. "Jill, what the fuck are you doing?"

"No," said Boner, his voice low and steady, the authority of it stopping Catch. "Leave her alone."

My eyes rose to meet my old man's.

"Do it," he said.

He knew what I needed to do. He understood what I wanted to do, no matter how low or bad or dirty, and he was giving it to me.

Creeper's body tensed then jerked, his one bloodied eye glaring at me, his breaths short and ragged.

"This is for my daughter."

And for me.

I thrust the knife into his side, and he let out a moaning hiss. I twisted it and pulled it back. My arm shook, my heart pounded. I handed the blood-covered blade to Boner, and he leaned in closer to me.

My bloodstained fingertips touched his cheek. "Break his bones for us, baby," I whispered.

A large hand went around my forearm and pulled me back. Lock walked me to the door and handed me off to Bear. All I saw as I left the room were my old man's incredible eyes holding mine and gleaming.

FORTY-FIVE

JILL

TODAY, IN AN EFFORT TO WIN SMILES FROM BONER, I'd made him flan. I'd wanted to prepare something special for him, so I'd decided on the caramel custard, which was practically the national obsession of Argentina. It was a simple enough recipe. Eggs, milk, sugar, and a real vanilla bean with a dash of lime juice and lots of whisking. Luckily, Rae had a top-of-the-line KitchenAid mixer, and it had made the entire process of making the custard a snap. I'd also bought a special round pan to bake it in. And as Argentineans paired their flan with dulce de leche sauce, I'd made that, too. That was a lot of caramel in one sensual dessert.

Grace and Lock had come over to Boner's and surprised us with a dinner of barbecued ribs and fries from a local joint.

A couple of hours later, Lock rose from the table after Grace and I had cleared the dishes. "We're off."

"Aren't you going to stay for dessert?" I asked.

"We've got to hit the road early tomorrow. I've got a lead on a 1970 El Camino and a '68 Corvette up in Bismarck."

Boner's forehead puckered. "That be serious."

"That be right," replied Lock, stretching his arms over his head and then circling them around his wife, who stood in front of him.

"And I'm going with," Grace said, stroking her old man's arm. "It's been way too long since we've done an overnight bike trip, and I'm really looking forward to it."

"Do what you can before this one arrives." I laughed, pointing at my belly.

Grace's face lit up. "Exactly."

We said our good-nights, and I locked the door after them.

I touched Boner's arm. "You have room for dessert?"

He rubbed at the back of his neck with a hand. "I'm beat, gonna head on upstairs."

There was that gloominess again.

"Please, Boner. I made it special for you. Just have a taste?"

I brushed his lips with mine, determined to nudge at that moodiness of his.

"You go relax on the sofa, and I'll bring you your surprise."

His eyebrows rose. "Surprise?"

"You'll see."

In the kitchen, I extricated the custard from its pan onto a large plate, the caramel sauce dripping down the custard tower and pooling in the dish. I poured the thick dulce de leche into a small bowl and added two spoons. I figured personal dishes were unnecessary.

I brought everything into the living room, setting it on the coffee table before Boner.

He stared at it.

He stared at me.

He stared back at the dessert.

"It's flan," I said.

"Flan?"

"Flan."

The word was beginning to sound ridiculous. It reminded me of when I was a kid and I would repeat words hundreds of times over on purpose with my best friend. The words would lose their meaning and familiarity and simply turn into a silly tumble of sounds, making us laugh.

"It's a custard," I said.

Another blank look.

"You know, like pudding? They call it créme caramel in France and flan in Spain and Latin America." I shifted my weight. "I thought you'd like it."

Mission Status: Epic Fail.

He picked up a spoon and sliced into the glistening wobbly mound of creaminess, scooping a generous helping into his mouth. His eyes widened, his thumb wiping at the corner of his lips. He scooped in another huge spoonful.

"Bone, have you ever had flan before?"

He shook his head as he dipped the spoon into the thick dulce de leche and licked at it with that tongue of his, his eyes on me. "I like it. It's a winner, baby."

"It's a favorite in Argentina. I thought—"

"You thought I'd had it before?" He rested a hand on his thigh and aimed his gaze at me.

"Yeah, I thought you might like—"

His green eyes flashed, his fingers tightening over the spoon handle. "You ever made flan before?"

"No."

He dropped the spoon in the plate and held out his hand to me, and I went to him. He pulled me down onto his lap, a hand cupping my jaw and then sliding around my neck.

"You made it special for me? Looked up a recipe for me?"

I nodded, my fingers combing through his short dark beard.

His mouth crashed on mine, and a caramel, cream, and Boner infusion exploded on my tongue. He pulled me in closer to his chest, his arms wrapping tighter around me, as if he couldn't get enough of me, of our taste, our heat, our kiss.

A whimper escaped my throat.

I pulled away from him and caught my breath. "I thought maybe your mom used to make it for you, and you'd enjoy it."

His forehead slid against mine. "She cooked a lot, but making desserts like this, not so much. She wanted to learn American shit. She used to make a lot of puddings, brownies, and cakes from boxes. Instant was a whole new concept for her, and she was fascinated by it. I sure didn't complain, but I don't remember a flan or this caramel sauce."

"Dulce de leche."

An eyebrow lifted. "Say it again."

"Dulce—"

His eyes went to my mouth. "Slower."

"De leche."

He made a noise in the back of his throat. "Baby, you gotta try your *flan*."

His pronunciation of the word made my insides ping. He brought a spoonful to my lips, and I took it in my mouth.

"Good, huh?"

I nodded, my gaze never leaving his. "Mmhmm."

He fed me again. "Did you take Spanish in school?"

"No, I took French," I replied.

He licked caramel from the corner of my mouth, and my eyes fluttered closed.

"Do you remember any Spanish?" I asked.

He fed me another spoonful, and the cool custard melted in my mouth, my throat burning with heat.

"I remember a few things."

"Tell me," I murmured, watching his lips take in a spoonful.

"My uncle had a few favorites he used to say to the women he brought home to fuck. One in particular used to make me laugh."

"What was it?"

"*Abrí las piernas.* Spread your legs."

"He had to tell them that?"

Boner laughed. "That fucker was always telling people what to do. Never let up. You'd think that one was a little obvious, right?"

His brows drew together, and I rubbed my finger over the indents, smoothing them out.

"I remember nice ones though," he said, his voice softer. "Really nice."

"Tell me."

He gently kissed the smile forming on my lips. "*Mi corazón.*"

"My heart."

He nodded. "*Mi cielo.*"

"Don't know."

"My sky or heaven."

He fed me another spoonful, and I stared into his eyes as I swallowed the luscious sweet custard perfectly scented with vanilla.

"*Mi vida.*"

"My life?"

"Yeah."

He put down the spoon and kissed the edge of my lips, and my head tilted back, as if some magnetic force emanating from him had willed it.

"*Mi amor,*" he whispered, laying soft kisses against my throat.

I spun in throbbing pink *corazones*, deep blue *cielos*, cool green *vidas*.

"*Mi amor.*" His breath was hot on my neck. He sucked on my earlobe as his fingers traced dizzying trails down the delicate skin of my throat.

"Bone."

He kissed me again, his hand at my throat, soft, slow kisses that pulled on my tongue, on my lips, on my soul.

"You wrote me a poem," I whispered.

"Yeah."

"You left it for me, here on the table."

A shadow passed over his eyes, and he kissed me again, his fingers cradling my face.

I breathed in the warm scent of his skin. "I love my poem."

His chuckle hummed in my chest.

"And I love you."

His forehead slid to mine, his eyes shut. "Firefly."

I held him tighter.

He cleared his throat. "You know, I don't want this dulce de leche to go to waste."

I glanced at him, my fingers lingering on his chest. "It did take me forever to make."

I nuzzled the swell of his pec, and he let out a shaky breath.

"Got an idea," he whispered.

"I hope it's a tasty idea to fully appreciate my effort and the flavor?"

"Grab the bowl."

I grabbed the small bowl with the thick caramel. He took my hand, and we charged up the stairs to his bedroom.

There, we experienced the sweet glory of dulce de leche and practiced our Argentinian Spanish, all at the same time.

Lo más...que rico, baby.

Yes, it was the best.

So delicious.

So damn good.

FORTY-SIX

JILL

Boner and I were getting married.

He hadn't exactly proposed or asked. Over a quick cup of coffee one afternoon at the Meager Grand Cafe, he had suddenly taken in a deep breath and pronounced: "I wanna marry you, Firefly."

I'd squealed and hugged him, knocking over his double espresso and my mocha latte.

"Is that a yes?" he asked, holding me tight.

I only burst into tears.

Oh, it would have been nice to have the baby first, to lose the extra pounds, to wear the perfect dress, to ride his bike to the ceremony and back. But what mattered was that we were together and couldn't live without each other. What mattered was that both of us were finally ready to make a new life, and that life was with each other.

We decided to have our ceremony in the majestic lush beauty of Sylvan Lake. The tall spires of the evergreens were our cathedral, the green grass our velvet carpet, the unusual granite boulders and hulking rock formations rising from the ground our silent witnesses. We made the effort and got there very early on a weekday morning to be able to have the secluded small spot we'd chosen to ourselves, and we were so glad we did.

Only the One-Eyed Jacks along with Rae and Tania attended. We arrived and a mist rolled over the still, sapphire water. The cool, crisp mountain air was laced with the almost butterscotch-like sweet fragrance of the ponderosa pine. At first, none of us spoke, taking in the perfect sacred hush. The colors of the morning bloomed over us, their tones and hues depending on the shifting shadows of the clouds and the strength of the sunlight. Pure magic.

Grace was my matron of honor, and Lock was Boner's best man. Strolling up the aisle formed by Boner's brothers, Tania held Becca by the hand, and they threw white rose petals on everyone.

My dress was a Bohemian-style piece that Lenore had made for me using a vintage dress she'd found. A plunging V-neckline, ruched chiffon bodice with hand-sewn corded lace appliqué, and a low back set off my assets. The skirt was made of antique-looking beige chiffon. Pearl-shaped buttons made a line down the back. My gown was ethereal, flowy, and oh-so comfortable in my progressed state of pregnancy.

As a gift, Grace had given me a thin pale-gold cashmere shrug to wear over my bare shoulders to keep me warm in the cool morning air. And I had made myself a special headpiece, a long chain dotted with tiny crystals that hung down the back of my long hair like a necklace. I felt like a fairy-tale princess in the woods.

My soon-to-be husband's wide-eyed stare and parted lips confirmed that he liked what he saw as Lock walked me down the aisle. I could've sworn Lock's arm was shaking just a little under mine.

Boner wore a vintage black tuxedo coat with tails over his colors and one of those body hugging V neck T-shirts I had gotten him. My dashing dark prince. When he took my one hand in both of his, he didn't let go until after we'd said our vows and he put the white-gold wedding band we'd chosen together on my finger, and I put one on his. Our rings were made of two coiled snakes with a tiny skull at the center where the snake heads met. On my ring, a diamond dotted one eye of the skull.

The justice of the peace declared us legal. Husband and wife. Old man and old lady.

We kissed, and Boner whispered in my ear, "That bright life just came true, Firefly."

I kissed him again.

Everyone cheered and small champagne bottles popped open. I had one quick sip and kissed my husband right away. I wanted to lock the warm taste of him and the crisp sweetness of the champagne—this very moment—in my heart and senses forever.

We made our way back to where everyone had parked their bikes and cars.

Boner stopped in his tracks, his arm tightening around me even more. I followed his line of sight.

"Holy wow!" I blurted.

Dig's 1968 black Camaro gleamed in the sunlight. That Camaro had been his pride and joy from all accounts. After Dig had been killed, Boner had taken it, but he never took it out, never drove it, although he kept it secured at the club all these years.

Now, here she was, glossy beyond belief, full of attitude, slick bravado, and sexy swagger. Stealth in motion. Breathtaking.

Boner turned to Lock. "What did you do?" His voice heavy with emotion, censure, shock.

Lock's huge dark eyes held his. Grace twisted her arms around one of Lock's.

"It's a beautiful piece, and it's meant to be enjoyed, meant to be ridden. That's what he bought it for," Lock said. "I was with him when he found it. You would've thought he'd won the damn lottery. It was a piece of junk he could barely afford, but he had to have it. He took his time rebuilding it with Wreck, loved taking it out, loved how it felt in his hands. It made him laugh, made him roar. You were the only one he'd let drive it, apart from Wreck."

"You stole the keys once and took it for a joyride, you little shit," said Boner.

We laughed.

Lock grinned, his large hands jamming into the front pockets of his black jeans. The renegade teenager was still pleased with himself all these years later. "Yeah, I did. I didn't even have my license yet, but that was how irresistible she was." He glanced at the car and then back at Boner. "I wanted to make her irresistible for you. You wouldn't let anyone touch her after he died." He took in a breath, tilting his head, his lips pressing together for a moment. "It's time you take her out, man. He would've wanted you to. He would've wanted you to laugh and roar behind that wheel, just like he did, like we did together."

Lock took Grace's hand in his and they stepped toward us. "She's got a professionally built 454 CID engine, turbo transmission. Original bucket seats with upgraded interior. Fresh paint, subtle silver stripes around the nose and down the sides, hand-buffed."

Silence, but for the wind kicking up in the tall trees soaring around us.

Boner tore his gaze away from Lock and stared at the car. "The Raven is back," he said, his voice so low that I could barely hear it.

"The Raven is back." Lock held out the keys. "Take your old lady home, Boner."

Boner lunged at Lock, and the two of them hugged tightly. Grace and I held each other's watery gazes.

I didn't think my heart could burst again today, but it did right then.

My old man took the keys and got me in his Camaro. We led a long line of bikes through the mountain-carved tunnels and eroded granite pillars of the Needles Highway, over the hairpin curves, and down the long winding road through the Black Hills back to Meager.

Back home.

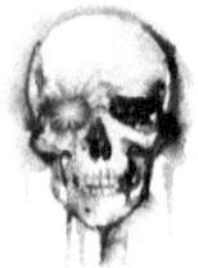

A week after the wedding, Boner took me to the Jacks' favorite tattoo parlor in Deadwood owned by their long time friend, Ronny. Looking through Ronny's amazing array of artwork, I secretly made plans to get fireflies tattooed on my rear and up over my back after I had the baby. Today, Boner had a plan for a special tattoo for himself. He had Ronny brand the poem he had written for me over his heart and down his torso.

I was speechless.

I was humbled.

I was honored.

I was in so much deep fucking love.

There have been many more poems since—some long and some short ditties. A few are nonsensical, a few are philosophical; yet, for the most part, they all express joy, not sorrow, not pain. So many are dirty, but all of them are simply true expressions of whatever Boner is feeling in that instant. He hides them for me to find around our house. I've found them in Becca's drawers, in the bathroom medicine cabinet, in between the bottles in my spice rack, in my makeup bag, inside a rain boot, in my pillowcase, in my underwear.

But that poem, the first poem, is still the most special one of all. I lay kisses over it on his chest every night before I fall asleep in his arms and every morning when I wake up, folded in his embrace.

Every morning.

I've captured my firefly
At long, long last
And she glows
She glows
Like a star in the dark
Like a flame in the cold
Heat in my lost soul
My Firefly
At long, long last
No prisoner to take
No lid to close
She is free
yet she glows in my heart,
For my heart has no walls,
It's clearer than glass.
And she shines within me,
The wild light of my dark night.
I swallowed her tears,
I took them in then threw them at the sky
and made them rays of light.

EPILOGUE

BONER

Jill entwined her fingers with mine as the nurse attached a wide belt over her huge belly. The quick thumps of Super-baby's heartbeat filled the delivery room, and Grace and Jill squeezed each other's hands.

The heart—alive, pumping, circulating blood, maintaining life for this little being, working so hard to do the thing it had been created for.

My breath bottled up in my chest, and my legs suddenly felt weak.

"Mi corazón." My mother's elegant throaty voice came back to me, her hand ruffling through the thick waves of my hair, her final kisses of the day caressing my face before sleep would claim me. Without those gifts from her each night, something was always missing. The night would be empty.

My heart.

An odd floating sensation overtook me, and the baby's quick heartbeat pulsed with my own. I rocked back on the heels of my boots.

This was Grace and Lock's baby.

This was urgent life staking its claim among us.

I wanted to match it, sing with it, breathe with that heartbeat.

Can you hear it, Dig?

"Honey? Are you okay?" Jill asked, raising her head.

"Yeah," I breathed, kissing her hand in mine. "Yeah, I'm good."

My eyes went to Lock, his lips pressed together, his sleek black hair in his eyes.

The two weeks leading up to the baby's due date, Jill and I had been very responsible in following the doctor's orders to help

Mother Nature do her thing. Jill had taken long walks around our property, and we'd fucked every chance we got.

Jill would come loud and hard each time. "I'm telling you, there's nothing like pregnancy hormones. I wish I could jump you myself, but that's physically impossible these days."

I'd stroked the side of her hip. "No worries there, Firefly."

She'd grinned lazily at me from our bed.

The day before Jill's due date, her contractions had started coming frequently, and we'd headed for the hospital. The urge to push had overwhelmed her, and her water had broken in the truck.

Now, with my wife bracing herself against me and with Grace and Lock on her other side, Jill got into her breathing and pushing zone and used her diaphragm muscles—just like the seminar we'd faithfully attended with Grace had taught us—to push Super-baby out in under three tries.

I had my eyes on the doctor as the last of the baby's body squeezed out of Jill.

The doctor's face split into a huge grin. "It's a boy!"

"It's a boy? A boy?" Jill shouted.

"Oh my God, it's a boy!" Grace exclaimed, her skin flushed, her hands flying to her mouth.

Lock clasped his arms around her and kissed the side of her face hard, whispering in her ear. She closed her eyes and pressed against him, a hand to his jaw, tears streaming down her cheeks. He rocked his wife, his wet eyes meeting mine.

Squalling and sharp cries pierced the air, uncurling around us. Lock's lips trembled, a smile wobbling the edges.

"You did it, baby. You did it." I kissed Jill's sweaty red cheek and her forehead. "You did it."

She let out choppy breaths. "I did it. Sweet Jesus, we *all* did it."

The doctor rose and gestured at Grace. "Here you go, Mommy." She laid the baby in Grace's arms and turned to Lock. "Are you ready, Dad?"

He wiped at his eyes and planted a kiss on the side of his wife's face, his thumb rubbing through a fallen tear.

"I love you," he rasped.

Lock took the small clamp tool in his grip from a nurse, and a sob escaped Grace's mouth. He cut the umbilical cord on his son's body and bent and kissed his head.

Jill sank back into my arms, laughing.
Laughing.

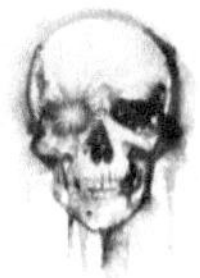

Over a month after Grace's baby was born, I got home early one afternoon, and Jill was curled up in the bay window seat, staring out the window, with her journal, a purple pen, a sketch of a necklace on the floor beside her. Her hands lay over her now much, much smaller belly.

I tucked in behind her without a word and took her in my arms, my face pressing against hers. The sun cast its orange glow over us as it dipped lower at the edge of the sky. "What are you thinking?"

"Nothing. Just…"

"What?"

She let out a sigh, her shoulders dropping. "It's strange."

"Nothing's strange."

"I don't want to feel strange. But I do." Her breath hitched. "There's this void…"

"I know," I whispered, brushing my lips against her hair. "It's only natural."

She muffled a sob. "I'm glad it's over, that it all worked out, but a part of me is sad."

"It's okay to be sad, sweetheart. It's not wrong."

"It feels wrong. I don't want it to feel wrong. It's not about missing the baby as much as it's the whole experience that I'm missing. I don't know how to put it into words," she said, her voice hoarse.

"For nine months, you carried that baby in your body along with so many people's wishes and dreams. A long, rich journey came to an end. You're saying good-bye."

Tears erupted from her, and she cried silently with her face buried in my arm as I held her. I planted kisses on the fireflies inked along her shoulder and neck.

"The good news is, we all live here together," I said. "You're not gonna lose out on that bond, Firefly—with Grace or being her boy's favorite aunt—right?"

"That's right." She sniffed. "I'm really glad about that. Grace and I have gotten so close. I don't want to lose that."

"You won't. I guarantee you, she feels the same way." I kissed the top of her head. "Anyway, now is that time you've been talking about for so long. The Jill-on-the-go time. Jill-chases-her-dreams time."

"Cuckoo!" Becca jumped in front of us.

"There you are, sweets." Jill wiped at her eyes. "Did you have a good nap?"

Becca nodded and stretched her hands out to me. Jill sat up as I picked up Becs and brought her onto my lap.

My free hand went to Jill's stomach, and she leaned her head against my shoulder, holding her daughter's hand.

"Firefly, I want to fill you with us. How does that fit into your dreams?"

She met my gaze, her eyes shining. "I've got my dreams right here, Santi. They all came true."

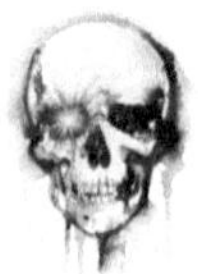

JILL

Two years later, Boner and I had our own child—a boy who was blessed to have those remarkable green eyes of his grandmother and father.

Nicolás is three years old now, and he and his dad chase a soccer ball on our front lawn, the two of them laughing loudly, both of their long manes of dark hair flying. Becca lets go of my hand to run after her baby brother and his ball, her laughter joining theirs. Pure joy shines on my husband's face.

Unfettered, free.

Our son kicks the ball hard down the hill and, jumping up and down, waves wildly at me, filling the air with his loud screeches and whoops.

In this very moment, I know that Nicolás's eyes will never doubt, never know the darkness his father or I had. They will live in this beautiful light that his parents have fought so hard for.

This I know, deep in my bones. Those eyes will feel and see and reflect our bright.

Always.

OTHER BOOKS BY CAT PORTER

Lock & Key

Random & Rare

Blood & Rust—Coming Soon

Wolfsgate

ABOUT THE AUTHOR

CAT PORTER was born and raised in New York City, but also spent a few years in Texas and Europe along the way. As an introverted, only child, she had very big, but very secret dreams for herself. She graduated from Vassar College, was a struggling actress, an art gallery girl, special events planner, freelance writer, restaurant hostess, and had all sorts of other crazy jobs all hours of the day and night to help make those dreams come true. She has two children's books traditionally published under her maiden name. She now lives on a beach outside of Athens, Greece with her husband and three children, and freaks out regularly and still daydreams way too much. She is addicted to reading, cafes on the beach, Instagram, Pearl Jam, the History Channel, her husband's homemade red wine, really dark chocolate, and her Nespresso coffee machine. Oh, and Jamie & Claire Fraser and those Vikings...never mind. Writing keeps her somewhat sane, extremely happy, and a productive member of society.

Cat Online

Facebook: www.facebook.com/catporterauthor

Website: www.catporter.eu

Newsletter: http://eepurl.com/biiKNT

Twitter: @catporter103

TSU: www.tsu.co/CatPorterAuthor

Goodreads:
www.goodreads.com/author/show/8286871.Cat_Porter

Instagram: instagram.com/catporter.author

Pinterest: www.pinterest.com/catporter103

Email: catporter103@gmail.com

ACKNOWLEDGMENTS

I COULD NOT HAVE MADE THIS DREAM COME TRUE without a great many wonderful, supportive and very smart people who deserve my big hugs and my sincerest thanks:

To Jovana Shirley for your keen insights, clarity, and enthusiasm, and the magical sweep of your editing and design wands.

Lots of hugs and kisses to Najla Qamber for yet another wonderful collaboration and for making my ideas and last minute epiphanies a breathtaking reality. Too much fun!

To Billy Blue of Blue Bayer Design NYC for the use of your amazing pirate dragon silver sworn bone pendant featured on the cover and in my story and for your enthusiasm. Everything came together with this gorgeous piece of piracy.

To Jenn whose friendship and deep heart knows no bounds—lost without you. To Alison for cheering me on and for your organizational skills on my behalf an ocean away. To my goddesses, Natalie, Ellen, Lena, Larri, Sue, Andrea, Tina, Sharon, Lori, Kandace—endless rivers of love for your friendship, support, laughter, intensity, and pearls of wisdom.

To my terrific beta readers Alison, Judy, Lena, Natalie, Needa, Sharon, Rachel, Tina, Jenn. Thank you for taking the time to help me with so much care and thoughtfulness and for putting up with my new versions. To Sharon and Penny for their guidance in the ways of Spanish and Argentina. Special thanks to Deana for her VS memories.

Huge thanks to Melissa, Sharon, Linda, and Jesey of Sassy, Savvy, Fabulous PR for their professionalism, support, guidance, enthusiasm, and friendship.

Big smooches to my author friends, Lauren Gilley, Needa Warrant (yes, keep kicking my ass, please), Leylah Attar, BL Berry, Daryl Banner, Lana Grayson, Autumn Jones Lake, and Lorelei James for their friendship, support, and insane sanity that matches my own.

To my fabulous Cat Callers, love you hard! To the Facebook groups that have welcomed me so warmly and the reader friends I've met this past year for their enthusiasm, sharing, and soooo much laughter, like Amy Figas, Sammy, Cindy, Kimber, Shanda, Stephanie, Iza, Jessica, Jan, Toni, Angie, MJ, Jo, Tracie, Caroline, Dawn, and many many more wonderful women. A very special thanks to Angel Dust, Mary Orr, and Donna whose tireless work and devotion amaze me on a daily basis.

To the wonderful blogging women of The Book Bellas, Dirty Book Girls, Guilty Pleasures, EDGy Reviews, Kinky Book Obsessions, Kindle Friends Forever, Divas Book Lounge, Book Gossip, I Love Book Love, Book Babes Unite, Maryse, Perusing Princesses, IScream Books, RedHotRomance, and Totally Booked, among many, many other blogs. The incredible, tireless work these wonderful women do on their blogs in the name of reading and woman power mean so very much to me as an author and a reader and always will.

To my husband for his support and most especially to my three children who put up with my crazy at all hours and thankfully laugh along with me at that crazy, giving me hugs and gentle reminders to feed them and pick them up from school. (Yes, I have been known to forget.) You're my everything.

To my readers, this is truly nothing without you. Thank you for letting my words whisper in your ears and in your hearts. You make it all the sweeter. I love hearing from you on Facebook, Twitter, and Instagram. Visit my Pinterest page where I have dedicated boards for all my books, and I hope you enjoy them much as I do pinning them into creation. (Yes, yes, I'm still addicted!) And when you get a chance, please do leave a review wherever you may roam. All are very much appreciated and vital to a book's journey out in the big world.

xx, C

www.ingramcontent.com/pod-product-compliance
Lightning Source LLC
Chambersburg PA
CBHW031151120726
47905CB00006B/1906